CLASSIC LIBRARY

SELECTED ESSAYS

G. K. CHESTERTON

A Wilco Book

Outstanding works of universal interest

© *Wilco* 2005
This edition printed in 2009

ISBN NO : 978818252038X

SELECTED ESSAYS
G. K. Chesterton
Complete and Unabridged

Published by
Wilco
Publishing House
ITTS House, 33, Sri Saibaba Marg
Kala Ghoda, Mumbai - India
Tel: (91-22) 2204 1420 / 2284 2574
Fax: (91-22) 2204 1429
E-mail: wilcos@vsnl.com

Printed and bound in India

INTRODUCTION

WHEN Gilbert Chesterton and I became friends, during our early schooldays, he was already in the habit of writing essays. His parents' house in Kensington was a place which, happily for me, I came to know almost as well as he did; and in the sitting-rooms of that house, in the hall, in the conservatory, on the table under the big tree in the garden, one was always likely to find at least one MS book with a few or many of its pages filled by his sprawling, energetic writing, the embryo of that remarkable calligraphy which was to become so well known in the world of letters. In China through the ages, we are told, a poet or scholar used to consider the realistic beauty of the characters traced by his brush-paintings as quite as important as the meaning conveyed by them. There was always something of this feeling in G.K.C. during the many years before he formed the habit of dictating to a secretary, and that habit made no difference to the grotesque shapeliness of everything written with his own hand. His signature was like a picture, a pleasure to the eye, if not particularly legible: he would quote in regard to it the Tennysonian line, '*With many a curve my banks I fret*' *.

If in those boyhood days the traces of literary activity were lying about everywhere, it was in his own big bedroom at the top of the house that they were concentrated. All along one wall of this room ran a big shelf which was packed with MS books. The writing within, always done in pencil, consisted of essays mainly, though the output of verse was already beginning, there were some fragments of plays, and a much fatter book was devoted to a vast work of extravagant fiction in which we collaborated, writing alternate chapters. Whenever I asked what he had been writing about since our previous meeting he would tell me, but only very unwillingly would he let me read it: to the end of his days he hated to have his work read by anyone else when he was present, and to have it read aloud was torture for him.

The task which Miss Dorothy Collins has undertaken in this book, and carried out as I think so admirably, is the providing of a

---

* *With many a curve my banks I fret, And many a fairy foreland set*
By many a field and fallow, With willow-weed and mallow.
– *The Brook* By English poet Alfred (Lord) Tennyson (1809-1892).

sort of quintessence of Chesterton the essayist. The actual number of essays published by him during his literary life would be hard to compute, for they appeared in so many periodicals, but it must certainly run into thousands, for his Saturday article in the *Daily News* was a regular feature for over a dozen years, and his page in the *Illustrated London News,* begun as a regular feature in 1905, was contributed week by week until the day of his death in 1936.

There was abundance of material, then, for the volumes of essays by G.K.C. which have appeared from time to time. What we have here is a representative selection from the best of that enormous production of eloquent, provocative, splendidly graphic and admirably humorous prose writing. And it is to be remembered that this was the work that he really lived for, as well as lived by. He was publishing at the same time a flood of other work in the shape of fiction, verse, history, biography, theology, criticism, drama and pure nonsense. These were his books, written as such; and he always undervalued them. The best that he could find to write about his own novels was, 'I have spoilt a number of jolly good ideas in my time.' When a friend of mine brought to him a copy of *Orthodoxy* – hailed everywhere as a vividly original work of Christian apologetics – and asked him to inscribe his name in it, he wrote on the title-page, 'Bosh. By G.K. Chesterton'. Of one of the finest poems of the century he could write: 'I have done my best to deface and spoil the purity of the White Horse by writing an interminable ballad about it'; and once, when someone proposed to read aloud from that ballad to a company of friends, its author seized the book, kicked it under an arm-chair, sat in the chair, and defied anyone to rescue his masterpiece.

The truth was that he insisted all his life that he was a journalist. He could not be a novelist, because he 'liked to see ideas or notions wrestling naked, as it were, and not dressed up in a masquerade as men and women'. Although there was so much that he could do with his pen, he could be nothing with his whole heart but a journalist. What he meant by being a journalist was being engaged in direct democratic appeal to the reading public about disputed or disputable questions of any sort or kind. Not many journalists, it is true, answer to this description; still, there are journalists who answer to it, and who are sometimes called, with more precision, publicists. G.K.C., then, was a journalist in this sense, and in the sense, also, that he made his living by writing for the Press; for what he earned by that means was the backbone of his income.

To live in this way was his deliberate choice. There can be no doubt of that, for it was a hard life, and a much easier one lay ready to his hand. As a writer of books, as a poet, he had an assured position and an inexhaustible fund of ideas; the friends who desired him to make the most of that position were many. Bernard Shaw used to prod him in the direction of the theatre. But G.K.C. preferred the existence of a regular contributor to the Press, bound by iron rules as to space and time. Getting his copy to the office before it was too late was often a struggle. Having to think of a deadline at all was always an inconvenience. His travels were fairly extensive, including two visits to the United States; but they never interrupted the flow of his weekly essays. A large number, perhaps as many as twenty-five, were written in advance, others were dictated in hotel bedrooms wherever he happened to be. In his later years, after the establishment of *G.K's Weekly,* it required regular contributions from him; and often there were articles to be written for the *Universe.*

It was a style to which a number of delicate minds could never be reconciled. In the days before that style had to be accepted as an inevitable feature of the English literary landscape, his editors used to receive many letters protesting passionately against the work of a writer who treated even the most serious subjects with levity, and could not possibly believe in his own nonsense. The notion at the bottom of this sort of objection was, no doubt, that serious subjects are dull, and that it is therefore unbecoming to be anything but dull in writing about them. Useless for G.K.C. to protest, as he sometimes did in print, that he was in earnest about everything he wrote, and never in his life said a thing merely because he thought it was amusing. One of the best of his few apologies for his style may he found at the end of the essay placed first in this collection: the one about Gargoyles. Here he says, speaking of his own writings, that these monsters are meant for the gargoyles of a definite cathedral!'

INTRODUCTION

'I have to carve the gargoyles, because I can carve nothing else; I leave to others the angels and the arches and the spires. But I am very sure of the style of the architecture and of the consecration of the church.'

In this book one may find matter almost purely literary, such as the account given of the manner in which the poet Gray probably did write the 'Elegy in a Country Churchyard', as distinct from the manner in which innocent minds suppose him to have written it – sitting on a tombstone in Stoke Poges. Or there is the social-political appraisement of the writings of Anthony Trollope. There are many essays of an interest; mainly historical-political, such as the essay on Poland or that on 'Our Latin Relations'. There are essays which are entirely concerned with morals, such as that 'On Experience' – one of the most Chestertonian things in the book, with so much of that regrettable introduction of humour into the discussion of serious subjects – or that on 'The Contented Man', so full of wisdom and understanding, containing the typical Chestertonian passage:

'True contentment is a thing as active as agriculture. It is the power of getting out of any situation all that there is in it. It is arduous and it is rare.'

There are also to be found in these pages essays which are simply exercises in fun. No other writer that ever lived could have produced 'What I Found in My Pockets'– that unknown treasury explored by G.K.C. for the first time when he had nothing to read on a dull railway journey. And who else could have written that triumph of nonsense, the essay called simply 'Cheese', with its cloud-capped pinnacles of ridiculous fantasy adorning a lifelong practical knowledge of the subject?

G.K.C.'s essays have always been my top favourite and I cherish them for sheer excellence.

E. C. BENTLEY

About the Author

GILBERT KEITH CHESTERTON

(1874-1936)

G.K. Chesterton was born in London, England, in a well-to-do family. After schooling and college education in arts, he decided not to practice art professionally, but instead, elected to go into journalistic writing. Modestly, he called himself a mere 'rollicking journalist,' but in reality, was a prolific and gifted writer in virtually every field of literature. Chesterton, a man of strong opinions, was enormously talented at defending his views. Though his beliefs were at variance with contemporary luminaries like George Bernard Shaw and H.G. Wells, his exuberant personality nonetheless enabled him to maintain close relationship with them. Together with Hilaire Belloc he opposed the Socialism of Shaw and Wells, and the imperialism of Kipling, becoming the robust champion of Traditionalism. The duo revolted against the sordidness of industrialization and complex moral issues, preferring the orthodoxy and authority.

G.K. Chesterton was one of the few journalists to oppose the Boer War*. GKC's works of social and literary criticism: *Robert Browning* (1903), *Charles Dickens* (1906), and *The Victorian Age in Literature* (1913) were interspaced with powerful fiction: *The Napoleon of Notting Hill* (1904) and the

---

* Fought between Great Britain and two Boer [Afrikaner] republics, namely the South Africans and the Orange Free State, from 1899 to 1902. It was caused by the Boers' refusal to grant political rights in the interior mining districts, to the aggressive British settlers. The British prevailed, but only on resorting to the 'scorched-earth' policy that bold people like GKC criticized openly.

popular allegorical novel *The Man who was Thursday* (1908). He fearlessly attacked what was the most progressive of all ideas: the notion that the humans were destined to breed a superior version of themselves. The wisdom of his once 'reactionary' views was historically demonstrated later in the Nazi experience.

GKC's poetry ranged from the comic to serious ballads. During the dark era of 1940s when Britain single-handedly faced the armed threats of Nazi Germany, this quatrain from his 'Ballad of the White Horse' (1911), was oft-quoted:

> *I tell you naught for your comfort,*
> *Yea, naught for your desire,*
> *Save that the sky grows darker yet*
> *And the sea rises higher.*

Chesterton's 'Father Brown' tales of suspense and mystery, written between 1911 and 1936, are still in demand even today. Certainly not seen as a political thinker, GKC's political influence on the world leaders has been reckonable – particularly his 'small is beautiful' slogan, and his abhorrence of concentrated wealth and power. Fun-loving and gregarious, Chesterton did once entertain thoughts of suicide but took solace in Christianity for the answers to the dilemmas and paradoxes in life. Converting later to Roman Catholicism in 1922, he showed keen interest in theology and religious argument.

G.K. Chesterton died in June 1936 in Beaconsfield, Buckinghamshire. During his entire life between 1905 and 1936 he wrote almost daily for his contractual obligations, particularly for *G.K.'s Weekly* and the *Universe*. He saw publication of a staggering 60 books, and as many as another ten were brought out after his death.

CONTENTS

On Gargoyles

ALONE AT some distance from the wasting walls of a disused abbey I found half sunken in the grass the grey and goggle-eyed visage of one of those graven monsters that made the ornamental waterspouts in the cathedrals of the Middle Ages. It lay there, scoured by ancient rains or striped by recent fungus, but still looking like the head of some huge dragon slain by a primeval hero. And as I looked at it, I thought of the meaning of the grotesque, and passed into some symbolic reverie of the three great stages of art.

* * *

I

Once upon a time there lived upon an island a merry and innocent people, mostly shepherds and tillers of the earth. They were republicans, like all primitive and simple souls; they talked over their affairs under a tree, and the nearest approach they had to a personal ruler was a sort of priest or white witch who said their prayers for them. They worshipped the sun, not idolatrously, but as the golden crown of the god whom all such infants see almost as plainly as the sun.

Now this priest was told by his people to build a great tower, pointing to the sky in salutation of the Sun-god; and he pondered long and heavily before he picked his materials. For he was resolved to use nothing that was not almost as clear and exquisite as sunshine itself; he would use nothing that was not washed as white as the rain can wash the heavens, nothing that did not sparkle as spotlessly as that crown of God. He would have nothing grotesque or obscure; he would not have even anything emphatic or even anything mysterious. He would have all the arches as light as laughter and as candid as logic. He built the temple in three concentric courts, which were cooler and more exquisite in substance each than the other. For the outer wall was a hedge of white lilies, ranked so thick that a green stalk was hardly to be seen; and the wall within that was of crystal, which smashed the sun into a million stars. And the wall within that, which was the tower itself, was a tower of pure water, forced up in an everlasting fountain and upon the very tip and crest of that foaming spire; was one big and blazing diamond, which the water tossed up eternally and caught again as a child catches a ball.

'Now,' said the priest, 'I have made a tower which is a little worthy of the sun.'

II

But about this time the island was caught in a swarm of pirates; and the shepherds had to turn themselves into rude warriors and seamen; and at first they were utterly broken-down in blood and shame; and the pirates might have taken the jewel flung up for ever from their sacred fount. And then, after years of horror and humiliation, they gained a little and began to conquer because they did not mind defeat. And the pride of the pirates went sick within them after a few unexpected foils; and at last the invasion rolled back into the empty seas and the island was delivered. And for some reason after this men began to talk quite differently about the temple and the sun. Some, indeed, said, 'You must not touch the temple; it is classical; it is perfect, since it admits no imperfections.' But the others answered, 'In that it differs from the sun, that shines on the evil and the good and on mud and monsters everywhere. The temple is of the noon; it is made of white marble clouds and sapphire sky. But the sun is not always of the noon. The sun dies daily; every night he is crucified in blood and fire.'

Now the priest had taught and fought through all the war, and his hair had grown white, but his eyes had grown young.

And he said, 'I was wrong and they are right. The sun, the symbol of our father, gives life to all those earthly things that are full of ugliness and energy. All the exaggerations are right, if they exaggerate the right thing. Let us point to heaven with tusks and horns and fins and trunks and tails so long as they all point to heaven. The ugly animals praise God as much as the beautiful. The frog's eyes stand out of his head because he is staring at heaven. The giraffe's neck is long because he is stretching towards heaven. The donkey has ears to hear – let him hear.'

And under the new inspiration they planned a gorgeous cathedral in the Gothic manner, with all the animals of the earth crawling over it, and all the possible ugly things making up one common beauty, because they all appealed to the god. The columns of the temple were carved like the necks of giraffes; the dome was like an ugly tortoise; and the highest pinnacle was a monkey standing on his head with his tail pointing at the sun. And yet the whole was beautiful, because it was lifted up in one living and religious gesture as a man lifts his hands in prayer.

III

But this great plan was never properly completed. The people had brought up on great wagons the heavy tortoise roof and the huge necks of stone, and all the thousand and one oddities that made up that unity, the owls and the efts and the crocodiles and the kangaroos, which hideous by themselves might have been magnificent if reared in one definite proportion and dedicated to the sun. For this was Gothic, this was romantic, this was Christian art; this was the whole advance of Shakespeare upon Sophocles.* And that symbol which was to crown it all, the ape upside down, was really Christian; for man is the ape upside down.

---

* Greek playwright (496-406 BC), who along with Aeschylus and Euripides wrote great tragedies in the era of classical Athens.

But the rich, who had grown riotous in the long peace, obstructed the things, and in some squabble a stone struck the priest on the head and he lost his memory. He saw piled in front of him frogs and elephants, monkeys and giraffes, toadstools and sharks, all the ugly things of the universe which he had collected to do honour to God. But he forgot why he had collected them. He could not remember the design or the object. He piled them all wildly into one heap fifty feet high; and when he had done it all, the rich and influential went into a passion of applause and cried, 'This is real art! This is Realism! This is things as they really are!'

*   *   *

That, I fancy, is the only true origin of Realism. Realism is simply Romanticism that has lost its reason. This is not so merely in the sense of insanity but of suicide. It has lost its reason; that is its reason for existing. The old Greeks summoned godlike things to worship their god. The medieval Christians summoned all things to worship theirs, dwarfs and pelicans, monkeys and madmen. The modern realists summon all these million creatures to worship their god; and then have no god for them to worship. Paganism was in art a pure beauty; that was the dawn. Christianity was a beauty created by controlling a million monsters of ugliness; and that in my belief was the zenith and the noon. Modern art and science practically mean having the million monsters and being unable to control them; and I will venture to call that the disruption and the decay. The finest lengths of the Elgin marbles consist of splendid horses going to the temple of a virgin. Christianity, with its gargoyles and grotesques, really amounted to saying this: that a donkey could go before all the horses of the world when it was really going to the temple. Romance means a holy donkey going to the temple. Realism means a lost donkey going nowhere.

The fragments of futile journalism or fleeting impression which are here collected are very like the wrecks and riven blocks that were piled in a heap round my imaginary priest of the sun. They are very like that grey and gaping head of stone that I found overgrown with the grass. Yet I will venture to make even of these trivial fragments the high boast that I am a medievalist and not a modern. That is, I really have a notion of why I have collected all the nonsensical things there are. I have not the patience nor perhaps the constructive intelligence to state the connecting link between all these chaotic papers. But it could be stated. This row of shapeless and ungainly monsters which I now set before the reader does not consist of separate idols cut out capriciously in lonely valleys or various islands. These monsters are meant for the gargoyles of a definite cathedral. I have to carve the gargoyles, because I can carve nothing else; I leave to others the angels and the arches and the spires. But I am very sure of the style of the architecture and of the consecration of the church.

The Contented Man

THE WORD content is not inspiring nowadays; rather it is irritating because it is dull. It prepares the mind for a little sermon in the style of the Vicar of Wakefield about how you and I should be satisfied with our countrified innocence and our simple village sports. The word, however, has two meanings, somewhat singularly connected; the 'sweet content' of the poet and the 'cubic content' of the mathematician. Some distinguish these by stressing the different syllables. Thus, it might happen to any of us, at some social juncture, to remark gaily, 'Of the content of the King of the Cannibal Islands' stewpot I am con*tent* to be ignorant'; or 'Not con*tent* with measuring the cubic *con*tent of my safe, you are stealing the spoons.' And there really is an analogy between the mathematical and the moral use of the term, for lack of the observation of which the latter has been much weakened and misused.

The preaching of contentment is in disrepute, well deserved in so far that the moral is really quite inapplicable to the anarchy and insane peril of our tall and toppling cities. Content suggests some kind of security; and it is not strange that our workers should often think about rising above their position, since they have so continually to think about sinking below it. The philanthropist who urges the poor to saving and simple pleasures, deserves all the derision that he gets. To advise people to be content with what they have got may or may not be sound moral philosophy.

But to urge people to be content with what they haven't got is a piece of impudence hard for even the English poor to pardon. But though the creed of content is unsuited to certain special riddles and wrongs, it remains true for the normal of mortal life. We speak of divine discontent; discontent may sometimes be a divine thing, but content must always be the human thing. It may be true that a particular man, in his relation to his master or his neighbour, to his country or his enemies, will do well to be fiercely unsatisfied or thirsting for an angry justice. But it is not true, no sane person can call it true, that man as a whole in his general attitude towards the world, in his posture towards death or green fields, towards the weather or the baby, will be wise to cultivate dissatisfaction. In a broad estimate of our earthly experience, the great truism on the tablet remains: he must not covet his neighbour's ox, nor his ass, nor anything that is his. In highly complex and scientific civilizations, nine times out of ten, he only wants his own ass back.

* * *

But I wish to urge the case for cubic content; in which (even more than in moral content) I take a personal interest. Now, moral content has been undervalued and neglected because of its separation from the other meaning. It has become a negative rather than a positive thing. In some accounts of contentment it seems to be little more than a meek despair.

But this is not the true meaning of the term; it should stand for the idea of a positive and thorough appreciation of the content of anything; for feeling the substance and rot merely the surface of experience. 'Content' ought to mean in English, as it does in French, being pleased; placidly, perhaps, but still positively pleased. Being contented with bread and cheese ought not to mean not caring what you eat. It ought to mean caring for bread and cheese; handling and enjoying the cubic content of the bread and cheese and adding it to your own. Being content with an attic ought not to mean being unable to move from it and resigned to living in it. It ought to mean appreciating what there is to appreciate in such a position; such as the quaint and elvish slope of the ceiling or the sublime aerial view of the opposite chimney-pots. And in this sense contentment is a real and even an active virtue; it is not only affirmative, but creative. The poet in the attic does not forget the attic in poetic musings; he remembers whatever the attic has of poetry; he realizes how high, how starry, how cool, how unadorned and simple in short, how Attic is the attic.

True contentment is a thing as active as agriculture. It is the power of getting out of any situation all that there is in it. It is arduous and it is rare. The absence of this digestive talent is what makes so cold and incredible the tales of so many people who say they have been 'through' things; when it is evident that they have come out on the other side quite unchanged. A man might have gone 'through' a plum pudding as a bullet might go through a plum pudding; it depends on the size of the pudding – and the man. But the awful and sacred question is 'Has the pudding been through him?' Has he tasted, appreciated, and absorbed the solid pudding, with its three dimensions and its three thousand tastes and smells? Can he offer himself to the eyes of men as one who has cubically conquered and contained a pudding?

* * *

In the same way we may ask of those who profess to have passed through trivial or tragic experiences whether they have absorbed the content of them; whether they licked up such living water as there was. It is a pertinent question in connexion with many modern problems.

Thus the young genius says, 'I have lived in my dreary and squalid village before I found success in Paris or Vienna.' The sound philosopher will answer, 'You have never lived in your village, or you would not call it dreary and squalid.'

Thus the Imperialist, the Colonial idealist (who commonly speaks and always thinks with a Yankee accent), will say, 'I've been right away from these little muddy islands, and seen God's great seas and prairies.' The sound philosopher will reply, 'You have never been in these islands; you have never seen the weald of Sussex or the plain of Salisbury; otherwise you could never have called them either muddy or little.'

Thus the Suffragette will say, 'I have passed through the paltry duties of pots and pans, the drudgery of the vulgar kitchen; but I have come out to intellectual liberty.' The sound philosopher will answer, 'You have never passed through the kitchen, or you never would call it vulgar. Wiser and stronger women than you have really seen a poetry in pots and pans; naturally, because there is a poetry in them.' It is right for the village violinist to climb into fame in Paris or Vienna; it is right for the stray Englishman to climb across the high shoulder of the world; it is right for the woman to climb into whatever *cathedrae* or high places she can allow to her sexual dignity. But it is wrong that any of these climbers should kick the ladder by which they have climbed. But indeed these bitter people who record their experiences really record their lack of experiences. It is the countryman who has not succeeded in being a countryman who comes up to London. It is the clerk who has not succeeded in being a clerk who tries (on vegetarian principles) to be a countryman. And the woman with a past is generally a woman angry about the past she never had.

When you have really exhausted an experience you always reverence and love it. The two things that nearly all of us have thoroughly and really been through are childhood and youth. And though we would not have them back again on any account, we feel that they are both beautiful, because we have drunk them dry.

The End of the World

FOR SOME time I had been wandering in quiet streets in the curious town of Besançon, which stands like a sort of peninsula in a horseshoe of river. You may learn from the guide-books that it was the birthplace of Victor Hugo, and that it is a military station with many forts, near to the French frontier. But you will not learn from guide-books that the very tiles on the roofs seem to be of some quainter and more delicate colour than the tiles of all the other towns of the world; that the tiles look like the little clouds of some strange sunset, or like the lustrous scales of some strange fish. They will not tell you that in this town the eye cannot rest on anything without finding it in some way attractive and even elvish, a carved face at a street corner, a gleam of green fields through a stunted arch, or some unexpected colour for the enamel of a spire or dome.

* * *

Evening was coming on and in the light of it all these colours so simple and yet so subtle seemed more and more to fit together and make a fairy tale. I sat down outside a cafe with a row of little toy trees in front of it, and presently the driver of a fly (as we should call it) came to the same place. He was one of those very large and dark Frenchmen, a type not common but yet typical of France; the Rabelaisian Frenchman, huge, swarthy, purple-faced, a walking wine-barrel; he was a sort of Southern Falstaff, if one can imagine Falstaff anything but English. And, indeed, there was a vital difference, typical of two nations. For while Falstaff would have been shaking with hilarity like a huge jelly, full of the broad face of the London streets, this Frenchman was rather solemn and dignified than otherwise – as if pleasure were a kind of pagan religion. After some talk which was full of the admirable civility and equality of French civilization, he suggested without either eagerness or embarrassment that he should take me in his fly for an hour's ride in the hills beyond the town. And though it was growing late I consented; for there was one long white road under an archway and round a hill that dragged me like a long white cord. We drove through the strong, squat gateway that was made by the Romans, and I remember the coincidence like a sort of omen that as we passed out of the city I heard simultaneously the three sounds which are the trinity of France. They make what some poet calls 'a tangled trinity', and I am not going to disentangle it. Whatever those three things mean, how or why they co-exist; whether they can be reconciled or perhaps are reconciled already; the three sounds I heard then by an accident all at once make up the French mystery. For the brass band in the Casino gardens behind me was playing with a sort of passionate levity some ramping tune from a Parisian comic opera, and while this was going on I heard also the bugles on the hills above, that told of terrible loyalties and men always arming in the gate of France; and I heard also, fainter than these sounds and through them all, the Angelus.*

* * *

After this coincidence of symbols I had a curious sense of having left France behind me, or, perhaps, even the civilized world. And, indeed, there was something in the landscape wild enough to encourage such a fancy. I have seen perhaps higher mountains, but I have never seen higher rocks; I have never seen height so near, so abrupt and sensational, splinters of rock that stood up like the spires of churches, cliffs that fell sudden and straight as Satan fell from heaven. There was also a quality in the ride which was not only astonishing, but rather bewildering; a quality which many must have noticed if they have driven or ridden rapidly up mountain roads. I mean a sense

---

* A devotional commemoration of the Incarnation said in the mornings, noons and evenings, by the followers of the Western Church.

of gigantic gyration, as of the whole earth turning about one's head. It is quite inadequate to say that the hills rose and fell like enormous waves. Rather the hills seemed to turn about me like the enormous sails of a windmill, a vast wheel of monstrous archangelic wings. As we drove on and up into the gathering purple of the sunset this dizziness increased, confounding things above with things below. Wide walls of wooded rock stood out above my head like a roof I stared at them until I fancied that I was staring down at a wooded plain. Below me steeps of green swept down to the river. I stared at them until I fancied that they swept up to the sky. The purple darkened, night drew nearer; it seemed only to cut clearer the chasms and draw higher the spires of that nightmare landscape. Above me in the twilight was the huge black bulk of the driver, and his broad, blank back was as mysterious as the back of Death in Watt's picture. I felt that I was growing too fantastic, and I sought to speak of ordinary things. I called out to the driver in French, 'Where are you taking me?' and it is a literal and solemn fact that he answered me in the same language without turning round, 'To the end of the world.'

I did not answer. I let him drag the vehicle up dark, steep ways, until I saw lights under a low roof of little trees and two children, one oddly beautiful, playing at ball. Then we found ourselves filling up the strict main street of a tiny hamlet, and across the wall of its inn was written in large letters, *Le Bout du Monde* – 'the end of the world'.

The driver and I sat down outside that inn without a word, as if all ceremonies were natural and understood in that ultimate place. I ordered bread for both of us, and red wine, that was good but had no name. On the other side of the road was a little plain church with a cross on top of it and a cock on top of the cross. This seemed to me a very good end of the world; if the story of the world ended here it ended well. Then I wondered whether I myself should really be content to end here, where most certainly there were the best things of Christendom – a church and children's games and decent soil and a tavern for men to talk with men. But as I thought a singular doubt and desire grew slowly in me, and at last I started up.

'Are you not satisfied?' asked my companion. 'No', I said, 'I am not satisfied even at the end of the world'.

Then, after a silence, I said, 'Because you see there are two ends of the world. And this is the wrong end of the world; at least the wrong one for me. This is the French end of the world. I want the other end of the world. Drive me to the other end of the world.'

'The other end of the world?' he asked. 'Where is that?'

'It is in Walham Green', I whispered hoarsely. 'You see it on the London omnibuses: 'World's End and Walham Green'. Oh, I know how good this is; I love your vine-yards and your free peasantry, but I want the English end of the world. I love you like a brother, but I want an English cabman, who will be funny and ask me what his fare "is". Your bugles stir my blood, but I want to see a London policeman. Take, oh, take me to see a London policeman.'

He stood quite dark and still against the end of the sunset, and I could not tell whether he understood or not. I got back into his carriage.

'You will understand', I said, 'if ever you are an exile, even for pleasure. The child to his mother, the man to his country, as a countryman of yours once said. But since, perhaps, it is rather too long a drive to the English end of the world, we may as well drive back to Besançon.'

Only as the stars came out among those immortal hills I wept for Walham Green.

The Glory of Grey

I SUPPOSE, that, taking this summer as a whole, people will not call it an appropriate time for praising the English climate. But for my part I will praise the English climate till I die – even if I die of the English climate. There is no weather so good as English weather. Nay, in a real sense there is no weather at all anywhere but in England. In France you have much sun and some rain; in Italy you have hot winds and cold winds; in Scotland and Ireland you have rain, either thick or thin; in America you have hells of heat and cold, and in the Tropics you have sunstrokes varied by thunderbolts. But all these you have on a broad and brutal scale, and you settle down into contentment or despair. Only in our own romantic country do you have the strictly romantic thing called Weather; beautiful and changing as a woman. The great English landscape painters (neglected now like everything that is English) have this salient distinction: that the Weather is not the atmosphere of their pictures; it is the subject of their pictures. They paint portraits of the Weather. The Weather sat to Constable. The Weather posed for Turner; and a deuce of a pose it was. This cannot truly be said of the greatest of their continental models or rivals. Poussin and Claude* painted objects, ancient cities or perfect Arcadian shepherds through a clear medium of the climate. But in the English painters Weather is the hero; with Turner an Adelphi hero, taunting, flashing and fighting, melodramatic but really magnificent. The English climate, a tall and terrible protagonist, robed in rain and thunder and snow and sunlight, fills the whole canvas and the whole foreground. I admit the superiority of many other French things besides French art. But I will not yield an inch on the superiority of English weather and

* Both were French painters. Nicolas Poussin (1594-1665) spent his entire career in Rome, and the works of Lorrain Claude (1600-1682) greatly influenced the European artists.

weather-painting. Why, the French have not even got a word for Weather; and you must ask for the weather in French as if you were asking for the time in English.

Then, again, variety of climate should always go with stability of abode. The weather in the desert is monotonous; and as a natural consequence the Arabs wander about, hoping it may be different somewhere. But an Englishman's house is not only his castle; it is his fairy castle. Clouds and colours of every varied dawn and eve are perpetually touching and turning it from clay to gold, or from gold to ivory. There is a line of woodland beyond a corner of my garden which is literally different on every one of the three hundred and sixty-five days. Sometimes it seems as near as a hedge, and sometimes as far as a faint and fiery evening cloud. The same principle (by the way) applies to the difficult problem of wives. Variability is one of the virtues of a woman. It avoids the crude requirement of polygamy. So long as you have one good wife you are sure to have a spiritual harem.

Now, among the heresies that are spoken in this matter is the habit of calling a grey day a 'colourless' day. Grey is a colour, and can be a very powerful and pleasing colour. There is also an insulting style of speech about 'one grey day just like another'. You might as well talk about one green tree just like another. A grey clouded sky is indeed a canopy between us and the sun; so is a green tree, if it comes to that. But the grey umbrellas differ as much as the green in their style and shape, in their tint and tilt. One day may be grey like steel, and another grey like dove's plumage. One may seem grey like the smoke of substantial kitchens. No things could seem further apart than the doubt of grey and the decision of scarlet. Yet grey and red can mingle, as they do in the morning clouds; and also in a sort of warm smoky stone of which they build the little towns in the west country. In those towns even the houses, that are wholly grey have a glow in them as if their secret, firesides were such furnaces of hospitality as faintly to transfuse the walls like walls of cloud. And wandering in those westland parts I did once really find a sign-post pointing up a steep crooked path to a town that was called Clouds. I did not climb up to it; I feared that either the town would not be good enough for the name, or I should not be good enough for the town. Anyhow, the little hamlets of the warm grey stone have a geniality which is not achieved by all the artistic scarlet of the suburbs; as if it were better to warm one's hands at the ashes of Glastonbury than at the painted flames of Croydon.

Again, the enemies of grey (those astute, daring and evil-minded men) are fond of bringing forward the argument that colours suffer in grey weather, and that strong sunlight is necessary to all the hues of heaven and earth. Here again there are two words to be said; and it is essential to distinguish. It is true that sun is needed to burnish and bring into bloom the tertiary and dubious colours; the colour of peat, pea-soap, Impressionist sketches, brown velvet coats, olives, grey and blue slates, the complexions of vegetarians, the tinge of volcanic rock, chocolate, cocoa, mud, soot, slime, old boots; the delicate shades of these do need the sunlight to bring out the faint beauty that often clings to them. But if you have a healthy negro taste in colour, if you choke your garden with poppies and geraniums, if you paint your house sky-blue and scarlet, if you wear, let us say, a golden top-hat and a crimson frock-coat, you will not only be visible on the greyest day, but you will notice that your costume and environment produce a certain singular effect. You will find, I mean, that rich colours actually look more luminous on a grey day, because they are seen against a sombre background and seem to be burning with a lustre of their own. Against a dark sky all flowers look like fireworks. There is something strange about them, at once vivid and secret, like flowers traced in fire in the phantasmal garden of a witch. A bright blue sky is necessarily the high light of the picture; and its brightness kills all the bright blue flowers. But on a grey day the larkspur looks like fallen heaven; the red daisies are really the red lost eyes of day; and the sunflower is the vice-regent of the sun.

Lastly, there is this value about the colour that men call colourless; that it suggests in some way the mixed and troubled average of existence, especially in its quality of strife and expectation and promise. Grey is a colour that always seems on the eve of changing to some other colour; of brightening into blue or blanching into white or bursting into green and gold. So we may be perpetually reminded of the indefinite hope that is in doubt itself; and when there is grey weather in our hills or grey hairs in our heads, perhaps they may still remind us of the morning.

Cheese

MY FORTHCOMING work in five volumes, 'The Neglect of Cheese in European Literature', is a work of such unprecedented and laborious detail that it is doubtful if I shall live to finish it. Some overflowings from such a fountain of information may therefore be permitted to sprinkle these pages. I cannot yet wholly explain the neglect to which I refer. Poets have been mysteriously silent on the subject of cheese. Virgil, if I remember right, refers to it several times, but with too much Roman restraint. He does not let himself go on cheese. The only other poet I can think of just now who seems to have had some sensibility on the point was the nameless author of the nursery rhyme which says: 'If all the trees were bread and cheese' – which is, indeed, a rich and gigantic vision of the higher gluttony. If all the trees were bread and cheese there would be considerable deforestation in any part of England where I was living. Wild and wide woodlands would reel and fade before me as rapidly as they ran after Orpheus. Except Virgil and this anonymous rhymer, I can recall no verse about cheese. Yet it has every quality which we require in exalted poetry. It is a short, strong word; it rhymes to 'breeze' and 'seas' (an essential point); that it is emphatic in sound is admitted even by the civilization of the modern cities. For their citizens, with no apparent intention except emphasis, will often say, 'Cheese it!' or even 'Quite the cheese'. The substance itself is imaginative. It is ancient – sometimes in the individual case, always in the type and custom. It is simple, being directly derived from milk, which is one of the ancestral drinks, not likely to be corrupted with soda-water. You know, I hope (though I myself have only just thought of it), that the four rivers of Eden were milk, water, wine, and ale. Aerated waters only appeared after the Fall.

But cheese has another quality, which is also the very soul of song. Once in endeavouring to lecture in several places at once,

I made an eccentric journey across England, a journey of so irregular and even illogical shape that it necessitated my having lunch on four successive days in four roadside inns in four different counties. In each inn they had nothing but bread and cheese; nor can I imagine why a man should want more than bread and cheese, if he can get enough of it. In each inn the cheese was good; and in each inn it was different. There was a noble Wensleydale cheese in Yorkshire, a Cheshire cheese in Cheshire, and so on. Now, it is just here that true poetic civilization differs from that paltry and mechanical civilization which holds us all in bondage. Bad customs are universal and rigid, like modern militarism. Good customs are universal and varied, like native chivalry and self-defence. Both the good and bad civilization cover us as with a canopy, and protect us from all that is outside. But a good civilization spreads over us freely like a tree, varying and yielding because it is alive. A bad civilization stands up and sticks out above us like an umbrella – artificial, mathematical in shape; not merely universal, but uniform. So it is with the contrast between the substances that vary and the substances that are the same wherever they penetrate. By a wise doom of heaven men were commanded to eat cheese, but not the same cheese. Being really universal it varies from valley to valley. But if, let us say, we compare cheese with soap (that vastly inferior substance), we shall see that soap tends more and more to be merely Smith's Soap or Brown's Soap, sent automatically all over the world. If the Red Indians have soap it is Smith's Soap. If the Grand Lama has soap it is Brown's Soap. There is nothing subtly and strangely Buddhist, nothing tenderly Tibetan about his soap. I fancy the Grand Lama does not eat cheese (he is not worthy), but if he does it is probably a local cheese, having some relation to his life and outlook. Safety matches, tinned foods, patent medicines are sent all over the world; but they are not produced all over the world. Therefore there is in them a mere dead identity, never that soft play of slight variation which exists in things produced everywhere out of the soil, in the milk of the kine, or the fruits of the orchard. You can get a whisky and soda at every outpost of the Empire; that is why so many Empire-builders go mad. But you are not tasting or touching any environment, as in the cider of Devonshire or the grapes of the Rhine. You are not approaching Nature in one of her myriad tints of mood, as in the holy act of eating cheese.

When I had done my pilgrimage in the four wayside public-houses, I reached one of the great northern cities, and there I proceeded, with great rapidity and complete inconsistency, to a large and elaborate restaurant, where I knew I could get many other things besides bread and cheese. I could get that also, however, or at least I expected to get it; but I was sharply reminded that I had entered Babylon, and left England behind. The waiter brought me cheese, indeed, but cheese cut up into contemptibly small pieces; and it is the awful fact that, instead of Christian bread, he brought me biscuits. Biscuits – to one who had eaten the cheese of four great countrysides! Biscuits – to one who had proved anew for himself the sanctity of the ancient wedding between cheese and bread! I addressed the waiter in warm and moving terms. I asked him who he was, that he should put asunder those whom Humanity had joined. I asked him if he did not feel, as an artist, that a solid but yielding substance like cheese went naturally with a solid; yielding substance like bread; to eat it off biscuits is like eating it off slates. I asked him if, when he said his prayers, he was so supercilious as to pray for his daily biscuits. He gave me generally to understand that he was only obeying a custom of Modern Society. I have therefore resolved to raise my voice, not against the waiter, but against Modern Society, for this huge and unparalleled modern wrong.

✦━━━●━━━━━━●━━✦

On the Classics

IN A moment of fine frenzy a young man has stood up and declared that 'the study of Latin and Greek is not of much use in the battle of life', and gone on to demand that the young should be instructed chiefly in the science of Health – that is, in the facts and the functions of the body. The young man in question will be gratified to know that I, for one, consistently neglected to do any work at the school in which I was supposed to be learning Latin and Greek, though I am not sure that the mere fact of idleness and ignorance can be said to have armed and drilled me for the battle of life. But, when I consider such armour or armament, some faint memories come to me from the learning that I neglected. There flits across my mind the phrase *aes triplex*,* and I remember how Stevenson used it for a title to his essay defending a cheerful contempt for medical fussing; and how he cited the example of Dr. Johnson, who dreaded death and yet disdained any vigilance against disease; and whose 'heart, bound with triple brass, did not recoil before the prospect of twenty-seven individual cups of tea'. It is, doubtless, terrible to think that Stevenson took his Stoical image of triple brass from a Latin poet; and still more terrible to think that Johnson would have approved of Stevenson for quoting the Latin poets. But though Stevenson and Johnson were superficially about as different as any two men could be in everything except in this weakness for traditional scholarship, I do not think that either of them can be said to have come off so badly in fighting the battle of life.

The trouble about always trying to preserve the health of the body is that it is so difficult to do it without destroying the health of the mind. Health is the most unhealthy of topics: Those who support such hygienic culture always profess to be very practical, and compare their own healthy materialism with the visionary futilities of everybody connected with the classics from Julius

* Triple brass armour.

Caesar to Johnson. But, in fact, it is in practice that their practical ideal breaks down. There is no difficulty about talking and writing in general terms of the facts of nature, or what are commonly called the God-given functions of man. It is when people really begin to teach these things, as if they were algebra or geography, that they discover a surprising number of difficulties – not to say diseases. Upon this point of practical application I will only mention one example out of the statement referred to above. The young man in question frankly admits that he would dislike having to read a list of hideous malformations or foul diseases to an infant school or a row of staring babies. He says that this might, doubtless, be inadvisable, and lead to morbid fears and fancies. Anyhow, he disapproves of such physiology in the nursery; every man has a sane spot somewhere. But he goes on to say that big boys, presumably towards the end of their school career, should have learnt to balance and appreciate such knowledge; and it is such knowledge which they ought above all things to know.

Now it seems to me that the argument is very much the other way. The period when many boys, we might almost say most boys, are capable of morbidly misusing a medical knowledge is exactly the period at which he proposes to give it to them. I imagine it would do, in comparison, precious little harm to a child of five. If you talk to a child about an aortic aneurysm,* he will not be frightened; he will only be bored. If you talk to a boy of fifteen or sixteen about it, and give only a few fragmentary hints of what it is like, he will very probably come to the rapid conclusion that he has got one. All that is necessary is to have odd sensations round the heart; and digestion, or indigestion, will do that at any time of life, but rather specially at the time when digestion is tried by unripe apples or cob nuts before lunch. Youth is a period when the wildest external carelessness often runs parallel to the most

*An abnormal dilation of a blood vessel.

gloomy and concentrated internal cares. An enormous number of normal youths are quite abnormal for a time. Their imagination is working inwards and on nothing more commonly than on imaginary maladies, to throw a medical encyclopaedia at the head of a young man in this condition is simply to provide him with a handbook of 'One Thousand Ways of Going Mad.' A doctor once told me that even among medical students there is a perceptible proportion of this medical mania; and they have all the correcting elements of a special vocation, of a scientific atmosphere and of more complete and therefore more balanced knowledge. Ordinary people receiving an ordinary smattering of such knowledge are very likely indeed to find that little knowledge is a dangerous thing.

But the essential truth is that those who talk to us about facts have not faced the chief fact of all and, indeed, the fact is also a paradox. Facts as facts do not always create a spirit of reality, because reality is a spirit. Facts by themselves can often feed the flame of madness, because sanity is a spirit. Consider the huge accumulations of detail piled up by men who have some crazy hobby of believing that Herodotus wrote Homer or that the Great Pyramid was a prophecy of the Great War. Consider the concrete circumstances and connected narratives that can often be given at vast lengths and in laborious detail by men who suffer from a delusion of being persecuted, or being disinherited, or being the rightful King of England. These men are maddened by material facts; they are lunatics not by their fancies but by having learned too many facts. What they lack is proportion: a thing as invisible as beauty, as inscrutable as God. And when we thus realize the real problem of morbidity and medicine we may begin to catch a far-off glimpse of something distant, but not quite so dispensable as we had supposed; and find ourselves once more faintly conscious of the presence of the case for Classical Education, so useless in the battle of life.

What culture does, or ought to do, is to give a health of the mind that is parallel to the health of the body. It is ultimately a matter of intellectual instincts that are almost like bodily instincts. A sane man knows when something would drive him mad, just as a man standing up knows at what angle he would fall down. He does not have to calculate the angle with a mathematical instrument, or fall flat on his nose forty times in a series of scientific experiments. The body, like the mind, knows its own equilibrium. But it knows it better than the mind; because the problem is simpler, and the physical instincts are less paralysed by false teaching. Now the true teaching, which strengthens and steadies the mind so that it knows and rejects madness at sight, has, in fact, come down to us very largely from the culture of those great languages in which were written the works of the last Stoics and the first Saints, the Greek Testament and the Roman Law.

To be of the company of such men, to have the mind filled with such words, to remember the tone of their orators or the gesture of their statues, is to feel a steadying power upon the spirit and a love of large spaces and large ideas, rather than of little lunacies and secrecies. It is something that understands at once modesty and dignity; something that is never servility and never pride. It is the power in the mind that can keep order among the virtues often almost as dangerous as the vices. No catalogue of facts will give it; yet we can hear it instantly in the sound of some random Roman verse. That is why the great men I have named, so different in their natures, felt that the classics did count somehow in the battle of life. When Johnson says, "The shepherd in Virgil became acquainted with love, and found him a native of the rocks,' we know that his rage against Chesterfield will never go beyond a grand restrain; when Stevenson says, 'We have heard perhaps too much of lesser matters. Here is the poor, here is the open air. *Itur in antiquam silvam,'* we know that for such a mind lunacies will always be lesser matters and sanity be like the open air.

—————————

* (Lat.) They go into the ancient wood.

A Cab Ride across Country

SOWN SOMEWHERE far off in the shallow dales of Hertfordshire there lies a village of great beauty, and I doubt not of admirable virtue, but of eccentric and unbalanced literary taste, which asked the present writer to come down to it on Sunday afternoon and give an address. Now it was very difficult to get down to it at all on Sunday afternoon, owing to the indescribable state into which our national laws and customs have fallen in connexion with the seventh day. It is not Puritanism; it is simply anarchy. I should have some sympathy with the Jewish Sabbath, if it were a Jewish Sabbath, and that for three reasons. First, that religion is an intrinsically sympathetic thing; second, that I cannot conceive any religion worth calling a religion without fixed and material observances; and third, that the particular observance of sitting still and doing no work is one that suits my temperament down to the ground.

But the absurdity of the modern English convention is that it does not let a man sit still; it only perpetually trips him up when it has forced him to walk about. Our Sabbatarianism does not forbid us to ask a man in Battersea to come and talk in Hertfordshire; it only prevents his getting there. I can understand that a deity might be worshipped with joys, with flowers, and fireworks in the old European style. I can understand that a deity might be worshipped with sorrows. But I cannot imagine any deity being worshipped with inconveniences. Let the good Moslem go to Mecca, or let him abide in his tent, according to his feeling for religious symbols. But surely Allah cannot see anything particularly dignified in his servant being misled by the time-table, finding that the old Mecca express is not running, missing his connexion at Baghdad, or having to wait three hours in a small side station outside Damascus.

So it was with me on this occasion. I found there was no telegraph service at all to this place; I found there was only one weak thread of train-service. Now if this had been the authority of real English religion, I should have submitted to it at once. If I believed that the telegraph clerk could not send the telegram because he was at that moment rigid in an ecstasy of prayer, I should think all telegrams unimportant in comparison. If I could believe that railway porters when relieved from their duties rushed with passion to the nearest place of worship, I should say that all lectures and everything else ought to give way to such a consideration. I should not complain if the national faith forbade me to make any appointments of labour or self-expression on the Sabbath. But, as it is, it only tells me that I may very probably keep the Sabbath by not keeping the appointment.

* * *

But I must resume the sad details of my tale. I found that there was only one train in the whole of that Sunday by which I could even get within several hours or several miles of the time or place. I therefore went to the telephone, which is one of my favourite toys, and down which I have shouted many valuable, but prematurely arrested, monologues upon art and morals. I remember a mild shock of surprise when I dis-covered that one could use the telephone on Sunday; I did not expect it to be cut off, but I expected it to buzz more than on ordinary days, to the advancement of our national religion. Through this instrument, in fewer words than usual, and with a comparative economy of epigram I ordered a taxi-cab to take me to the railway station. I have not a word to say in general either against telephones or taxi-cabs; they seem to me two of the purest and most poetic of the creations of modern scientific civilization. Unfortunately, when the taxi-cab started, it did exactly what modern scientific civilization has done – it broke down, The result of this was that when I arrived at King's Cross my only train was gone; there was a Sabbath calm in the station, a calm in the eyes of the porters, and in my breast if calm at all, if any calm, a calm despair.

There was not, however, very much calm of any sort in my breast on first making the discovery; and it was turned to blinding horror when I learnt that I could not even send a telegram to the organizers of the meeting. To leave my entertainers in the lurch was sufficiently exasperating; to leave them without any intimation was simply low. I reasoned with the official. I said, 'Do you really mean to say that if my brother were dying and my mother in this place, I could not communicate with her?' He was a man of literal and laborious mind; he asked me if my brother was dying. I answered that he was in excellent and even offensive health, but that I was inquiring upon a question of principle. What would happen if England were invaded, or if I alone knew how to turn aside a comet or an earthquake? He waved away these hypotheses in the most irresponsible spirit, but he was quite certain that telegrams could not reach this particular village. Then something exploded in me; that element of the outrageous which is the mother of all adventures sprang up ungovernable, and I decided that I would not take a cab merely because some of my remote ancestors had been Calvinists. I would keep my appointment if I lost all my money and all my wits. I went out into the quiet London street, where my quiet London cab was still waiting for its fare in the cold and misty morning. I placed myself comfortably in the London cab and told the London driver to drive me to the other end of Hertfordshire. And he did.

* * *

I shall not forget that drive. It was doubtful whether, even in a motor-cab, the thing was possible with any consideration for the driver, not to speak of some slight consideration for the people in the road. I urged the driver to eat and drink something before he started, but he said (with I know not what pride of profession or delicate sense of adventure) that he would rather do it when we arrived – if we ever did. I was by no means so refined; I bought a varied selection of pork-pies at a little shop that was open (why was that shop open? – it is all a mystery), and ate them as we went along. The beginning was sombre and irritating. I was annoyed, not with people but with things, like a baby; with the motor for breaking down and with Sunday for being Sunday. And the sight of the northern slums expanded and ennobled, but did not decrease my gloom: Whitechapel has an Oriental gaudiness in its squalor; Battersea and Camberwell have an indescribable bustle of democracy; but the poor parts of North London. . . . . well, perhaps I saw them wrongly under that ashen morning and on that foolish errand.

It was one of those days which more than once this year broke the retreat of winter; a winter day that began too late to be spring. We were already clear of the obstructing crowds, and quickening our pace through a borderland of market gardens and isolated public houses, when the grey showed golden patches and a good light began to glitter on everything. The cab went quicker and quicker. The open land whirled wider and wider; but I did not lose that sense of being battled with and thwarted that I had felt in the thronged slums. Rather the feeling increased, because of the great difficulty of space and time. The faster went the car, the fiercer and thicker I felt the fight.

The whole landscape seemed charging at me – and just missing me. The tall, shining grass went by like showers of arrows; the very trees seemed like lances hurled at my heart, and shaving it by a hair's breadth. Across some vast, smooth valley I saw a beech-tree by the white road stand up little and defiant. It grew bigger and bigger with blinding rapidity. It charged me like a tilting knight, seemed to hack at my head, and pass by. Sometimes, when we went round a curve of road, the effect was yet more awful. It seemed as if some tree or windmill swung round to smite like a boomerang. The sun by this time was a blazing fact; and I saw that all Nature is chivalrous and militant. We do wrong to seek peace in Nature; we should rather seek the nobler sort of war; and see all the trees as green banners.

* * *

I made my speech, arriving just when everybody was deciding to leave. When my cab came reeling into the market-place they decided, with evident disappointment, to remain. Over the lecture I draw a veil. When I came back home I was called to the telephone, and a meek voice expressed regret for the failure of the motor-cab, and even said something about any reasonable payment. 'Payment!' I cried down the telephone. 'Whom can I pay for my own superb experience? What is the usual charge for seeing the clouds shattered by the sun? What is the market price of a tree blue on the skyline and then blinding white in the sun? Mention your price for that windmill that stood behind the hollyhocks in the garden. Let me pay you for......' Here it was, I think, that we were cut off.

About Voltaire

ALL CHRISTIAN history began with that great social occasion when Pilate and Herod[1] shook hands. Hitherto, as everybody knew in Society circles, they had hardly been on speaking terms. Something led them to seek each other's support, a vague sense of social crisis, though very little was happening except the execution of an ordinary batch of criminals. The two rulers were reconciled on the very day when one of these convicts was crucified. That is what many people mean by Peace, and the substitution of a reign of Love for one of Hatred. Whether or no there is honour among thieves, there is always a certain social interdependence and solidarity among murderers; and those sixteenth-century ruffians who conspired to assassinate Riccio or Darnley[2] were always very careful to put their names, and especially each other's names, to what they called a 'band', so that at the worst they might all hang together. Many political friendships – nay, even broad democratic comradeships, are of this nature; and their representatives are really distressed when we decline to identify this form of Love with the original mystical idea of Charity.

It sometimes seems to me that history is dominated and determined by these evil friendships. As all Christian history begins with the happy reconciliation of Herod and Pilate, so all modern history, in the recent revolutionary sense, begins with that strange friendship which ended in a quarrel, as the first quarrel had ended in a friendship. I mean that the two elements of destruction, which make the modern world more and more

1 Pontius Pilate, the Roman prefect of Judaea (d. 36 AD) who had ordered the crucifixion of Jesus; and Herod the Great (73-4 BC), Jewish king of Judaea who had murdered his wife and sons, just to retain power.
2 Lord Darnley, orig. Henry Stewart (1545-1567). English nobleman, husband of Mary, Queen of Scots, and father of James I. A pretender to the Scottish throne, Henry wed his cousin Mary in 1565 despite the opposition of Elizabeth I. He played a sinister role in the murder of Mary's secretary, David Riccio, but was himself murdered at the instigation of Earl of Bothwell James Hepburn. The Earl thereafter soon married Mary.

incalculable, were loosened with the light of that forgotten day when a lean French gentleman in a large wig, by name M. Arouet, travelled north with much annoyance to find the palace of a Prussian king far away in the freezing Baltic plain. The strict title of the King in dynastic chronicles is Frederick the Second, but he is better known as Frederick the Great. The actual name of the Frenchman was Arouet, but he is better known as Voltaire. The meeting of these two men, in the mid winter of eighteenth-century scepticism and secularism, is a sort of spiritual marriage which brought forth the modern world; *monstrum horrendum, informe, ingens, cui lumen ademptum.* But because that birth was monstrous and evil, and because true friendship and love are not evil, it did not come into the world to create one united thing, but two conflicting things; which, between them, were to shake the world to pieces. From Voltaire the Latins were to learn a raging scepticism. From Frederick the Teutons were to learn a raging pride.

We may note at the start that neither of them cared very much about their own countries or traditions. Frederick was a German who refused even to learn German. Voltaire was a Frenchman who wrote a foul lampoon about Joan of Arc. They were cosmopolitans; they were not in any sense patriots. But there is this difference; that the patriot does, however stupidly, like the country: whereas the cosmopolitan does not in the least like the cosmos. They neither of them pretended to like anything very much. Voltaire was the more really humane of the two; but Frederick also could talk on occasion the cold humanitarianism that was the cant of his age. But Voltaire, even at his best, really began that modern mood that has blighted all the humanitarianism he honestly supported. He started the horrible habit of helping human beings only through pitying them, and never through respecting them. Through him the oppression of the poor became a sort of cruelty to animals, and the loss of all that mystical sense that to wrong the image of God is to insult the ambassador of a King.

Nevertheless, I believe that Voltaire had a heart; I think that Frederick was most heartless when he was most humane. Anyhow, these two great sceptics met on the level, on the dead solid plain, as dull as the Baltic Plain; on the basis that there is no God, or no God who is concerned with men any more than with mites in cheese. On this basis they agreed; on this basis they disagreed; their quarrel was personal and trivial, but it ended by launching two European forces against each other, both rooted in the same unbelief. Voltaire said in effect: 'I will show you that the sneers of a sceptic can produce a Revolution and a Republic and everywhere the overthrowing of thrones.' And Frederick answered: 'And I will show you that this same sneering scepticism can be used as easily to resist Reform, let alone Revolution; that scepticism can be the basis of support for the most tyrannical of thrones, for the bare brute domination of a master over his slaves.' So they said farewell, and have since been sundered by two centuries of war; they said farewell, but presumably did not say 'adieu'.

Of every such evil seed it may be noted that the seed is different from the flower, and the flower from the fruit. A demon of distortion always twists it even out of its own unnatural nature. It may turn into almost anything, except anything really good. It is, to use the playful term of affection which Professor Freud applies to his baby, 'a polymorphous pervert'. These things not only do not produce the special good they promise; they do not produce even the special evil they threaten. The Voltairean revolt promised to produce, and even began to produce, the rise of mobs and overthrow of thrones; but it was not the final form of scepticism. The actual effect of what we call democracy has been the disappearance of the mob. We might say there were mobs at the beginning of the Revolution and no mobs at the end of it. That Voltairean influence has not ended in the rule of mobs, but in the rule of secret societies. It has falsified politics throughout the Latin world, till the recent Italian Counter-Revolution. Voltaire has produced hypocritical and pompous professional politicians, at whom he would have been the first to jeer. But on his side, as I have said, there does linger a certain humane and civilized sentiment which is not unreal. Only it is right to remember what has really gone wrong on his side of the Continental quarrel, when we are recording the much wilder and wickeder wrong on the other side of it.

For the evil spirit of Frederick the Great has produced, not only all other evils, but what might seem the very opposite evil. He who worshipped nothing has become a god who is quite blindly worshipped. He who cared nothing for Germany has become the battle cry of madmen who care for nothing except Germany. He who was a cold cosmopolitan has heated seven times a hell of narrow national and tribal fury which at this moment menaces mankind with a war that may be the end of the world. But the root of both perversions is in the common ground of atheist irresponsibility; there was nothing to stop the sceptic from turning democracy into secrecy; there was nothing to stop him interpreting liberty as the infinite licence of tyranny. The spiritual zero of Christendom was at that freezing instant when those two dry, thin, hatchet-faced men looked in each other's hollow eyes and saw the sneer that was as eternal as the smile of a skull. Between them, they have nearly killed the thing by which we live.

These two points of peril or centres of unrest, the intellectual unrest of the Latins and the very unintellectual unrest of the Teutons, do doubtless both contribute to the instability of international relations, and threaten us all the more because they threaten each other. But when we have made every allowance for there being, in that sense, dangers on both sides, the main modern fact emerges that the danger is mostly on one side, and that we have long been taught to look for it only on the other side. Much of Western opinion, especially English and

American, has been trained to have a vague horror of Voltaire, often combined with a still vaguer respect for Frederick. No Wesleyans are likely to confuse Wesley with Voltaire. No Primitive Methodist is under the impression that Voltaire was a Primitive Methodist. But many such Protestant ministers really were under the impression that Frederick the Great was a Protestant Hero. None of them realized that Frederick was the greater atheist of the two. None of them certainly foresaw that Frederick, in the long run, would turn out to be the greater anarchist of the two. In short, nobody foresaw what everybody afterwards saw: the French Republic becoming a conservative force, and the Prussian Kingdom a purely destructive and lawless force. Victorians like Carlyle[1] actually talked about pious Prussia, as if Blucher[2] had been a saint or Moltke[3] a mystic. General Göring[4] may be trusted to teach us better, till we learn at last that nothing is so anarchical as discipline divorced from authority; that is, from right.

1 Scottish historian and essayist Thomas Carlyle (1795-1881), the author of *The French Revolution* (3 vols., 1837).
2 Gebhard von Blücher (1742-1819), Prussian military leader who commanded Prussian forces in the Battle of Waterloo, coordinating his army with the allied forces under the duke of Wellington to bring about Napoleon's defeat.
3 Helmuth von Moltke (1848-1916), German general till the outbreak of World War I. His errors led to the halt of the German offensive in the Battle of the Marne (1914). He was relieved of his command and died a broken man two years later.
4 Hermann Göering (1893-1946), German Nazi leader who established the Gestapo. As the head of the German air force (Luftwaffe) he failed to win the Battle of Britain. Göring had a vast art collection confiscated from Jews. In 1946 he was condemned to death at the Nuremberg Trials, but in a state of complete breakdown, committed suicide.

About Shamelessness

THERE ARE some who actually like the Country dialects which State education is systematically destroying. There are some who actually prefer them to the Cockney dialect which State education is systematically spreading. For that is perhaps the most practical and successful effect of our present scheme of public instruction, that the village children no longer talk like ignorant inhabitants of Sussex or Suffolk; they now talk like enlightened inhabitants of Hoxton and Houndsditch. Among the eccentric reactionaries who have actually observed this change with regret, a further and more curious fact has also been remarked more than once. An Anglican country parson, a friend of mine, once told me that it was not only a loss of pronunciation, but also of perception. 'They not only can't say the word, but they can't hear it,' was the way he put it. Supposing that the virtuous vicar in question had been so ill-advised as to teach his infant school to recite, let us say, the 'Dolores' of Swinburne – which I admit is not extremely probable – their intonation would be different, but without any intention to differ. The vicar would say, 'Ringed round with a flame of fair faces.' And the Sunday School children would obediently repeat, 'Ringed rarnd with a flime of fair fices', with a solid certainty and assurance that this was exactly what he had said. However laboriously he might entreat them to say 'faces', they would say 'fices' and it would sound to them exactly like 'faces'.

In short, this sort of thing is not a variation or a form of variety; on the contrary, it is an inability to see that there is any variety. It is not a difference in the sense of a distinction; on the contrary, it is a sudden failure in the power to make any distinction. Whatever is distinct may possible be distinguished. And Burns and Barnes did manage to be distinguished, in the particular form of distinction commonly called dialect. But the change here in question is something much more formless and much more formidable than anything that could arise from the most uncouth or unlucky of local or rustic accents. It is a certain loss of sharpness, in the ear as well as the tongue; not only a flattening of the speech, but a deadening of the hearing. And though it is in itself a relatively small matter, especially as compared with many parallel matters, it is exactly this quality that makes it symbolic in the social problems of today. For one of the deepest troubles of the day is this fact; that something is being commended as a new taste which is simply the condition which finds everything tasteless. It is sometimes offered almost as if it were a new sense; but it is not really even a new sensibility; it is rather a pride in a new insensibility.

For instance, when some old piece of decorum is abolished, rightly or wrongly, it is always supposed to be completely justified if people become just as dull in accepting the indecency as they were in accepting the decency. If it can be said that the grandchildren 'soon get used' to something that would have made the grandfathers fight duels to the death, it is always assumed that the grandchildren have found a new mode of living, whereas those who fought the duel to the death were already dead. But the psychological fact is exactly the other way. The duelists may have been fastidious or even fantastic, but they were frightfully alive. That is why they died. Their sensibilities were vivid and intense, by the only true test of the finer sensibilities, or even of the five senses. And that is that they could feel the difference between one thing and another. It is the livelier eye that can see the difference between peacock-blue and peacock-green; it is the more fatigued eye that may see them both as something very like grey. It is the quicker ear that can detect in any speech the shade between innocence and irony, or between irony and insult. It is the duller ear that hears all the notes as monotone, and therefore monotonous. Even the swaggering person, who was supposed to turn up his nose at everything, was at least in a position to sniff the different smells of the world, and perhaps to detect their difference.

There is the drearier and more detached sort of pride of the other sort of man, who may be said to turn his nose down at everything. For that also is only a more depressing way of turning everything down. It is not a mark of purity of taste, but of absence of taste, to think that cocoa is as good as claret; and even in the field of morals it may well have the ultimate Nemesis of thinking cocaine as good as cocoa. Even the mere senses, in the merely sensual sense, attest to this truth about vivacity going with differentiation. It is no answer, therefore, to say that you have persuaded a whole crowd of hygienic hikers to be content with cocoa; any more than to say that you have persuaded a whole crowd of drug-fiends to be content with cocaine. Neither of them is the better for pursuing a course which spoils the palate, and probably robs them of a reasonable taste in vintages. But what most modern people do not see is that this dullness in diet, and similar things, is exactly parallel to the dull and indifferent anarchy in manners and morals. Do not be proud of the fact that your grandmother was shocked at something which you are accustomed to seeing or hearing without being shocked. There are two meanings of the word 'nervous', and it is not even a physical superiority to be actually without nerves. It may mean that your grandmother was an extremely lively and vital animal, and that you are a paralytic.

We are constantly told, for instance, by the very prosaic paralytics who call themselves Nudists, that people 'soon get used' to being degraded, in that particular, to the habits of the beasts of the field. I have no doubt they do; just as they soon get used to being drunkards or drug-fields or jail-birds or people talking Cockney instead of talking English. Where the argument of the apologist entirely fails is in showing that it is *better* to get used to an inferior status after losing a superior one. In a hundred ways, recent legislation has ridden roughshod over the instincts of innocent and simple and yet very sensible people. There was a feeling, strangely enough, that men and women might not feel very comfortable when they met as total strangers to discuss some depraved and perhaps disgusting aspect of their natural sex relation. This has already given a good deal of quiet trouble on juries, and we have not seen the end of the trouble yet. Now, it will be noted that the objection to female juries never was an objection to juries being female. There always were female juries. From the first days of legislation a number of matrons were empanelled to decide certain points among each other. The case against mixed juries was a case of embarrassment; and that embarrassment is far more intelligent, far more civilized far more subtle, far more psychological than the priggish brutality that disregards it, But, in any case, it will serve here as an illustration of what I mean. The question is not whether the embarrassment can be so far overcome somehow that a good many people can discharge the duty somehow. The question is whether the blunting of the sentiment really is a victory for human culture, and not rather a defeat for human culture. Just as the question is not whether millions of little boys, in different districts with different dialects, can all be taught the same dialect of the Whitechapel Road, but whether that dialect is better than others; and whether it is a good thing to lose the sense of difference between dialects.

For what we do at least know, in the most fundamental fashion, is that man is man by the possession of these fastidious fancies; from which the free thinking haddock is entirely emancipated, and by which the latitudinarian turnip is never troubled. To lose the sense of repugnance from one thing, or regard for another, is exactly so far as it goes to relapse into the vegetation or to return to the dust. But for about fifty or sixty years nearly all our culture and controversial trend has been conducted on the assumption that, as long as we could get used to any sort of caddishness, we could be perfectly contented in being cads. I do not say that all the results of the process have been wrong. But I do say that the test of the process has been wrong from first to last; for it is not a case against the citizen that a man can grow *accustomed* to being either a savage or a slave.

❖─────❖

On War Memorials

I HAPPENED recently to renew my acquaintance with Edinburgh Rock; I refer to the remarkable fortress and not the more remarkable foodstuff of that name. The latter, indeed, I am far from despiring. There seems even to be something terrible in giving that stark and rugged title to a sweetmeat; as if a child were invited to nibble at Gibraltar or take a big bite out of St. Michael's Mount. Anyhow, that citadel, which is like a city within a city, contains a new and unique building, which is like a castle within a castle. It is the War Memorial of Scotland, and, to my mind, one of the few great War Memorials that are worthy of the greatness of the War. And the train of rambling reflections which it started left me with a profound renewal of all my own original belief in what would now, by comparison, be called little and local things. I have lived through the times when many intelligent and idealistic men hoped that the World War would be an introduction to the World State. But I myself am more convinced than ever that the World War occurred because nations were too big, and not because they were too small. It occurred especially because big nations wished to be bigger, or, in other words, because each State wanted to be the World State. But it occurred, above all, because about things so vast there comes to be something cold and hollow and impersonal. It was *not* merely a war of nations; it was a war of warring Internationalists.

Now, the Scottish War Memorial has a personality. It is the personality of a people, not merely the impersonality of people I would not raise here, least of all in any unsympathetic spilt, the purely aesthetic debates about the Cenotaph. But, after all, a Cenotaph is by definition an empty tomb, and it affects me individually as a very empty tomb, I would not call it cold and hollow and impersonal in any abusive sense. But it is by its very nature hollow; it is by a deliberate artistic policy impersonal; and the effect of this, on some people at least, is that it is rather cold. The point is that this effect was produced intentionally, and almost inevitably, by the avoidance of anything that could be distinctive of any creed any province any profession, or branch of the service It is in that sense cosmopolitan, and therefore colourless; in being the meeting place of so many races and religions, it can hardly help having something of the hollowness of the heart of the whirlpool, or reminding us of a temple of the winds, offering an intermediate and cold hospitality to all the winds of the world. I know all that there is to be said for such severities of classic architecture; but at least those who most admire the Cenotaph must admire it as architecture, and not as sculpture. Now, the Edinburgh War Memorial is full of sculpture, as a medieval church is full of such carving and craftsmanship; and the word 'full' does really correspond to a sense of fullness. And one effect of that sort of Gothic fullness is that a thing can be great when it is small.

Now, a thing like the Cenotaph can hardly be great when it is small. Even as it is, to my instinct, it is too small. What I fancy really feel about it is that it might be very fine, in its own way, if it were as big as the Great Pyramid and stood against a background as bare the great desert. It might then be entirely artistic and appropriate, for the artist's own purpose, that it should be as bare as the sky or as inhuman as the wilderness. But if we are talking about the human and historical quality of these things, then there will be surely more value in a piece of varied and yet concentrated craftsmanship, such as that which has been achieved by this group of Scottish craftsmen. A carving must be carving of something, if not of somebody. And the peculiar liveliness of local life and work lies in the fact that it is always dealing With something, describing something, struggling with the particular difficulties of something or somebody. There is a spirit that can only be called Gossip about a Gothic cathedral and its carvings. It may deal it caricatures, but it does not deal much in those abstract diagrams that can be much more misleading than caricatures. And, without at all narrowing my artistic tastes to this one type or school of work, I will confess to an undiminished partiality for it, because of its extraordinary vitality and vivacity. It is the liveliness of localism, even the liveliness of littleness. It arises when craftsmen have particular positive traditions of the workshop or the shrine, or when there is, for instance, as there still is in Scotland, a living memory of the lineage of particular families, and not only the families of the rich. For no family that is really respected consistently, as a family, can ever be entirely snobbish. The vast voting majority of the very richest family consists of poor relations.

These rambling reflections first began to ramble at the sight of a stone Unicorn, the ancient bearer of the Scottish arms, which stands outside the entrance to the memorial chapel. I thought it was a strong piece of work, simplified, but far from conventional, even in the artistic sense. But what took the eye, as typical of the spirit of which I speak, was the bold but harmonious way in which the artist had dealt with the difficulty of the conventional spike sticking out of the forehead of the sacred monster. The artist had bent the horn back by sheer strength, so to speak – at least by sheer strength of imagination – so that it followed with a wilder curve of its own the strong curve of the horse's neck. And I thought to myself that this was typical of the true spirit of craftsmanship, especially of craftsmanship dealing with definite and traditional symbols. The sculptor had really wrestled with the Unicorn, like a legendary hero wrestling with a fabulous animal. That is, she had really wrestled with a problem of presenting something positive that had to be presented, and yet in a new and more perfect form of presentation. She had made something new out of the old Unicorn; but she had not made anything else except a Unicorn. There was something symbolic in the fact that she had taken that wild, unearthly horse by the horn and forced it back into the contours of her own design. This is only one example out of many, and there are hundreds of such examples, wherever good workmen are doing real work with real images and ideas. Because they are real images and ideas, they can be treated: but they must be treated with. They must be taken on certain terms, and partly on their own terms. Because they are wild things they can be tamed, but only by the true Unicorn-tamer, who is even more daring than the Lion-tamer.

That is why the traditional art is the truly creative art. That is why it is truly more creative than the negative abstractions which tend, of their nature, not merely to anarchy, but to nothingness. And that is why a glimpse of these things encouraged me in my own lifelong belief in particularism, and the tales and traditions of a people. Where there are traditions there are tests; where there are traditions there are tasks and practical problems; but they are always stimulants to the spirit and cunning and imagination of man. They are always more fruitful, in the long run than the work of those who strike outwards to draw a design of nothing on the dark canvas of night. The Unicorn brings forth Unicorns, and all sorts of new and varied Unicorns, and one of them will be different because it is a stone Unicorn and another because it is a bronze Unicorn. But there are no foals born to the Nightmare.

On Funeral Customs

I HAVE been cheering myself lately with a very bright and pleasant book on the subject of death and burial. It is called *Funeral Customs: Their Origin and Development,* by Bertaram S. Puckle, and the point of view of the writer is interesting because in a sense, it is individual. He does not write in the usual supercilious way about superstition, indirectly identifying it with religion. He is rather concerned to show that it is not religion which is responsible for superstition. He quotes the very simple forms actually required by ecclesiastical authorities, and contracts them with the mass of fussy formalities, old and new, that have been added without any authority at all. To this extent he is undoubtedly quite right. The nightmarish pomp which seemed so nonsensical to Dickens, the tall black plumes, the long black streamers, the horrible marionettes of mutes – all that sort of thing was often carried out with religious solemnity, but it had nothing to do with religion. Those forms were never imposed by the Church; they were always imposed by the world. They were signs of worldliness and not of unworldliness; being almost always devoted to proclaiming the pride and pedigree and social rank of the dead man: all the things which religion declares to be obviously useless to him when he is dead. We may agree that it was always a worldly gloom and a worldly solemnity. St. Augustine said it, as he said so many things, a long while ago. He who uttered the '*Pereant qui ante nos.*'* etc, must have provoked many other people to say it. He says somewhere that funeral customs are not tributes to the dead but to the living. But perhaps it is not quite so indefensible to pay tributes to the living. If the demand comes not from the Church but from the world, it may be that the worldly are not always quite just to the world. There is more to be said than Mr. Puckle allows for, even for the boast of heraldry, the pomp of power, altogether apart from the long-drawn anthem swelling the note

* (Lat.) 'May they perish who have expressed our bright ideas before us.'

of praise. On the whole, however, we may well be grateful to a writer who will point out that religion has not complicated human customs, but rather simplified them. I remarked many years ago that the most ritualistic service in the world is a very simple matter, concerned with plain things like fire and water or bread and wine, compared with the existing ritualism observed by butlers and waiters in serving a long dinner.

But why will even the most intelligent people insist on saying that every obvious human custom is a relic of some base and barbaric custom? Here, for instance, the writer suggests that leading the favourite charger of a general behind his hearse is a 'survival' of some primitive habit of sacrificing an animal on the grave. This seems to me exactly like saying that taking off our hats to a lady is a survival of having our heads cut off, when we were suitors for a fairy princess. In one sense the connexion is quite correct. Taking off hats is a sign of respect to the lady, in a society where ladies are supposed to be respected. And cutting off heads, in the fairy-tale, was a sign that respect for that particular lady was perhaps almost carried to excess. But there is no reason to suppose that the idea would not have existed in its saner form, even if it had never been carried to excess. Similarly, it is natural to associate the horse with the glory of the warrior; and people were doubtless moved by some such emotion, even if they went so far as to kill the horse to his greater glory. But if nobody had ever thought of killing the horse, thousands of people would still have thought of leading the horse. They would have thought of it because it is a perfectly natural thing to think of. Where a higher type of society thinks chiefly of the dignity and solemn beauty of the occasion, it is the occasion of a procession. Where a lower or wilder type of society thinks chiefly of the doom and terror of the occasion, it is the occasion of a sacrifice. Both are of course, in one sense feeling the intensity and importance of the occasion. That is why they both do something to celebrate it. But I can never see why we should say that the sane form of it is a variation of the savage form, any more than that the savage form is a variation of the sane form. It seems to me much more true to say that the natural introduction of the horse is sometimes degraded into the unnatural immolation of the horse, than to put it the other way round, and say that the immolation introduces the introduction. The presence of the horse behind the hearse is a normal thing, which has sometimes in the past taken an abnormal form. In other words, this explanation of putting the horse behind the hearse is an excellent example of putting the cart before the horse.

This fallacy, which is not peculiar to this writer, but is indeed rather refreshingly rare in him, is always the result of not using our own imagination: that is, our own inside knowledge of mankind! In other words, it comes from not really believing in the brotherhood of men. For there is no value in a version of the brotherhood of men which does not cover troglodytes and cannibals. People do solemn things because they think the occasion is solemn; and they do dreadful things because they think the occasion is dreadful. But there is no particular sense in saying that they do solemn things merely because they once did dreadful things. There is no need to explain ritual by remote extravagances; because it does not need any explanation It explains itself. It explains all sorts of other things much better than definitions or abstractions explain them. To scatter flowers on a grave is simply a way in which an ordinary person can express in gesture things that only a very great poet could express in words. I decline to believe that those who do it necessarily believe that the dead man can smell. I doubt whether even those who did it in pre-historic times necessarily thought that the dead man could smell. Strange as it may seem, I do not think they were thinking in that vivid, vicarious fashion about the dead man's feelings. I think they were relieving their own feelings. 'Funeral customs are a tribute not to the dead but to the living,' said St. Augustine.

But those who write about primitive man's feelings always seem to start with the assumption that he had no feelings. He did everything that we do for sentimental reasons; but we are always told that he did it far totally different reasons. I have never been able to see the sense of this argument at all. Some men sometimes did dark and diabolical things then; and some men sometimes do dark and diabolical things now. Decadents in Paris attend a Black Mass, which is often a sort of parody of human sacrifice. But if somebody tells me that High Mass at the Madeleine, with Marshal Foch* in the front pew, is a *survival* of the Black Mass in the den of the decadents, I shall take the liberty of disbelieving him. It is obviously more reasonable to call the bad thing a relic of the good one than vice versa. And I do not see why any number of people should have not conceived the common human notion of having a horse as the companion of a hero, quite apart from special ideas, which undoubtedly existed on special occasions, of terror and blood-offering and similar expiation. It is simply a question of the order in which the ideas occur to the mind; and I see no reason to suppose that the abnormal always occurs before the normal, or the inhuman before the human.

I do not profess to be reviewing a book, but only taking a text for an article; but there are, of course, any number of things in this sort of book that would provide texts for any number of articles. For instance, I have never read anything at all adequate about the very beautiful and profound tradition of the 'soul-cake' or 'souling cake' connected with the ceremony of All Soul's Eve. The passage about it in this book is necessarily brief but very compact and contains some valuable information. It also contains a version which I had not seen of that very touching appeal in which there is all the tender irony of the Christian idea. The last lines are given here thus:

> If you ain't got a penny,
> a ha'penny will do,
> If you ain't got a ha'penny,
> then God bless you.

---

* French Commander of the Allied forces in the World War I, Ferdinand Foch (1851-1929). The author's essay dedicated exclusively to Foch appears on page 79.

I have always thought there was something very moving in that last gesture, admitting the man addressed into the brother-hood of the poor.

Here again it is really a matter of inside information. I mean information which we may obtain merely by diving inside ourselves. It is doubtless probable that the 'soul-cake' is some sort of substitute for the funeral baked meats of which Shakespeare speaks. But it is not to be understood merely by looking it up in old books, even in Shakespeare. It is to be understood by imagining the moral atmosphere for ourselves. Mr. Puckle has some very sensible remarks about the effect of War Shrines: and how they silently ended the long protest of two or three centuries against prayers for the dead. But if anybody will put himself in the position of one praying for the dead, or, better still, simply pray for them, he will not have the smallest difficulty in understanding why the same people at the same time offered prayers for the dead and gave pennies to the poor. The truth is that the science of folk-lore has suffered terribly from oblivion of one fact: that folklorists also are folk. It is not in that sense a science like entomology or conchology or ornithology. A man must study a beetle from the outside; because it is quite difficult to get inside a beetle. Men must be objective about a winkle; they must regard it as an object; some even regard it as an unpleasant object. They cannot all become winkles; but they have all been born men. They ought to have an Inner Light, as the Quakers say, about all the things that men have done, which they cannot expect to have about the social activities of winkles. And a great deal of what is called enlightenment seems largely to consist of extinguishing this inner illumination; or, in other words, sinning against the light.

The Fairy Pickwick

In THE PICKWICK PAPERS Dickens sprang suddenly from a comparatively low level to a very high one. To the level of *Sketches by Boz* he never afterwards descended. To the level of *The Pickwick Papers* it is doubtful if he ever afterwards rose. *Pickwick,* indeed, is not a good novel; but it is not a bad novel either, for it is not a novel at all. In one sense, indeed, it is something nobler than a novel, for no novel with a plot and a proper termination could emit that sense of everlasting youth – a sense as of the gods gone wandering in England. This is not a novel, for all novels have an end; and *Pickwick,* properly speaking, has no end – he is equal unto the angels. The point at which, as a fact, we find the printed matter terminates is not an end in any artistic sense of the word. Even as a boy I believed there were some more pages that were torn out of my copy, and I am looking for them still. The book might have been cut short anywhere else. It might have been cut short after Mr. Pickwick was released by Mr. Nupkins, or after Mr. Pickwick was fished out of the water, or at a hundred other places. And we should still have known that this was not really the story's end. We should have known that Mr. Pickwick was still having the same high adventures on the same high roads. As it happens, the book ends after Mr. Pickwick has taken a house in the neighbourhood of Dulwich. But we know he did not stop there. We know he broke out, that he took again the road of the high adventures; we know that if we take it ourselves in any acre of England, we may come suddenly upon him in a lane.

But the relation of *Pickwick* to the strict form of fiction demands a further word, which should indeed be said in any case before the consideration of any or all of the Dickens tales. Dickens's work is not to be reckoned in novels at all. Dickens's work is to be reckoned always by characters. Sometimes by groups, oftener by episodes, but never by novels. You cannot discuss whether *Nicholas Nickleby* is a good novel, or whether

Our Mutual Friend is a bad novel. Strictly, there is no such novel as *Nicholas Nickleby*. There is no such novel as *Our Mutual Friend*. They are simply lengths cut from the flowing and mixed substance called Dickens – a substance of which any given length will be certain to contain a given proportion of brilliant and of bad stuff. You can say, according to your opinions, 'the Crummies part is perfect', or 'the Boffins are a mistake', just as a man watching a river go by him could count here a floating flower, and there a streak of scum. But you cannot artistically divide the output into books. The best of his work can be found in the worst of his works. *The Tale of Two Cities* is a good novel; *Little Dorrit* is not a good novel. But the description of 'The Circumlocution Office' in *Little Dorrit* is quite as good as the description of 'Tellson's Bank' in *The Tale of Two Cities*. *The Old Curiosity Shop* is not as good as *David Copperfield*, but Swiveller is quite as good as Micawber. Nor is there any reason why these superb creatures, as a general rule, should be in one novel any more than another. There is no reason why Sam Weller, in the course of his wanderings, should not wander into *Nicholas Nickleby*. There is no reason why Major Bagstock, in his brisk way, should not walk straight out of *Dombey and Son* and straight into *Martin Chuzzlewit* To this generalization some modification should be added *Pickwick* stands by itself, as being the only book which Dickens wrote of himself; and *The Tale of Two Cities* stands by itself as being the only book in which Dickens slightly altered himself. But as a whole, this should be firmly grasped, that the units of Dickens, the primary elements are not the stories, but the characters who affect the stories – or, more often still, the characters who do not affect the stories.

This is a plain matter; but, unless it be stated and felt, Dickens may be greatly misunderstood and greatly underrated. For not only is his whole machinery directed to facilitating the self-display of certain characters, but something more deep and more un-modern still is also true of him. It is also true that all the *moving* machinery exists only to display entirely *static* character.

Things in the Dickens story shift and change only in order to give us glimpses of great characters that do not change at all. If we had a sequel of *Pickwick* ten years afterwards, Pickwick would be exactly the same age. We know he would not have fallen into that strange and beautiful second childhood which soothed and simplified the end of Colonel Newcome. Newcome, throughout the book, is in an atmosphere of time: Pickwick, throughout the book, is not. This will probably be taken by most modern people as praise of Thackeray and dispraise of Dickens. But this only shows how few modern people understand Dickens. It also shows how few understand the faiths and fables of mankind. The matter can only be roughly stated in one way. Dickens did not strictly make a literature; he made a mythology

Dickens was a mythologist rather than a novelist; he was the last of the mythologists, and perhaps the greatest. He did not always manage to make his characters men, but he always managed, at the least, to make them gods. They are creatures like Punch or Father Christmas. They live statically, in a perpetual summer of being themselves. It was not the aim of Dickens to show the effect of time and circumstance upon a character; it was not even his aim to show the effect of a character on time and circumstance. It is worth remark, in passing, that whenever he tried to describe change in a character, he made a mess of it, as in the repentance of Dombey or the apparent deterioration of Boffin. It was his aim to show character hung in a kind of happy void, in a world apart from time – yes, and essentially apart from circumstance, though the phrase may seem odd in connexion with the godlike horseplay of *Pickwick*. But all the Pickwickian events, wild as they often are, were only designed to display the greater wildness of souls, or sometimes merely to bring the reader within touch, so to speak, of that wildness. The author would have fired Mr. Pickwick out of a cannon to get him to Wardle's by Christmas; he would have taken the roof off to drop him into Bob Sawyer's parry. But once put Pickwick at Wardle's, with his punch and a group of gorgeous personalities, and nothing will move him from his chair. Once he is at Sawyer's party, he forgets how he got there; he forgets Mrs. Bardell and all his story. For the story was but an incantation to call up a god, and the god (Mr. Jack Hopkins) is present in divine power. Once the great characters are face to face, the ladder by which they climbed is forgotten and falls down, the structure of the story drops to pieces, the plot is a abandoned; the other characters deserted at every kind of crisis; the whole crowded thoroughfare of the tale is blocked by two or three talkers, who take their immortal case as if they were already in Paradise. For they do not exist for the story; the story exists for them; and they know it.

To every man alive, one must hope, it has in some manner happened that he has talked with his more fascinating friends round a table on some night when all the numerous personalities unfolded themselves like great tropical flowers. All fell into their parts as in some delightful impromptu play. Every man was more himself than he had ever been in this vale of tears. Every man was a beautiful caricature of himself. The man who has known such nights will understand the exaggerations of *Pickwick*. The man who has not known such nights will not enjoy *Pickwick* nor (I imagine) heaven. For, as I have said, Dickens is, in this matter, close to popular religion, which is the ultimate and reliable religion. He conceives an endless joy; he conceives creatures as permanent as Puck or Pan – creatures whose will to live, aeons upon aeons* cannot satisfy. He is not come, as a writer, that his creatures may copy life and copy its narrowness; he is come that they may have life, and that they may have it more abundantly. It is absurd indeed that Christians should be called the enemies of life because they wish life to last forever; it is more absurd still to call the old comic writers dull because they wished their unchanging characters to last for ever. Both popular religion, with its endless joys, and the old comic story, with its endless

* An immeasurably or indefinitely long period of time.

jokes, have in our time faded together. We are too weak to desire that undying vigour. We believe that you can have too much of a good thing – a blasphemous belief, which at one blow wrecks all the heavens that men have hoped for. The grand old defiers of God were not afraid of an eternity of torment. We have come to be afraid of an eternity of joy. It is not my business here to take sides in this division between those who like life and long novels and those who like death and short stories; my only business is to point out that those who see in Dickens's unchanging characters and recurring catchwords, a mere stiffness and lack of living movement, miss the point and nature of his work. His tradition is another tradition altogether; his aim is another aim altogether to those of the modern novelists who trace the alchemy of experience and the autumn tints of character. He is there, like the common people of all ages, to make deities; he is there, as I have said, to exaggerate life in the direction of life. The spirit he at bottom celebrates is that of two friends drinking wine together and talking through the night. But for him they are two deathless friends talking through an endless night and pouring wine from an inexhaustible bottle.

This, then, is the first firm fact to grasp about *Pickwick* – about *Pickwick* more than about any of the other stories. It is, first and foremost, a supernatural story. Mr. Pickwick was a fairy. So was old Mr. Weller. This does not imply that they were suited to swing in a trapeze of gossamer; it merely implies that if they had fallen out of it on their heads they would not have died. But, to speak more strictly, Mr. Samuel Pickwick is not the fairy; he is the fairy prince; that is to say, he is the abstract wanderer and wonderer, the Ulysses of comedy; the half-human and half-elfin creature-human enough to wander, human enough to wonder, but still sustained with that merry fatalism that is natural to immortal beings – sustained by that hint of divinity which tells him in the darkest hour that he is doomed to live happily ever afterwards. He has set out walking to the end of the world, but he knows he will find an inn there.......

Pickwick, I have said, is a romance of adventure and Samuel Pickwick is the romantic adventurer. So much is indeed obvious. But the strange and stirring discovery which Dickens made was this -- that having chosen a fat old man of the middle classes as a good thing of which to make a butt, he found that a fat old man of the middle classes is the very best thing of which to make a romantic adventurer. *Pickwick* is supremely original in that it is the adventures of an old man. It is a fairy-tale in which the victor is not the youngest of the three brothers, but one of the oldest of their uncles. The result is both noble and new and true. There is nothing which so much needs simplicity as adventure. And there is no one who so much possesses simplicity as an honest and elderly man of business. For romance he is better than a troop of young troubadours; for the swaggering young fellow anticipates his adventures just as he anticipates his income. Hence both the adventures and the income, when he comes up to them, are not there. But a man in late middle-age has grown used to the plain necessities, and his first holiday is a second youth. A good man, as Thackeray said with such thorough and searching truth, grows simpler as he grows older. Samuel Pickwick in his youth was probably an insufferable young coxcomb. He knew then, or thought he knew, all about the confidence tricks of swindlers like Jingle. He knew then, or thought he knew, all the amatory designs of sly ladies like Mrs. Bardell. But years and real life have relieved him of this idle and evil knowledge. He has had the high good luck in losing the follies of youth to lose the wisdom of youth also. Dickens has caught, in a manner at once wild and convincing, this queer innocence of the afternoon of life. The round, moon-like face, the round, moon-like spectacles of Samuel Pickwick move through the tale as emblems of a certain spherical simplicity. They are fixed in that grave surprise that may be seen in babies: that grave surprise which is the only real happiness that is possible to man. Pickwick's round face is like a round and honourable mirror, in which are reflected all the fantasies of

earthly existence; for surprise is, strictly speaking, the only kind
of reflection. All this grew gradually on Dickens. It is odd to
recall to our minds the original plan, the plan of the Nimrod
Club, and the author who was to be wholly occupied in playing
practical jokes on his characters. He had chosen (or somebody
else had chosen) that corpulent old simpleton as a person
peculiarly fitted to fall down trap-doors, to shoot over butter
slides, to struggle with apple-pie beds, to be tipped out of carts
and dipped into horse-ponds. But Dickens, and Dickens only,
discovered as he went on how fitted the old fat man was to
rescue ladies, to defy tyrants, to dance, to leap, to experiment
with life, to be a *deus ex machina** an even a knight errant
Dickens made this discovery Dickens went into the Pickwick
Club to scoff, and Dickens remained to pray. . . . .

Pickwick goes through life with that godlike gullibility
which is the key to all adventures. The greenhorn is the ultimate
victor in everything; it is he that gets the most out of life.
Because Pickwick is led away by Jingle, he will be led to the
White Hart Inn, and see the only Weller cleaning boots in the
courtyard. Because he, is bamboozled by Dodson and Fogg, he
will enter the prison house like a paladin, and rescue the man and
the woman who have wronged him most. His soul will never
starve for exploits or excitements who is wise enough to be
made a fool of. He will make himself happy in the traps that have
been laid for him; he will roll in their nets and sleep. All doors
will fly open to him who has a mildness more defiant than mere
courage. The whole is unerringly expressed in one fortunate
phrase – he will be always 'taken in'. To be taken in everywhere
is to see the inside of everything. It is the hospitality of
circumstance. With torches and trumpets, like a guest, the
greenhorn is taken in by Life. And the sceptic is cast out by it.

* A stage device in Greek and Roman drama in which a god appeared in the sky by
means of a crane (Greek, *mechane*) to resolve the runaway plot of a play.

About Widows

WIDOWS HAVE always been regarded as an alarming and avenging tribe. In the background of history, back to the time of barbarism, they stand like rigid statues with uplifted arms, calling down the vengeance of heaven upon slayers and spoilers; it was especially their wrongs that the knight was pledged to vindicate when he received the accolade; it is still to the righting of their grievances that the King is bound by the Coronation Oath. They have been nobly treated in ancient tragedy and even in more recent romance; as in that story of the Highland Widow which is always classed with Scott's worst, apparently because it is one of his best. The atmosphere changed from tragedy to comedy, with the coming of the more comfortable sentimentality of the nineteenth century. The conception of the comic widow, as distinct from the tragic widow, a conception started long before by the arresting originality of Chaucer, touching that recurrent widow the Wife of Bath, underwent another broadening and flattening in passing from the comedy of Chaucer to the comedy of Dickens. Tony Weller became the voice of mankind, uttering its ancient fear of widows. And now the widow has entered on a third phase in relation to literature: after the tragedy of Sophocles and Scott the comedy of Chaucer and Dickens. The widow has become literary herself; and reminded us that we might have had the memoirs of Mrs. Chaucer or the autobiography of Mrs. Dickens. Hitherto, the method has been simple enough. As next to nothing is known about Philippa Chaucer, and there is nothing very much to be said about her, there has been a mysterious assumption that there was nothing to be said for her. It has been oddly assumed that any Chaucerian jokes about wives must be jokes against his own wife; in defiance of the obvious fact that most of the same sort of jokes against wives were made by medieval clerics, who had no wives at all. On the other hand as the wife of Charles

Dickens wrote nothing at all to speak of, about the story of her life, a modern critic has been so obliging as to write it for her, entirely out of his own head.

But the third and most formidable phase of the widow in literature requires special and rather grave consideration. At least two, if not three or four, of the wives of distinguished men of letters recently dead have almost simultaneously published their impressions of their own and their husbands' private lives. It is not my primary purpose here to discuss the propriety of this new domestic habit; beyond saying that nothing would ever induce me personally to have anything to do with it. But the deeper causes of this difference of opinion are here rather more interesting than the difference itself. For the causes seem to me to go rather deep, into a new and even unnatural view of life and art. The question might be put for debate in many forms, but perhaps the simplest form of all, to which it ultimately works back, can be found in the old debating-club query of 'Is Life Worth Living?' For there seem to be more and more people who put it to themselves, consciously or unconsciously, in the form of 'Is Life Worth Writing About?'

In other words, it is supposed that all this publicity of self-revelation represents an interest in private life. Sometimes, it may be admitted perhaps, an excessive interest in private life. But it seems to me to indicate a lack of interest in private life. That is, it is a lack of intensity of interest in life as a thing to be lived, and a limitation of the interest to a biography as a thing to be written. If we happen to object to 'the sale of Keats' love-letters by auction', as did Oscar Wilde; or to the clown and knave who would not let the bones of Shakespeare rest, as did Alfred Tennyson; or to those who would cut a man's house in two to watch him in his parlour or bedroom, as did Robert Browing. . . . . if you happen to express some of the regrets felt by these eminent Victorians, you will now always find yourself confronted with one general idea. It is the idea that the love-letters were *wasted* if they were not sold to an illiterate millionaire from Nebraska; or that the poet's private emotions and meditations are *wasted* if somebody does not spy upon him walking in his garden; or that life inside the house is *wasted* if people outside the house know nothing about it. And this seems to me to mean a lack of appreciation, not only of private life, but of life itself. Literary expression is a very valuable part of human experience; but this is making human experience merely a part of literary expression. And though it is done by the most refined persons, and often from really fine motives, it seems to me to drift unconsciously with the whole of that modern tide of mere sale and exchange that has been the curse of all our recent history. I do not mean, of course, that there is any need to denounce every woman who happens to be a widow, who may happen to write something about some man who happens to be an artist, even if he also happens to be her husband. It is a question of the way in which the thing is done; and above all of the way in which the thing is defended. And where it is defended on the ground that anything left private is merely buried and lost, that defence is utterly indefensible. It does really imply that nobody has any inner life; that human happiness is not the need of human beings; that man is not an end to himself, subject only to the glory of God; or, in short, that biography was not made for man but man for biography.

What amuses me about this fallacy of the intellectual and the superior persons is how very near it is to the fallacy of the hucksters and the go-getters and the most vulgar sort of capitalist exploiters. For they hold as their chief heresy, in a coarser form, the fundamental falsehood that things are not made to be used but made to be sold. All the collapse of their commercial system in our own time has been due to that fallacy of forcing things on a market where there was no market; of continually increasing the power of supply without increasing the power of demand; or briefly, of always considering the man who sells the potato and never considering the man who eats it. And just as we need much more of the subsistence farm, or the worker who simply produces for his own consumption, so we need much more of what may be called in moral matters the subsistence family; that is, the private family that can be really excited about its private life: the household that is interested in itself It is all nonsense to say that such a thing is impossible. Even by the test of literature, there is a whole mass of literature which witnesses both to its actuality and to its attractiveness. But life is much more real than literature. What Stevenson called the great theorem of the livableness of life can be solved without incessant distractions either of publicity or dissipation. It cannot be conducted without reasonable holidays and changes of scene or occupation; nor can anything else. But it can certainly be conducted; and it can certainly be interesting and even exciting. Now, to suggest that a love-letter or a family joke or a secret language among children is never really important until it is edited and published, is to imply only too much of the suggestion of so many memories: that a man is only interesting when he is dead. For the whole world of mere stunts and scoops and trading and self-advertisement is spiritually a world utterly dead; although it is very noisy. It is, in the very precise and literal meaning of the phrase, a howling wilderness.

On Flags

IN RECENT times the flags of all nations have tended to run to stripes, whether they were the narrow stripes of the American flag or the broad stripes of the French flag. Despite all we say, often truly enough, about the complexity of the modern world, there is a real sense in which modern things tend to simplicity; and sometimes to too much simplicity. In that fashion of tricolours which was started by the more or less rationalistic revolt of the French nation at the end of the eighteenth century, there is much of such harsh simplicity. There is something perhaps of the mathematical spirit of the pure logician; marching into battle under a banner that is like a diagram of Euclid. His nearest approach to heraldry is a picture of parallel straight lines which cannot meet. It is as if there were lifted above the lances and the sabres an ensign in the form of an isosceles triangle or a flag cut in a pattern to illustrate the square on the hypotenuse. That French flag of the three colours has been so gloriously coloured with heroism and martyrdom and the romance of revolution; with splendid victories and with defeats more splendid than victories, that it has become vividly romantic in retrospect; and more magnificent than all the eagles and leopards of the kings. But it is not at all improbable that those who originally designed it were men moving about in the cold innocence of the dawn of rationalism, who supposed that they were planning something as purely rational as the pattern of a machine. They may have cut up the flag into sections as they cut up the country into departments, ignoring the romantic traditions of the old provinces of France. They may have done it as calmly and confidently as they broke up the old crowns and coins of the great duchies into the exact equality of the decimal system. But romance has reappeared, not only in spite of the rational republic, but actually in the form of the rational republic. And the other nations, that have copied France in this as in so many other things, have varied the conception and the colours in ways that are more symbolic than anything required for the practical numbering of the nation. The black and gold and scarlet of the flag of Flanders carries the memory of the lion of Brabant; there is a significant hope of unity in the orange strip at the end of the new Irish flag; it might be called the Unceltic Fringe. And it was not for nothing, nor without another and even better sort of hope in the augury, that even into the new tricolour of Cavour and Garibaldi there crept a chivalric shield bearing the symbol of the cross.

Perhaps this modern simplification in political symbols might be compared not only to the simplification in science but to the simplification in art. Stevenson said that a geometrical problem was an exact and luminous parallel to a work of art; and many of the artists of his period undoubtedly loved to simplify their art to such an extreme. In those days the critics often complained that the pictures of Whistler were mere bands of flat colour, a slab of grey for the sky and a slab of green for the sea; the whole having indeed something of the same flatness as the flags. Whistler, that very militant person, might well be said to have marched into battle waving a tricolour of grey; black and Chinese white. But here again the same general principle holds; and even simplicity preserved the tendency to variety; and especially to national variety. It was soon found that character could not be simplified for nothing or rationalized out of existence. And in no case was this more marked than in the very countries where science was supposed to be most abstract or art most impersonal. Nothing, for instance, could be more impersonal than impressionism; but anybody studying its origins will receive a very French impression. Both in science and art it was found that even a universal simplification did not get rid of a fundamental division, like the three divisions in the simplest tricolour flag.

But there is a special truth in this symbol which specially affects the intercourse of nations. It may be stated under the same figure of speech. The Belgian flag may be, as Whistler would put it, an arrangement in black and yellow and red, or the Italian a different effect produced by the introduction of white and green. But there are flags that are arrangements in the same colours: only that they are differently arranged. And this is perhaps the nearest metaphor by which we can describe a very vital and even dangerous similarity and dissimilarity. The French republican flag is of red, white and blue; but so, for that matter, is the Union Jack; so also is the Stars and Stripes. When Napoleon forced the English out of Toulon, when Nelson broke the French at Trafalgar, the glorious battle-flags reared against each other in that heroic combat were both tricolours of the same blended hues. When the victory of the *Chesapeake* raised Old Glory for a moment above the mistress of the seas, it was still a new flag but an old tricolour. And the hearty old English Tories, who loved to sing over their port the patriotic song which ran 'Three Cheers for the Red, White and Blue', would have been considerably annoyed, not to say agitated, if some polite Frenchman had bowed in acknowledgment of this compliment to the Republic and the Revolution. They would have been still more annoyed if some breezy and brotherly Anglo-Saxon from Alabama had expressed his gratification at finding that the old country had got wise to the go ahead virtues of the Stars and Stripes. All the colours would indeed be the same; all would be familiar with the look of blue or red; and any Anglo-Saxon might, if he liked, compare the blue to the sea which was common to the two nations or the red to the blood that is thicker than water. But the fact remains that what affects people in practice is not the things they use but the pictures that they make. In this sense form is much more powerful than colour. Men see a sign, an emblem, an object, before they see the polychrome elements that make it up. And, as I have already suggested, these things are an allegory.

What affects men sharply about a foreign nation is not so much finding or not finding familiar things; it is rather not finding them in the familiar place. It is not so much that he cannot find red, white and blue on the French or American flag; but that he always finds red where he expects blue, and blue where he expects white. The actual mixture of human and ethical elements in the different countries is not so very different.

The amount of good and evil is pretty much what it is everywhere in the moral balance and mortal battle of the soul of man. In that sense we may say that every nation is an arrangement in black and white. And yet that historical allusion would be an excellent historical illustration. All through the eighteenth and early nineteenth centuries America and England were astonished at each other; not because either was complete or consistent, but because each had inequality where the other expected equality. The English knew that they had not got rid of a squirearchy,* which many of them already wanted to get rid of; but they said to themselves with satisfaction that if they had squires, at least they did not have slaves. The Americans admitted that they had not got rid of the slaves; many of them admitted it with regret or shame; but they felt that if they had slaves, at least they also had citizens. They felt that, in comparison, England had no notion even of the nature of citizens. These cross-purposes can be seen in the great national figures of both nations. An advanced democrat like Jefferson still has slaves. An antiquated Tory like Johnson is yet horrified at slavery. But Jefferson could not conceive how Johnson could submit to an old fool like George III. Still less could he understand the acceptation of aristocracy; as little as the other could understand the acceptation of slavery. We might almost say that in the one case there were lords and no slaves and in the other slaves and no lords. But that sort of misunderstanding always perplexes the mutual understanding of nations. And in no case is this stronger than in the present relations of England and America. I have deliberately taken an old and familiar example, as I have taken an obvious and popular metaphor, to make clear this point about the difference between elements and the relation of elements, between colours and the arrangement of colours. And in these days when people are talking so much about the necessity of peace and international sympathy, I suggest it as one of the problems on which there has been much talking and perhaps not quite enough thinking.

* The class of landed gentry.

About Beggars and Soldiers

IT AMUSES me to think that, amid all the invocations of Christmas and invocations to Christmas charity, I am probably in a minority in uttering any particular and positive eulogy of Christmas waits. It is common enough to celebrate the jovial season by making jokes about Christmas waits, but they are generally in the same vein as the jokes about Christmas bills. It is constantly said in the newspapers (and therefore it must be true) that we have everywhere increased in social sympathies and sentiments of human brotherhood, and it is sometimes even said that all classes are drawing together in mutual understanding. I am sure I hope it may be so; and indeed I think that in certain special social aspects it is so. But I notice that in many houses where a previous generation accepted waits and carol-singers, even if they grumbled at them in secret, with all the external courtesy and resignation of Duke Theseus listening to the play of Pyramus and Thisbe in *A Midsummer Night's Dream,* many of a later generation have grown less patient and less polite. I also notice that over whole vast districts of the modern urban civilization whole streets are plastered with placards forbidding hawkers and street cries; lest the ancient institution of the pedlar or the last of the old music of London should disturb those within who are intently occupied, let us hope, in studying books on evolutionary ethics by Cambridge economists which demonstrate so radiantly the need of social contacts and the removal of all barriers between class and class. Having read a vast number of that sort of book in my time, I am still not entirely satisfied that, in every respect, they are invariably more human and amusing than the talk of Autolycus or the tune of 'Cherry Ripe'.

But there is a special case for carol-singers, because they come at a time when our whole tradition has always told us to be charitable to strangers, even to beggars. Of course carol-singers are not in any sense whatever beggars. They are people offering something in return for money; we may not happen to think it is worth the money, and I happen to think exactly the same of about three quarters of the things that are most boomed and pushed in the modern business market. But in so far as many of us do pay for the entertainment, even when we do not particularly want the entertainment, and do it from motives of charity, the waits or carol-singers can in that sense be put into the same class as beggars, and sink instantly to the abject and degraded condition of Homer or St. Francis of Assisi. And it is in a sense about this problem of beggars, or of those who in one aspect are in the position of beggars, that I am disposed to raise a very general question and remark on a general comparison.

I happen myself to represent, more or less, a general moral philosophy which until very lately was the general moral philosophy of most nations and even most confessions in Europe. And in nothing was that general tradition of our fathers more criticized by our contemporaries than in its alleged contentment with casual and sporadic charity; or, in other words, the habit of giving money to beggars. Now, there is a rather interesting parallel here, between the nineteenth-century attitude towards the problem of the beggar and the twentieth-century attitude towards the problem of the soldier. Only too often, and to the deep disgrace of governments, they were the same individuals. There was a beggars' rhyme in my boyhood that ran: 'Here comes a poor soldier from Botany Bay; What have you got to give him today?' In the eyes of many modern scientific humanitarians and philanthropists (who certainly would have nothing to give him), he would be blasted with a sort of series and crescendo of crimes; horrible because he was a beggar; horrible because he was a convict, from Botany Bay or any other convict settlement; and most horrible of all because he was a soldier. But both in his character of a beggar and his character of a soldier he offers an opportunity for explaining a certain old fashioned point of view which I fancy the majority of modern people do not understand at all.

Those modern people who, much more than any ancient people, have refused and repulsed beggars as such were not merely brutal or stingy. The thing was perhaps at its worst in the blackest time of industrial individualism, when even the theories were brutal and stingy; we might almost say, in some cases, that the ideals were brutal and stingy. But this would be unjust to a very large number of the theorists and idealists who really did believe in plausible theories and ideals. The first theory that held the field was something like this; that it was uneconomic and therefore unethical to patch up the position of people who were in the wrong position and even in the wrong place. The theory was that such a person could eventually find his place when the whole economic community could find its level, and each person was achieving the cheapest production at the proper profit or price. The ideal, however vague, was that of a community in which everybody was living productively and profitably, and nobody was living unproductively and unprofitably. Given that ideal, or any real belief in that ideal, it is not difficult to see that the beggar appears an anomaly that ought to disappear. Unfortunately, the ideal has disappeared and the beggar has remained. Nobody now believes that mere individualism and competition will ever, of themselves work out to that economic paradise of give and take. The death of that delusion was hastened by the Socialists. And whatever be wrong with Socialism, it was entirely right about what is wrong with Individualism. But the Socialist, quite as much as the Individualist, necessarily and naturally regarded the beggar as an anomaly to be abolished. His way of abolishing him was to plan out a series of Utopias in which the State would find everybody the best work and pay everybody the best wages. I am not criticizing those Utopias just now, or rather I am only criticizing them on one small point. So far as this argument goes there is nothing against them, except that they have not happened. Even among the Bolshevists, where something happened, it was not the abolition of beggary, whether this was the fault of the Bolshevists or no. A rich man in the Ukraine famine would be faced with just the same problem of beggars as a rich man in the Irish famine. Now, when one theory after another thus rises and falls, and one Utopian promise after another is made and broken, is it not comprehensible that some of us think it well to save even a solitary man from starvation, while the world is making up its mind how many centuries it will take for starvation to disappear?

As I have hinted, there is something of the same notion in tolerating the soldier as in tolerating the beggar. Nobody wants anybody to beg or anybody to fight. But when promise after promise of universal peace is broken, and conference after conference abandons the task of establishing international justice, is it so very odd that some people should still want something to defend national justice, in the sense of justice to their own nation? And if the beggar and the soldier seem to remain, *since* they seem to remain – then I do most strongly feel that it is better that they should not be regarded merely as blots or pests, but rather in the light of the traditional virtues associated with the tragedy; the one in the light of charity and the other of chivalry, I do not expect every one, or possibly anyone, to agree entirely with this view, but I hope that somebody will at least accept the compromise in the case of Carol-Singers or Waits.

On Mr. Thomas Gray*

A NEWSPAPER appeared with the news, which it seemed to regard as exciting and even alarming news, that Gray did not write the 'Elegy in a Country Churchyard' in the churchyard of Stoke Poges, but in some other country churchyard of the same sort in the same country. What effect the news will have on the particular type of American tourist who has chipped pieces off trees and tombstones, when he finds that the chips come from the wrong trees, or the wrong tombstones. I do not feel impelled to inquire. Nor, indeed, do I know whether the new theory is proved or not. Nor do I care whether the new theory is proved or not. What is most certainly proved, if it needed any proving, is the complete lack of imagination, in many journalists and archaeologists, about how any poet writes any poem.

In such a controversy it is implied, generally on both sides, that what happens is something like this. The poet comes and sits on a tombstone, or wherever he was supposed to sit in the one and only churchyard of Stoke Poges, or whatever place be the rival of Stoke Poges. He hears the Curfew: and there is a dreadful about and dispute about whether anybody sitting among the tombs of Stoke Poges can hear the Curfew, which does really rung from Windsor, though I imagine it sounds pretty much like any other bell at evening. Then the poet produces a portable pen and ink, preferably a large quill and a scroll (the poet in question lived before the time of fountain-pens), and writes down the first line: "The curfew tolls the knell of parting day.' Then he looks round to make quite sure that there are some lowing herds winding over that particular lea, that the ploughman is present and doing his duty in plodding homeward his weary way, and that all the other fittings are in

---

* British poet Thomas Gray (1716-1771). He wrote poems of wistful melancholy filled with truisms phrased in striking, quotable lines. He is best remembered for 'An Elegy Written in a Country Church Yard' (1751).

the offing. Latter, he will have to insist peremptorily on an ivy-mantled tower being in the immediate neighbourhood, inhabited by an (if possible) moping owl. It will not be the only owl involved in the business. If there are not all these correct conditions provided on the spot, he will not be able to write the Elegy. If, on the other hand, they are all there and everything has been properly provided, he will then write the whole of the Elegy, steadily, right through, and not roll up his scroll or rise from his tombstone until he has left the unfortunate young man in the poem finally safe in the bosom of his Father and his God. Then he will go home to tea; and I should imagine he would need it, after so prolonged and sustained a literary effort achieved in such damp and clammy conditions. That, with very little exaggeration, is what is really suggested by those who talk about Gray writing the poem in this place or that place, and under this or that condition of local colour.

Now, I should have thought that anybody would know that poetry is not written like that. But perhaps, in this case, even a bad poet is better than a good critic. Anybody who has ever written any verse, good, bad, or indifferent, will know that calculations of this sort are calculations about the in-calculable. Gray might have written the poem, or any part of the poem, in any place on the map; he might have visited the New Stoke Poges or the Old Stoke Poges, or quite probably both, or possibly neither. But, if I may be allowed to pick out one thread of speculation from a thousand threads of possibility, I would suggest that the Elegy in a Country Churchyard, even if it did refer to one particular churchyard, is very likely to have been begun, continued, and ended rather like this:

Mr. Thomas Gray was sitting one evening in a coffee-house; let us hope a coffee-house that did not confine itself to coffee. Something or other, a fiddle or a few glasses of wine, or a good dinner, had thrown him into a mood of musing, of pleasant musing, through touched with a manly and generous melancholy.

His thoughts turned round and round, as they do at such times, the tantalizing old riddle of what we really felt about life and death; about the toy God gave us which is beautiful and brittle, yet certainly not trivial. He said to himself: 'After all' who doesn't really feel that it really matters, with all its botherations?. . . . .A queer business . . . . .pleasing. . . . . anxious. . . . .' Then something stirred quicker within him, and he said to himself, in warm poetic emotion —

> For who tytumpty tumpty tumpty tum.
> This pleasing anxious being e'er resigned

Then his impulse gathered speed and power; and he struck the table and said the next line straight off —

> Left the warm precincts of the cheerful day.

He said that line several times. He liked it very much. Then it was a matter of form, certainly a matter of facility, to put the tail on the verse —

> Nor cast one longing, ling'ring look behind.

Then he got up and put on his hat. He left the warm precincts of the cheerful coffee-house, and went home and forgot all about it.

Some time afterwards, perhaps quite a long time afterwards, he was walking in the countryside at dusk. It is quite possible that he was walking in Stoke Poges, or through Stoke Poges, or through any number of other places in the neighbourhood. Perhaps he did hear the Curfew, or what he thought was the Curfew, or what he pretended was the Curfew. He made up another verse or two about the twilight landscape, full of the same spirit of stoical thankfulness and general resignation. Then he noticed, with great joy, that they would work into the same metre as the lines he had made up in the coffee-house. They were very much in the same mood. But he did not write many of the verses in the churchyard. Possibly he did not write any of the verses in the churchyard. It is more likely that the third act has for its scene Mr. Gray's private study, lined with classics in old leather bindings, and adorned with the celebrated cat and the bowl of goldfish. There he jotted down disjointed verses, and began to put them together; until it looked as if they might some day make a poem. But, subject to any information that may exist on the subject, it would not in the ordinary way surprise me to learn that it was a devil of a long time before they did make a poem. It is most likely, in the abstract, that he got sick of it halfway through, and chucked it away, and found it again years afterwards. It is extremely likely that there was another very long interval, when he was just finishing it, but could not finish finishing it. Many a man writing such a poem has held it up for a year for want of one verse. Nor would the newspaper assist him, in such a difficulty, by pointing out that there was another churchyard much more suitable than that of Stoke Poges.

Now, it is possible – nay, it is probable – that there is not one word of truth in this particular description of the proceedings of Mr. Gray. I have not read any of the literary and biographical records of Mr. Gray, at least for a long time; and there are plenty of records to read. It is quite likely that there are details of his daily life that destroy altogether the details I have here suggested. It is even possible that, by some amazing eccentricity, he did write the whole thing in a churchyard: or, by some unscrupulous exaggeration, pretended that he had done so. But my story is a great deal nearer to the normal story of the production of a poem than any story that supposes particular places and conditions to be *necessary* to the poem. Even if Gray did write with all the stage properties stuck up around him, the lowing cow the plodding ploughman, the moping owl, they were not the materials of the poem; and he would probably have written pretty much the same sort of poem without them. All this business of clues and tests is not criticism. It is a very good thing that people are applying literature to detective stories and detectives. But it is not a good thing to apply detectives to literature. Gray's unmistakable footmark or favourite tobacco-ash may be found in Stoke Poges or anywhere else. But it is not in those ashes that there lived his wonted fires.

The real relation of Gray's great poem to the present stage of our history will probably not be understood until a later stage. Yet the poem is a monument, a trophy, and, at the same time, a beacon or signal, standing up as solid and significant as the monument stands up in the Stoke Poges fields. Many poems have been written since, and grown more fashionable, if not more famous, which have not the particular meaning for the modern world stored up in this very storied urn. For Gray wrote at the very beginning of a certain literary epoch of which we, perhaps, stand at the very end. He represented that softening of the Classic which slowly turned it into the Romantic. We represent that ultimate hardening of the Romantic which has turned it into the Realistic. Both changes have, of course, been criticized in their time by the more conservative critics. Dr Johnson said probably with a partly humorous impatience, that Gray had only proved that he 'could be dull in a new way'. And most of us will agree that the modern realistic writers, who have in their turn replaced the romantic writers, have indubitably discovered a marvellous and amazing number of new ways of being dull.

But the change, as it hung uncompleted in Gray, strangely resembled the twilight changes of that landscape which the poem describes. Indeed, the whole episode has a curious, almost uncanny, harmony that even includes coincidence. Concerned as he was with a fine shape of twilight, it is even odd that his name was Gray. The whole legend is like that of something colourless and classical fading into mere shadow. For something was, indeed, fading before the eyes of Thomas Gray, the poet, and it was something that he did not wish to see fade. It may be noted that the first impression, especially in the first verses, is one of things moving away from the poet and leaving him alone. We see only the back of the ploughman, so to speak, as he plods away into the darkness; the herds of cattle have the perspective of vanishing things; for a whole world was indeed passing out of the sight and reach of that learned and sensitive and secluded gentleman, who represented the culture of eighteenth century England, and could only watch a twilight transformation which he could not understand. For when the ploughman comes back out of that twilight, he will come back different. He will be either a scientific works-manager or an entirely new kind of agrarian citizen, great as in the first day of Rome; a free peasant or a servant of alien machinery; but never the same again.

I am not very fond of committees and societies of specialists or amateurs who sit upon this or that sort of problem; but in the particular problem of the preservation of the rural and culture traditions of our own countryside, I can not see at the moment that any other machinery is possible. And it seems to me that the Penn-Gray Society is a good example of a machine suited to its work and doing work that is wanted. The trouble is that the typical cultured Englishman, like Gray or the traditional admirer of Gray, was generally a certain kind of gentleman, of the sort that had some kind of country seat. Since then, to continue the figure, the gentleman with the country seat has rather fallen between two stools. He is no longer so rich and powerful as a landlord. He generally has not become so rich and powerful as a local politician. There were any number of men, of course, who appreciated the country without owning a country seat. But if they were not the sort of men to own a country seat, still less were they the sort of men to stand for a country council. And, as the old organization of England went, the organization that has been gradually dying since the days of Gray, men of this artistic sort were mostly attached in some more or less indirect way to the gentry. That is the point; that, for good or ill, it was the system peculiar to a gentry. It was never, for instance, the system peculiar to a peasantry. When there is anything like a peasantry, even as there is in Scotland, it was possible to produce a peasant poet like Burns. And the memory of a peasant like Burns would be preserved by other peasants, even if there were nobody else to preserve it. But nobody could expect the agricultural labourers to preserve the memory of a scholar like Gray. It is amusing to remember that Burns put a verse from the Elegy as a motto to his own homely and pungent picture of peasant life; as some thought, consciously stressing the contrast between his own rea ism and the scholar's classicism:

> Let not Ambition mock their useful toil,
> Their homely joys, and destiny obscure;
> Nor Grandeur hear, with a disdainful smile,
> The short and simple annals of the poor.

Indeed, I rather fancy that, in citing those rather patronizing lines, it was the poor poet who had the disdainful smile.

But we must take the rough with the smooth in that noble aristocratic story that has made South England like a garden among the nations. And with it weakened the only organization for protecting the art and antiquities of rural life. Gray could not be a popular poet like Burns; at least, not in that sort of rural life. Perhaps there is a hint of it in his own phrase; that the Village Matron would have remained mute and inglorious. Perhaps he deliberately did not finish the tale of the Village Hampden, who was possibly a poacher but could not possibly be a peasant. Anyhow, the old organization of culture has weakened; and the new organization of local politics is not an organization of culture. There can be a culture of peasants, but not a culture of petty politicians. In this dilemma there is nothing to be done except to work through groups of sympathetic individuals students or artists or lovers of landscape, who take the trouble to support each other in defending the tradition of the national history and poetry. Otherwise the whole country will be swept bare for the sort of motorist to whom every object is an obstacle to rushing from nowhere to nowhere. Roads will not be roads, for there will be no places for them to go to; there will be only those ominously called arterial, and resembling, indeed, those open and spouting arteries that are an inevitable sign of death. I should say the ultimate moral is that we ought to have made up our minds between real aristocracy and real democracy, and should have either preserved a gentry or created a peasantry. But the immediate moral is that we must preserve what we can of all that reminds us that rural life was a civilization and not a savagery, and especially support such groups as the society here in question, which is defending the great tradition of Gray.

*About Impenitence**

WELL AWARE of how offensive I make myself, and with what loathing I may well be regarded, in this sentimental age which pretends to be cynical, and in this poetical nation which pretends to be practical, I shall nevertheless continue to practise in public a very repulsive trick or habit – the habit of drawing distinctions; or distinguishing between things that are quite different, even when they are assumed to be the same, I cannot be content with being a Unionist or a Universalist or a Unitarian. I have again and again blasphemed against and denied the perfect oneness of chalk and cheese; and drawn fanciful distinctions, ornithological or technological, between hawks and handsaws. For in truth I believe that the only way to say anything definite is to define it, and all definition is by limitation and exclusion; and that the only way to say something distinct is to say something distinguishable; and distinguishable from everything else. In short, I think that a man does not know what he is saying until he knows what he is not saying.

At this moment, if we were to judge by a general direction, by a vague unanimity existing in very varying degrees, and consisting of opinions rather similar but not the same, we should certainly say there was a universal wave of pacifism, just as in 1914 there was a general wave of patriotism. And when I say pacifism, I do not mean peace. It is possible, as I happen to know, to think pacifism a very direct menace to peace. But I am not debating these political points here. My point here is merely that this public sentiment, in so far as it exists, is made up of very varied materials, and also of distinctly different views. Now, whatever we may think of those views, regarded as general political views, it will be well to pick out of them certain really preposterous propositions, as one would weed a path of soil.

* Being unrepentant.

Neither side of any controversy can be the better for mere confusion and delusion; still less for the confusion of one delusion with another, or of a delusion with a defensible opinion. There are many forms of pacifism which are quite defensible opinions, though I personally might be more inclined to attack than to defend them. There are any number of forms of peace policy which I should profoundly respect; and some with which I entirely agree. But one or two fancies have begun to form in the chaos which are simply fragments of fixed and frozen nonsense.

I have explained that I believe in drawing distinctions; or what is called splitting hairs. I do not believe in saying breezily that a fungus is pretty much the same as a fungoid, even if you are hungry and in a hurry to have mushrooms for breakfast; or agreeing heartily that a rhombus is the same as a rhomboid, because you have to hustle the geometricians in some plans for housing or surveying. I think the first sort of practicality will probably end with a number of people being poisoned with toadstools, or worse; and the latter with un-geometrical houses falling down on un-geometrical though practical men of action. And I wish to point out that you cannot conduct a policy of pacifism, or of anything else, unless you will consent to distinguish one idea from another; and to find out where your own ideas came from, and with what other ideas they conflict. This weeding of the weaker or wilder ideas out of the mind is simply a practical piece of gardening which applies to any sort of garden, even the garden of peace; even to a garden planted with nothing but olives, and undefiled with a single leaf of the laurel.

For instance, there is a wild hypothesis now hardening in the minds of many which has nothing to do with any philosophical case for pacifism, let alone peace. It is the notion that not fighting, as such, would prevent somebody else from fighting, or from taking all he wanted without fighting. It assumes that every pacifist is some strange sort of blend of a lion-tamer and a mesmerist, who would hold up invading armies

with his glittering eye, like the Ancient Mariner. The pacifist
would paralyse the militarist in all his actions, both militant and
post-militant. Now, there is no sort of sense or even meaning in
this notion at all. It is a muddle and mixture of a number of other
and older pacific traditions, all of them much more reasonable
and some of them quite right. Some of them are ancient attitudes
of the saint or sage towards all sorts of misfortune; some of
them are more or less mystical experiments in psychology,
suitable to exceptional cases; some of them are mere dregs of
dramatic or romantic situations, out of particular novels, plays
or short stories. There have been many great and good men in
the past who have said that they would never need to resist
spoliation or invasion, or would not care if it was irresistible. But
they were almost always one of two types, and were thinking
only of one of two truths. In some of them it meant: 'My mind
to me a kingdom is. The inner life is so deep and precious that I
do not care if I am beggared or made an outlaw or even a slave.'
In the others it meant: 'I know that my avenger liveth. The
judgment of this world may beggar or enslave me but I shall
have justice when I appeal to a higher court.' Both these moral
attitudes mean something and something worthy of all possible
respect. But neither of these two types was ever such a fool as
to say that he *could* not be beggared or enslaved, merely
because he stood stock still like a post and did not resist beggary
or enslavement. Neither of them was so silly as to suppose that
there were cot men in the world, wicked or resolute or fanatical
or mechanically servile enough, to do unpleasant things to them,
while they were content to do nothing. The Stoic claimed to
endure pain with patience; but he never claimed that his patience
would prevent anybody causing him pain. The martyr endured
tortures to affirm his belief in truth; but he never asserted his
disbelief in torture. The hazy notion that has been gathering
more and more substance in the modern mind is quite different
and is really unreasonable. Men who have no intention of
abandoning their country's wealth, not to mention their own,

men who rightly insist on comfort for their countrymen and not infrequently for themselves, still seem to have formed a strange idea that they can keep all these things in all conceivable circumstances, solely and entirely by refusing to defend them. They seem to fancy they could bring the whole reign of violence and pride to an end, instantly and entirely, merely by doing nothing. Any party will be better for abandoning that delusion.

Oddly enough, the only exceptional hint of truth in this theory of establishing Peace is the same notion which made rude barbaric groups sometimes establish Trial by Battle. It was the notion that, under some very vivid and awful conditions, the man who knew he was in the wrong might lose his nerve. There was a story about that wicked man, Godwin the father of Harold, which illustrates the idea; and Scott used it as a dramatic turn in the death of the Templar. It did occasionally happen then; it might just conceivably happen now. But it happened because everybody believed in God, everybody thought the same about perjury and blasphemy, and a theory of justice was common to those who vindicated and those who violated it. In the present utter severance in fundamental ideas I cannot see why even this exceptional trick should work at all. The pacifists are only a sect; and Europe is boiling over with equally sincere militarist and imperialist sects. Does anybody believe that Hitler or Stalin or Mussolini would ruin all his plans because a Quaker did not propose to interfere with them?

On Foch[1]

I AM always amused to notice that in this post-war society, when everybody is talking about internationalism, everybody seems to be more narrow and national than ever. It is gratifying to know that Foch appreciated the great military virtues of Haig; but it is not the most philosophical aspect of a historical character. It is interesting to know that Foch was a friend of Sir Henry Wilson; but for future historians it will be at least equally true to say that Sir Henry Wilson was a friend of Foch. It is doubtless impressive to be told by a professional politician that Foch could not have done more for us if he had been an English general; but perhaps it is as well to remember that he was not an English general, and that he will not be judged in future centuries entirely and exclusively by how he got on with the English. The truth is that there never was a man whose importance in history depended so much on a full understanding of the whole Continental problem as Ferdinand Foch. He was a good Frenchman, and therefore respected those of the English who were good Englishmen. But a man can hardly measure the meaning of the story without being a good European.

I am one of those who think that a man will hardly be a good European unless he is a good Englishman or a good Frenchman, or in each several case full of his own national culture. There was a great deal about Foch that was intensely and peculiarly French. Nobody but a Frenchman would have launched that direct and yet dazzling epigram in the midst of the Battle of the Marne;[2] 'Mr. Right gives way: my left retreats; situation excellent; I attack.' Where that phrase was so typically French is that it has three separate meanings, and

1 Ferdinand Foch (1851-1929), French Commander of the Allied forces in the First World War.
2 Sep. 6-12, 1914. The Franco-Bristish alliance fought the Germans at Marne River 50 k.m. off Paris. The Germans then retreated and remained dug-in (into trenches) for next 3 years.

they are all true. A superficial person will take it as a fine piece of faronade, a romantic defiance and refusal to accept defeat. A more sagacious person will see that it is a piece of irony almost worthy of Voltaire, and that Foch sees the joke of the boast better than anybody. The most sagacious person of all will observe that it was also a piece of cold, hard, scientific fact. It really was true that the Germans pursuing the Allied retreat on one side, and checking the attempted envelopment on the other, created the strain and the weak point at which Foch suddenly struck. That is the French genius; to say things that only look witty and are also wise. That is the achievement of all French literature and philosophy: it is the supreme and splendid triumph of looking shallow, and being deep.

But there was also a quality in him that was more than French: a quality that was represented by his religion and his restraint and the way in which he stood apart from the politics of his country and of other countries, He was full of tradition; and the best part of tradition is unconscious. The final flower of tradition is instinct. He embodied better than anybody else the fact that is now forgotten, and without which the whole story is formless and senseless – the fact that it was a defensive war. It is always quite easy to forget the advantages gained by a defensive war. A defensive war is always the most defensible and the least easy to defend. The reason is obvious enough. If a man goes out to knock another man down and take his watch, and if he succeeds, he will at least have the watch to show. But the other man, if he successfully defends himself, will have nothing to show; except perhaps a Black eye or a broken umbrella. He will not have added to the watches in his own possession; he will only have the old, slow and faulty time-piece that he always had, and everybody expected him to have.

Disappointment after a defensive war is quite inevitable, and quite irrational. But Foch represented an old morality which regarded it as the only kind of war that was really justifiable.

This quiet and unadvertised man, who made no noise among the noisy controversies of post-war Europe, was nevertheless one of the fixed points, one of the calculable nuclei, of the oldest controversy in the world. He was to be counted on to stand for the ancient and normal morals of Christendom, which so many other great man have been driven either to misunderstand or to misrepresent. In the matter of the way of doing things, of the technique and science of his own profession, he was all in favour of dash and originality. But in the matter of what ought to be done, of what is the real reason for doing anything, of what we are all ultimately trying to do, he was as simple as a saint – and as sane. He might have said, like that other great Frenchman, also so daring and successful in modern applications of a science, 'My scientific studies have left me with the faith of a Breton peasant; and I do not doubt that further studies would give me the faith, of a Breton peasant's wife.'

Something in our age prevents direct and simple genius of this sort appearing on its real scale. For about fifty or sixty years the names counted famous have been largely of those who argued about what should be done and why. The men called great – sometimes really great and sometimes only great as charlatans – were Carlyle and Nietzsche and Ibsen and Tolstoy and Hardy and Bernard Shaw. But in history as a whole the scale of greatness was somewhat different. Men who did great things, granted the obvious motives of piety and patriotism and glory and the service of the gods, filled the large space of the story; Alexander and Caesar and Godfrey and Napoleon. Both cults are open to corruption; but when the older cult returns, as it will, it will be known that a man died quietly some time ago who delivered Europe with a single blow.

On Holland

I HAVE recently had occasion to visit a country I had never visited before; though it is one of the nearest to us in geography, and quite the nearest in history. I knew nothing about Holland except from pictures, and it was natural that the first impression should be that it had stolen its landscapes from the National Gallery. Perhaps, indeed, the National Gallery ought really to be called the International Gallery. It is odd in these days of the cant of cosmopolitanism, when so many things are called international that will always be national, that we should make such a patriotic claim for a place full of foreign pictures. A collection of Raphaels and Rembrandts* is called the National Gallery, while a little shop in a little village is called the International Stores. But it struck me that the fact of the Dutch genius having reached its highest glory in painting does make an important distinction between that country and our own, which is in many ways so similar, Holland has been described by her painters, and England by her poets. This has made the island State yet more insular. The one mode of expression is necessarily more cosmopolitan than the other, Pictures need not be translated. Poems cannot be translated, 'The moan of doves in immemorial elms, the murmur of innumerable bees,' is perfectly inaudible to anybody who does not know English. But Hobbema's Avenue stands open to all tourists, and is not blocked by a fence against anyone who does not know Dutch or Flemish. The Dutch do indeed improve their advantage by talking half a-dozen languages very well; but that is never quite the same thing. The duty of patriots is to make comprehensible the love of country; and the difficulty with poets is that they can only talk their native tongue; which is like a secret language of lovers.

I had a very inadequate idea of the grandeur of Holland, which has something of the grandeur of Venice. Amsterdam,

* Raffaello Sanzio (1483-1520), Italian architect and painter; and van Rijn Rembrandt (1606-1669), Dutch painter and etcher.

indeed, is very like Venice; but I myself, having long improved my mind with sensational fiction of the Oppenheim order, had only vaguely associated it with diamonds and Jews, and persons who murder the Jews to obtain the diamonds. But the traveller walks rather amid the ruins of a great State than the restrictions of a small one. Everywhere is the sort of magnificence that always marks an aristocracy founded on colonies and commerce, which marked Venice in the sixteenth and England in the eighteenth century, the private houses like palaces, and the personal genius for portrait-painting. But as Dutch dignity is connected with Dutch decay, an Englishman looks at it with an unquiet mind. It is as though he looked not at things of the past, but of the future.

Of course, when we speak of England falling to the position of Holland, we must allow for those who might fairly talk of England rising to the position of Holland. It is by no means unlikely that Holland is now happier than England. It is quite certain that in a general way the small nations are now happier than the great nations. It may be dull to be a Switzer as compared with being a Frenchman, which has always been in all ages a very exciting occupation. But it is certainly probable that Switzerland is better governed than France; though France is better governed than many of the modern industrial States. Switzerland is better governed because it is easier to govern. It has none of the problems of militarism, of frontiers, of foreign policy, of great traditional controversies about religion and politics. It may or may not be better to be a French citizen than a Swiss citizen; it is certainly safer to be a Swiss peasant than to be a French peasant. The Danes have much more solid prosperity now that they are peasants; though it is possible that they had more international influence and importance when they were pirates.

It is certain that the Dutch had more international influence and importance when they were merchant seamen and colonists, which, in those days especially, sometimes approximated to being pirates. But it is by no means certain that the Dutch have not more comfort and contentment now. This preliminary proviso must be made and admitted before any such criticism. There is a perfectly serious historical and economic case for anybody who says that by far the brightest hope for a great nation now is that by luck or skill it may somehow become a small one.

Nevertheless, nearly every normal person does feel, rightly or wrongly, that he wishes to keep his own great nation great, very much as any man would wish to allow his father to keep the position of a gentleman, however sincerely he himself might have praised the position of a peasant. These things are not easy to analyse, but they are even less easy to ignore. The thing is perhaps most accurately taught in a casual turn of phrase in the old and spirited verses about the British soldier in China.

The Englishman feels that not through *him* shall England come to shame, or even to diminishment. If it be indeed better for his country to fall, the thing shall be done either by a providence that is wiser, or by a posterity that is baser than he. The thing shall come from a heaven above him or from an abyss very much beneath; but not from the man himself in the momentous hour of the fate of his fatherland. As Victor Hugo said, when his old enemy, Louis Napoleon, surrendered at Sedan. 'Any prophet who had foreseen it would have been a traitor.'

Perhaps the morality of the thing is simple enough after all; and there move through my mind old phrases, about things of which it may be written that they come, but woe unto them by whom they come! However this may be, most men feel – and certainly I feel – that such an ancient glory should not abdicate. But by the same instinct I felt, with a shiver of realism, that it has lately come nearer and nearer to abdication, Holland only went the way that every great State has gone of which the greatness was purely commercial and colonial; which did not, when the time came, take thought for peasantry and popular religion, and all the more rooted things. Goldsmith, in *The Vicar of Wakefield,* pointed out that the mercantile aristocracies of England and Holland were alike forgetting the populace. England was then in her noon of glory, and Holland in her sunset; and that was a hundred years ago. The mark of this mercantile decline is that it is always gradual and almost unconscious. The Dutch cities contain hotels that were once obviously aristocratic mansions; but our own aristocratic mansions are already being turned into hotels. There are Rembrandts in the National Gallery; but the 'Blue Boy' is already in the United States.

I do not believe in a fate that falls on men however they act; but I do believe in a fate that falls on them unless they act. If I treated the matter merely as one of necessity and the nature of things, I should say that England was following her sister States of Venice and Holland. If I had ever talked all the mean materialism about living nations and dying nations, I should say that England was certainly dying. But I do not believe that a nation dies save by suicide. To the very last every problem is a problem of will; and if we wilt we can be whole. But it involves facing our own failures as well as counting our successes; it means *not* depending entirely on commerce and colonies; it means balancing our mercantile morals with more peasant religion and peasant equality; it means ceasing to be content to rule the sea, and making some sort of effort to return to the land.

The Book of Job

THE BOOK of Job is among the other Old Testament Books both a philosophical riddle and a historical riddle. It is the philosophical riddle that concerns us in such an introduction as this; so we may dismiss first the few words of general explanation or warning which should be said about the historical aspect. Controversy has long raged about which parts of this epic belong to its original scheme and which are interpolations of considerably later date. The doctors disagree, as it is the business of doctors to do; but upon the whole, trend of investigation has always been in the direction of maintaining that the parts interpolated, if any, were the prose prologue and epilogue and possibly the speech of the young man who comes in with an apology at the end, I do not profess to be competent to decide such questions. But whatever decision the reader may come to concerning them, there is a general truth to be remembered in this connexion. When you deal with any ancient artistic creation do not suppose that it is anything against it that it grew gradually. The Book of Job may have grown gradually just as Westminster Abbey grew gradually. But the people who made the old folk poetry, like the people who made Westminster Abbey, did not attach that importance to the actual date and the actual author, that importance which is entirely the creation of the almost insane individualism of modern times. We may put aside the case of Job, as one complicated with religious difficulties, and take any other, say the case of The Iliad. Many people have maintained the characteristic formula of modern scepticism, that Homer was not written by Homer, but by another person of the same name. Just in the same way many have maintained that Moses was not Moses but another person called Moses. But the thing really to be remembered in the matter of The Iliad is that if other people did interpolate the passages, the thing did not create the same sense of shock as would be created by such proceedings in these individualistic times. The creation of the tribal epic was to some extent regarded as a tribal work, like the building of the tribal temple. Believe then, if you will, that the prologue of Job and the epilogue and the speech of Elihu are things inserted after the original work was composed. But do not suppose that such insertions have that obvious and spurious character which would belong to any insertions in a modern individualistic book. Do not regard the insertions as you would regard a chapter in George Meredith which you afterwards found had not been written by George Meredith, or half a scene in Ibsen which you found had been cunningly sneaked in by Mr. William Archer. Remember that this old world which made these old poems like *The Iliad* and Job, always kept the tradition of what it was making. A man could almost leave a poem to his son to be finished as he would have finished it, just as a man could leave a field to his son, to be reaped as he would have reaped it. What is called Homeric unity may be a fact or not. *The Iliad* may have been written by one man. It may have been written by a hundred men. But let us remember that there was more unity in those times in a hundred men than there is unity now in one man. Then a city was like one man. Now one man is like a city in civil war.

Without going, therefore, into questions of unity as understood by the scholars, we may say of the scholarly riddle that the book has unity in the sense that all great traditional creations have unity; in the sense that Canterbury Cathedral has unity. And the same is broadly true of what I have called the philosophical riddle. There is a real sense in which the Book of Job stands apart from most of the books included in the canon of the Old Testament. But here again those are wrong who insist on the entire absence of unity. Those are wrong who maintain that the Old Testament is a mere loose library; that it has no consistency or aim. Whether the result was achieved by some supernal spiritual truth, or by a steady national tradition, or merely by an ingenious selection in after times, the books of the Old Testament have a quite perceptible unity. To attempt to understand the Old Testament without realizing this main idea is as absurd as it would be to study one of Shakespeare's plays without realizing that the author of them had any philosophical object at all. It is as if a man were to read the history of Hamlet, Prince of Denmark, thinking all the time that he was reading what really purported to be the history of an old Danish pirate prince. Such a reader would not realize at all that Hamlet's procrastination was on the part of the poet intentional. He would merely say, 'How long Shakespeare's hero does take to kill his enemy'. So speak the Bible-smashers, who are unfortunately always at bottom Bible worshippers. They do not understand the special tone and intention of the Old Testament; they do not understand its main idea, which is the idea of all men being merely the instruments of a higher power.

Those, for instance, who complain of the atrocities and treacheries of the judges and prophets of Israel have really got a notion in their head that has nothing to do with the subject. They are too Christian. They are reading back into the pre-Christian scriptures a purely Christian idea – the idea of saints, the idea that the chief instruments of God are very particularly good men. This is a deeper, a more daring, and a more interesting idea than the old Jewish one. It is the idea that innocence has about it something terrible which in the long run makes and remakes empires and the world. But the Old Testament idea was much more what may be called the commonsense idea, that strength is strength, that cunning is cunning, that worldly success is worldly success, and that Jehovah uses these things for His own ultimate purpose, just as He uses natural forces or physical elements. He uses the strength of a hero as He uses that of a Mammoth – without any particular respects for the Mammoth. I cannot comprehend how it is that so many simple-minded sceptics have read such stories as the fraud of Jacob and supposed that the man who wrote it (whoever he was) did not know that Jacob was a sneak just as well as we do. The primeval human sense of honour does not change so much as that. But these simple-minded sceptics are, like the majority of modern sceptics, Christians. They fancy that the patriarchs must be meant for patterns; they fancy that Jacob was being set up as some kind of saint; and in that case I do not wonder that they are a little startled. That is not the atmosphere of the Old Testament at all. The heroes of the Old Testament are not the sons of God, but the slaves of God, gigantic and terrible slaves, like the genii, who were the slaves of Aladdin.

The central idea of the great part of the Old Testament may be called the idea of the loneliness of God. God is not only the chief character of the Old Testament; God is properly the only character in the Old Testament. Compared with His clearness of purpose all the other wills are heavy and automatic, like those of animals; compared with His actuality all the sons of flesh are shadows. Again and again the note is struck, 'With whom hath he taken counsel?' 'I have trodden the wine press alone, and of the peoples there was no man with me'. All the patriarchs and prophets are merely His tools or weapons; for the Lord is a man of war. He uses Joshua like an axe or Moses like a measuring-rod. For Him Samson is only a sword and Isaiah a trumpet. The saints of Christianity are supposed to be like God, to be, as it were, little statuettes of Him. The Old Testament hero is no more supposed to be of the same nature as God than a saw or a hammer is supposed to be of the same shape as the carpenter. This is the main key and characteristic of the Hebrew scriptures as a whole. There are, indeed, in those scriptures innumerable instances of the sort of rugged humour, keen emotion, and powerful individuality which is never wanting in great primitive prose and poetry. Nevertheless the main characteristic remains; the sense not merely that God is stronger than man, not merely that God is more secret than man, but that He means more, that He knows better what He is doing, that compared with Him we have something of the vagueness, the unreason, and the vagrancy of the beasts that perish. 'It is He that sitteth above the earth, and the inhabitants thereof are as grasshoppers'. We might almost put it thus. The book is so intent upon asserting the personality of God that it almost asserts the impersonality of man. Unless this gigantic cosmic brain has conceived a thing, that thing is insecure and void; man has not enough tenacity to ensure its continuance. 'Except the Lord build the house their labour is but lost that build it. Except the Lord keep the city the watchman watcheth but in vain'.

Everywhere else, then, the Old Testament positively rejoices in the obliteration of man in comparison with the divine purpose. The Book of Job stands definitely alone because the Book of Job definitely asks, 'But what is the purpose of God?' Is it worth the sacrifice even of our miserable humanity? Of course it is easy enough to wipe out our own paltry wills for the sake of a will that is grander and kinder. Let God use His tools; let God break His tools. But what is He doing and what are they being broken for? It is because of this question that we have to attack as a philosophical riddle the riddle of the Book of Job.

The present importance of the Book of Job cannot be expressed adequately even by saying that it is the most interesting of ancient books. We may almost say of the Book of Job that it is the most interesting of modern books. In truth, of course, neither of the two phrases covers the matter, because fundamental human religion and fundamental human irreligion are both at once old and new; philosophy is either eternal or it is not philosophy. The modern habit of saying, 'This is my opinion, but I may be wrong', is entirely irrational. If I say that it may be wrong I say that it is not my opinion. The modern habit of saying, 'Every man has a different philosophy; this is my philosophy and it suits me': the habit of saying this is mere weak-mindedness. A cosmic philosophy is not constructed to fit a man; a cosmic philosophy is constructed to fit a cosmos. A man can no more possess a private religion than he can possess a private sun and moon.

The first of the intellectual beauties of the Book of Job is that it is all concerned with this desire to know the actuality; the desire to know what is, and not merely what seems. If moderns were writing the book we should probably find that Job and his comforters got on quite well together by the simple operation of referring their differences to what is called the temperament, saying that the comforters were by nature 'optimists' and Job by nature a 'pessimist'. And they would be quite comfortable, as people can often be, for some time at least, by agreeing to say what is obviously untrue. For if the word 'pessimist' means anything at all, then emphatically Job is not a pessimist. His case alone is sufficient to refute the modern absurdity of referring everything to physical temperament. Job does not in any sense look at life in a gloomy way. If wishing to be happy and being quite ready to be happy constitute an optimist, Job is an optimist; he is an outraged and insulted optimist. He wishes the universe to justify itself. not because he wishes it to be caught out, but because he really wishes it to be justified. He demands an explanation from God, but be does not do it at all in the spirit in which Hampden might demand an explanation from Charles I. He does it in the spirit in which a wife might demand an explanation from her husband whom she really respected. He remonstrates with his Maker because he is proud of his Maker. He even speaks of the Almighty as his enemy, but he never doubts, at the back of his mind, that his enemy has some kind of a case which he does not understand. In a fine and famous blasphemy he says, 'Oh, that mine adversary had written a book!' It never really occurs to him that it could possibly be a bad book. He is anxious to be convinced, that is, he thinks that God could convince him. In short, we may say again that if the word optimist means anything (which I doubt) Job is an optimist. He shakes the pillars of the world and strikes insanely at the heavens; he lashes the stars, but it is not to silence them; it is to make them speak.

In the same way we may speak of the official optimists, the Comforters of Job. Again, if the word pessimist means anything (which I doubt) the comforters of Job may be called pessimists rather than optimists. All that they really believe is not that God is good but that God is so strong that it is much more judicious to call Him good. It would be the exaggeration of censure to call them evolutionists; but they have something of the vital error of the evolutionary optimist. They will keep on saying that everything in the universe fits into everything else; as if there were anything comforting about a number of nasty things all fitting into each other. We shall see later how God in the great climax of the poem turns this particular argument upside down.

When, at the end of the poem, God enters (somewhat abruptly), is struck the sudden and splendid note which makes the thing as great as it is. All the human beings through the story, and Job especially, have been asking questions of God. A more trivial poet would have made God enter in some sense or other in order to answer the questions. By a touch truly to be called inspired, when God enters, it is to ask a number more questions on His own account, In this drama of scepticism God Himself takes up the role of sceptic. He does what all the great voices defending religion have always done. He does, for instance, what Socrates did. He turns rationalism against itself. He seems to say that if it comes to asking questions, He can ask some questions which will fling down and flatten out all conceivable human questioners. The poet by an exquisite intuition has made, God ironically accept a kind of controversial equality with His accusers. He is willing to regard it as if it were a fair intellectual duel: 'Gird up now thy loins like a man; for I will demand of thee, and answer thou me.' The ever-lasting adopts an enormous and sardonic humility. He is quite willing to be prosecuted. He only asks for the right which every prosecuted person possesses; He asks to be allowed to cross-examine the witness for the prosecution. And He carries yet further the correctness of the legal parallel. For the first question, essentially speaking, which He asks of Job is the question that any criminal accused by Job would be most entitled to ask. He asks Job who He is. And Job, being a man of candid intellect, takes a little time to consider, and comes to the conclusion that he does not know.

This is the first great fact to notice about the speech of God, which is the culmination of the inquiry. It represents all human sceptics routed by a higher scepticism. It is this method, used sometimes by supreme and sometimes by mediocre minds, that has ever since been the logical weapon of the true mystic. Socrates, as I have said, used it when he showed that if you only allowed him enough sophistry he could destroy all the sophists. Jesus Christ used it when He reminded the Sadducees, who could not imagine the nature of marriage in heaven, that if it came to that they had not really imagined the nature of marriage at all. In the break up of Christian theology in the eighteenth century, Butler used it, when he pointed out that rationalistic arguments could be used as much against vague religion as against doctrinal religion, as much against rationalist ethics as against Christian ethics. It is the root and reason of the fact that men who have religious faith have also philosophic doubt, like Cardinal Newman, Mr. Balfour, or Mr. Mallock. These are the small streams of the delta; the Book of Job is the first great cataract that creates the river. In dealing with the arrogant asserter of doubt, it is not the right method to tell him to stop doubting. It is rather the right method to tell him to go on doubting, to doubt a little more, to doubt every day newer and wilder things in the universe, until at last, by some strange enlightenment, he may begin to doubt himself.

This, I say, is the first fact touching the speech; the fine inspiration by which God comes in at the end, not to answer riddles, but to propound them. The other great fact which, taken together with this one, makes the whole work religious instead of merely philosophical, is that other great surprise which makes Job suddenly satisfied with the mere presentation of something impenetrable. Verbally speaking the enigmas of Jehovah seem darker and more desolate than the enigmas of Job; yet Job was comfortless before the speech of Jehovah and is comforted after it. He has been told nothing, but he feels the terrible and tingling atmosphere of something which is too good to be told. The refusal of God to explain His design is itself a burning hint of His design. The riddles of God are more satisfying than the solutions of man.

Thirdly, of course, it is one of the splendid strokes that God rebukes alike the man who accused, and the men who defended Him; that He knocks down pessimists and optimists with the same hammer.

And it is in connexion with the mechanical and supercilious comforters of Job that there occurs the still deeper and finer inversion of which I have spoken. The mechanical optimist endeavours to justify the universe avowedly upon the ground that it is a rational and consecutive pattern. He points out that the fine thing about the world is that it can all be explained. That is one point, if I may put it so, on which God, in return, is explicit to the point of violence God says, in effect, that if there is one fine thing about the world, as far as men are concerned, it is that it cannot be explained. He insists on the inexplicableness of everything: 'Hath the rain a father? . . . Out of whose womb came the ice?' He goes farther, and insists on the positive and palpable unreason of things: 'Hast thou sent the rain upon the desert where no man is, and upon the wilderness wherein there is no man?' God will make man see things, if it is only against the black background of nonentity. God will make Job see a starting universe if He can only do it by making Job see an idiotic universe. To startle man God becomes for an instant a blasphemer; one might almost say that God becomes for an instant an atheist. He unrolls before Job a long panorama of created things, the horse, the eagle, the raven, the wild ass, the peacock, the ostrich, the crocodile. He so describes each of them that it sounds like a monster walking in the sun. The whole is a sort of psalm or rhapsody of the sense of wonder. The maker of all things is astonished at the things He has Himself made.

This we may call the third point. Job puts forward a note of interrogation; God answers with a note of exclamation. Instead of proving to Job that it is an explicable world. He insists that it is a much stranger world than Job ever thought it was. Lastly, the poet has achieved in this speech, with that unconscious artistic accuracy found in so many of the simpler epics, another and much more delicate thing. Without once relaxing the rigid impenetrability of Jehovah is His deliberate declaration, he has contrived to let fall here and there in the metaphors, in the parenthetical imagery, sudden and splendid suggestions that the secret of God is a bright and not a sad one – semi-accidental suggestions, like light seen for an instant through the cracks of a closed door. It would be difficult to praise too highly, in a purely poetical sense, the instinctive exactitude and ease with which these more optimistic insinuations are let fall in other connexions, as if the Almighty Himself were scarcely aware that He was letting them out. For instance, there is that famous passage where Jehovah with devastating sarcasm asks Job where he was when the foundations of the world were laid, and then (as if merely fixing a date) mentions the time when the sons of God shouted for joy. One cannot help feeling, even upon this meagre information, that they must have had something to shout about. Or again, when God is speaking of snow and hail in the mere catalogue of the physical cosmos, He speaks of them as a treasury that He has laid up against the day of battle – a hint of some huge Armageddon in which evil shall be at last over-thrown.

Nothing could be better, artistically speaking, than this optimism breaking through agnosticism like fiery gold round the edges of a black cloud. Those who look superficially at: the barbaric origin of the epic may think it fanciful to read so much artistic significance into its casual similes or accidental phrases. But no one who is well acquainted with great examples of semi-barbaric poetry, as in the Song of Roland or the old ballads, will fall into this mistake. No one who knows what primitive poetry is, can fail to realize that while its conscious form is simple some of its finer effects are subtle. *The Iliad* contrives to express the idea that Hector and Sarpedon have a certain tone or tint of sad and chivalrous resignation, not bitter enough to be called pessimism and not jovial enough to be called optimism: Homer could never have said this in elaborate words. But somehow he contrives to say it in simple words. The Song of Roland contrives to express the idea that Christianity imposes upon its heroes a paradox: a paradox of great humility in the matter of their sins combined with great ferocity in the matter of their ideas. Of course the Song of Roland could not say this; but it conveys this. In the same way the Book of Job must be credited with many subtle effects which were in the author's soul without: being, perhaps, in the author's mind. And of these by far the most important remains even yet to be started. I do not know, and I doubt whether even scholars know, if the Book of Job had a great effect or had any effect upon the after development of Jewish thought. But if it did have any effect it may have saved them from an enormous collapse and decay. Here in this book the question is really asked whether God invariably punishes vice with terrestrial punishment and rewards virtue with terrestrial prosperity. If the Jews had answered that question wrong they might have lost at their influence in human history. They might have sunk even down to the level of modern well-educated society. For when once people have begun to believe that prosperity is the reward of virtue their next calamity is obvious. If prosperity is regarded as the reward of virtue it will be regarded as the symptom of virtue. Men will leave off the heavy task of making good men successful. They will adopt the easier task of making our successful men good. This, which has happened throughout modern commerce and journalism, is the ultimate Nemesis of the wicked optimism of the comforters of Job. If the Jews could be saved from it, the Book of Job saved them. The Book of Job is chiefly remarkable, as I have insisted throughout, for the fact that it does not end in a way that is conventionally satisfactory. Job is not told that his misfortunes were due to his sins or a part of any plan for his improvement. But in the prologue we see Job tormented not because he was the worst of men, but because he was the best. It is the lesson of the whole work that man is most comforted by paradoxes; and it is by all human testimony the most reassuring I need not suggest what a high and strange history awaited this paradox of the best man in the worst fortune. I need not say that in the freest and most philosophical sense there is one Old Testament figure who is truly a type; or say what is prefigured in the wounds of Job.

On Sightseeing

I HAVE often done my best to consider, in various aspects, what is really the matter with Sightseeing. Or rather, I hope, I have done my best to consider what is the matter with me, when I find myself faintly fatigued by Sightseeing. For it is always wiser to consider not so much why a thing is not enjoyable, as why we ourselves do not enjoy it. In the case of Sightseeing, I have only got so far as to be quite certain that the fault is not in the Sights and is not in the Sightseers. This would seem to drive the speculative philosopher back upon the dreadful and shocking conclusion that the fault is entirely in me. But, before accepting so destructive a deduction, I think there are some further modifications to be made and some further distinctions to be drawn in this matter.

The mere fact that a mob is going to see a monument ought not in itself to depress an imaginative and sympathetic mind. On the contrary, such a mind ought to perceive that there is something of the same mystery or majesty in the mob as in the monument. It is a weakness to fail in feeling that a statue standing on a pedestal above a street, the statue of a hero, carved by an artist, for the honour and glory of a city, is, so far as it goes, a marvellous and impressive work of man. But it is far more of a weakness to fail in feeling that a hundred statues walking about the street, alive with the miracle of a mysterious vitality, are a marvellous and impressive work of God. In so far as that ultimate argument affects the matter, the sightseer might almost as well travel to see the sightseers as to see the sights. There are, of course, vulgar and repulsive sightseers. There are, for that matter, vulgar and repulsive statues. But this cannot be a complete excuse for my own lamentable coldness; for I have felt it creeping over me in the presence of the most earnest and refined sightseers, engaged in inspecting the most classical and correct statues. Indeed (if I must make the disgraceful confession in the interests of intellectual discovery), I will own that I have felt this mysterious wave of weariness pass over me rather *more* often when the elegant and distinguished Archdeacon was explaining the tombs to the Guild of Golden Thoughts than when an ordinary shouting showman was showing them to a jolly rabble of trippers with beer bottles and concertinas. I am very much troubled with this unnatural insensibility of mind; and I have made many attempts, none of them quite successful, to trace my mental malady to its origin. But I am not sure that some hint of the truth may not be found in the first popular example that I gave – the example of a statue standing in a street.

Now, men have stuck up statues in streets as part of the general and ancient instinct of popular monumental art, which they exhibited in erecting pillars, building pyramids, making monoliths and obelisks, and such things, from the beginning of the world. And the conception may be broadly stated thus – that this sort of sight was meant for two different kinds of sightseers. First, the monument was meant to be seen accidentally; it was set up purposely in order to be seen accidentally. In other words, a striking tower on a hill, an arresting statue on a pedestal, a remarkable relief over an archway, or any other piece of public art, was intended for the traveller, and even especially for the chance traveller. It was meant for the passerby, perhaps in the hope that he would not merely pass by; perhaps in the hope that he would pause, and possibly even meditate. But he would be meditating not only on something that he had never seen before, but on something that he had never expected to see. The statue would almost spring out upon him like a stage brigand. The archway would arrest him and almost bar his path like a barricade. He would suddenly see the high tower like a sort of signal; like a rocket suddenly sent up to convey a message, and almost a warning. This is the way in which many popular monuments have been seen; and this, some

may agree with me in thinking, is pretty much the best way to
see them. No man will ever forget the sights he really saw when
he was not a sightseer. Every man remembers the thing that
struck him like a thunderbolt of an instant, though it had stood
there waiting for him as the memorial of an aeon. But whether or
no this be the best way of treating popular memorials, it is not
the only way, and certainly has not been the only popular way.
Historic relics, as a whole, have been treated differently in history
as a whole. But, in history as a whole, the other way of seeing
such sights was not what we commonly call sight-seeing.

We might put the point this way: that the two ways of
visiting the statue or the shrine were the way of the Traveller
and the way of the Pilgrim. But the way of the Pilgrim almost
always involved the way of the Pilgrimage. It was a ritual or
ceremonial way; the way of a procession which had indeed
come to see that shrine, but had not come to see anything else.
The pilgrim does not feel, as the tourist does often quite
naturally feel, that he has had his tour interrupted by something
that does not happen to interest him. The pilgrimage must
interest him, or he would never have been a pilgrim. He knows
exactly what he wants to do; and, what is perhaps even more
valuable, he knows for certain when he has done it. He cannot
be dragged on from one thing to another; from one thing that
interests him mildly to another thing that bores him stiff. He has
undertaken a certain expedition with a certain logical end; an end
both in the sense of a purpose and in the sense of a termination.
For a certain mystical reason of his own he wanted to visit a
certain monument or shrine; and, now he has visited it, he is free
to visit the nearest public house or any other place he pleases.

But all this is altered, because we have passed from the age
of monuments to the age of museums. We have been afflicted
with the modern idea of collecting all sorts of totally different
things, with totally different types of interest, including a good
many of no apparent interest at all, and stuffing them all into one

building, that the stranger may stray among a hundred distracting monuments or the pilgrim be lost among a hundred hostile shrines. When the traveller saw the statue of the hero, he did not see written on the pedestal: 'This way to the Collection of Tropical Fungi', in which he possibly felt no interest at all. When the pilgrim found his way to the shrine, he did not find that the priest was eagerly waving him on to a glass case filled with the specimens of the local earthworms. Fungi and earthworms may be, and indeed are, exceedingly interesting things in themselves; but they are not things which men seek in the same mood which sends them to look at the statues of heroes or the shrines of saints. With the establishment of that entirely modern thing, the Museum, we have a new conception, which, like so many modern conceptions, is based on a blunder in psychology and a blindness to the true interests of culture. The Museum is not meant either for the wanderer to see by accident or for the pilgrim to see with awe. It is meant for the mere slave of a routine of self-education to stuff himself with every sort of incongruous intellectual food in one indigestible meal. It is meant for the mere Sightseer, the man who must see all the sights.

Of course, I am only speaking of this kind of sight as it affects this kind of sightseer. I do not deny that museums and galleries and other collections serve a more serious purpose for specialists who can select special things. But the modern popular practice of which I complain is bad, not because it is popular, but because it is modern. It was not made by any of the ancestral instincts of mankind; either the instinct that erected the crucifix by the wayside, to arrest the wayfarer, or the instinct that erected the crucifix in the cathedral to be the goal of the worshipper. It is not the product of popular imagination, but of what is called popular education; the cold and compulsory culture which is not, and never will be, popular.

On Trollope*: Historian

I WAS recently reading an article on Anthony Trollope, one of the many that have appeared in literary magazines since critics have discovered that his work can be treated as literature, when they used to treat it as fiction. He is a rather rare example of a man who has been taken more seriously after his death than in his presence. The Victorians tended to regard Trollope as light literature, and Thackeray and even Dickens as more serious literature. The modern critics, rightly or wrongly, are disposed to treat Trollope more seriously, and even Dickens and Thackeray more lightly. Of course, Trollope is treated in both fashions, according to the taste of the critic. Mr. Hugh Walpole has cultivated the Trollope style both by precept and example; and Father Ronald Knox has made a most elaborate and detailed map of Barsetshire, and annotated it with stern queries about why Dr. Thorne took so long to get to Plumstead Episcopi, or what Mr. Gresham was doing on the wrong road to Framley Parsonage. These are not the right examples; for I, alas! have not the powerful detective and documentary brain of Father Knox. But it is broadly true that Trollope has again attracted many people from many aspects. And yet there is one aspect of Trollope which I think has been entirely neglected, and which I think is of very great and vital importance to the history of England.

The critic in question says of Trollope, truly enough in the main: 'He scarcely concerned himself with the lower orders'. We may say that the whole system of English squirearchy scarcely concerned itself with the lower orders; or only in the same vague and well-meaning way as Trollope. But when the critic adds, 'His values were those of the middle class', he misses the point – the point which I think important about English history. It is not really true, as a whole, that his characters were middle class. It might be said more truly that

* English novelist Anthony Trollope (1815-1882).

Dickens dealt largely with the middle class, though doubtless more largely with the lower middle class, and even the lower class. But Trollope really deals with the upper middle class in so far as it is attached to the upper class. Squire Gresham was not middle class; and I fancy Archdeacon Grantley would have been very much surprised to be told he was. I draw a veil over the fury of Mrs. Proudie, who would probably, I admit, have been even more indignant at the description if it happened to be true. Dr. Thorne was, in the ordinary sense, of the professional middle class; but we are never allowed to forget that his family was older and prouder than the De Courcys. Most of the Government clerks are of the more or less aristocratic class from which Government clerks were, and to some extent still are, chiefly drawn. In other words, we shall not learn the first historical lesson from Trollope till we realize that he bears witness to England as an aristocratic State; and not, as our friends the Communists would say, as a *bourgeois* State. But there is a further development of this historical truth, which I think rather curious. Trollope bears witness to a big historical fact about our past, and does it all the more solidly and sincerely because he has no notion that he is doing it at all.

I know it was the fashion in the Victorian times to say that England was represented by its Great Middle Class and not by its aristocracy. That was the artfulness of its aristocracy. Never did a governing class govern to completely, by saying it did not govern at all. The middle class Englishman was always pushed into the foreground; while the rulers remained in the background. It was the middle-class Englishman who wrote letters to *The Times;* it was not he who informed *The Times.* It was the middle-class man who went to the political meeting; it was not he who sent down the candidate. The governing class governed by the perfectly simple principle of keeping all the important things to themselves; and giving the papers and the public unimportant things to discuss. When Earl Balfour (one of the last great survivals of the governing class) said languidly that he never read the newspapers, everybody laughed, as if he had said that he could not read the alphabet. In fact, of course, he never read the newspapers because he had read the State papers. Why should he read all the nonsense that was served out to the public, when he knew all the real secrets which were kept as secrets of State?

But when we have realized that the England of Trollope was still an aristocratic England, there is a further distinction, which Trollope never notices, but always makes clear. His evidence is alone enough to upset Macaulay and Green and the whole Whig theory of our history taught in the schools. The really interesting fact to be inferred from Trollope is this. Nineteenth-century England is *not* a country in which we have a populace led by a Liberal middle class on one side and a powerful Tory nobility led by dukes and earls on the other. The division of the parties is totally different, and unconsciously betrays the real secret, not only of the nineteenth, but of the eighteenth and seventeenth centuries. It betrays the truth about the Glorious Revolution of 1688, and the nature of the new system which it really introduced. The Crown did not pass from James II to William III. Like many stolen treasures, it was cut up; it was cut up into coronets.

Let anybody, reading Trollope carefully, note what the real division between the parties was. There is a large proportion of minor gentry, who may be called middle class, if we will, who are certainly numerous and not very rich: doctors, parsons, small squires, and yeomen and all sorts of plain and hard-working people. Now *these* people are all Tories. They inherit the old Tory tradition of loyalty to a king, which belonged to purely middle class people like Dr. Johnson or Dr. Goldsmith. For above all these people, like gods on Olympus, like higher beings living on a loftier plane, there are two or three people who are of prodigious public importance, like emperors or kings. The tone of everybody else in talking about them implies the remote condescension of a sovereign. The obvious example is the Duke of Omnium. He is spoken of as playing a great princely part like a prince. We need not deny him the credit, but we need not disguise the fact that his importance rested on being what we call a millionaires. More presentable, I admit, than the millionaires why are flattered today. But he is ruler of all England because he is gigantically rich. Now *this* kind of man is always a Whig.*

What the serious historians have disguised, the frivolous novelist has detected. Their histories are fiction and his fiction in history. That is the truth; and that is Trollope's unconscious witness to what the Whigs really did in English history; why they were able to overthrow the Stuarts; why they were able to dominate the common traditional Tories like Dr. Thorne. What the Revolution did was obviously not to establish a democracy; not even to establish a normal and national gentry; no even to establish a mere rustic squirearchy. It was to establish certain great magnates, whose wealth and power was far out of proportion to that of the ordinary gentleman, let alone the ordinary citizen. They owned everything, and Trollope knew it. What other possible meaning is there in the title of *The Duke of Omnium?* Thackeray also knew it. What possible other meaning is there in that fine satiric flourish, 'I am not a Whig . . . but oh, how I should like to bell'? Even the waiters and couriers on the Continent knew it. What other meaning was in the Arabian Nights legend of the English Milord? Everybody seems to have known it, except the people who taught history in the schools and universities of England.

---

* Between the 17th through the 19th centuries, the Whigs as a political group sought to limit the Royal authority and strived to increase parliamentary power in England.

On Poland

THERE ARE certain things in this world that are at once intensely loved and intensely hated. They are naturally things of a strong character and either very good or very bad. They generally give a great deal of trouble to everybody; and a special sort of trouble to those who try to destroy them. But they give most trouble of all to those who try to ignore them. Some hate them so insanely as to deny their very existence; but the void made by that negation continues to exasperate those who have made it, till they are like men choked with a vacuum. They declare that it shall be nameless and then never cease to cure its name. This curious case is perhaps best illustrated by examples. One example of it is Ireland. Another example is Poland.

Within ten minutes of my stepping from the train on to Polish territory, I had heard two phrases; phrases which struck the precise note which thus inspires one half of the world and infuriates the other half. Most men have an immediate reaction to them, one way or the other; they think them spirited and generous or they would think them extravagant and futile. We were received by a sort of escort of Polish cavalry; and one of the officers made a speech in French; a very fine speech in very good French. In the course of it he used the first of these two typical expressions, 'I will not talk of the chief friend of Poland. God is the chief friend of Poland.' And he afterwards said, in a more playful and conversational moment, 'After all, there are only two trades for a man: a poet and a soldier of cavalry.' He said it humorously, and with the delicate implication, 'You are a poet and I am a soldier of cavalry. So there we are!' I said that, allowing for the difficulty of anybody having anything to eat, if this were literally true, I entirely accepted the sentiment and heartily agreed with it. But I know there are some people who would not understand it even enough to disagree with it. I know that some people would hotly and even furiously refuse even to see the joke of it. There is something in that particular sort of romance, or (if you will) in that particular sort of swagger, which moves them quite genuinely to a violent irritation. It is an irritation common among rationalists among the drier sort of dons, and among the duller sort of public servants. It is one of the real working prejudices of the world.

Now if all those Polish officers had been Prussian officers if their swagger had consisted of silently pushing people off the kerbstone, if their ceremony had consisted not in making good speeches but in standing in row quite speechless, if their faces had been like painted wood and their heads and bodies puffed up with nothing but an east wind of pride, they would not have irritated this sort of critic in this sort of way. They would have soothed him, with a vague sense that is what seem to him absurd, is the idea of the soldier civilized, the man who is no more ashamed of the military art than of any other art, but who is interested in other arts beside the military art; and interested in them all like an artist. That the man in uniform should make a speech, and, worst of all, a good speech, seems comic, like a policeman composing a sonnet. That he should connect a horse soldier with a poet appears meaningless, like connecting a butcher with a Buddhist monk. In one historic word, these people have and have always hated the cavalier. They hate the cavalier especially when he writes cavalier songs. They hate the knight when he is also a troubadour; especially when he always swaggers about with both rapier and guitar. They can understand Ironsides solemnly killing people in the fear of the Lord, as they can understand Prussian soldiers solemnly killing people in the fear of the War-Lord. But they cannot tolerate the combination of wit and culture and courtesy with this business of killing; it really seems to them provocative and preposterous. It seems especially preposterous when the cavalier adds to all his other dazzling inconsistencies by being quite as religious as the Ironside. The last touch is put to their angry bewilderment, when the man who has talked gaily as if nobody mattered except lancers and lyric poets, says with the same simplicity and gaiety, 'The one friend of our country is God,'

These critics commonly say that they are irritated with this romantic type because it always fails; so they are naturally even more irritated when it very frequently succeeds. People who are ready to shed tears of sympathy, when the windmills overthrow Don Quixote, are very angry indeed when Don Quixote really overthrows the windmills. People who are prepared to give a vain blessing to a forlorn hope are not unnaturally annoyed to find that the forlorn hope is comparatively hopeful, and not entirely forlorn. Even the most genial of these realists, Mr. Bernard Shaw, would be a little vexed if he had to reverse the whole moral of *Arms and the Man* and admit that the Arms counted for a little less and the Man for a little more. He would be slightly put out, perhaps, if the celebrated artillery duel really took place; and the sentimental Sergius blew the realistic Bluntzschli to pieces. But that is almost exactly what has really happened in modern Europe today. That is what happened, for instance, when the practical Mr. Broadbent went bankrupt in his other Island.

When the Poles defeated the Bolshevists in the field of battle, it was precisely that. It was the old chivalric tradition defeating everything that is modern, everything that is necessitarian, everything that is mechanical in method and materialistic in philosophy. It was the Marxian notion that everything is inevitable, defeated by the Christian notion that nothing is inevitable – no, not even what has already happened. Mr. Belloc has put the Polish ideal into lines dedicated to a great Polish shrine:

> Hope of the half-defeated; house of gold,
> Shrine of the sword and tower of ivory.

I am not dealing with such great matters, but describing an aspect and an experience; and before I leave these Polish cavaliers, I may remark that I had another chance of seeing them at the jumping competition in the Concours Hippique; and I will only mention one incident and leave it; for it is something of a parable. The course consisted of the usual high obstacles; but there was one which was apparently of a novel pattern and practically insuperable. Anyhow, one after another in that long

procession of admirable riders, French, Polish, and Italian, failed at this final test till failure, came to be treated as a matter of course. There were, of course, other misfortunes that were not a matter of course; even under the best conditions the race is not always to the swift; even experts on such occasions differ about the degrees of merits and misfortunes; and I am not likely to offer myself as an expert at a horse show. One of the lancers playfully asked me if I was going to compete. I made the obvious answer that, mounted on my favourite elephant, I would undertake to step over many of the fences, though certainly not the last fence of all, which I doubt if a giraffe could bestride. But the general feeling seemed to be that I should be more useful as an obstacle than a surmounter of obstacles; and that if I lay down on the course, it might be even worse than the worst obstacle. Otherwise, I am an outsider in these things and only describe what I saw; and on that, as I say, even doctors may disagree. There was some amusement and some pity for one young Pole, who was, I believe, a novice or relatively untired person, whose mount in some fashion stumbled, so that the rider was shot over the horse's head. At least I thought he was shot over the horse's head; and then discovered, amid some amazing and jerky gyrations, that he was what can only be called clinging to the horse's ears. While the horse danced about the course in a *degage*** manner, the rider seemed to crawl down his neck in some incredible way and rolled back into the saddle. He found one stirrup and tried in vain to find the other. Then he gave it up; the stirrup, not the race. He cleared a fairly low obstacle before him, and then, seeming to gather a wild impetus from nowhere, with one stirrup flying loose and swaying in the saddle, he charged the last impossible barrier, and, first of all that company, went over it like a bird. And someone said at my elbow with a sharp exclamation, in English, 'That's just like the Poles!'

Hope of the half-defeated; house of gold . . . .

---

* Free of constraint: nonchalant

On New Capitals

I WONDER that no historian has written a great historical monograph bearing some such title as *The New City* or perhaps *The Second City* or more specifically *The City of the King*. Perhaps none of the titles fully explains what should be explained in the book. It would describe a certain action which differed with differing conditions; but occurred again and again all over the world, or at any rate all over Europe. Briefly, it may be called moving from the old capital to the new capital. The old capital was naturally the seat of tradition, and generally of religion. The new capital was naturally the seat of fashion, because it was generally the seat of royalty. A sort of ancient archetypal form of it exists at the very back or beginning of the whole history of Christendom; in that great exodus of the Roman Emperor from Rome; the passage of Constantine to Constantinople.

The impression first struck me as I stood among the baroque buildings and classical squares of Warsaw. But I remembered that I had something of the same impression and memory standing in the streets of Madrid. Warsaw and Madrid, as the two opposite ends of civilized Europe, both illustrate this curious passage in the history of our civilization. Both are practically products of the seventeenth and eighteenth centuries. Both are practically products of that 'kingcraft' or sense of the supreme importance of the secular prince, which marked the time after the religious schism and the failure of the religious wars. The princes had so little link with their own past, and sometimes so much confidence in their own future, that they left behind them the sacred cities of the dead kings and the dead saints and heroes, as if they were nothing but cities of the dead. They began to build new cities of their own, for purely political or financial reasons; full of the rationalism of the Renaissance. These towns that were meant to be novelties are now necessarily much less interesting as antiquities. There is at least one Polish city much more national than the capital of Poland. There are several cities much more Spanish than the capital of Spain.

France is the working model of Europe; like a clock with the clockwork showing clearly in a glass-case. There the movements occur rapidly, sharply, and logically, which appear elsewhere more slowly, more confusedly, and more at large. And French history exhibits a sort of extreme case of this process. It was impossible to dethrone Paris; even by taking the throne away from under it, so to speak. But the eighteenth century king did try the trick of taking the throne away; though he did not take it very far. He set it up in Versailles; and something in the proximity and the contrast exhibits more vividly than elsewhere the ultimate futility of the affair. Paris was far too powerful as the ancient popular and religious capital, which had once at the command of the populace shut its gates against the king, until he had returned to the religion. The populace continued to count even when the religion had turned to irreligion; it was still, so to speak, a sort of religion of irreligion. The French king went to his new town late: and he left it early. We might even say that he left it abruptly. We might confidently say that when he had left it, there was nothing left. The French revolution was always regarded as an innovation; but it is worth noting that if it was the triumph of the new faction, it was also the triumph of the old town. It is curious that while the last court was being held amid the latest and most florid classical ornaments of the Age of Reason, the tocsins* of revolution were being rung from old Gothic towers and the rebels were assuming, with deeper irony than they knew, the names of old fraternities of monks and friars. It is

* Alarm bells.

worth noting, I say, because what happened in the French Revolution has also happened in the more extreme example of the Russian Revolution. Even where the religion turns to irreligion, even where the irreligion sometimes turns to a sort of religion of devil-worship, the most ancient shrine and citadel in some mysterious manner retains and even recovers its power. Even for the desecrators of all shrines it acts as a shrine. Popular instincts return to it, even when worse or wilder instincts are let loose. The artificial creation of the last few centuries vanishes like Versailles in the conflagration. We no longer talk of St. Petersburg; we no longer talk very much even of Petrograd. The city of Peter the Great has lost its greatness; and once again, after many centuries, when we talk of Muscovy we talk of Moscow. Moscow is again, as the Russian poet said, the heart of Russia; even if the heart is broken.

These extremes are not felt in cases like that of Madrid or that of Warsaw; because the process was more natural and gradual and the nation more united and less challenged by internal hatreds. But even in the milder cases I should never be surprised to find that at some time in the future there was a return to the older civic centres. However this may be, it is certain that the older civic centres are generally the more interesting; and sometimes more interested, in the future as well as in the past. Now that Moscow has fallen to the Bolshevists as Constantinople fell to the Moslems, we might almost say of its fate, considered as a Christian capital, that both those imperial experiments have ended. We might almost say, in some mystical sense, that Byzantium may yet go back to Rome. In the rising fortunes of countries like Spain and Poland it is quite possible that further resurrections may take place, and that cities left for dead may begin once more to live even a modern life. In the case of Poland, of course, the more traditional and even mystical site is the town of Cracow. It has always been, and still is, of very great national and international importance as a University town. But it is also the original Royal capital; and the seat of the kings at the moment when Polish kingship had perhaps its highest influence in Europe. There still clings to it something of the quality that belonged to a city of palaces as well as a city of colleges or chapels. Warsaw has become the modern capital of a republic; but there still lies upon Cracow the shadow of a crown.

But what gives to Cracow a sort of sharp outline of spires and turrets against the background of history is the fact that it is a seat of culture on the edge of the uncultivated wilds. The city, like the nation, is a sort of outpost, and the contrast is of the sort that belongs to capes and islands and the edges of things. That balance of the mind that we call philosophy is here balanced on the edge of an abyss. That great gift of civilization which we call learning, and that greater gift of civilization which is the art of carrying learning lightly, is here poised only with a sort of perilous grace. The Germans who do not carry learning lightly, and the wild Slavs, who do not carry it at all, press upon that more slender and subtle experiment with the weight of less living things. In Cracow can be seen all those crafts and schools of art with which we are familiar in the Western culture, in the free cities of Flanders or the cathedrals of Normandy. But we see them there thrust up against a vast and vague hostility which is something altogether alien to us and different from the internal quarrels of Flemish burghers or Norman knights. For centuries the Tartars rolled around these towers a torrent of Asiatic barbarism. There is little change in the position today; except that the barbarism is called Bolshevism. Sections of the city wall are still shown, which were guarded by the guilds, each lining its part of the wall; first the tanners and then the shoe-makers and then the glaziers, and so on round the whole circle. Guilds of that type existed all over Europe; but when they went out to battle, it was commonly against other guilds or against the feudal nobility, as in the flaming victory of Courtrai, But here in Cracow the guildsmen standing on that wall looked out across a wilderness that faced away into the formless east, where strange gods were worshipped under strange skies. Out of that mystery of the sunrise a strange horseman came riding from the legendary country of Cathay; and he felt himself to be in the ends of the earth. And from the tower of the city a trumpet is still blown every hour to the four winds of heaven as if uttering the defiance of civilization besieged. Only the trumpet peal breaks on the last note; to commemorate a medieval trumpeter slain by a Tartar arrow. And so odd and moving is the break that a man listening today can fancy that he hears not only the trumpet, but the bolt of the barbarian singing by.

What I found in my Pocket

ONCE WHEN I was very young I met one of those men who have made the Empire what it is – a man in an astrachan* coat, with an astrachan moustache – a tight, black, curly moustache. Whether he put on the moustache with the coat, or whether his Napoleonic will enabled him not only to grow a moustache in the usual place, but also to grow little moustaches all over his clothes, I do not know. I only remember that he said to me the following words: 'A man can't get on nowadays by hanging about with his hands in his pockets.' I made reply with the quite obvious flippancy that perhaps a man got on by having his hands in other people's pockets. Whereupon he began to argue about Moral Evolution, so I suppose what I said had some truth in it. But the incident now comes back to me, and connects itself with another incident – if you can call it an incident – which happened to me only the other day.

I have only once in my life picked a pocket, and then (perhaps through some absent-mindedness) I picked my own. My act can really with some reason be so described. For in taking things out of my pocket I had at least one of the more tense and quivering emotions of the thief; I had a complete ignorance and a profound curiosity as to what I should find there. Perhaps it would be the exaggeration of eulogy to call me a tidy person. But I can always pretty satisfactorily account for all my possessions. I can always tell where they are, and what I have done with them, so long as I can keep them out of my pockets. If once anything slips into these unknown abysses, I wave it a sad Virgilian farewell. I suppose that the things that I have dropped into my pockets are still there; the same presumption applies to the things that I have dropped into the sea. But I regard the riches stored in both these bottomless

* Karakul or curled wool of Russian origin.

chasms with the same reverent ignorance. They tell us that on the last day the sea will give up its dead; and I suppose that on the same occasion long strings and strings of extraordinary things will come running out of my pockets. But I have quite forgotten what any of them are; and there is really nothing (excepting the money) that I shall be at all surprised at finding among them.

Such at least has hitherto been my state of innocence. I here only wish briefly to recall the special, extraordinary, and hitherto unprecedented circumstances which led me in cold blood, and being of sound mind, to turn out my packets. I was locked up in a third-class carriage for a rather long journey. The time was towards evening, but it might have been anything, for everything resembling earth or sky or light or shade was painted out as if with a great wet brush by an unshifting sheet of quite colourless rain. I had no books or newspapers. I had not even a pencil and a scrap of paper with which to write a religious epic. There were no advertisements on the walls of the carriage, otherwise I could have plunged into the study of them, for any collections of printed words is quite enough to suggest infinite complexities of mental ingenuity. When I find myself opposite the words 'Sunlight Soap' I can exhaust all the aspects of Sun Worship, Apollo, and summer poetry before I go on to the less congenial subject of soap. But there was no printed word or picture anywhere; there was nothing but blank wood inside the carriage and blank wet without. Now I deny most energetically that anything is, or can be, uninteresting. So I stared at the joints of the walls and seats, and began thinking hard on the fascinating subject of wood. Just as I had begun to realize why, perhaps, it was that Christ was a carpenter, rather than a bricklayer, or a baker, or anything else, I suddenly started upright, and remembered my pockets I was carrying about with me an unknown treasury. I had a British Museum and a South Kensington collection of unknown curios hung all over me in different places. I began to take the things out.

The first thing I came upon consisted of piles and heaps of Battersea tram tickets. There were enough to equip a paper chase. They shook down in showers like confetti. Primarily, of course, they touched my patriotic emotions, and brought tears to my eyes; also they provided me with the printed matter I required, for I found on the back of them some short but striking little scientific essays about some kind of pill. Comparatively speaking, in my then destitution, those tickets might be regarded as a small but well-chosen scientific library. Should my railway journey continue (which seemed likely at the time) for a few months longer, I could imagine myself throwing myself into the controversial aspects of the pill, composing replies and rejoinders pro and con upon the data furnished to me. But after all it was the symbolic quality of the tickets that moved me most. For as certainly as the Cross of St. George means English patriotism, those scraps of paper meant all that municipal patriotism which is now, perhaps, the greatest hope of England.

The next thing that I took out was a pocket-knife. A pocket-knife, I need hardly say, would require a thick book full of moral meditations all to itself. A knife typifies one of the most primary of those practical origins upon which as upon low, thick pillars all our human civilization reposes. Metals, the mystery of the thing called iron and of the thing called steel, led me off half dazed into a kind of dream I saw into the entrails of dim, damp woods: where the first man, among all the common stones, found the strange stone I saw a vague and violent battle, in which stone axes broke and stone knives were splintered against something shining and new in the hand of one desperate man. I heard all the hammers on all the anvils of the earth. I saw all the swords of feudal and all the wheels of industrial war. For the knife is only a short sword; and the pocket-knife is a secret sword. I opened it and looked at that brilliant and terrible tongue which we call a blade; and I thought that perhaps it was the symbol of the oldest of the needs of man. The next moment I knew that I was wrong; for the thing that came next in my pocket was a box of matches. Then I saw fire which is stronger even than steel, the old fierce female thing, the thing we all love, but dare not touch.

The next thing I found was a piece of chalk; and I saw in it all the art and all the frescoes of the world, The next was a coin of a very modest value; and I saw in it not only the image and superscription of our own Cæsar, but all government and order since the world began. But I have not space to say what were the items in the long and splendid procession of poetical symbols that came pouring out. I cannot tell you all the things that were in my pocket. I can tell you one thing, however, that I could not find in my pocket that vital and absolutely essential piece of paper now demanded by the frowning railway official. I allude here to my railway ticket!

The Dickensian

HE WAS a quiet man, dressed in dark clothes, with a large limp straw hat; with something almost military in his moustache and whiskers, but with a quite unmilitary stoop and very dreamy eyes. He was gazing with a rather gloomy interest at the cluster, one might almost say the tangle, of small shipping which grew thicker as our little pleasure boat crawled up into Yarmouth Harbour. A boat entering this harbour, as every one knows, does not enter in front of the town like a foreigner, but creeps round at the back like a traitor taking the town in the rear. The passage of the river seems almost too narrow for its traffic, and in consequence the bigger ships look colossal. As we passed under a timber ship from Norway, which seemed to block up the heavens like a cathedral, the man in a straw hat pointed to an old wooden figure-head carved like a woman, and said like one continuing a conversation, 'Now, why have they left off having them? They didn't do anyone any harm'.

I replied with some flippancy about the captain's wife being jealous; but I knew in my heart that the man had struck a deep note. There has been something in our most recent civilization which is mysteriously hostile to such healthy and poetic symbols.

'They hate anything like that, which is human and pretty', he continued, exactly echoing my thoughts. 'I believe they broke up all the jolly old figure-heads with hatchets and enjoyed doing it'.

'Like Mr. Quilp', I answered, 'when he battered the wooden Admiral with the poker'.

His whole face suddenly became alive, and for the first time he stood erect and stared at me.

'Do you come to Yarmouth for that?' he asked.

'For what?'

'For Dickens', he answered, and drummed with his foot on the deck.

'No', I answered; 'I come for fun, though that is much the same thing'.

'I always come', he answered quietly, 'to find Peggotty's boat. It isn't here'.

And when he said that I understood him perfectly.

There are two Yarmouths; I daresay there are two hundred to the people who live there. I myself have never come to the end of the list of Batterseas. But there are two to the stranger and tourist; the poor part, which is dignified, and the prosperous part, which is savagely vulgar. My new friend haunted the first of these like a ghost; to the latter he would only distantly allude.

'The place is very much spoilt now. . . .trippers, you know', he would say, not at all scornfully, but simple sadly. That was the nearest he would go to an admission of the monstrous watering place that lay along the front, outblazing the sun, and more deafening than the sea. But behind – out of earshot of this uproar – there are lanes so narrow that they seem like secret entrances to some hidden place of repose. There are squares so brimful of silence that to plunge into one of them is like plunging into a pool. In these places the man and I paced up and down talking about Dickens, or, rather, doing what all true Dickensians do, telling each other verbatim long passages which both of us knew quite well already. We were really in the atmosphere of the older England. Fishermen passed us who might well have been characters like Peggotty; we went into a musty curiosity shop and bought pipe-stoppers carved into figures from Pickwick. The evening was settling down between all the buildings with that slow gold that seems to soak everything, when we went into the church.

In the growing darkness of the church, my eye caught the coloured windows which on that clear golden evening were flaming with all the passionate heraldry of the most fierce and ecstatic of Christian art. At length I said to my companion –

'Do you see that angel over there? I think it must be meant for the angel at the sepulchre'.

He saw that I was somewhat singularly moved, and he raised his eyebrows.

'I daresay', he said. 'What is there odd about that?'

After a pause I said, 'Do you remember what the angel at the sepulchre said?'

'Not particularly', he answered; but where are you off to in such a hurry?'

I walked him rapidly out of the still square, past the fishermen's almshouses, towards the coast, he still inquiring indignantly where I was going.

'I am going', I said, 'to put pennies in automatic machines on the beach. I am going to listen to the niggers. I am going to have my photograph taken. I am going to drink ginger-beer out of its original bottle. I will buy some picture post-cards. I do want a boat. I am ready to listen to a concertina, and but for the defects of my education should be ready to play it. I am willing to ride on a donkey; that is, if the donkey is willing I am willing to be a donkey; for all this was commanded me by the angel in the stained-glass window'.

'I really think', said the Dickensian, 'that I had better put you in charge of your relations'.

'Sir,' I answered, 'there are certain writers to whom humanity owes much, whose talent is yet of so shy or delicate or retrospective a type that we do well to link it with certain quaint places or certain perishing associations. It would not be unnatural to look for the spirit of Horace Walpole at Strawberry Hill, or even for the shade of Thackeray in Old Kensington. But let us have no antiquarianism about Dickens, for Dickens is not an antiquity. Dickens looks not backward, but forward, he might look at our modern mobs with satire, or with fury, but he would love to look at them. He might lash our democracy, but it would be because like a democrat, he asked much from it. We will not have all his books bound up under the title of *The Old Curiosity Shop*. Rather we will have them all bound up under the title of *Great Expectations*. Wherever humanity is he would have us face it and make something of it, swallow it with a holy cannibalism, and assimilate it with the digestion of a giant. We must take these trippers as he would have taken them, and tear out of them their tragedy and their farce. Do you remember now what the angel said at the sepulchre? Why seek ye the living; among the dead? He is not here; He is risen'.

With that we came out suddenly on the wide stretch of the sands, which were black with the knobs and masses of our laughing and quite desperate democracy. And the sunset, which was now in its final glory, flung far over all of them a red flush and glitter like the gigantic firelight of Dickens. In that strange evening light every figure looked at once grotesque and attractive, as if he had a story to tell. I heard a little girl (who was being throttled by another little girl) say by way of self-vindication, 'My sister-in-law' has got four rings aside her weddin'-ring!'

I stood and listened for more, but my friend went away.

On Philosophy versus Fiction

LOOKING BACK on a wild and wasted life, I realize that I have especially sinned in neglecting to read novels. I mean the really novel novels; for such old lumber as Dickens and Jane Austen I know fairly well. If instead of trifling away my time over pamphlets about Collectivism or Co-operation, plunging for mere pleasure into the unhealthy excitement of theological debates with dons, or enjoying the empty mirth of statistics about Poland and Czechoslovakia, I had quietly sat at home doing my duty and reading every novel as it came out, I might be a more serious and earnest man than I am today. If instead of loitering to laugh over something, merely because it happened to be laughable, I had walked stiffly and sternly on to the Circulating Library, and put myself under the tuition of our more passionate lady novelists, I might by this time be as intense as they. If instead of leading a riotous life, scrapping with Mr. Shaw about Socialism, or Dean Inge about Science, I had believed everything I was told about marriage by an unmarried young woman in an avowedly imaginary story, I might now have a more undisturbed faith and simplicity. Novels are the great monument of the amazing credulity of the modern mind; for people believe them quite seriously even though they do not pretend to be true.

But it is really true, alas! that I have failed to follow adequately the development of serious fiction. I do not admit that I have entirely failed to follow the development of serious facts. Not only have I discussed Labour with Socialists, or Science with Scientists, but I have argued with myself about other things, so new and true that I cannot get anybody else to argue about them. The world-wide power of trusts, for instance, is a thing that is never attacked and never defended. It seems to have been completed without ever having been proposed; we might say without ever having been begun. The small shopkeeper has been destroyed in the twentieth century, as the small yeoman was destroyed in the eighteenth century. But for the yeoman there was protest and regret; great poets sang his dirge, and great orators like Cobbett* died trying to avenge his death. But the modern destructive changes seem to be too new to be noticed. Perhaps they are too enormous to be seen. No; I do not think it can be fairly said that I have neglected the most recent realities of the real world. It seems rather the real world that neglects them.

Nor do I confess, thank heaven, to the more odious vice of neglecting funny or frivolous fiction; whether in the sense of reading everything from the first story of Mr. Jacobs to the last story of Mr. Wodehouse; or in that richer sense in which the joke consists entirely of a corpse, a blood-stained hat-peg, or the mysterious footprints of a three-legged man in the garden. I have been a munificent patron of fiction of that description; and have even presented the public with a corpse or two of my own. In short, the limitation of my literary experience is altogether on the side of the modern serious novel; especially that very serious novel which is all about the psychology of flirting and jilting and going to jazz dances. I have read hundreds of books bearing titles like *Socialism: the Way Out;* or *Society: the Way In;* or *Japanese Light on the Paulus Mythus;* or *Cannibalism the Clue to Catholicism;* or *Parricide: a Contribution to Progress;* or *The Traffic Problem: the Example of Greenland;* or *Must we Drink?;* or *Should We Eat?;* or *Do We Breathe?* and all those grave and baffling questions. I have also read hundreds of books bearing titles like *Who Killed Humphrey Higgleswick?;* or *The Blood on the Blotting-paper;* or *The Secret of Piccadilly Circus;* or *The Clue of the Stolen Toothbrush;* and so on and so on. But I have *not* read with sufficient regularity, diligence and piety all

---

* William Cobbett (1763-1835), English journalist and champion of the cause of traditional rural England against the adverse changes wrought by the Industrial Revolution. His reactionary views on the ideal society were very popular.

those other books that bear titles like *The Grass-widowhood of Grace Bellow*; or *The Seventh Honeymoon of Sylphide Squeak*; or *Dear Lady Divorce*; or *The Sex of Samuel Stubbin*; or *Harold Hatrack, Soul-Thief*; or *The Hypnotist of Insomnia Smith*. All these grave and laborious, and often carefully written books come out season after season; and somehow I have missed them. Sometimes they miss me, even when hurled at my head by publishers. It were vain to deny that I sometimes deliberately avoid them. I have a reason, of a reasonable sort; for I do not think it is a really reasonable reason merely to say that they bore me. For I did once really try to read them; and I got lost. One reason is that I think there is in all literature a sort of purpose; quite different from the mere moralizing that is generally meant by a novel with a purpose. There is something in the plan of the idea that is straight like a backbone and pointing like an arrow. It is meant to go somewhere, or at least to point somewhere; to its end, not only in the modern sense of an ending, but in the medieval sense of a fruition. Now, I think that many of the less intellectual stories have kept this, where the more intellectual stories have lost it. The writer of detective stories, having once asked who killed Humphrey Higgleswick, must, after all, end by telling us who did it, even by the mean subterfuge of saying it was Humphrey Higgleswick. But the serious novelist asks a question that he does not answer. The sex of Samuel Stubbin may even remain in considerable doubt, in some of the more emotional passages, and the seventh honeymoon of Sylphide seems to have nothing to do with the probable prospect of her eighth. It is the custom of these writers to scoff at the old sentimental novel or novelette, in which the story always ended happily to the sound of church bells. But, judged by the highest standards of heroic or great literature, like the Greek tragedies or the great epics, the novelette was really far superior to the novel. It set itself to reach a certain goal – the marriage of two persons, with all its really vital culmination in the founding of a family and a vow to God; and all other incidents were interesting because they pointed to a consummation which was, by legitimate hypothesis, a grand consummation.

But the modern refusal both of the religious vow and the romantic hope has broken the backbone of the business altogether, and it is only an assorted bag of bones. People are minutely described as experiencing one idiotic passion after another, passions which they themselves recognize as idiotic and which even their own wretched philosophy forbids them to regard as steps towards any end. The sentimental novelette was a simplified and limited convention of the thing; in which for the sake of argument, marriage was made the prize. Of course marriage is not the only thing that happens in life; and somebody else may study another section with another goal. They cannot point to the human happiness which the romantics associated with gaining the prize. They cannot point to the heavenly happiness which the religious associated with keeping the vow. They are driven back entirely on the microscopic description of these aimless appetites in themselves. And, microscopically studied in themselves, they are not very interesting to a middle-aged man with plenty of other things to think about. In short, the old literature, both great and trivial, was built on the idea that there is a purpose in life, even if it is not always completed in this life; and it really was interesting to follow the stages of such a purpose; from the meeting to the wedding, from the wedding to the bells, and from the bells to the church. But modern philosophy has taken the life out of modern fiction. It is simply dissolving into separate fragments and then into formlessness; and deserves much more than the romantic novel the modern reproach of being 'sloppy'.

Our Latin Relations

IT IS odd how often one may hear, in the middle of a very old and genuine English town, the remark that it looks like a foreign town. I heard it only yesterday, standing on the ramparts of the noble hill of Rye, which overlooks the flats like a Mount of St. Michael left inland. Most people know that Rye contains a medieval monument which might almost be called a medieval prophecy – a prophecy of modern things more awful than anything medieval. It is an ancient tower, which has not only always been marked on maps with the name of Ypres, but has always been actually pronounced by the name of Wipers. Nothing could mark a thing as more continuously national than that Englishmen sundered by vast centuries should actually make the same mistake and should mispronounce the same word in the same way.

There is in this small point a paradox we must understand, especially just now, if we are to have a really patriotic foreign policy. It is very unlucky that for some time our teaching of history has been rather the un-teaching of history, because it has been the un-teaching of tradition. Our histories told us we were Teuton;* our legends told us we were Roman – and, as usual, the legends were right. It is not only true that England is nowhere more really English than where she is Roman – it is even true that she is nowhere more really English than where she is French. To make only the chance example, with which I began above, you could find nothing more national, more typical, more traditional, as a real piece of English history, than the very phrase, 'The Cinq Ports'. And it is all the more English because the word 'cinq' is French and the word 'port' is Latin. A Teutonist professor, full of some folly about 'folk-speech', might insist on our calling them 'The Five Harbours',

---

* Descendants of the religious order founded in the Middle Ages (1189 AD) in eastern Europe to nurse the sick in Palestine during the Third Crusade.

or (for all I know) 'The Five Holes'. But his version would be less popular, and only more pedantic. The Latin was always the popular element, which may not sound so odd if we happen to remember that the very word 'popular' is Latin.

Thus our alliance with the French and the Italians is not something to be supported for the sake of the last five years. It is something to be solidified for the sake of more than a thousand. The fact has been hidden by the historical accident that we have often been the antagonists of the French in particular rivalries for particular things. But we were always much nearer to the French when we were their antagonists than to the Germans when we were their allies. There was much more resemblance between a knight like the Black Prince and a knight like Bertrand du Guesclin than there ever was between a sailor like Nelson and a soldier like Blucher. A town like Rye is full of memories of fighting with the French, especially in the Middle Ages; of raids to and fro across the narrow seas, in which the bells of the coast town churches were captured and recaptured; and there are spirited stories about the Abbot of Battle, worthy to be turned into ballads. But the very fact of these coast-town raids suggests that it was coast against coast, and even seaman against seaman. But the whole point of Prussian war was that it was an inland thing the whole point of English war that it was an island thing. The alliance with Prussia was never either popular or natural it was wholly aristocratic and artificial. Compared with that the medieval war was as friendly as a medieval tournament. Nor was it peculiar to the case of France; it was true of all we call Latin – all that remains of the Roman Empire. The Latins, even when treated as foes in politics, were treated almost as friends in popular tradition. The English sailors sang in their idle moments, 'Farewell and adieu to you, fine Spanish ladies', even when they had devoted their working hours to singing the ballads of the fine Spanish gentlemen. The children in the nurseries sang in imaginative triumph, 'The King of Spain's daughter came to visit me', though their Elizabethan parents might have been lightning the beacons and calling out the train-bands[1] to prevent the King of Spain's son, the noble Don John of Austria from paying them such a visit. A thousand nursery rhymes and nonsense tags testify to a vast tradition that Southern Europe was the world to which we belonged. We belonged to a system of which Rome was the sun, and of which the old Roman provinces were planets. We were never meant to pursue a meteor out of empty space, the comet of Teutonism. Our place was in an order and a watch of stars, though one star might differ from another in glory. Our place was with that red star of Gaul which might well bear the name of Mars; or that morning and evening star which the Latins themselves named Lucifer, last to fade and first to return in every twilight of history; Italy, the light of the world.

A Latin alliance is founded on our history, though not on our historians. The French and English who fought each other round these southern harbours were also ready to help each other, and often did help each other. Not only did they frequently go crusading together against the Turks, but they would have been ready at any moment to go crusading against the Prussians. Chaucer was exceedingly English, and therefore partly French; and he sends his ideal knight to fight the heathen in Prussia. Froissart[2] was highly French, and therefore respectful to the English; and he says that the French and English always do courtesy, but the Germans? Never. The truth is that all the old English traditions, scholarly and legendary, chivalric and vulgar, were at one in referring back to Roman culture, until we come to a new crop of very crude pedants in the nineteenth century.

Most of them were prigs, and many of them were snobs – for it was largely a Court fashion, spread by Court poets and

1 A corruption of 'trained band' of soldiers, a 17th century Militia in England.
2 French court historian and poet Jean Froissart (1333-1401). He chronicled the Hundred Years' War from 1325 to 1400, including events in Flanders, Spain, Portugal, France, and England.

Court chaplains. It was like a huge, hideous gilded German monument; and, fortunately, it has already fallen down. But I think it undesirable that the mere discredited litter and lumber of it, left lying about, should for ever prevent us from building anything else.

Even after the ghastly enlightenment of the war there are people who cannot clear their minds of the nation that the Prussian is the Progressive. They think he is progressing now, because he is picking up new things. Picking up new things is not the way to progress, any more than picking up grass by the roots is the way to make it grow. The northern barbarian always has picked up new things especially when they were other people's things. It was still only picking up new things, whether it was picking pockets or picking brains. And there was always one other note about the new things – that they never lived to be old. The barbarians followed the creed of Arius as they followed the ensign of Attila.[1] But nobody remembers Attila as everybody remembered Alfred;[2] and though some modern people object to hearing the Athanasian Creed, they have no opportunity of objecting to hearing the Arian Creed. The enthusiasms of semi-savages do not last.

---

1 King of the Huns (died 453 A.D.). He was one of the most notorious of the barbarian rulers who assailed the Roman Empire. His last invasion of Italy in 452 culminated in famine and plague. His depredations, appearing like divine punishment, earned him the epithet *Flagellum Dei* or *Scourge of God*.
2 Known as Alfred the Great (849-899), he was king of Wessex in southwestern England. Alfred drew up an important code of laws and promoted literacy and learning.

The Secret of a Train

I WILL not say that this story is true; because, as you will soon see, it is all truth and no story. It has no explanation and no conclusion; it is, like most of the other things we encounter in life, a fragment of something else, which would be intensely exciting if it were rot too large to be seen. For the perplexity of life arises from there being too many interesting things in it for us to be interested properly in any of them. What we call its triviality is really the tag-ends of numberless tales; ordinary and unmeaning existence is like ten thousand thrilling detective stories mixed up with a spoon. My experience was a fragment of this nature, and it is, at any rate, not fictitious. Not only am I not making up the incidents (what there were of them), but I am not making up the atmosphere or the landscape, which were the whole horror of the thing. I remember them vividly, and they were truly as I shall now describe.

About noon of an ashen autumn day some years ago I was standing outside the station at Oxford intending to take the train to London. And for some reason, out of idleness or the emptiness of my mind or the emptiness of the pale grey sky, or the cold, a kind of caprice fell upon me that I would not go by that train at all, but would step out on the road and walk at least some part of the way to London. I do not know if other people are made like me in this matter; but for me it is always dreary weather, what may be called useless weather that stings into life a sense of action and romance. On bright blue days I do not want anything to happen; the world is complete and beautiful, a thing for contemplation. I no more ask for adventures under that turquoise dome than I ask for adventures in church. But when the background of man's life is a grey background, then in the name of man's sacred supremacy, I desire to paint on it in fire and gore. When the heavens fail man refuses to fail; when the sky seems to have written on it, in letters of lead and pale silver, the decree that nothing shall happen, then the immortal soul, the prince of the creatures, rises up and decrees that something shall happen, if it be only the slaughter of a policeman. But this is a digressive way of stating what I have said already – that the bleak sky awoke in me a hunger for some change of plans, that the monotonous weather seemed to render unbearable the use of the monotonous train, and that I set out into the country lanes out of the town of Oxford. It was, perhaps, at that moment that a strange curse came upon me out of the city and the sky, whereby it was decreed that years afterwards I should, in an article in the *Daily News,* talk about Sir George Trevelyan* in connexion with Oxford, when I knew perfectly well that he went to Cambridge.

As I crossed the country everything was ghostly and colourless. The fields that should have been green were as grey as the skies; the tree-tops that should have been green were as grey as the clouds and as cloudy. And when I had walked for some hours the evening was closing in. A sickly sunset clung weakly to the horizon, as if pale with reluctance to leave the world in the dark. And as it faded more and more the skies seemed to come closer and to threaten. The clouds which had been merely sullen became swollen; and then they loosened and let down the dark curtains of the rain. The rain was blinding and seemed to beat like blows from an enemy at close quarters; the skies seemed bending over and bawling in my ears. I walked on many more miles before I met a man; in that distance my mind had been made up; and when I met him I asked him if anywhere in the neighbourhood I could pick up the train for Paddington. He directed me to a small silent station (I cannot even remember the name of it) which stood well away from the road and looked as lonely as a hut on the Andes. I do not think I have ever seen such a type of time and sadness and scepticism and everything

---

* English historian Sir George Macauley Trevelyan (1876-1962). He is known for books appreciating the Whig tradition and on British history.

devilish as that station was: it looked as if it had always been raining there ever since the creation of the world. The water streamed from the soaking wood of it as if it were not water at all, but some loathsome liquid corruption of the wood itself; as if the solid station were eternally falling to pieces and pouring away in filth. It took me nearly ten minutes to find a man in the station. When I did he was a dull one, and when I asked him if there was a train to Paddington his answer was sleepy and vague. As far as I understood him, he said there would be a train in half an hour. I sat down and lit a cigar and waived, watching the last tail of the tattered sunset and listening to the everlasting rain. It may have been in half an hour or less that a train came rather slowly into the station. It was an unnaturally dark train; I could not see a light anywhere in the long black body of it, and I could not see any guard running beside it. I was reduced to walking up to the engine and calling out to the stoker to ask if the train was going to London, 'Well – yes, sir,' he said, with an unaccountable kind of reluctance. 'It is going to London but – ' It was just starting, and I jumped into the first carriage: it was pitch dark. I sat there smoking and wondering, as we steamed through the continually darkening landscape, lined with desolate poplars, until we slowed down and stopped, irrationally, in the middle of a field. I heard a heavy noise as of someone clambering off the train, and a dark, ragged head suddenly put itself into my window. 'Excuse me, sir', said the stoker, 'but I think perhaps – well, perhaps you ought to know – there's a dead man in this train'.

Had I been a true artist, a person of exquisite susceptibilities and nothing else, I should have been bound, no doubt, to be finally overwhelmed with this sensational touch, and to have insisted on getting out and walking. As it was, I regret to say, I expressed myself politely, but firmly, to the effect that I didn't care much so long as the train took me to Paddington. But when the train had started with its unknown burden I did do one thing, and do it quite instinctively, without stopping to think, or to think more than a flash. I threw away my cigar. Something that is as old as man and has to do with all mourning and ceremonial told me to do it. There was something un-necessarily horrible, it seemed to me, in the idea of there being only two men in that train, one of them dead and the other smoking a cigar. And as the red and gold of the butt end of it faded like a funeral torch trampled out at some symbolic moment of a procession, I realized how immortal ritual is. I realized the origin and essence of all ritual. That in the presence of those sacred riddles about which we can say nothing, it is often more decent merely to do something. And I realized that ritual will always mean throwing away something; *destroying* our corn or wine upon the altar of our gods.

When the train panted at last into Paddington Station I sprang out of it with a suddenly released curiosity. There was a barrier and officials guarding the rear part of the train; no one was allowed to press towards it. They were guarding and biding something; perhaps death in some too shocking form, perhaps something like the Merstham matter,* so mixed up with human mystery and wickedness that the law has to give it a sort of sanctity; perhaps something worse than either. I went out gladly enough into the streets and saw the lamps shining on the laughing faces. Nor have I ever known from that day to this into what strange story I wandered or what frightful thing was my companion in the dark.

---

* Merstham matter: In 1905 a murder took place of one Mary Money in the Merstham rail tunnel, casting the doubt on the safety of rail travel in those days.

On St. George Revivified

THE DISADVANTAGE of men not knowing the past is that they do not know the present. History is a hill or high point of vantage, from which alone men see the town in which they live or the age in which they are living. Without some such contrast or comparison, without some such shifting of the point of view, we should see nothing whatever of our own social surroundings. We should take them for granted, as the only possible social surroundings. We should be as unconscious of them as we are, for the most part, of the hair growing on our heads or the air passing through our lungs. It is the variety of the human story that brings out sharply the last turn that the road has taken, and it is the view under the arch of the gateway which tells us that we are entering a town.

Yet this sense of the past is curiously patchy among the most intelligent and instructed people, especially in modern England. Among a hundred such scraps and snippets, I saw this morning a literary competition in an exceedingly high-brow weekly, a prize being awarded for a conversation between a modern interviewer and St. George. And I was struck by the fact that clever, and even brilliant, contributors missed much of the point, even about the modern interviewer, by missing the point about the ancient saint. I am not setting up as an authority on either. I am not pretending to be learned; nor is there here any question of learning. It is a question of quite superficial information, but of information that is fairly well spread over the whole surface. I have not been right slap bang through *The Decline and Fall of the Roman Empire* lately, any more than had Mr. Silas Wegg; I have not read every word of the *Acta Sanctorum* within the last week or so; I have not even read very closely the relatively modern romance of *The Seven Champions of Christendom* I have nothing but general information; but it is fairly general. What surprises me in people younger, brighter, and more progressively educated than myself, is that their general information is very patchy.   -

Now, it is unfair to say that they know nothing about St. George, because it may fairly be answered that there is nothing to be known about St. George. In one sense, nobody knows who St. George was; we only know who he was not. The only clear and solid fact about him is that he certainly was *not* what Gibbon said he was; the contractor of Cappadocia.[1] He was merely recorded as a common soldier of the legions martyred with multitudes under Diocletian;[2] nor is there any particular reason to doubt that he was. All the rest is legend, though legend is often very valuable to history. And I mean by general information the sense of the life in legends; how they grow; where they come from; why they remain. I know what saints were supposed to be; what patron saints were supposed to do; how they often did it for the most diverse groups, ages after their death; how other saints besides George dealt with dragons; how other nations besides England invoked St. George; how the saints were before the knights; how the knights were before the nations; and so on. In short, I have picked up quite crudely what Mr. Wells calls an Outline of History; but a more scientifically educated generation still seems to have only snippets of history; the lie out of Gibbon; the legend about the dragon; the phrase 'St. George for Merry England', and such isolated items. The result is a curious sort of narrowness, even about the problem of the present or the immediate past. For instance, one quite intelligent contributor apparently identified St. George, as somebody supposed to have lived in 'Merry England', and explained that his period (whatever it was supposed to be) was not really merry, because there was a great deal of mud in the streets, or people lived in mud hovels. Apart from everything

1 Ancient district of east Asia minor, now in central Turkey, which became a bulwark of the Byzantine empire.
2 Alludes to Gaius Diocletianus (245-316 AD), Roman emperor who restored efficient rule after prolonged anarchy.

else, I call it narrow for a man to suppose that Mud is the opposite of Merryment. Did he never make any mud-pies? Was he not much merrier making them than contributing to intellectual weeklies?

But the essential point is this. Everybody thought the joke must be found in showing how unlike St George's time was to ours. I think it would be a much better joke to show how extremely like St. George's time was to ours. But the writers are hampered in this by being extremely vague about what was St. George's time. Now, a man in the later Roman Empire, like George the Martyr, would have seen all round him an ancient world that was astonishingly like the modern world. Whether or no Merry England was a suitable phrase for medievalism, whether or no medievalism was all mud, it is quite certain that the Empire of Diocletian was not all mud. Imperial Rome was not all mud, but all marble, all mortar and massive building, all piles and tanks and engineering, all sorts of elaborate equipment of luxury or hygiene. And among all those palatial baths and towering aqueducts, George would probably be thinking pretty much what many an intelligent man is thinking now – that man does not live by soap alone; and that hygiene, or even health, is not much good unless you can take a healthy view of it – or, better still, feel a healthy indifference to it.

Suppose, for instance, that the soldier George had read some of the satires on fashionable society that were produced in that old Pagan world. He would find fact after fact and fashion after fashion exactly parallel to our own. He would find Juvenal making fun of fashionable ladies who join in masculine sports or adventures in a spirit of self-advertisement. The Roman satirist describes how grand Roman ladies would appear as gladiators in the arena, sacrificing not only modesty, but the manners of their rank, in order to be in the limelight. That exact fashionable blend of Feminism and Publicity did really exist in the real epoch of the real St. George; almost exactly as it exists today. Or suppose the

Roman soldier read the religious and philosophical literature circulating through the Roman Empire. He would find all that we call New Religions now, already called New Religions then. He would find idealists who were vegetarians, like Apolionius of Tyana;[1] theosophists who had learned all about Reincarnation from Brahmins and Hindu seers; prophets of the Simple Life in the drawing rooms of duchesses, talking about the secrets of health, wealth, and wisdom; promises of a new Universal Religion, which should include all beliefs without any particular belief in any of them. If the real original St. George did find himself interviewed by a modern newspaperman, he would think that hardly anything in the newspaper was new. He would not think primarily that he had come into a strange world, far away from dragons and princesses and medieval armour. He would think he had got back into the old bewildered and decaying world of the last phase of Paganism, loud with denials of religion and louder with the howlings of superstition. He would find everything in Juvenal[2] – except Juvenal. He would find quite as many absurd lady gladiators – only not so many people calling them absurd. He would be quite at home, thinking himself back in the old Diocletian Empire – and he would prepare for death.

---

1 He was from Tyana in Cappadocia, Asia Minor. His life and teachings were believed to have been appropriated to construct Christianity, and the name of Jesus was then being used in place of Apollonius to hide the truth, according to this outlandish belief.
2 Decimus Junius Juvenalis (55-130 A.D.), Roman poet.

The Wrong Incendiary

I STOOD looking at the Coronation Procession – I mean the one in Beaconsfield, not the rather elephantine imitation of it which, I believe, had some success in London – and I was seriously impressed. Most of my life is passed in discovering with a deadly surprise that I was quite right. Never before have I realized how right I was in maintaining that the small area expressed the real patriotism; the smaller the field the taller the tower. There were things in our local procession that did not (one might even reverently say, could not) occur in the London procession. One of the most prominent citizens in our procession (for instance) had his face blacked. Another rode on a pony which wore pink and blue trousers, I was not present at the Metropolitan affair, and therefore my assertion is subject to such correction as the eye-witness may always offer to the absentee. But, I believe with some firmness that no such features occurred in the London pageant.

But it is not of the local celebration that I would speak, but of something that occurred before it. In the field beyond the end of my garden the materials for a bonfire had been heaped; a hill of every kind of rubbish and refuse and things that nobody wants; broken chairs, dead trees, rags, shavings, newspapers, new religions, in pamphlet form, reports of the Eugenic Congress, and so on. All this refuse, material and mental, it was our purpose to purify and change to holy flame on the day when the King was crowned. The following is an account of the rather strange thing that really happened. I do not know whether it was any sort of symbol; but I narrate it just as it befell.

In the middle of the night I woke up slowly and listened to what I supposed to be the heavy crunching of a cart-wheel along a road of loose stones. Then it grew louder, and I thought somebody was shooting out cartloads of stones; then it seemed as if the shock was breaking big stones into pieces. Then I realized that under this sound there was also a strange, sleepy, almost inaudible roar; and that on top of it every now and then came pigmy pops like a battle of penny pistols. Then I knew what it was. I went to the window; and a great firelight flung across two meadows smote me where I stood. 'Oh, my holy aunt,' I thought, 'they've mistaken the Coronation Day.'

And yet when I eyed the transfigured scene it did not seem exactly like a bonfire or any ritual illumination. It was too chaotic, and too close to the houses of the town. All one side of a cottage was painted pink with the giant brush of flame; the next side, by contrast, was painted as black as tar. Along the front of this ran a blackening rim or rampart edged with a restless red ribbon that danced and doubled and devoured like a scarlet snake and beyond it was nothing but a deathly fullness of light.

I put on some clothes and went down the road; all the dull or startling noises in that din of burning growing louder and louder as I walked. The heaviest sound was that of an incessant cracking and crunching, as if some giant with teeth of stone was breaking up the bones of the world. I had not yet come within sight of the real heart and habitat of the fire; but the strong red light, like an unnatural midnights sunset, powdered the greyest grass with gold and flushed the few tall trees up to the last fingers of their foliage. Behind them the night was black and cavernous; and one could only trace faintly the ashen horizon beyond the dark and magic Wilton woods. As I went, a workman on a bicycle shot a rood past me; then staggered from his machine and shouted to me to tell him where the fire was. I answered that I was going to see, but thought it was the cottages by the wood-yard. He said, 'My God!' and vanished.

A little farther on I found grass and pavement soaking and flooded, and the red and yellow flames repainted in pools and puddles. Beyond were dim huddles of people and a small distant voice shouting out orders. The fire engines were at work. I went on among the red reflections, which seemed like subterranean fires; I had a singular sensation of being in a very important dream. Oddly enough, this was increased when I found that most of my friends and neighbours were entangled in the crowd. Only in dreams do we see familiar faces so vividly against a black background of midnight. I was glad to find (for the workman cyclist's sake) that the fire was not in the houses by the wood-yard, but in the wood-yard itself. There was no fear for human life, and the thing was seemingly accidental, though there were the usual ugly whispers about rivalry and revenge. But for all that I could not shake off my dream-drugged soul a swollen, tragic, portentous sort of sensation, that it all had something to do with the crowning of the English King, and the glory or the end of England. It was not till I saw the puddles and the ashes in broad daylight next morning that I was fundamentally certain that my midnight adventure had not happened outside this world.

But I was more arrogant than the ancient Emperors Pharaoh or Nebuchadnezzar, for I attempted to interpret my own dream. The fire was feeding upon solid stacks of unused beech or pine, grey and white piles of virgin wood. It was an orgy of mere waste; thousands of good things were being killed before they had ever existed. Doors, tables, walking sticks, wheelbarrows, and wooden swords for boys, Dutch dolls for girls – I could hear the cry of each uncreated thing as it expired in the flames. And then I thought of that other noble tower of needless things that stood in the field beyond my garden; the bonfire, the mountain of vanities, that is meant for burning; and how it stood dark and lonely in the meadow, and the birds hopped on its corners and the dew touched and spangled its twigs. And I remembered that there are two kinds of fires, the Bad Fire and the Good Fire – the last must surely be the meaning of Bonfire. And the paradox is that the Good Fire is made of bad things, of things that we do not want; but the Bad Fire is made of good things, of things that we do want; like all that wealth of wood that might have made dolls and chairs and tables, but was only making a hueless ash.

And then I saw, in my vision, that just as there are two fires, so there are two revolutions. And I saw that the whole mad modern world is a race between them. Which will happen first – the revolution in which bad things shall perish, or that other revolution in which good things shall perish also? One is the riot that all good men, even the most conservative, really dream of, when the sneer shall be struck from the face of the well-fed: when the wine of honour shall be poured down the throat of despair; when we shall, so far as to the sons of flesh is possible, take tyranny and usury and public treason and bind them into bundles and burn them. And the other is the disruption that may come prematurely, negatively, and suddenly in the night; like the fire in my little town.

It may come because the mere strain of modern life is unbearable; and in it even the things that men do desire may break down; marriage and fair ownership and worship and the mysterious worth of man. The two revolutions, white and black, are racing each other like two railway trains; I cannot guess the issue – but even as I thought of it, the tallest turret of the timber stooped and faltered and came down in a cataract of noises. And the fire, finding passage, went up with a spout like a fountain. It stood far up among the stars for an instant, a blazing pillar of brass fit for a pagan conqueror, so high that one could fancy it visible away among the goblin trees of Burnham or along the terraces of the Chiltern Hills.

On Travel's Surprises

TRAVELLERS' TALES are supposed to be tall tales; but I have always found them fall short. I have nearly always felt that the real monument or landscape, when I saw it for myself, was something stranger and more striking than the indirect impression of reading. The old tale against traveller's tales was that they magnified everything; that every lizard became a dragon and every savage tribe a race of giants. But my experience is that travellers in a strange land, especially if they have travelled in it long, tend too much to forget its strangeness. They become concerned with a dust of details, and tend to take the green lizards as casually as the green leaves. The danger is rather, I think, that a man can live in a tribe of gigantic savages, and grow to remark and record all sorts of details about their tribal taxes or their coinage of tusks or hides, and, at the end of his detailed narrative, forget even to mention that they were giants. For there *are* things too big and obvious to be remembered.

There have, indeed, been many cases in which travellers have been accused of telling lies, which have often afterwards turned out to be truths. Modern research, which has justified so many medieval reputations, has made some reparation even to medieval travellers. It was Marco Polo, I think, who reported that he had met in Africa men who had the heads of dogs. And most modern critics treated it as a manifest fairy-tale, as if he claimed to have seen birds with the heads of elephants. But it is very likely indeed that the traveller saw baboons, or some of the larger apes; and his description is really more scientific and exact than the common popular impression about men and monkeys. For the higher apes have not that sort of hollow, half-human visage which we see in the little monkeys: they often have an aggressive and solid projection of nose and jaw, like the nozzle or muzzle of a dog. But even here the principle of comparison is true. It is one thing to read in a book about dog-headed men and believe it or not as we choose: it must have been quite another to see the first of the huge hairy anthropoids – monstrous, mysterious erect; a premature provocation to the myth of the Missing Link. And I repeat that foreign sights have mostly affected me as the first ape must have affected the first explorer; not necessarily as something beautiful of charming, but certainly as something very surprising and entirely unexpected. When I first saw St. Mark's, Venice, I am by no means sure that I liked it; but I am quite sure that I was surprised by it; that it was not only quite different from anything I had ever seen, but quite different from anything I had ever expected. I thought it looked liked Aladdin's Palace in a pantomime. And the impression was not altogether false; for a man standing in that great merchant city of the Western Mediterranean is, by a paradox, standing deep in the golden gate of the East. There was always something a little too Oriental about the Venetian republic; and this, it has been suggested, was why it did, in a sense, fall like Carthage rather than survive like Rome. But, however that may be, the Christian who first looks at the Christian Church of St. Mark's is as startled as if it were a Chinese pagoda. Yet I had often seen pictures of it; photographs, and even coloured photographs; but these never conveyed how extraordinary the thing really is. For the extraordinary thing is that anything so fantastic should be solid.

The queer thing is that what one would expect to be the first thing mentioned is generally the last thing mentioned. I had heard a thousand things about Jerusalem ever since my babyhood, and seen views of it, and plans of it, and read controversies about it. But, somehow or other, I had never got hold of the first fact that it is a mountain city. A city that is set upon a hill cannot be hid; but somehow it seems as if the hill could be hid. All the photographs and descriptions I had seen were like glimpses of an Eastern bazaar; and suggested all the accompaniments of heat and stagnation and flat desert sands.

Whereas the real city, relatively speaking, is much more like a castle on the crags of the Rhine, or set high among the rocks of Spain. From Spain itself it would be easy to take similar examples. I knew that the Escorial was a palace; I did not knew that it looks much more like a prison; but especially I did not knew the strange journey into the mountains by which it is reached, with the consequent sense of separation and unearthly loneliness in that huge habitation of a moody King. In short, I have sometimes positively disliked the famous spectacles of travel. But the thing I disliked was always utterly different from the thing that I was expected to like; so utterly different that I generally came at last to like it.

I had another experience of the same sort recently; I suddenly saw Canada. I had visited it before; but I had never seen it before. On the former occasion I crossed the frontier from the United States; and there is nothing particularly interesting about the frontier. . . . On the second occasion I went up the St. Lawrence to Montreal. This also was a thing I had heard of often enough; but nothing I had ever heard of gave me any rumour of the reality. As is usual in such cases, the point of the experience is almost always missed. The point of the experience is that the traveller is carried far northward, almost as if he was going to the North Pole, or at least to find the North-West Passage. He sees icebergs and the Northern Lights and the whales of the northern waters; a hundred signs recall to him the Arctic adventures of which he read as a boy. Then the slip takes a sharp turn, which seems like one of the sharpest turns in navigation, and enters a new, an enormous, and yet a secret world. He feels, as the first explorers must have felt, that it is really a world set apart; that he had never guessed the earth contained anything so vast yet so concealed. And the impression is now increased when there begin to appear upon the narrowing coasts of that inland sea villages and the spires of churches that are not altogether like anything he has left behind. It is as if there were another Mediterranean, with another civilization in all its ports and shrines. So a man sails up the great St. Lawrence, wondering more and more, until the broad river seems to split about the great rock of Quebec.

I fancied that there might be here the beginning and the end of a quarrel I remember in my youth. Mr. Rudyard Kipling wrote a poem in praise of Canada, which very much annoyed the Canadians. Many of them stated with great sternness that, if he praised them any more, they would give him a good hard knock. The ground of the offence was that he had referred to the Dominion of Canada as 'Our Lady of the Snows'. This was held to imply that Canada has no local industry except snowballing; that her principal exports are icebergs; and that the typical Canadian citizen is a sort of furry and inarticulate Eskimo. One Canadian poet haughtily replied that Canada contained glowing maple woods in which England might be lost. One Canadian painter painted an ironical allegory, representing the spirit of the Dominion sitting on a pile of gorgeous fruits and varied products of the sun, and entitled the picture, 'Our Lady of the Snows'. I am no Imperialist in particular, but the days of my skirmishes with Mr. Kipling about Imperialism are long past, and I am affected by the thought of leaving Mr. Kipling and Canada in an embrace of reconciliation. I would therefore suggest that the impression of Arctic magnificence may be partly due to the fact that, though Canada is not made of snow, in a sense her gates are of ice. And though her woods are really as beautiful as any Canadian painter or poet can depict them, the true traveller really does have an impression of having travelled beyond the North Pole to find them.

On Experience

IT WILL be remarked that Experience which was once claimed by the aged is now claimed exclusively by the young. There used to be a system of morals and metaphysics that was specially known as the Experience Philosophy, but those who advanced it were grim rationalists and utilitarians who were already old in years, or more commonly old before their time. We all now know that Experience now stands rather for the philosophy of those who claim to be young long after their time. But they preach something that may in a sense be called an Experience Philosophy; though some of the experiences seem to me the reverse of philosophical. So far as I can make it out, it consists of two dogmas; first, that there is no such thing as right or wrong; and secondly, that they themselves have a right to experience. How they manage to have any rights if there is no such thing as right, I do not know; nor do they. But perhaps the philosophy was best summed up in a phrase I saw recently in a very interesting and important American magazine; quoted from one of the more wild and fanciful of the American critics. I have not the text before me, but the substance of the remark was this. The critic demanded indignantly to know how many ordinary American novelists had any Experiences outside those of earning their bread, pottering about in a farm or a farm house, helping to mind the baby, etc. The question struck me as striking at the very root of all the rot and corruption and imbecility of the times.

On the face of it, of course, the whole question is rather a joke; only that these gay pleasure seekers and revellers in the joy of life have seldom been known to see a joke. We might politely inquire exactly how much Experience is needed to equip a novelist to write novels. How many marks does he get for being vamped or for being intoxicated; and which are the particular discreditable acts by which he can get credit? How many liaisons give him this singular rank as a literary liaison officer; and how many double lives does it take to constitute Life? Is it only after a fourth divorce that he may write his first novel? For my part, I do not see why the same principle should not be applied to all the other Ten Commandments as well as to that particular Commandment. It should surely be obvious that if love affairs are necessary to the writing of this particular sort of love story, then it follows that a life of crime is necessary to the writing of any kind of crime story. I have myself made arrangements (on paper) for no less than fifty-two murders in my time; they took the form of short stories and I shall expose myself to the withering contempt of the young sages of Experience when I confess that I am not really a murderer, and have never yet committed an actual murder. And what about all the other forms of criminal Experience? Must a writer be a forger; and manufacture other men's names, before he is allowed to make his own? Must there be a journalistic apprenticeship in picking pockets, as well as in picking brains; and have we to look to the establishment of an Academy of Anarchy, with the power of conferring degrees? Novelists might proudly print after their names the letters indicating the degrees they had taken; such as F Y.B., meaning 'Five Years for Burglary', or T.N.H., for 'Twice Nearly Hanged'. Altogether, it may be said that writers do not rob, but it may be fortunate that robbers do not write; it is possible that the wild and wicked criminal might after all make almost as dull a novelist as the novelist.

It would also be easy enough to attract the fallacy upon the facts. Everybody who has any real experience knows that good writing should not necessarily come from people with many experiences. Some of the art which is closest to life has been produced under marked limitations of living. Its prestige has generally lasted longer than the splash made by sensational social figures. Jane Austen has already survived Georges Sand. Even the most modern critic, if he is really a critic, will admit that Jane Austen is really realistic in a sense in which Georges Sand is only romantic. She was indeed a flaming, fashionable figure created entirely by the Romantic Movement; but Jane Austen did not belong to any movement; she does not move; but she stays. And though I do not agree with the too common depreciation of Byron, it is true that all his somewhat excessive experience, in the new or juvenile sense, has not prevented people feeling him to be the very reverse of realistic; and in some ways strangely unreal.

But there is, of course, a much deeper objection to the whole of this new sort of Experience Philosophy; which is quite sufficiently exposed in the very examples I quoted from the magazine. There are certainly all sorts of experiences; some great and some small. But the small ones are those which the critic imagines to be great; and the great ones are those that he contemptuously dismisses as small. There are no more universal affairs than those which he imagines to be little and local. There are no events more tremendous than those which he regards as trivial. There are no experiences more exciting than those which he duly imagines to be dull. To take his own example, a literary man who cannot see that a baby is marvellous could not see that anything was marvellous. He has certainly no earthly logical reason for regarding a movie vamp as marvellous. The movie vamp is only what happens to the baby when it goes wrong; but, from a really imaginative and intellectual standpoint, there is nothing marvellous about either of them except what is already marvellous in the mere existence of the baby. But this sort of moralist or immoralist has a queer, half-baked prejudice; to the effect that there is no good in anything until it has gone bad. It is supposed to be a part of Experience for the woman to be a vamp; but not for the woman to be a mother. Although it states us all in the face, as a stark fact of common sense; that child-bearing really is an experience, and a highly realistic experience; while the other sort of experiment may not really be an experience at all. It may be in the exact sense mere play acting; and, as the game is now played, the main preoccupation is to prevent its ending with an addition to the cast of characters.

Whatever happens, it must not be the means of bringing on the scene a new, breathing, thinking, conscious creature like a baby. That would not be life.

Now, if there is one thing of which I have been certain since my boyhood, and grow more certain as I advance in age, it is that nothing is poetical if plain daylight is not poetical; and no monster should amaze us if the normal man does not amaze. All this talk of waiting for experiences in order to write, is simply a confession of incapacity to experience anything. It is a confession of never having felt the big facts; in such experiences as babyhood and the baby. A paralytic of this deaf and dumb description imagines he can be healed in strange waters or after strange wanderings; and announces himself ready to drink poisons that they may stimulate him like drugs. But it is futile for him to suppose that this sort of quackery will teach him how to be a writer; for he has been from the first admittedly blind to everything that is worth writing about. He will find nothing in the wilderness but the broken shards or ruins of what should have been sacred in his own home; and if he can really make nothing of the second he will certainly make nothing of the first. The whole theory rests on a ridiculous confusion, by which it is supposed that certain primary principles or relations will become interesting when they are damaged, but are bound to be depressing when they are intact.

None of those who are perpetually suggesting this view ever state it thus plainly; for they are incapable of making plain statements, just as they are incapable of feeling plain things. But the point they have to prove, if they really want their Experience Philosophy accepted by those who do not care for catch words, is that the high perils, pleasures, and creative joys of life do not occur on the high road of life; but only in certain crooked and rambling by-paths made entirely by people who have lost their way. As yet they have not even begun to prove it; and in any case, and in every sense, it could be disproved by a baby.

The Gardener and the Guinea

STRICTLY SPEAKING, there is no such thing as an English Peasant. Indeed, the type can only exist in community, so much does it depend on co-operation and common laws. One must not think primarily of a French Peasant, any more than of a German Measle. The plural of the word is its proper form; you cannot have a Peasant till you have a peasantry. The essence of the Peasant ideal is equality; and you cannot be equal all by yourself.

Nevertheless, because human nature always craves and half creates the things necessary to its happiness, there are approximations and suggestions of the possibility of such a race even here. The nearest approach I know to the temper of a Peasant in England is that of the country gardener; not, of course, the great scientific gardener attached to the great houses; he is a rich man's servant like any other. I mean the small jobbing-gardener who works for two or three moderate-sized gardens: who works on his own; who sometimes even owns his house; and who frequently owns his tools. This kind of man has really some of the characteristics of the true Peasant – especially the characteristics that people don't like. He has none of that irresponsible mirth which is the consolation of most poor men in England. The gardener is even disliked sometimes by the owners of the shrubs and flowers; because (like Micaiah) he prophesises not good concerning them, but evil. The English gardener is grim, critical, self-respecting; sometimes even economical. Nor is this (as the reader's lightening wit will flash back at me) merely because the English gardener is always a Scotch gardener. The type does exist in pure South England blood and speech; I have spoken to the type. I was speaking to the type only the other evening, when a rather odd little incident occurred.

It was one of those wonderful evenings in which the sky was warm and radiant while the earth was still comparatively cold and wet. But it is of the essence of Spring to be unexpected; as in that heroic and hackneyed line about coming 'before the swallow dares'. Spring never is Spring unless it comes too soon. And on a day like that one might pray without any profanity, that Spring might come on earth, as it was in heaven. The gardener was gardening. I was not gardening. It is needless to explain the causes of this difference; it would be to tell the tremendous history of two souls. It is needless because there is a more immediate explanation of the case; the gardener and I, if not equal in agreement, were at least equal in difference. It is quite certain that he would not have allowed me to touch the garden if I had gone down on my knees to him. And it is by no means certain that I should have consented to touch the garden if he had gone down on his knees to me. His activity and my idleness, therefore, went on steadily side-by-side through the long sunset hours.

And all the time I was thinking what a shame it was that he was not sticking his spade into his own garden, instead of mine; he knew about the earth and the underworld of seeds, the resurrection of Spring and the flowers that appear in order like a procession marshalled by a herald. He possessed the garden intellectually and spiritually, while I only possessed it politically. I know more about flowers than coal-owners knew about coal; for at least I pay them honour when they are brought above the surface of the earth. I knew more about gardens than railway shareholders seem to know about railways; for at least I know that it needs a man to make a garden; a man whose name is Adam. But as I walked on that grass my ignorance overwhelmed me – and yet that phrase is false, because it suggests something like a storm from the sky above. It is truer to say that my ignorance exploded underneath me, like a mine dug long before; and indeed it was dug before the beginning of the ages. Green bombs of bulbs and seeds were bursting underneath me everywhere; and, so far as my knowledge went, they had been laid by a conspirator. I trod quite uneasily on this uprush of the earth; the Spring is always only a fruitful earthquake. With the land all-alive under me I began to wonder more and more why this man, who had made the garden, did not own the garden. If I stuck a spade into the ground, I should be astonished at what I found there . . . and just as I thought this I saw that the gardener was astonished too.

Just as I was wondering why the man who used the spade did not profit by the spade, he brought me something he had found actually in my soul. It was a thin worm gold piece of the Georges, of the sort which are called, I believe. Spade Guineas. Anyhow, a piece of gold.

If you do not see the parable as I saw it just then, I doubt if I can explain it just now. He could make a hundred other round yellow fruits; and this flat yellow one is the only sort that I can make. How it came there I have not a notion – unless Edmund Burke dropped it in his hurry to get back to Butler's Court. But there it was; this is a cold recital of facts. There may be a whole pirate's treasure lying under the earth there, for all I know or care; for there is no interest in a treasure without a Treasure Island to sail to. If there is a treasure it will never be found, for I am not interested in wealth beyond the dreams of avarice – since I know that avarice has no dreams, but only insomnia. And, for the other party, my gardener would never consent to dig up the garden.

Nevertheless, I was overwhelmed with intellectual emotions when I saw that answer to my question; the question of why the garden did not belong to the gardener. No better epigram could be put in reply than simply putting the Spade Guinea beside the Spade. This was the only underground seed that I could understand. Only by having a little more of that dull, battered yellow substance could I manage to be idle while he was active. I am not altogether idle myself; but the fact remains that the power is in the thin slip of metal we call the Spade Guinea, not in the strong square and curve of metal which we call the Spade. And then I suddenly remembered that as had found gold on my ground by accident, so richer men in the north and west countries had found coal in their ground, also by accident.

I told the gardener that he had found the thing he ought to keep it, but that if he cared to sell it to me it could be valued properly, and then sold. He said, at first with characteristic independence, that he would like to keep it. He said it would make a brooch for his wife. But a little later he brought it back to me without explanation. I could not get a ray of light on the reason of his refusal; but he looked lowering and unhappy. Had he some mystical instinct that it is just such accidental and irrational wealth that it is the doom of all peasantries? Perhaps he dimly felt that the boy's pirate tales are true; and that buried treasure is a thing for robbers and not for producers. Perhaps he thought there was a curse on such capital; on the coal of the coal-owners, on the gold of the gold-seekers. Perhaps there is.

The Bluff of the Big Shops

TWICE IN my life has an editor told me in so many words that he dared not print what I had written, because it would offend the advertisers in his 'paper. The presence of such pressure exists everywhere in a more silent and subtle form. But I have a great respect for the honesty of this particular editor; for it was evidently as near to complete honesty as the editor of an important weekly magazine can possibly go. He told the truth about the falsehood he had to tell.

On both these occasions he denied me liberty of expression because I said that the widely advertised stores and large shops were really worse than little shops. That, it may be interesting to note, is one of the things that a man is now forbidden to say; perhaps the only thing he is really forbidden to say. If it had been an attack on Government, it would have been tolerated. If it had been an attack on God, it would have been respectfully and tactfully applauded. If I had been abusing marriage or patriotism or public decency I should have been heralded in headlines and allowed to sprawl across Sunday newspapers. But the big newspaper is not likely to attack the big shop; being itself a big shop in its own way and more and more a monument of monopoly. But it will be well if I repeat here in a book what I found it impossible to repeat in an article. I think the big shop is a bad shop. I think it had not only in a moral but a mercantile sense; that is, I think shopping there is not only a bad action but a bad bargain. I think the monster emporium is not only vulgar and insolent, but incompetent and uncomfortable; and I deny that its large organization is efficient. Large organization is loose organization. Nay, it would be almost as true to say that organization is always disorganization. The only thing perfectly organic is an organism; like that grotesque and obscure organism called a man. He alone can be quite certain of doing what he wants;

beyond him, every extra man may be an extra mistake. As applied to things like shops, the whole thing is an utter fallacy. Some things like armies have to be organized; and therefore do their very best to be well organized. You must have a long rigid line stretched out to guard a frontier; and therefore you stretch it right. But it is not true that you must have a long rigid line of people trimming hats or tying bouquets, in order that they may be trimmed or tied neatly. The work is much more likely to be neat if it is done by a particular craftsman for a particular customer with particular ribbons and flowers. The person told to trim the hat will never do it quite suitably to the person who wants it trimmed; and the hundredth person told to do it will do if badly, as he does. If we collected all the stories from all the housewives and householders about the big shops sending the wrong goods, smashing the right goods, forgetting to send any sort of goods, we should behold a welter of inefficiency. There are far more blunders in a big shop than ever happen in a small shop, where the individual customer can curse the individual shopkeeper. Confronted with modern trading efficiency the customer is silent; well aware of that organization's talent for sacking the wrong man. In short, organization is a necessary evil which in this case is not necessary.

I have begun these notes with a note on the big shops because they are things near to us and familiar to us all. I need not dwell on other and still more entertaining claims made for the colossal combination of departments. One of the funniest is the statement that it is convenient to get everything in the same shop. That is to say, it is convenient to walk the length of the street, so long as you walk indoors, or more frequently underground, instead of walking the same distance in the open air from one little shop to another. The truth is that the monopolists' shops are really very convenient – to the monopolist. They have all the advantage of concentrating business as they concentrate wealth, in fewer and fewer of the citizens. Their wealth sometimes permits them to pay tolerable wages; their wealth also permits them to buy up better businesses and advertise worse goods. But that their own goods are better nobody has ever even begun to show: and most of us know any number of concrete cases where they are definitely worse. Now I expressed this opinion of my own (so shocking to the magazine editor and his advertisers) not only because it is an example of my general thesis that small properties should be revived, but because it is essential to the realization of another and much more curious truth. It concerns the psychology of all these things; of mere size, of mere wealth, of mere advertisement and arrogance. And it gives us the first working model of the way in which things are done today and the way in which (please God) they may be undone tomorrow.

There is one obvious and enormous and entirely neglected general fact to be noted before we consider the laws chiefly needed to renew the State. And that is the fact that one considerable revolution could be made without any laws at all. It does not concern any existing law, but rather an existing superstition. And the curious thing is that its upholders boast that it is a superstition. The other day I saw and very thoroughly enjoyed a popular play called *It Pays to Advertise;* which is all about a young businessman who tries to break up the soap monopoly of his father, a more old-fashioned businessman, by the wildest application of American theories of the psychology of advertising. One thing that struck me as rather interesting about it was this. It was quite good comedy to give the old man and the young man our sympathy in turn. It was quite good farce to make the old man and the young man each alternately look a fool. But nobody seemed to feel what I felt to be the most outstanding and obvious points of folly. They scoffed at the old man because he was old;

because he was old-fashioned; because he himself was healthy enough to scoff at the monkey tricks of their mad advertisements. But nobody really criticized him for having made a corner, for which he might once have stood in a pillory. Nobody seemed to have enough instinct for independence and human dignity to be irritated at the idea that one purse-proud old man could prevent us all from having an ordinary human commodity if he chose. And as with the old man, so it was with the young man. He had been taught by his American friend that advertisement can hypnotize the human brain; that people are dragged by a deadly fascination into the doors of a shop as into the mouth of a snake; that the subconscious is captured and the will paralysed by repetition; that we are all made to move like mechanical dolls when a Yankee advertiser says, 'Do it Now'. But it never seemed to occur to anybody to resent this. Nobody seemed sufficiently alive to be annoyed. The young man was made game of because he was poor; because he was bankrupt; because he was driven to the shifts of bankruptcy; and so on. But he did not seem to know he was by his own boast a mesmerist and a mystagogue; a destroyer of reason and will; an enemy of truth and liberty.

I think such people exaggerate the extent to which it pays to advertise; even if there is only the devil to pay. But in one sense this psychological case for advertising is of great practical importance to any programme of reform. The American advertisers have got hold of the wrong end of the stick; but it is a stick that can be used to beat something else besides their own absurd big drum. It is a stick that can be used also to beat their own absurd business philosophy. They are always telling us that the success of modern commerce depends on creating an atmosphere, on manufacturing a mentality, on assuming a point of view. In short, they insist that their commerce is not merely commercial, or even economic or political, but purely psychological. I hope they will go on saying it; for then some day everybody may suddenly see that it is true.

For the success of big shops and such things really is psychology; not to say psycho-analysis; or, in other words nightmare. It is not real and, therefore, not reliable. This point concerns merely our immediate attitude, at the moment and on the spot, towards the whole plutocratic occupation of which such publicity is the gaudy banner. The very first thing to do, before we come to any of our proposals that are political and legal, is something that really is (to use their beloved word) entirely psychological. The very first thing to do is to tell these American poker-players that they do not know how to play poker. For they not only bluff but they boast that they are bluffing. In so far as it really is a question of an instant psychological method, there must be, and there is, an immediate psychological answer. In other words, because they are admittedly bluffing, we can call their bluff.

I said recently that any practical programme for restoring normal property consists of two parts, which current can't would call destructive and constructive; but which might more truly be called defensive and offensive. The first is stopping the mere mad stampede towards monopoly, before the last traditions of property and liberty are lost. It is with that preliminary problem of resisting the world's trend towards being more monopolist, that I am first of all dealing here. Now, when we ask what we can do, here and now, against the actual growth of monopoly, we are always given a very simple answer. We are told that we can do nothing. By a natural and inevitable operation the large things are swallowing the small, as large fish might swallow little fish. The trust can absorb what it likes, like a dragon devouring what it likes, because it is already the largest creature left alive in the land. Some people are so finally resolved to accept this result that they actually condescend to regret it. They are so convinced that it is fate that they will even admit that it is fatality. The fatalists almost become sentimentalists when looking at the little shop that is being bought up by the big company. They are ready to weep, so long as it is admitted that they weep because they weep in vain. They are willing to admit that the loss of a little toy-shop of their childhood, or a little tea-shop of their youth, is even in the true sense a tragedy. For a tragedy means always a man's struggle with that which is stronger than man. And it is the feet of the gods themselves that are here trampling on our traditions; it is death and doom themselves that have broken our little toys like sticks; for against the stars of destiny none shall prevail. It is amazing what a little bluff will do in this world.

For they go on saying that the big fish eats the little fish, without asking whether little fish swim up to big fish and ask to be eaten. They accept the devouring dragon without wondering whether a fashionable crowd of princesses ran after the dragon to be devoured. They have never heard of a fashion; and do not know the difference between fashion and fate. The necessitarians have here carefully chosen the one example of something that is certainly *not* necessary, whatever else is necessary. They have chosen the one thing that does happen still to be free, as a proof of the unbreakable chains in which all things are bound. Very little is left free in the modern world; but private buying and selling are still supposed to be free; and indeed still are free; if anyone has a will free enough to use his freedom. Children may be driven by force to a particular school. Men may be driven by force away from a public-house. All sorts of people, for all sorts of new and nonsensical reasons, may be driven by force to a prison. But nobody is yet driven by force to a particular shop. Of all things in the world, the rush to the big shops is the thing that could be most easily stopped – by the people who rush there.

We do not know what may come later; but they cannot be driven there by bayonets just yet.

If we chose to make a vow, if we chose to make a league, for dealing only with little local shops and never with large centralized shops, the campaign could be every bit as practical as the Land Campaign in Ireland. It would probably be nearly as successful. It will be said, of course, that people will go to the best shop. I deny it; for Irish boycotters did not take the best offer. I deny that the big shop is the best shop; and I especially deny that people go there because it is the best shop. And if I be asked why, I answer at the end with the unanswerable fact with which I began at the beginning. I know it is not merely a matter of business, for the simple reason that the businessmen themselves tell me it is merely a matter of bluff. It is *they* who say that nothing succeeds like a mere appearance of success. It is *they* who say that publicity influences us without our will or knowledge. It is they who say that 'It Pays to Advertise'; that is, to tell people in a bullying way that they must 'Do it Now', when they need not do it at all.

About Bad Comparisons

I HAVE never quite understood the phrase that comparisons are odious; but anybody can see that even the very best of comparisons is only comparatively complimentary. A literal interpretation could turn most compliments into insults. It would not do to treat the poet as a botanist when he says, 'My love is like the red, red rose'. There are roses which would suggest rather too apoplectic a complexion and be rough on the lady. There are ladies of whom we might say that it was rough on the rose. The line in the modern version of 'Annie Laurie', 'Her neck is like the swan', always suggested to me a very startling and somewhat alarming alteration in the human form; but I believe that this line was a fake put in by the false modesty of somebody who was shocked by the beautiful simplicity of the older version. But there is another sense of the world 'comparative' in which it is liable to another somewhat parallel abuse or error. It is that grammatical classification of a thing in the three degrees of positive, comparative, and superlative; as illustrated in the bright little boy who gave the extension of an adverb in the form of 'Ill – Worse – Dead'. It will be noted that this, though founded on highly practical experience, is not exact as an example of grammatical logic.

Now, there are a great many phrases used in practice as comparatives which are not nearly so truly comparative as the trial of the little boy. I mean that many people suppose one thing to be an extension of another thing or an excess of another thing when it is really a totally different thing; and sometimes almost a contrary thing. For instance, some people have an instinctive itch of irritation against the word 'authority'. Either they suppose that authority is a pompous name for mere bullying, or else, at the best, they think that mere bullying is an excess of authority. But bullying is almost the opposite authority. Tyranny is the opposite of authority. For authority simply means right; and nothing is authoritative except what somebody has a right to do, and therefore is right in doing. It often happens in this imperfect world that he has the right to do it and not the power to do it. But he cannot have a shred of authority if he merely has the power to do it and has not the right to do it. If you think any form of mastery unjust it is enough to say that you do not like injustice; but there is no need to say that you do not like authority. For injustice, as such, cannot have any authority at all. Moreover, a man can only have authority by admitting something better than himself; and the bully does not get his claim from anybody but himself. It is not a question, therefore, of there being authority, and then tyranny, which is too much authority; for tyranny is no authority. Tyranny means too little authority; for though of course, an individual may use wrongly the power that may go with it, he is in that act disloyal to the law of right, which should be his own authority. To abuse authority is to attack authority. A policeman is no longer a policeman when he is bribed privately to arrest an innocent man; he is a private criminal. He is not exaggerating authority; he is reducing it to nothing.

Another example of the false comparative, which is really not a comparative but a contrary, is the distinction between avarice and thrift. Here, again, it is of course possible for an individual to pass from one to the other; but it is only by violating the other, not by exaggerating it. The two things are really opposites; but things do sometimes produce their opposites. Love may turn to hate; a man may begin by wanting to marry a woman and end by wanting to murder her. But love is none the less the opposite of hate; and even our most advanced thinkers would hardly say that marriage is the same as murder. A man, profligate in youth, may so poison himself as to become Puritan in old age. But the reaction is none the less a reaction because it is a morbid and exaggerated reaction In the same way a thrifty man may turn into a miser, but in turning into a miser he is ceasing to be a thrifty man. He is most emphatically not becoming more of a thrifty man. A miser is a man who is intercepted and misled in his pursuit of thrift and betrayed into turning to the pursuit of money. Madness of that sort always haunts the life of man, as a possible temptation and perversion. Idolatry is always a danger to the soul, and idolatry is the worship of the instrument. A man who thinks he is justified in drawing the sword for justice may be tempted of the devil and come to worship not the justice but the sword. That is what happened to poor Nietzsche, leading him to write that sentence which is still the motto of Prussianism and Prussia: 'You say a good cause justifies any war; but I say a good war justified any cause' The peasant who follows the plough may fall into the same temptation as the soldier who follows the sword: but both will be turning against their original purpose, even against their own purpose in using their own tools. For the peasant who thinks more of the moneybags than he does of the flour-sacks becomes less of a peasant in becoming more a miser. And the real soldier does not follow the sword, but follows the flag.

Thrift by derivation means thriving; and the miser is the man who does not thrive. The whole meaning of thrift is making the most of everything; and the miser does not make anything of anything. He is the man in whom the process, from the seed to the crop, stops at the intermediate mechanical stage of the money. He does not grow things to feed men; not even to feed one man; not even to feed himself. The miser is the man who starves himself, and everybody else, in order to worship wealth in its dead form, as distinct from its living form. He is occasionally found among peasants, as the bully is occasionally found among soldiers. But in that very fact, the one is a bad peasant and the other a bad soldier. In the rather morbid modern culture of the industrial towns there has arisen a habit of denouncing both these two types as if they always yielded to these temptations. But the towns also have their temptations; and the town critics have generally yielded to all of them. They do not understand either the peasants' sense of liberty or the soldiers' sense of loyalty; and they always assume that there is

nothing but avarice in the economic independence of the one, and nothing but brutality in the militant obedience of the other. An actual experience, either of peasants or of soldiers, will teach anybody that the aberrations of avarice or arrogance are exceptional. The general effect of discipline on decent soldiers is to make them very pleasant companions and rather more modest and pliable than the majority of men. The actual effect of thrift on most peasants is to make them inventive and intelligent in their ordinary hospitality and human intercourse. There is no difference between them and other simple and sociable human beings, except that they understand the rather important thing which economists call 'economy of consumption'.

A French or Flemish peasant woman will make much more out of the scraps in the kitchen, or the very weeds in the garden, than a proletarian will make out of the tinned food and advertised wares of a commercial city. But normally she will be quite as pleased, not to say proud, to put the results of her cookery before other people as if she were presiding over a fatigued cocktail party in Mayfair. But the test of her pretensions, of her pride – one might almost say of her profession – is concerned entirely with the practical product. For the healthy-minded peasant, more than anybody, the proof of the pudding is in the eating. She may become an unhealthy-minded peasant and think of nothing but the money; for the diseases of the soul are in the very air. Therefore, it will probably happen that every village will contain a miser – that is, a madman. But his madness has nothing to do with the sanity of thrift. Thrift in itself is always a thirst to make all things thrive, animal, vegetable, or mineral; to make them proper and produce; to prevent their being wasted, or, in ether words, destroyed. Whether particular people need to be warned of particular dangers touching the avarice that perverts thrift is a matter of moral education and religion; but the first principle is that the miser is not a more thrifty man but a much less thrifty man, for he wastes money more than a spendthrift.

The Architect of Spears

THE OTHER day, in the town of Lincoln, I suffered an optical illusion which accidentally revealed to me the strange greatness of the Gothic architecture. Its secret is not, I think, satisfactorily explained in most of the discussions on the subject. It is said that the Gothic eclipses the Classical by a certain richness and complexity, at once lively and mysterious. This is true; but Oriental decoration is equally rich and complex, yet it awakens a widely different sentiment. No man ever got out of a Oriental carpet the emotions that he got from a cathedral tower. Over all the exquisite ornaments of Arabia and India there is the presence of something stiff and heartless, of something tortured and silent. Dwarfed trees and crooked serpents, heavy flowers and hunchbacked birds accentuate by the very splendour and contrast of their colour the servility and monotony of their shapes. It is like the vision of a sneering sage, who sees the whole universe as a pattern. Certainly no one ever felt like this about Gothic, even if he happens to dislike it. Or again, some will say that it is the liberty of the Middle Ages in the use of the comic or even the coarse that makes Gothic more interesting than the Greek. There is more truth in this; indeed, there is real truth in it. Few of the old Christian cathedrals would have passed the Censor of Plays. We talk of the inimitable grandeur of the old cathedrals; but indeed it is rather their gaiety that we do not dare to imitate. We should be rather surprised if a chorister suddenly began singing 'Bill Bailey' in church. Yet that would be only doing in music what the medievals did in sculpture. They put into a Miserere* seat the very scenes that we put into a music-hall song; comic domestic scenes similar to the spilling of the beer and the hanging out of the washing. But though the gaiety of Gothic is one of its features, it also is not the secret of

---

* The first word of the Psalm (13c), (Lat.) be merciful.

its unique effect. We see a domestic topsy-turvydom in many Japanese sketches. But delightful as these are, with their fairy tree-tops, paper houses, and toddling, infantile inhabitants, the pleasure they give is of a kind quite different from the joy and energy of the gargoyles. Some have even been so shallow and illiterate as to maintain that our pleasure in medieval building is a mere pleasure in what is barbaric, in what is rough, shapeless, or crumbling like the rocks. This can be dismissed after the same fashion; South Sea idols, with painted eyes and radiating bristles, are a delight to the eye; but they do not affect it in at all the same way as Westminster Abbey. Some again (going to another and almost equally foolish extreme) ignore the coarse and comic in medievalism, and praise the pointed arch only for its utter purity and simplicity, as of a saint with his hands joined in prayer. Here, again the uniqueness is missed. There are Renaissance things (such as the ethereal silvery drawings of Raphael), there are even pagan things (such as the Praying Boy), which express as fresh and austere a piety. None of these explanations explain. And I never saw what was the real point about Gothic till I came into the town of Lincoln, and saw it behind a row of furniture vans.

I did not know they were furniture vans; at the first glance and in the smoky distance I thought they were a row of cottages. A low stone-wall cut off the wheels, and the vans were somewhat of the same colour as the yellowish clay or stone of the buildings around them. I had come across that interminable Eastern plain which is like the open sea, and all the more so because the one small hill and tower of Lincoln stands up in it like a lighthouse. I had climbed the sharp, crooked streets up to this ecclesiastical citadel; just in front of me was a flourishing and richly coloured kitchen garden; beyond that was the low stone wall; beyond that the row of vans that looked like houses; and beyond and above that, straight and swift and dark, light as a flight of birds, and terrible as the Tower of Babel, Lincoln Cathedral seemed to rise out of human sight.

As I looked at it I asked myself the questions that I have asked here; what was the soul in all those stones? They were varied, but it was not variety; they were solemn, but it was not solemnity; they were farcical, but it was not farce. What is it in them that thrills and soothes a man of our blood and history, that is not there in an Egyptian pyramid or an Indian temple or a Chinese pagoda? All of a sudden the vans I had mistaken for cottages began to move away to the left. In the start this gave to my eye and mind I really fancied that the Cathedral was moving towards the right. The two huge towers seemed to start striding across the plain like the two legs of some giant whose body was covered with clouds. Then I saw what it was.

The truth about Gothic is, first, that it is alive, and second, that it is on the march. It is the Church Militant; it is the only fighting architecture. All its spires are spears at rest; and all its stones are stones asleep in a catapult. In that instant of illusion, I could hear the arches clash like swords as they crossed each other. The mighty and numberless columns seemed to go swinging by like the huge feet of imperial elephants, The graven foliage wreathed and blew like banners going into battle; the silence was deafening with all the mingled noises of a military march; the great bell shock down, as the organ shook up, its thunder. The thirsty-throated gargoyles shouted like trumpets from all the roofs and pinnacles as they passed; and from the lectern in the core of the cathedral the eagle of the awful evangelist clashed his wings of brass.

And amid all the noises I seemed to hear the voice of a man shouting in the midst like one ordering regiments hither and thither in the fight; the voice of the great half-military master-builder; the architect of spears. I could almost fancy he wore armour while he made that church; and I knew indeed that, under a scriptural figure, he had borne in either hand the trowel and the sword.

I could imagine for the moment that the whole of that house of life had marched out of the sacred East, alive and inter-locked, like an army. Some Eastern nomad had found it solid and silent in the red circle of the desert. He had slept by it as by a world forgotten pyramid; and been woke at midnight by the wings of stone and brass, the tramping of the tall pillars, the trumpets of the waterspouts. On such a night every snake or sea-beast must have turned and twisted in every crypt or corner of the architecture. And the fiercely coloured saints marching eternally in the flamboyant windows would have carried their glorioles like torches across dark lands and distant sea; till the whole mountain of music and darkness and lights descended roaring on the lonely Lincoln hill. So for some hundred and sixty seconds I saw the battle-beauty of the Gothic; then the last furniture-van shifted itself away; and I saw only a church tower in a quite English town round which the English birds were floating.

The Irishman

THE OTHER day I went to see the Irish plays, recently acted by real Irishmen-peasants and poor folk – under the inspiration of Lady Gregory and Mr. W. B. Yeats. Over and above the excellence of the acting and the abstract merit of the plays (both of which were considerable), there emerged the strange and ironic interest which has been the source of so much fun and sin and sorrow – the interest of the Irishman in England. Since we have sinned by creating the Stage Irishman, it is fitting enough that we should all be rebuked by Irishmen on the stage. We have all seen some obvious English-man performing a Paddy.* It was, perhaps, a just punishment to see an obvious Paddy performing the comic and contemptible part of an English gentleman. I have now seen both, and I can lay my hand on my heart (though my knowledge of physiology is shaky about its position) and declare that the Irish English gentleman was an even more object and crawling figure than the English Irish servant. The Comic Irishman in the English plays was at least given credit for a kind of chaotic courage. The Comic Englishman in the Irish plays was represented not only as a fool, but as a nervous fool; a fussy and spasmodic prig, who could not be loved either for strength or weakness. But all this only illustrates the fundamental fact that both the national views are wrong; both the versions are perversions. The rollicking Irishman and the priggish Englishman are alike the mere myths generated by a misunderstanding. It would be rather nearer the truth if we spoke of the rollicking Englishman and the priggish Irishman. But even that would be wrong too.

Unless people are near in soul they had better not be near in neighbourhood. The Bible tells us to love our neighbours, and also to love our enemies; probably because they are generally the

---

* Paddy, Hiberno-English nickname for 'Patrick' an Irishman, – often taken to be offensive.

same people. And there is a real human reason for this. You think of a remote man merely as a man; that is, you think of him in the right way. Suppose I say to you suddenly – 'Oblige me by brooding on the soul of the man who lives at 351 High Street, Islington'. Perhaps (now I come to think of it) *you are* the man who lives at 351 High Street, Islington. In that case substitute some other unknown address and pursue the intellectual sport. Now you will probably be broadly right about the man in Islington whom you have never seen or heard of, because you will begin at the right end – the human end. The man in Islington is at least a man. The soul of the man in Islington is certainly a soul. He also has been bewildered and broadened by youth; he also has been tortured and intoxicated by love; he also is sublimely doubtful about death. You can think about the soul of that nameless man who is a mere number in Islington High Street. But you do not think about the soul of your next-door neighbour. He is not a man; he is an environment. He is the barking of a dog; he is the noise of a pianola; he is a dispute about a party wall; he is drains that are worse than yours, or roses that are better than yours. Now, all these are the wrong ends of a man; and a man, like many other things in this world, such as a cat-o' nine-tails, has a large number of wrong ends, and only one right one. These adjuncts are all tails, so to speak. A dog is a sort of curly tail to a man; a substitute for that which man so tragically lost at an early stage of evolution. And though I would rather myself go about trailing a dog behind me than tugging a pianola or towing a rose garden, yet this is a matter of taste, and they are all alike appendages or things dependent upon man. But besides his twenty tails, every man really has a head, a centre of identity, a soul. And the head of a man is even harder to find than the head of a Skye terrier, for man has nine hundred and ninety-nine wrong ends instead of one. It is no question of getting hold of the sow by the right ear; it is a question of getting hold of the hedgehog by the right quill, of the bird by the right feather, of the forest by the right leaf. It we have never known the forest we shall know at least that it is a forest, a thing grown grandly out of the earth; we shall realize the roots toiling in the terrestrial darkness, the trunks reared in the sylvan twilight.

But to find the forest is to find the fringe of the forest. To approach it from without is to see its mere accidental outline ragged against the sky. It is to come close enough to be superficial. The remote man, therefore, may stand for manhood; for the glory of birth or the dignity of death. But it is difficult to get Mr. Brown next door (with whom you have quarrelled about the creepers) to stand for these things in any satisfactorily symbolic attitude. You do not feel the glory of his birth; you are more likely to hint heatedly at its ingloriousness. You do not, on purple and silver evenings, dwell on the dignity and quietude of his death; you think of it, if at all, rather as sudden. And the same is true of historical separation and proximity. I look forward to the same death as a Chinaman; barring one or two Chinese tortures, perhaps. I look back to the same babyhood as an ancient Phoenician; unless, indeed, it were one of that special confirmation class of Sunday-school babies who were passed through the fire to Moloch.* But these distant or antique terrors seem merely tied on to the life; they are not part of its texture. Babylonian mothers (however they yielded to etiquette) probably loved their children; and Chinamen unquestionably reverenced their dead. It is far different when two peoples are close enough to each other to mistake all the acts and gestures of everyday life. It is far different when the Baptist baker in Islington thinks of Irish infancy, passed amid Popish priests and impossible fairies. It is far different when the tramp from Tipperary thinks of Irish death, coming often in dying hamlets, in distant colonies, in English prisons or on English gibbets. There

---

* Ancient Middle Eastern deity to whom children were sacrificed. A shrine to Moloch outside the walls of Jerusalem was destroyed during the reign of Josiah, the reformer king of Judah (640-609 B.C.).

childhood and death have lost all their reconciling qualities; the very details of them do not unite, but divide. Hence England and Ireland see the facts of each other without guessing the meaning of the facts. For instance, we may see the fact that an Irish housewife is careless. But we fancy falsely that this is because she is scatter-brained; whereas it is, on the contrary, because she is concentrated – on religion, or conspiracy, or tea. You may call her inefficient, but you certainly must not call her weak. In the same way, the Irish see the fact that the Englishman is unsociable; they do not see the reason, which is that he is romantic.

This seems to me the real striking value of such national sketches as those by Lady Gregory and Mr. Synge, which I saw last week. Here is a case where mere accidental realism, the thing written on the spot the 'slice of life', may, for once in a way, do some good. All the signals, all the flags, all the declaratory externals of Ireland we are almost certain to mistake If the Irishman speaks to us, we are sure to misunderstand him. But if we hear the Irishman talking to himself, it may begin to dawn on us that he is a man.

The Toy Theatre

THERE IS only one reason why all grown-up people do not play with toys: and it is a fair reason. The reason is that playing with toys takes so very much more time and trouble than anything else. Playing as children mean playing is the most serious thing in the world. And as soon as we have small duties or small sorrows we have to abandon to some extent so enormous and ambitious a plan of life. We have enough strength for politics and commerce and art and philosophy; we have not enough strength for play. This is the truth which every one will recognize who, as a child, has ever played with anything at all; anyone who has played with bricks, anyone who has played with dolls, anyone who has flayed with tin soldiers. My journalistic work, which earns money, is not pursued with such awful persistency as that work which earned nothing.

Take the case of bricks. If you publish a book tomorrow in twelve volumes (it would be just like you) on 'The Theory and Practice of European Architecture', your work may be laborious, but it is fundamentally frivolous. It is not serious as the work of a child piling one brick on the other is serious; for the simple reason that if your book is a bad book no one will ever be able ultimately and entirely to prove to you that it is a bad book. Whereas if his balance of bricks is a bad balance of bricks, it will simply tumble down. And if I know anything of children, he will set to work solemnly and sadly to build it up again. Whereas, if I know anything of authors, nothing would induce you to write your book again, or even to think of it again if you could help it.

Take the case of dolls. It is much easier to care for an educational cause than to care for a doll. It is as easy to write an article on education as to write an article on toffee or tramcars or anything else. But it is almost as difficult to look after a doll as to look after a child. The little girls that I meet in the little streets of Battersea worship their dolls in a way that reminds one not so much of play as idolatry. In some cases the love and care of the artistic symbol has actually become more important than the human reality which it was, I suppose, originally meant to symbolize.

I remember a Battersea little girl who wheeled her large baby sister stuffed into a doll's perambulator. When questioned on this course of conduct, she replied: 'I haven't got a dolly, and Baby is pretending to be my dolly.' Nature was indeed imitating art. First a doll had been a substitute for a child; afterwards a child was a mere substitute for a doll. But that opens other matters; the point is here that such devotion take up most of the brain and most of the life; much as if it were really the thing which it is supposed to symbolize. The point is that the man writing on motherhood is merely an educationalist; the child playing with a doll is a mother.

Take the case of soldiers. A man writing an article on military strategy is simply a man writing an article; a horrid sight. But a boy making a campaign with tin soldiers is like a general making a campaign with live soldiers. He must to the limit of his juvenile powers think about the thing; whereas the war correspondent need not think at all. I remember a war correspondent who remarked after the capture of Methuen: 'This renewed activity on the part of Delarey is probably due to his being short of stores' The same military critic had mentioned a few paragraphs before that Delarey was being hard pressed by a column which was pursuing him under command of Methuen. Methuen chased Delarey; and Delarey's activity was due to his being short of stores. Otherwise he would have stood quite still while he was being chased. I run after Jones with a hatcher, and if he turns round and tries to get rid of me the only possible explanation is that he has a very small balance at his bankers. I cannot believe that any boy playing at soldiers would be as idiotic as this. But then anyone playing at anything has to be serious. Whereas, as I have only too good reason to know, if you are writing an article you can say anything that comes into your head.

Broadly then, what keeps adults from joining in children's games is, generally speaking, not that they have no pleasure in them; it is simply that they have no leisure for them. It is that they cannot afford the expenditure of toil and time and consideration for so grand and grave a scheme. I have been myself attempting for some time past to complete a play in a small toy theatre, the sort of toy theatre that used to be called Penny Plain and Twopence Coloured; only that I drew and coloured the figures and scenes myself. Hence I was free from the degrading obligation of having to pay either a penny or twopence; I only had to pay a shilling a sheet for good cardboard and a shilling a box for bad watercolours. The kind of miniature stage I mean is probably familiar to every one; it is never more than a development of the stage which Skelt made and Stevenson celebrated.

But though I have worked much harder at the toy theatre than I ever worked at any tale or article, I cannot finish it; the work seems too heavy for me, I have to break off and betake myself to lighter employments; such as the biographies of great men. The play of 'St. George and the Dragon', over which I have burnt the midnight oil (you must colour the thing by lamplight because that is how it will be seen), still lacks, most conspicuously, alas! two wings of the Sultan's Palace, and also some comprehensible and workable way of getting up the curtain.

All this gives me a feeling touching the real meaning of immortality. In this world we cannot have pure pleasure. This is partly because pure pleasure would be dangerous to us and to our neighbours. But it is partly because pure pleasure is a great deal too much trouble. If I am ever in any other and better world, I hope that I shall have enough time to play with nothing but toy theatres; and I hope that I shall have enough divine and superhuman energy to act at least one play in them without a hitch.

Meanwhile the philosophy of toy theatres is worth anyone's consideration. All the essential morals which modern men need to learn could be deduced from this toy. Artistically considered, it reminds us of the main principle of art, the principle which is in most danger of being forgotten in our time. I mean the fact that art consists of limitation; the fact that art is limitation. Art does not consist in expanding things, Art consists of cutting things down, as I cut down with a pair of scissors my very ugly figures of St. George and the Dragon. Plato, who liked definite ideas, would like my cardboard dragon; for though the creature has few other artistic merits he is at least dragonish. The modern philosopher, who likes infinity, is quite welcome to a sheet of the plain cardboard. The most artistic thing about the theatrical art is the fact that the spectator looks at the whole thing through a window. This is true even of theatres inferior to my own; even at the Court Theatre or His Majesty's you are looking through a window; an unusually large window. But the advantage of the small theatre exactly is that you are looking through a small window. Has not every one noticed how sweet and startling and landscape looks when seen through an arch? This strong, square shape, this shutting off of everything else is not only an assistance to beauty; it is the essential of beauty. The most beautiful part of every picture is the frame.

This especially is true of the toy theatre; that, by reducing the scale of events it can introduce much larger events. Because it is small it could easily represent the earthquake in Jamaica. Because it is small it could easily represent the Day of Judgment. Exactly in so far as it is limited, so far it could play easily with falling cities or with falling stars. Meanwhile the big theatres are obliged to be economical because they are big. When we have understood this fact we shall have understood something of the reason why the world has always been first inspired by small nationalities. The vast Greek philosophy could fit easier into the small city of Athens than into the immense empire of Persia. Dante felt that there was room for Purgatory and Heaven and Hell. He would have been stified by the British Empire. Great empires are necessarily prosaic; for it is beyond human power to act a great poem upon so great a scale. You can only represent very big ideas in very small spaces. My toy theatre is as philosophical as the drama of Athens.

The Advantages of having One Leg

A FRIEND of mine who was visiting a poor woman in bereavement and casting about for some phrase of consolation that should not be either insolent or weak, said at last, 'I think one can live through these great sorrows and even be better. What wears one is the little worries'. 'That's quite right, mum', answered the old woman with emphasis, and I ought to know, seeing I've had ten of 'em'. It is, perhaps, in this sense that it is most true that little worries are most wearing. In its vaguer significance the phrase, though it contains a truth, contains also some possibilities of self-deception and error. People who have both small troubles and big ones have the right to say that they find the small ones most bitter; and it is undoubtedly true that the back which is bowed under loads incredible can feel a faint addition to those loads; a giant holding up the earth and all its animal creation might still find the grass-hopper a burden. But I am afraid that the maxim that the smallest worries are the worst is sometimes used or abused by people, because they have nothing but the very smallest worries. The lady may excuse herself for reviling the crumpled rose-leaf by reflecting with what extraordinary dignity she would wear the crown of thorns – if she had to. The gentleman may permit himself to curse the dinner and tell himself that he would behave much better if it were a mere matter of starvation. We need not deny that the grasshopper on man's shoulder is a burden; but we need not pay much respect to a gentleman who is always calling out that he would rather have an elephant when he knows there are no elephants in the country. We may concede that a straw may break the camel's back, but we like to know that it really is the last straw and not the first.

I grant that those who have serious wrongs have a real right to grumble, so long as they grumble about something else. It is a singular fact that if they are same they almost always do grumble about something else. To talk quite reasonably about your own quite real wrongs is the quickest way to go off your head. But people with great troubles talk about little ones, and the man who complains of the crumpled rose-leaf very often has his flesh full of the thorns. But if a man has commonly a very clear and happy daily life then I think we are justified in asking that he shall not make mountains out of molehills. I do not deny that molehills can sometimes be important. Small annoyances have this evil about them, that they can be more abrupt because they are more invisible; they cast no shadow before, they have no atmosphere. No one ever had a mystical premonition that he was going to tumble over a hassock. William III died by falling over a molehill; I do not suppose that with all his varied abilities he could have managed to fall over a mountain. But when all this is allowed for, I repeat that we may ask a happy man (not William III) to put up with pure inconveniences, and even make them part of his happiness. Of positive pain or positive poverty I do not here speak. I speak of those innumerable accidental limitations that are always falling across our path – bad weather, confinement to this or that house or room, failure of appointments or arrangements, waiting at railway stations, missing posts, finding unpunctuality when we want punctuality, or, what is worse, finding punctuality when we don't. It is of the poetic pleasures to be drawn from all these that I sing – I sing with confidence because I have recently been experimenting in the poetic pleasures which arise from having to sit in one chair with a sprained foot, with the only alternative course of standing on one leg like a stork. A stork is a poetic simile; therefore I eagerly adopted it.

To appreciate anything we must always isolate it, even if the thing itself symbolize something other than isolation. If we wish to see what a house is it must be a house in some uninhabited landscape. If we wish to depict what a man really is we must depict a man alone in a desert or on a dark sea sand. So long as he is a single figure he means all that humanity means; so long as he is solitary he means human society; so long as he is solitary he means sociability and comradeship. Add another figure and the picture is less human – not more so. One is company, two is none. If you wish to symbolize human building draw one dark tower on the horizon; if you wish to symbolize light let there be no star in the sky. Indeed, all through that strangely lit season which we call our day there is but one star in the sky – a large, fierce star which we call the sun. One sun is splendid; six suns would be only vulgar. One Tower of Giotto* is sublime; a row of Towers of Giotto would be only like a row of white posts. The poetry of art is in beholding the single tower; the poetry of nature in seeing the single tree; the poetry of love in following the single woman; the poetry of religion in worshipping the single star. And so, in the same pensive lucidity, I find the poetry of all human anatomy in standing on a single leg. To express complete and perfect leggishness the leg must stand in sublime isolation, like the tower in the wildness. As Ibsen so finely says, the strongest leg is that which stands most alone.

This lonely leg on which I rest has all the simplicity of some Doric column. The students of architecture tell us that the only legitimate use of a column is to support weight. This column of mine fulfils its legitimate functions. It supports weight. Being of an animal and organic consistency, it may even improve by the process, and during these few days that I am thus unequally balanced the helplessness or dislocation of the one leg may find compensation in the astonishing strength and classic beauty of the other leg. Mrs. Mountstuart Jenkinson in Mr. George Meredith's novel might pass by at any moment, and seeing me in the stork-like attitude would exclaim, with equal admiration and a more literal exactitude, 'He has a leg.' Notice how this famous literary phrase supports my contention touching this isolation of

---

* Named after di Bondone Giotto (1267-1337), the famed painter and decorator of Italian churches. He is considered the father of European painting.

any admirable thing. Mrs. Mountstuart Jenkinson, wishing to make a clear and perfect picture of human grace, said that Sir Willoughby Patterne had a leg. She delicately glossed over and concealed the clumsy and offensive fact that he had really two legs. Two legs were superfluous and irrelevant, a reflection, and a confusion. Two legs would have confused Mrs. Mountstuart Jenkinson like two Monuments in London. That having had one good leg he should have another – this would be to use vain repetitions as the Gentiles do. She would have been as much bewildered by him as if he had been a centipede.

All pessimism has a secret optimism for its object. All surrender of life, all denial of pleasure, all darkness, all austerity, all desolation has for its real aim this separation of something so that it may be poignantly and perfectly enjoyed. I feel grateful for the slight sprain which has introduced this mysterious and fascinating division between one of my feet and the other. The way to love anything is to realize how very much otherwise it might have been. The moral of the thing is wholly exhilarating. This world and all our powers in it are far more awful and beautiful than we ever know until some accident reminds us. If you wish to perceive that limitless felicity, limit yourself if only for a moment. If you wish to realize how fearfully and wonder-fully God's image is made, stand on one leg. If you want to realize the splendid vision of all visible things – wink the other eye.

The Romance of Rhyme

THE POET in the comic opera, it will be remembered (I hope), claimed for his aesthetic authority that 'Hey diddle diddle will rank as an idyll, if I pronounce it chaste'. In fact of a satire which still survives the fashion it satirized, it may require some moral courage seriously to pronounce it chaste, or to suggest that the nursery rhyme in question be really of some qualities of an idyll. Of its chastity, in the vulgar sense, there need be little dispute, despite the scandal of the elopement of the dish with the spoon, which would seem as free from grossness as the loves of the triangles. And though the incident of the cow may have something of the moon-struck ecstasy of Endymion,* that also has a silvery coldness about it worthy of the wilder aspects of Diana. The truth more seriously tenable is that this nursery rhyme is a complete and compact model of the nursery short story. The cow jumping over the moon fulfils to perfection the two essentials of such a story for children. It makes an effect that is fantastic out of objects that are familiar; and it makes a picture that is at once incredible and unmistakable. But it is yet more tenable, and here more to the point, that this nursery rhyme is emphatically a rhyme. Both the lilt and the jingle are just right for their purpose, and are worth whole libraries of elaborate literary verse for children. And the best proof of its vitality is that the satirist himself has unconsciously echoed the jingle even in making the joke. The metre of that nineteenth-century satire is the metre of the nursery rhyme. 'Hey diddle diddle, the car and the fiddle' and 'Hey diddle diddle will rank as an, idyll' are obviously both dancing to the same ancient tune; and that by no means the tune the old cow died of, but the more exhilarating air to which she jumped over the moon.

---

* This lengthy poem 'Endymion' was written by English Romantic poet John Keats (1795-1821) when he was just 23. Two years later he died of tuberculosis.

The whole history of the thing called rhyme can be found between those two things: the simple pleasure of rhyming 'diddle' to 'fiddle', and the more sophisticated pleasure of rhyming 'diddle' to 'idyll'. Now the fatal mistake about poetry, and more than half of the fatal mistake about humanity, consists in forgetting that we should have the first kind of pleasure as well as the second. It might be said that we should have the first pleasure as the basis of the second; or yet more truly, the first pleasure inside the second. The fatal metaphor of progress, which means leaving things behind us, has utterly obscured the real idea of growth, which means leaving things inside us. The heart of the tree remains the same, however many rings are added to it; and a man cannot leave his heart behind by running hard with his legs. In the core of all culture are the things that may be said, in every sense, to be learned by heart. In the innermost part of all poetry is the nursery rhyme, the nonsense that is too happy even to care about being nonsensica. It may lead on to the more elaborate nonsense of the Gilbertian line or even the far less poetic nonsense of some of the Browningesque rhymes. But the true enjoyment of poetry is always in having the simple pleasure as well as the subtle pleasure. Indeed it is on this primary point that so many of our artistic and other reforms seem to go wrong. What is the matter with the modern world is that it is trying to get simplicity in everything, except the soul. Where the soul really has simplicity it can be grateful for anything – even complexity. Many peasants have to be vegetarians, and their ordinary life is really a simple life. But the peasants do not despise a good dinner when they can get it; they wolf it down with enthusiasm, because they have not only the simple life but the simple spirit. And it is so with the modern modes of art which revert, very rightly, to what is 'primitive'. But their moral mistake is that they try to combine the ruggedness that should belong to simplicity with a superciliousness that should only belong to satiety. The last Futurist draughtmanship, for instance, evidently has the aim of drawing a tree as it might be drawn by a child of ten. I think the new artists would admit it; nor do I merely sneer at it. I am willing to admit, especially for the sake of argument, that there is a truth of philosophy and psychology in this attempt to attain the clarity even through the crudity of childhood. In this sense I can see what a man is driving at when he draws a tree merely as a stick with smaller sticks standing out of it. He may be trying to trace, in black and white or grey; a primeval and almost prenatal illumination; that it is very remarkable that a stick should exist, and still more remarkable that a stick should stick up or stick out. He may be similarly enchanted with his own stick of charcoal or grey chalk; he may be enraptured, as a child is, with the mere fact that it makes a mark on the paper – a highly poetic fact in itself. But the child does not despise the real tree for being different from his drawing of the tree. He does not despise Uncle Humphrey because that talented amateur can really draw a tree. He does not think less of the real sticks because they are live sticks, and can grow and branch and curve in a way uncommon in walking sticks. Because he has a single eye he can enjoy a double pleasure. This distinction, which seems strangely neglected, may be traced again in the drama and most other domains of art. Reformers insist that the audiences of simpler ages were content with bare boards or rudimentary scenery if they could hear Sophocles or Shakespeare talking a language of the gods. They were very properly contented with plain boards. But they were not discontented with pageants. The people who appreciated Antony's oration as such would have appreciated Aladdin's palace as such. They did not think gilding and spangles substitutes for poetry and philosophy, because they are not. But they did think gilding and spangles great and admirable gifts of God, because they are.

But the application of this distinction here is to the case of rhyme in poetry. And the application of it is that we should never be ashamed of enjoying a thing as a rhyme as well as enjoying it as a poem. And I think the modern poets who try to escape from the rhyming pleasure, in pursuit of a freer poetical pleasure, are making the same fundamentally fallacious attempt to combine simplicity with superiority. Such a poet is like a child who could take no pleasure in a tree because it looked like a tree, or a playgoer who could take no pleasure in the Forest of Arden because it looked like a forest. It is not impossible to find a sort of prig who professes that he could listen to literature in any scenery, but strongly objects to good scenery. And in poetical criticism and creation there has also appeared the prig who insists that any new poem must avoid the sort of melody that makes the beauty of any old song. Poets must put away childish things, including the child's pleasure in the mere sing-song of irrational rhyme. It may be hinted that when poets put away childish things they will put away poetry. But it may be well to say a world in further justification of rhyme as well as poetry, in the child as well as the poet. Now, the neglect of this nursery instinct would be a blunder, even if it were merely an animal instinct or an automatic instinct. If a rhyme were to a man merely what a bark is to a dog, or a crow to a cock, it would be clear that such natural things cannot be merely neglected. It is clear that a canine epic, about Argus instead of Ulysses, would have a beat ultimately consisting of barks. It is clear that a long poem like *Chantecler,* written by a real cock, would be to the tune of Cock-a-doodle-doo. But in truth the nursery rhyme has a nobler origin; if it be ancestral it is not animal; its principle is a primary one, not only in the body but in the soul.

Milton prefaced *Paradise Lost* with a ponderous condemnation of rhyme. And perhaps the finest and even the most familiar line in the whole of *Paradise Lost* is really a glorification of rhyme. 'Seasons return, but not to me return,' is not only an echo that has all the ring of a rhyme in its form, but it happens to contain nearly all the philosophy of rhyme in its spirit. The wonderful word 'return' has, not only in its sound but in its sense, a hint of the whole secret of song. It is not merely that its very form is a fine example of a certain quality in English, somewhat similar to that which Mrs. Meynell admirably analysed in the case of words like 'unforgiven'. It is that it describes poetry itself, not only in a mechanical but a moral sense. Song is not only a recurrence, it is a return. It does not merely, like the child in the nursery, take pleasure in seeing the wheels go round. It also wishes to go back as well as round; to go back to the nursery where such pleasures are found. Or to vary the metaphor slightly, it does not merely rejoice in the rotation of a wheel on the road, as if it were a fixed wheel in the air. It is not only the wheel but the wagon that is returning. That labouring caravan is always travelling towards some camping-ground that it has lost and cannot find again. No lover of poetry needs to be told that all poems are full of that noise of returning wheels; and none more than the poems of Milton himself. The whole truth is obvious, not merely in the poem, but even in the two words of the title. All poems might be bound in one book under the title of *Paradise Lost.* And the only object of writing *Paradise Lost* is to turn it, if only by a magic and momentary illusion, into *Paradise Regained.*

It is in this deeper significance of return that we must seek for the peculiar power in the recurrence we call rhyme. It would be easy enough to reply to Milton's strictures on rhyme in the spirit of a sensible if superficial liberality by saying that it takes all sorts to make a world, and especially the world of the poets. It is evident enough that Milton might have been right to dispense with rhyme without being right to despise it. It is obvious that the peculiar dignity of his religious epic would have been weakened if it had been a rhymed epic beginning:

> Of man's first disobedience and the fruit
> Of that forbidden tree whose mortal root.

But it is equally obvious that Milton himself would not have tripped on the light fantastic toe with quite so much charm and cheerfulness in the lines:

> But come thou Goddess fair and free
> In heaven yclept[1] Euphrosyne[2]

if the goddess had been yclept something else, as, for the sake of argument, Syrinx. Milton in his more reasonable moods would have allowed rhyme in theory a place in all poetry, as he allowed it in practice in his own poetry. But he would certainly have said at this time, and possibly at all times, that he allowed it an inferior place, or at least a secondary place. But is its place secondary; and is it in any sense inferior?

The romance of rhyme does not consist merely in the pleasure of a jingle, though this is a pleasure of which no man should be ashamed. Certainly most men take pleasure in it, whether or not they are ashamed of it. We see it in the older fashion of prolonging the chorus of a song with syllables like 'rumty turoty' or 'tooral looral'. We see it in the similar but later fashion of discussing whether a truth is objective or subjective, or whether a reform is constructive or destructive, or whether an argument is deductive or inductive: all beating witness to a very natural love for those nursery rhyme recurrences which make a sort of song without words, or at least without any kind of intellectual significance. But something much deeper is involved in the love of rhyme as distinct from other poetic forms, something which is perhaps too deep and subtle to be described. The nearest approximation to the truth I can think of is something like this; that while all forms of genuine verse recur, there is in rhyme a sense of return to exactly the same place. All modes of song go forward and backward like the tides

1 Past tense of CLEPE i.e. cried out (the name).
2 One of the three Graces.

of sea; but in the great sea of Homeric or Virgilian hexameters, the sea that carried the labouring ships of Ulysses and Aeneas, the thunder of the breakers is rhymic, but the margin of the foam is necessarily irregular and vague. In thyme there is rather a sense of water poured safely into one familiar well, or (to use a nobler metaphor) of ale poured safely into one familiar flagon. The armies of Homer and Virgil advance and retreat over a vast country, and suggest vast and very profound sentiments about it; about whether it is their own country or only a strange country. But when the old nameless ballad boldly rhymes 'the bonny ivy tree' to 'my ain countree' the vision at once dwindles and sharpens to a very vivid image of a single soldier passing under the ivy that darkness his own door. Rhythm deals with similarity, but rhyme with identity. Now in the one word *identity* are involved perhaps the deepest and certainly the dearest human things. He who is homesick does not desire houses or even homes. He who is lovesick does not want to see all the women with whom he might have fallen in love. Only he who is sea-sick, perhaps, may be said to have a cosmopolitan craving for all lands or any kind of land. And this is probably why sea-sickness, like cosmopolitanism, has never yet been a high inspiration to song. Songs, especially the most poignant of them, generally refer to some absolute, to some positive place or person for whom no similarity is a substitute. In such a case all approximation is merely asymptotic. The prodigal returns to his father's house and not the house next door, unless he is still an imperfectly sober prodigal; the lover desires his lady and not her twin sister, except in old complications of romance; and even the spiritualist is generally looking for a ghost and not merely for ghosts. I think the intolerable torture of spiritualism must be a doubt about identity. Anyhow, it will generally be found that where this call for the identical has been uttered most ringingly and unmistakably in literature, it has been uttered in rhyme. Another purpose for which this pointed and definite form is very much fitted is the expression of dogma, as distinct from doubt

or even opinion. This is why, with all allowance for a decline in
the most classical effects of the classical tongue, the rhymed
Latin of the medieval hymns does express what it had to express
in a very poignant poetical manner, as compared with the
reverent agnosticism so nobly uttered in the rolling unrhymed
metres of the ancients. For even if we regard the matter of the
medieval verses as a dream, it was at least a vivid dream, a
dream full of faces, a dream of love and of lost things. And
something of the same spirit runs in a vaguer way through
proverbs and phrases that are not exactly religious, but rather in
a rude sense philosophical, but which all move with the burden
of returning; things to be felt only in familiar fragments. . . . . *on
revient toujours*. . . . .it's the old story – it's love that makes the
world go round; and all roads lead to Rome: we might almost say
that all roads lead to rhyme.

Milton's revolt against rhyme must be read in the light of
history. Milton is the Renascence* frozen into a Puritan form:
the beginning of a period which was in a sense classic, but was
in a still more definite sense aristocratic. There the Classicist
was the artistic aristocrat because the Calvinist was the spiritual
aristocrat. The seventeenth century was intensely individualistic; it had both in the noble and the ignoble sense a respect
for persons. It had no respect whatever for popular traditions;
and it was in the midst of its purely logical and legal excitement
that most of the popular traditions died. The Parliament
appeared and the people disappeared. The arts were put under
patrons, where they had once been under patron saints. The
schools and colleges at once strengthened and narrowed the
New Learning, making it something rather peculiar to one
country and one class. A few men talked a great deal of good
Latin, where all men had once talked a little bad Latin. But they
talked even the good Latin so that no Latinist in the world could
understand them. They confined all study of the classics to that

* Renaissance

of the most classical period, and grossly exaggerated the barbarity and barrenness of patriotic Greek or medieval Latin. It is as if a man said that because the English translation of the Bible is perhaps the best English in the world, therefore Addison and Pater and Newman are not worth reading. We can imagine what men in such a mood would have said of the rude rhymed hexameters of the monks; and it is not unnatural that they should have felt a reaction against rhyme itself. For the history of rhyme is the history of something else, very vast and sometimes invisible, certainly somewhat indefinable, against which they were in aristocratic rebellion.

That thing is difficult to define in impartial modern terms. It might well be called Romance, and that even in a more technical sense, since it corresponds to the rise of the Romance languages as distinct from the Roman language. It might more truly be called Religion, for historically it was the gradual re-emergence of Europe through the Dark Ages,[1] because it still had one religion, though no longer one rule. It was, in short, the creation of Christendom. It may be called Legend, for it is true that the most overpowering presence in it is that of omnipresent and powerful popular legend; so that things that may never have happened, or, as some say, could never have happened, are nevertheless rooted in our racial memory like things that have happened to ourselves. The whole Arthurian Cycle,[2] for instance, seems something more real than reality. If the faces in that darkness of the Dark Ages, Lancelot and Arthur and Merlin and Modred, are indeed faces in a dream, they are like faces in a real dream: a dream in a bed and not a dream in a book. Subconsciously at least, I should be much less surprised if Arthur were to come again than I should be if the Superman were to come at all. Again, the thing might be called Gossip: a

---

1 A time when civilization suffers a decline. Here, (the European) period from
  AD 416 to 1000.
2 Relating to legendary King Arthur, believed to be a 6th-century Christian warrior.

noble name, having in it the name of God and one of the most generous and genial of the relations of men. For I suppose there has seldom been a time when such a mass of culture and good traditions of craft and song have been handed down orally, by one universal buzz of conversation, through countries of ignorance down to centuries of greater knowledge. Education must have been an eternal *viva voce* examination; but the men passed their examination. At least they went out in such rude sense masters of art as to create the Song of Roland and the round Roman arches that carry the weight of so many Gothic towers. Finally, of course, it can be called ignorance, barbarism, black superstition, a reaction towards obscurantism and old night; and such a view is eminently complete and satisfactory, only that it leaves behind it a sort of weak wonder as to why the very youngest poets do still go on writing poems about the sword of Arthur and the horn of Roland.

All this was but the beginning of a process which has two great points of interest. The first is the way in which the medieval movement did rebuild the old Roman civilization; the other was the way in which it did not. A strange interest attaches to the things which had never existed in the pagan culture and did appear in the Christian culture. I think it is true of most of them that they had a quality that can very approximately be described as popular, or perhaps as vulgar, as indeed we still talk of the languages which at that time liberated themselves from Latin as the vulgar tongues. And to many Classicists these things would appear to be vulgar in a more vulgar sense. They were vulgar in the sense of being vivid almost to excess, of making a very direct and unsophisticated appeal to the emotions. The first law of heraldry was to wear the heart upon the sleeve. Such medievalism was the reverse of mere mysticism, in the sense of mere mystery; it might more truly be described as sensationalism. One of these things, for instance, was a hot and even an impatient love of colour. I learned to paint before I could draw, and could afford the two pence colour long before I could manage the penny plain. It culminated at last, of course, in the energy and gaiety of the Gothic; but even the richness of Gothic rested on a certain psychological simplicity. We can contrast it with the classic by noting its popular passion for telling a story in stone. We may admit that a Doric portico is a poem, but no one would describe it as an anecdote. The time was to come when much of the imagery of the cathedrals was to be lost; but it would have mattered the less that it was defaced by its enemies if it had not been already neglected by its friends. It would have mattered less if the whole tide of taste among the rich had not turned against the old popular masterpieces. The Puritans defaced them, but the Cavaliers did not truly defend them. The Cavaliers also were aristocrats of the new classical culture, and used the word Gothic in the sense of barbaric. For the benefit of the Teutonists we may note in parenthesis that, if this phrase meant that Gothic was despised, it also meant that Goths were despised. But when the Cavaliers came back, after the Puritan interregnum, they restored not in the style of Pugin but in the style of Wren. The very thing we call the Restoration which was the restoration of King Charles, was also the restoration of St. Paul's. And it was a very modern restoration.

So far we might say that simple people do not like simple things. This is certainly true if we compare the classic with these highly-coloured things of medievalism, or all the vivid visions which first began to glow in the night of the Dark Ages. Now, one of these things was the romantic expedient called rhyme. And even in this, if we compare the two, we shall see something of the same paradox by which the simple like complexities and the complex like simplicities. The ignorant liked rich carvings and melodious and often ingenious rhymes. The learned liked bare walls and blank verse. But in

the case of rhyme it is peculiarly difficult to define the double
and yet very definite truth. It is difficult to define the sense in
which rhyme is artificial and the sense in which it is simple. In
truth it is simple because it is artificial. It is an artifice of the
kind enjoyed by children and other poetic people; it is a toy. As
a technical accomplishment it stands at the same distance
from the popular experience as the old popular sports. Like
swimming, like dancing, like drawing the bow, anybody can
do it, but nobody can do it without taking the trouble to do it;
and only a few can do it very well. In a hundred ways it was
akin to that simple and even humble energy that made all the
lost glory of the guilds. Thus their rhyme was useful as well
as ornamental. It was not merely a melody but also a
mnemonic; just as their towers were not merely trophies but
beacons and belfries. In another aspect rhyme is akin to
rhetoric, but of a very positive and emphatic sort; the
coincidence of sound giving the effect of saying. 'It is
certainly so.' Shakespeare realized this when he rounded off a
fierce or romantic scene with a rhymed couplet. I know that
some critics do not like this, but I think there is a moment
when a drama ought to become a melodrama. Then there is a
much older effect of rhyme that can only be called mystical,
which may seem the very opposite of the utilitarian, and
almost equally remote from the rhetorical. Yet it shares with
the former the tough texture of something not easily forgotten,
and with the later the touch of authority which is the aim of all
oratory. The thing I mean may be found in the fact that so
many of the old proverbial prophecies, from Merlin to Mother
Shipton, were handed down in rhyme. It can be found in the
very name of Thomas the Rhymer.

But the simplest way of putting this popular quality is in a
single word: it is a song. Rhyme corresponds to a melody so
simple that it goes straight like an arrow to the heart. Its
corresponds to a chorus so familiar and obvious that all men

can join in it, I am not disturbed by the suggestion that such an arrow of song, when it hits the hearts, may entirely miss the head. I am not concerned to deny that the chorus may sometimes be a drunken chorus, in which men have lost their heads to find their tongues. I am not defending but defining; I am trying to find words for a large but elusive distinction between certain things that are certainly poetry and certain other things which are also song. Of course it is only an accident that Horace opens his greatest series of odes by saying that he detests the profane populace and wishes to derive them from his temple of poetry. But it is the sort of accident that is almost an allegory. There is even a sense in which it has a practical side. When all is said, *could* a whole crowd of men sing the 'Descende Coelo', that noble ode, as a crowd can certainly sing the 'Dies Irae'*, or for that matter 'Down among the Dead Man'? Did Horace himself sing the Horatian odes in the sense in which Shakespeare could sing, or could hardly help singing, the Shakespearean songs? I do not know, having no kind of scholarship on these points. But I do not feel that it could have been at all the same thing; and my only purpose is to attempt a rude description of that thing. Rhyme is consonant to the particular kind of song that can be a popular song, whether pathetic or passionate or comic; and Milton is entitled to his true distinction; nobody is likely to sing *Paradise Lost* as if it were a song of that kind. I have tried to suggest my sympathy with rhyme, in terms true enough to be accepted by the other side as expressing their antipathy for it. I have admitted that rhyme is a toy and even a trick, of the sort that delights children. I have admitted that every rhyme is a nursery rhyme. What I will never admit is that anyone who is too big for the nursery is big enough for the Kingdom of God, though the God were only Apollo.

---

* A medieval Latin hymn on the Day of Judgment, sung in requiem masses.

A good critic should be like God in the great saying of a Scottish mystic. George Macdonald said that God was easy to please and hard to satisfy. That paradox is the poise of all good artistic appreciation. Without the first part of the paradox appreciation perishes, because it loses the power to appreciate. Good criticism, I repeat, combines the subtle pleasure in a thing being done well with the simple pleasure in it being done at all. It combines the pleasure of the scientific engineer in seeing how the wheels work together to a logical end with the pleasure of the baby in seeing the wheels go round. It combines the pleasure of the artistic draughtsman in the fact that his lines of charcoal, light and apparently loose, fall exactly right and in a perfect relation with the pleasure of the child in the fact that the charcoal makes marks of any kind on the paper. And in the same fashion it combines the critic's pleasure in a poem with the child's pleasure in a rhyme. The historical point about this kind of poetry, the rhymed romantic kind, is that it rose out of the Dark Ages with the whole of this huge popular power behind it, the human love of a song, a riddle, a proverb, a pun or a nursery rhyme; the sing-song of innumerable children's games, the chorus of thousand camp-fires and a thousand taverns. When poetry loses its link with all these people who are easily pleased it loses all its power of giving pleasure. When a poet looks down on a rhyme it is, I will not say as if he looked down on a daisy (which might seem possible to the more literal-minded), but rather as if he looked down on a lark because he had been up in a balloon. It is cutting away the very roots of poetry; it as revolting against nature because it is natural, against sunshine because it is bright, or mountains because they are high or moonrise because it is a mysterious. The freezing process began after the Reformation with a fastidious search for finer yet freer forms; today it has ended in formlessness.

But the joke of it is that even when it is formless it is still fastidious. The new anarchic artists are not ready to accept everything. They are not ready to accept anything except anarchy. Unless it observes the very latest conventions of unconventionality, they would rule out anything classic as coldly as any classic ever ruled out anything romantic. But the classic was a form; and there was even a time when it was a new form. The men who invented Sapphics did invent a new metre; the introduction of Elizabethan blank verse was a real revolution in literary form. But *vers libre,** or nine-tenths of it, is not a new metre any more than sleeping in a ditch is a new school of architecture. It is no more a revolution in literary form than eating meat raw is an innovation in cookery. It is not even original, because it is not creative; the artist does not invent anything, but only abolishes something. But the only point about it, that is to my present purpose, is expressed in the word 'pride'. It is not merely proud in the sense of being exultant, but proud in the sense of being disdainful. Such outlaws are more exclusive than aristocrats; and their anarchical arrogance goes far beyond the pride of Milton and the aristocrats of the New Learning. And this final refinement has completed the work which the saner aristocrats began, the work now most evident in the world: the separation of art from the people. I need not insist on the sensational and self-evident character of that separation. I need not recommend the modern poet to attempt to sing his *verse libres* in a public-house. I need not even urge the young Imagist to read out a number of his disconnected Images to a public meeting. The thing is not only admitted but admired. The old artist remained proud in spite of his unpopularity; the new artist is proud because of his unpopularity; perhaps it is his chief ground for pride.

Dwelling as I do in the Dark Ages, or at least among the medieval fairy-tales, I am yet moved to remember something I once read in a modern fairy-tale. As it happens, I have already used the name of George Macdonald; and in the best of his

* Free verse.

books there is a description of how a young miner in the mountains could always drive away the subterranean goblins if he could remember and repeat any kind of rhyme. The impromptu rhymes were often doggerel, as was the dog-Latin of many monkish hexameters or the burden of many rude Border ballads. But I have a notion that they drove away the devils, blue devils of pessimism and black devils of pride. Anyhow Madame Montessori,* who has apparently been deploring the educational effect of fairy-tales, would probably see in me a pitiable example of such early perversion, for that, image which was one of my first impressions seems likely enough to be one of my last; and when the noise of many new and original musical instruments, with strange shapes and still stranger noises, has passed away like a procession, I shall hear in the succeeding silence only a rustle and scramble among the rocks and a boy singing on the mountain.

---

* Italian educator Maria Montessori (1870-1952). Her system is based on belief in children's creative potential, their drive to learn, and their right to be treated as individuals. It relies on the use of *didactic apparatuses* to cultivate hand-eye coordination, self-directedness, and sensitivity to pre-mathematical and pre-literary instruction.

On the Englishman Abroad

IT WAS an old objection to the Englishman abroad that he made himself too much at home. He was accused of treating a first-class foreign hotel as if it were only a fourth-class English hotel; and of brawling in it as if it were a bad variety of public-house. If there was a truth in the charge, it has since been transferred to a more vigorous type of vulgarian; and compared with a certain sort of American traveller, the English tripper might be mistaken for a civilized man. He has even taken on the colour of his Continental surroundings and is indistinguishable from what he himself would once have described as 'the natives'. It might almost be regarded as a form of going *fantee*.* But there is one particular aspect of the old accusation, which seems to me much more curious and puzzling than any other. It is that when the Englishman did blunder or bully, in demanding certain things merely because they were familiar, they were not really the things that had long been familiar to him; or to his fathers. I can understand the Englishman asking for English things; the odd thing is that it was not for the most English things that he asked. Some of the most English things he had already lost in England, and could hardly hope to find in Europe. Most of the things he did hope to find in Europe, he had only recently found even in England. When he asked for a drink, he asked for a Scotch drink; he even submitted to the intolerable national humiliation of calling it Scotch. When he asked for a game, he asked for a Scotch game; he looked to see whole landscapes transformed by the game of golf; which he himself had hardly played for ten years. He did not go about looking for cricket, which, he had played for six hundred years. And just as he asked for Scotch links instead of cricket-finds, and Scotch whisky instead of ale, so he expected a number of appliances

* To adopt the ways of the native people.

and conveniences which were often much less English than American; and sometimes much less English than German, It would perhaps be pressing the argument fantastically far to say that even tea is originally a thing as Oriental as hashish. But certainly an Englishman demanding tea in all the cafes of the Continent was as unreasonable as a Chinaman demanding opium in all the public houses of the Old Kent Road. He was at least comparable to a Frenchman roaring to have red wine included in his bill in a series of tea-shops in Tooting. But I am not so much complaining of the old fashioned Englishman who asked for something like the 'five o'clock' which was recognized as English. I am rather complaining of a new-fashioned English-man who would insist on American ice-cream sodas in the plains of Russia, while refusing tea because it was taken with lemon or served in a samovar. This bizarre contradiction and combination of the blind acceptance of some foreign things and the blind refusal of others does seem to me a mystery to be added to what is perhaps the most mysterious national character in Christendom. That a man from Market Harborough should miss the oldest things in Old England when travelling in Lithuania, may be intelligible and pardonable enough. That a man from Market Harborough should miss the newest things in New York, and be seriously surprised not to find them among Lithuanian peasants, is even more extraordinary than that he should want them himself.

But there goes along with this English eccentricity an even more serious English error. The things of which England has most reason to be proud are the things which England has preserved out of the ancient culture of the Christian world, when all the rest of that world has neglected them. They are at once unique and universal triumphs and trophies of the national life. They are things that are English in the sense that the English have kept them; but human in the sense that all humanity ought to have kept them. They are European in the sense of really belonging to the whole white civilization; they are English in the sense of having been largely lost in Europe. And I have heard Englishmen boasting of all sorts of absurd things, from the possession of German blood to the possession of Jewish politicians and I have never heard a single Englishman say a single word about a single one of these really English things.

One obvious case, for example, is that of having a fire in the old Latin sense of a focus. The idea of the hearth is one to be found in ancient Roman culture, and therefore in all the European cultures that have come from it. The idea of the hearth is to be found everywhere; but the hearth; is not to be found everywhere. It is now most easily and universally to be found in England. And it is a strange irony that the French poet or the Italian orator, full of the splendours of the great pagan past, naturally speaks of a man fighting for his hearth and his altar; when he himself in practice has as much neglected hearths as we have neglected altars. And the only man in Christendom who really retains a hearth is one who has unfortunately rather dropped out of the habit of fighting for it. I do not mean, of course, that there are not really firesides scattered everywhere throughout Europe, especially among the poor, who always retain the highest and proudest traditions of the past. I am talking of a matter of proportion; of the preponderating presence of the custom in one place rather than another; and in this sense it is certain that it preponderates in England more than in any other country. Almost everywhere else the much more artificial and prosaic institution called the stove has become solidly established. In every eternal and essential sense, there is simply no comparison between that open domestic altar, on which the visible flame dances and illuminates, and the mere material habit of shutting up heat in a big box. The comparison is as sharp as that between the wild but splendid pagan custom of burning a dead man on a tower of timber, so that he went up to the sky in a column of fire and cloud, and the paltry paganism of our own time, which is content with the thing called cremation. Similarly there is about the stove all the essential utilitarian ugliness of the oven. There must always be something more magnificent about an open furnace, even from the standpoint of Shadrach, Meshach, and Abednego.* Theirs was perhaps a rather heroic form of affection for the fireside. But, in comparison, we can all feel that there is something cold and desolate about the condition of the unhappy foreigner, who cannot really hope to sit in the glow of a fireside except by the extreme experiment of sitting his house on fire.

Now I appeal to all those who have sung a hundred English songs, heard a hundred English speeches, read a hundred English books of more or less breezy or bombastic patriotism, to say whether they have ever seen the continuity of this Christian custom properly praised as a matter of pride among the English. And this strange gap in our glory seems to me another example of something that I noted recently; the dangerous lack of an intensive national feeling in this country; and above all a much too supine surrender to other influences; from Germany; from Scotland; and above all from America.

I have taken only one domestic detail here, for the sake of clearness; but of course the principle could be extended to any number of larger examples of the same truth. The English inn, although a most Christian institution, was something more than an institution of Christendom. It was in its day a thing very specially English. I say it was; for I very much fear that capitalist monopoly and prohibitionist madness have between them turned it into something historical. It may be that the public-house will soon be dead enough to become a glorious historical monument. But the point to be noted here is the comparison with other countries, which had similar institutions,

---

* *Daniel* 3: 16-18. The three-some defied king Nebuchadnezzar and sought to be delivered from the burning furnace.

yet never had exactly the same institution. Sometimes, as in the case of the open hearth or fireside, they really had the same institution; and yet never had it so long. But anyone travelling in foreign countries can note that new things are not erected on the basis of this particular old thing. We have spoilt the English inn; but at least we had it to spoil; and many national traditions, admirable in other ways, have had something much less admirable to spoil. In Europe, especially in outlying parts of Europe, we may see the latest modern machinery introduced without any of that intermediate type of comfort and convenience. The new American barbarism is applied direct to the oldest European barbarism. That interlude of moderate and mellow civilization has never been known. Men of many countries, both new and old, could only see it by coming to England; and even then they might come too late. The English might have already destroyed the last glories of England. When I think of these things, I still stand astounded at the strange quality of my countrymen; at their arrogance and especially at their modesty.

A Defence of Dramatic Unities

INJUSTICE IS done to the old classical rules of artistic criticism, because we do not treat them as artistic criticism. We first turn them into police regulations, and then complain of them for being so. But I suspect, with the submission proper to ignorance, that the art canons of Aristotle and others were much more generally artistic, in the sense of atmospheric. We allow a romantic critic to be as dogmatic as Ruskin, and still feel that he is not really being so despotic as Boileau.[1] If a modern, like Maeterlinck,[2] says that all drama is in an open door at the end of an empty passage, we do not take it literally, like a notice requiring an extra exit in case of fire. But if an ancient, like Horace, says that all drama demands a closed door, which shall hide Medea[3] while she murders her children, then we do receive it as something rigid and formal, like the order to close the shutters on air-raid nights. Now how far the classical critics took their rules absolutely I do not know. But I am substantially sure that there is a true instinct at the back of them, whatever exceptions be allowed at the edges. The unities of time and place, that is the idea of keeping figures and events within the frame of a few hours or a few yards, is naturally derided as a specially artificial affront to the intellect. But I am sure it is an especially true suggestion to the imagination. It is exactly in the artistic atmosphere, where rules and reasons are so hard to define, that this unification would be most easy to defend. This limitation to a few scenes and actors really has something in it that pleases the imagination and not the reason. There are

1 Nicolas Boileau (1636-1711), French poet and literary critic who upheld the classical standards in both French and English.
2 Maurice comte Maeterlinck (1862-1949), Belgian playwright and poet who wrote Symbolist poetry and was also popular for write-ups on scientific topics.
3 Daughter of King Aeetes in Greek mythology who commits fratricide, and also kills her own children just to avenge the breach of faith by her husband.

instances in which it may be broken boldly; there are types of art to which it does not apply at all. But wherever it can be satisfied, something not superficial but rather subconscious is satisfied. Something resists us that is the strange soul of single places; the shadow of haunting ghosts or of household gods. Like all such things, it is indescribable when it is successful; it is easier to describe the disregard of it as unsuccessful. Thus Stevenson's masterpiece, *The Master of Ballantra,* always seems to me to fall into two parts, the finer which revolves round Durisdeer and the other which rambles through India and America. The slender and sinister figure in black, standing on the shore or vanishing from the shrubbery, does really seem to have come from the ends of the earth.

In the chapters of travel he only serves to show that, for a boy's adventure tale, a good villain makes a bad hero. And even about Hamlet I am so heretical as to be almost classical; I doubt whether the exile in England does not rather dwarf than dignify the prisoner of Denmark. I am not sure that he got anything out of the pirates he could not have got out of the players. And I am very sure indeed that this figure in black, like the other, produces a true through intangible effect of tragedy when, and because, we see him against the great grey background of the house of his fathers. In a word it is what Mr. J. B Yeats, the poet's stimulating parent, calls in his excellent book of essays 'the drama of the home'. The drama is domestic, and is dramatic because it is domestic.

We might say that superior literature is centripetal, while inferior literature is centrifugal. But oddly enough, the same truth may be found by studying inferior as well as superior literature. What is true of a Shakespearean play is equally true of a shilling shocker. The shocker is at its worst when it wanders, and escapes through new scenes and new characters. The shocker is at its best when it shocks by something familiar; a figure or fact which is already known through not understood. A good detective story also can keep the classic unities; or otherwise play the game. I for one devour detective stories; I am delighted when the dagger of the curate is found to be the final clue to the death of the vicar. But there is a point of honour for the author; he may conceal the curate's crime, but he must not conceal the curate. I feel I am cheated when the last chapter hints for the first time that the vicar had a curate. I am annoyed when a curate, who is a total stranger to me, is produced from a cupboard or a box in style at once abrupt and belated. I am annoyed most of all when the new curate is only the tool of a terrible secret society remifying from Moscow or Thibet. These cosmopolitan complications are the dull and not the dramatic element in the ingenious tales of Mr. Oppenheim or Mr. Le Queux. They entirely spoil the fine domesticity of a good murder. It is unsportsmanlike to call spies from the ends of the earth, as it is to call spirits from the vasty deep, in a story that does not imply them from the start. And this because the supply is infinite; and the infinite, as Coventry Patmore well said, is generally alien to art. Everybody knows that the universe contains enough spies or enough spectres to kill the most healthy and vigorous vicar. The drama of detection is in discovering how he can be killed decently and economically, within the classic unities of time and place.

In short, the good mystery story should narrow its circles like an eagle about to swoop. The spiral should curve inwards and not outwards. And this inward movement is in true poetic mysteries as well as mere police mystifications. It will be assumed that I am joking if I say there is a serious social meaning in this novel-reader's notion of keeping a crime in the family. It must seem mere nonsense to find a moral in this fancy, about washing gory linen at home. It will naturally be asked whether I have idealized the home merely as a good place for assassinations. I have not; any more than I have idealized the Church as a thing in which the curates can kill the vicars. Nevertheless the thing, like many things, is symbolic though it is not serious. And the objection to it implies a subtle misunderstanding, in many minds, of the whole case for the home as I have sometimes had occasion to urge it. When we defend the family we do not mean it is always a peaceful family; when we maintain the thesis of marriage we do not mean that it is always a happy marriage. We mean that it is the theatre of the spiritual drama, the place where things happen, especially the things that matter. It is not so much the place where a man kills his wife as the place where he can take the equally sensational step of not killing his wife. There is truth in the cynicism that calls marriage a trial; but even the cynic will admit that a trial may end in an acquittal. And the reason that the family has this central and crucial character is the same reason that makes it in politics the only prop of liberty, The family is the test of freedom; because the family is the only thing that the free man makes for himself and by himself. Other institutions must largely be made for him by strangers, whether the institutions be despotic or democratic. There is no other way of organizing mankind which can give this power and dignity, not only to mankind, but to men. If anybody likes to put it so, we cannot really make all men democrats unless we make all men depots. That is to say, the co-operation of the commonwealth will be a mere automatic unanimity like that of insects, unless the citizen has some province of purely voluntary action; unless he is so far not only a citizen but a king. In the world of ethics this is called liberty; in the world of economics it is called property. And in the world of aesthetics, necessarily so much more dim and indefinable, it is darkly adumbrated in the old dramatic unities of place or time. It must indeed be a mistake in any case to treat such artistic rules as rigidly as if they were moral rules. It was an error if they ever were so treated; it may well be a question whether they were ever meant to be so treated. But when critics have suggested that these classical canons were a mere superficial varnish, it, may safety be said that it is the critics who are superficial. Modern artists would have been wiser if they had developed sympathetically some of the Aristotelian aesthetics, as medieval philosophers developed sympathetically the Aristotelian logic and ethics. For a more subtle study of the unities of time and place, for example, as outlined for the Greek drama, might have led us towards what is perhaps the last secret of all legend and literature. It might have suggested why poets, pagan or not, returned perpetually to the idea of happiness as a place for humanity as a person. It might suggest why the world is always seeking for absolutes that are not abstractions, why fairyland was always a land, and even the Superman was almost a man.

A Piece of Chalk

I REMEMBER one splendid morning, all blue and silver, in the summer holidays, when I reluctantly tore myself away from the task of doing nothing in particular, and put on a hat of some sort and picked up a walking-stick, and put six very bright coloured chalks in my pocket. I then went into the kitchen (which, along with the rest of the house, belonged to a very square and sensible old woman in a Sussex village), and asked the owner and occupant of the kitchen if she had any brown paper. She had a great deal; in fact, she had too much; and she mistook the purpose and the rationale of the existence of brown paper. She seemed to have an idea that if a person wanted brown paper he must be wanting to tie up parcels; which was the last thing I wanted to do; indeed, it is a thing which I have found to be beyond my mental capacity. Hence she dwelt very much on the varying qualities of toughness and endurance in the material. I explained to her that I only wanted to draw pictures on it, and that I did not want them to endure in the least; and that from my point of view, therefore, it was a question not of tough consistency, but of responsive surface, a thing comparatively irrelevant in a parcel. When she understood that I wanted to draw she offered to overwhelm me with note paper, apparently supposing that I did my notes and correspondence on old brown paper wrappers from motives of economy.

I then tried to explain the rather delicate logical shade, that I not only liked brown paper, but liked the quality of brownness in piper, just as I liked the quality of brownness in October woods, or in beer, or in the peat-streams of the North. Brown paper represents the primal twilight of the first toil of creation, and with a bright coloured chalk or two you can pick out points of fire in it, sparks of gold, and blood-red, and sea-green, like the fierce stars that sprang out of divine darkness. All this I said (in an off-hand way) to the old woman; and I put the brown paper in my pocket along with the chalks, and possibly other things. I suppose every one must have reflected how primeval and how poetical are the things that one carries in one's pocket; the pocket-knife, for instance, the type of all human tools, the infant of the sword. Once I planned to write a book of poems entirely about the things in my pocket. But I found it would be too long; and the age of the great epics is past.

With my stick and my knife, my chalks and my brown paper, I went out on to the great downs. I crawled across those colossal contours that express the best quality of England, because they are at the same time soft and strong. The smoothness of them has the same meaning as the smoothness of great cart-horses, or the smoothness of the beech-tree; it declares in the teeth of our timid and cruel theories that the mighty are merciful. As my eye swept the landscape, the landscape was as kindly as any of its cottages, but for power it was like an earthquake. The villages in the immense valley were safe, one could see, for centuries; yet the lifting of the whole land was like the lifting of one enormous wave to wash them all away.

I crossed one swell of living turf after another, looking for a place to sit down and draw. Do not, for heaven's sake, imagine I was going to sketch from Nature. I was going to draw devils and seraphim,* and blind old gods that men worshipped before the dawn of right, and saints in robes of angry crimson, and seas of strange green, and all the sacred or monstrous symbols that look so well in bright colours on brown paper. They are much better worth drawing than Nature; also they are much easier to draw. When a cow came slouching by in the field next to me, a mere artist might have drawn it; but I always get wrong in the hind legs of quadrupeds. So I drew the soul of the cow; which I saw there plainly walking before me in the sunlight; and the soul was all purple and silver, and had seven horns and the

* Seraphims are the highest ranking angels, and in art they appear red, symbolizing fire. In Christian, Jewish and Islamic legends, these angels with two or three pairs of wings guard the throne of god.

mystery that belongs to all the beasts. But though I could not with a crayon get the best out of the landscape, it does not follow that the landscape was not getting the best out of me. And this, I think, is the mistake that people make about the old poets who lived before Wordsworth, and were supposed not to care very much about Nature because they did not describe it much.

They preferred writing about great men to writing about great hills; but they sat on the great hills to write it. They gave out much less about Nature, but they drank in, perhaps, much more. They painted the white robes of their holy virgins with the blinding snow, at which they had stared all day. They blazoned the shields of their paladins with the purple and gold of many heraldic sunsets. The greenness of a thousand preen leaves clustered into the live green figure of Robin Hood, The blueness of a score of forgotten skies became the blue robes of the Virgin. The inspiration went in like sun-beams and came out like Apollo.

But as I sat scrawling these silly figures on the brown paper, it began to dawn on me, to my great disgust, that I had left one chalk, and that a most exquisite and essential chalk, behind. I searched all my pockets, but I could not find any white chalk. Now those who are acquainted with all the philosophy (nay, religion) which is typified in the art of drawing on brown paper, know that white is positive and essential. I cannot avoid remarking here upon a moral significance. One of the wise and awful truths which this brown-paper art reveals, is this, that white is a colour. It is not a mere absence of colour; it is a shining and affirmative thing, as fierce as red, as definite as black. When (so to speak) your pencil grows red-hot, it draws roses; when it grows white-hot, it draws stars. And one of the two or three defiant verities of the best religious morality, of real Christianity for example, is exactly this same thing; the chief assertion of religious morality is that white is a colour. Virtue is not the absence of vices or the avoidance of moral dangers; virtue is a vivid and separate thing, like pain or a particular smell.

Mercy does not mean not being cruel or sparing people revenge or punishment; it means a plain and positive thing like the sun, which one has either seen or not seen. Chastity does not mean abstention from sexual wrong; it means something naming, like Joan of Arc. In a word, God paints in many colours; but He never paints so gorgeously, I had almost said so gaudily, as when He paints in white. In a sense our age has realized this fact and expressed it in our sullen costume. For if it were really true that white was a blank and colourless thing, negative and non-committal, then white would be used instead of black and grey for the funeral dress of this pessimistic period. We should see city gentlemen in frock coats of spotless silver satin, with top hats as white as wonderful arum lilies. Which is not the case.

Meanwhile, I could not find my chalk.

I sat on the hill in a sort of despair. There was no town nearer than Chichester at which it was even remotely probable that there would be such a thing as an artist's colourman. And yet, without white, my absurd little pictures would be as pointless as the world would be if there were no good people in it. I started stupidly round, racking my brain for expedients. Then I suddenly stood up and roared with laughter, again and again, so that the cows started at me and called a committee. Imagine a man in the Sahara regretting that he had no sand for his hour-glass. Imagine a gentleman in mid-ocean wishing that he had brought some salt water with him for his chemical experiments. I was sitting on an immense warehouse of white chalk. The landscape was made entirely out of white chalk. White chalk was piled mere miles until it met the sky. I stooped and broke a piece of the rock I sat on; it did not mark so well as the shop chalks do; but it gave the effect. And I stood there in a trance of pleasure, realizing that this Southern England is not only a grand peninsula, and a tradition and a civilization; it is something even more admirable. It is a piece of chalk.

The Fear of the Film

LONG LISTS are being given of particular cases in which children have suffered in spirits or health from alleged horrors of the cinema. One child is said to have had a fit after seeing a film; another to have been sleepless with some fixed idea taken from a film; another to have killed his father with a carving knife through having seen a knife used in a film. This may possibly have occurred; and if it did; anybody of common sense would prefer to have details about that particular child rather than about that particular picture. But what is supposed to be the practical moral of it, in any case? Is it that the young should never see a story with a knife in it? Are they to be brought up in complete ignorance of 'The Merchant of Venice' because Shylock flourishes a knife for a highly disagreeable purpose? Are they never to hear of Macbeth, lest it should slowly dawn upon their trembling intelligence that it is a dagger that they see before them? It would be more practical to propose that a child should never see a real carving-knife, and still more practical that he should never see a real father. All that may come; the era of preventive and prophetic science has only begun. We must not be impatient. But when we come to the cases of morbid panic after some particular exhibition, there is yet more reason to clear the mind of cant. It is perfectly true that a child will have the horrors after seeing some particular detail. It is quite equally true that nobody can possibly predict what that detail will be. It certainly need not be anything so obvious as a murder or even a knife. I should have thought anybody who knew anything about children, or for that matter anybody who had been a child, would know that these nightmares are quite incalculable. The hint of horror may come by any chance in any connexion. If the cinema exhibited nothing but views of country vicarages or vegetarian restaurants, the ugly fancy is as likely to be stimulated by these things as by anything else. It is like seeing a face in the carpet; it makes no difference that it is the carpet at the vicarage.

I will give two examples from my own most personal circle; I could give hundreds from hearsay. I know a child who screamed steadily for hours if he had been taken past the Albert Memorial. This was not a precocious precision or excellence in his taste in architecture. Nor was it a premature protest against all that gimcrack German culture which nearly entangled us in the downfall of the barbaric tyranny. It was the fear of something which he himself described with lurid simplicity as the Cow with the India-rubber Tongue. It sounds rather a good title for a creepy short story. At the base of the Albert Memorial (I may explain for those who have never enjoyed that monument) are four groups of statuary representing Europe, Asia, Africa, and America. America especially is very overwhelming; borne onward on a snorting bison who plunges forward in a fury of western progress, and is surrounded with Red Indians, Mexicans, and all sorts of pioneers, pioneers armed to the teeth. The child passed this transatlantic tornado with complete coolness and indifference. Europe however is seated on a bull so mild as to look like a cow; the tip of its tongue is showing and happened to be discoloured by weather; suggesting, I suppose, a living thing coming out of the dead marble. Now nobody could possibly foretell that a weather stain would occur in that particular place, and fill that particular child with that particular fancy. Nobody is likely to propose meeting it by forbidding graven in ages, like the Moslems and the Jews. Nobody has said (as yet) that it is bad morals to make a picture of a cow. Nobody has even pleaded that it is bad manners for a cow to put its tongue out. These things are utterly beyond calculation; they are also beyond counting for they occur all over the place, not only to morbid children but to any children. I knew this particular child very well, being a rather older child myself at the time. He certainly was not congenitally timid or feeble-minded; for he risked going to prison to expose the Marconi Scandal* and died fighting in the Great War.

Here is another example out of scores. A little girl, now a very normal and cheerful young lady, had an insomnia of insane terror entirely arising from the lyric of 'Little Bo-Peep'. After an inquisition like that of the confessor or the psychoanalyst, it was found that the word 'bleating' had some obscure connexion in her mind with the word 'bleeding'. There was thus perhaps an added horror in the phrase 'heard'; in hearing rather than seeing the flowing of blood. Nobody could possibly provide against that sort of mistake. Nobody could prevent the little girl from hearing about sheep, any more than the little boy from hearing about cows. We might abolish all nursery rhymes; and as they are happy and popular and used with universal success, it is very likely that we shall. But the whole point of the mistake about that phrase is that it might have been a mistake about any phrase. We cannot foresee all the fancies that might arise, not only out of what we say, but of what we do not say. We cannot avoid promising a child a caramel lest he should think we say cannibal, or conceal the very word 'hill' lest it should sound like 'hell'.

All the catalogues and calculations offered us by the party of caution in this controversy are therefore quite worthless. It is perfectly true that examples can be given of a child being frightened of this, that or the other. But we can never be certain of his being frightened of the same thing twice. It is not on the negative side, by making lists of vetoes, that the danger can be avoided, it can never indeed be entirely avoided. We can only fortify the child on the positive side by giving him

---

* In 1911 British Prime Minister Herbert Asquith approved a plan for several wireless stations in the Empire and awarded the contract to Marconi Company of Godfrey Isaacs, a close friend of the Attorney General in Asquith's government. This act helped the Marconi shares to rise four-fold.

GKC's colleague Hilaire Belloc, the editor of the political weekly, *The Eye-Witness*, smelled the rat and exposed the corruption.

health and humour and a trust in God; not omitting (what will much mystify the moderns) an intelligent appreciation of the idea of authority, which is only the other side of confidence, and which alone can suddenly and summarily cast out such devils. But we may be sure that most modern people will not look at it in this way. They will think it more scientific to attempt to calculate the incalculable. So soon as they have realized that it is not so simple as it looks, they will try to map it out, however complicated it may be. When they discover that the terrible detail need not be a knife, but might just as well be a fork, they will only say there is a fork complex as well as a knife complex. And that increasing complexity of complexes is the net in which liberty will be taken.

Instead of seeing in the odd cases of the cow's tongue or the bleating sheep the peril of their past generalizations, they will see them only as starting points for new generalizations. They will get yet another theory out of it. And they will begin acting on the theory long before they have done thinking about it. They will start out with some new and crude conception that sculpture has made children scream or that nursery rhymes have made children sleepless; and the thing will be a clause in a programme of reform before it has begun to be a conclusion in a serious story of psychology. That is the practical problem about modern liberty which the critics will not see; of which eugenics is one example and all this amateur child-psychology is another. So long as an old morality was in black and white like a chess-board, even a man who wanted more of it made white was certain that no more of it would be made black. Now he is never certain what vices may not be released, but neither is he certain what virtues may be forbidden. Even if he did not think it wrong to run away with a married women, he knew that his neighbours only thought it wrong because the woman was married. They did not think it wrong to run away with a red-haired woman, or a left-handed woman, or a woman subject to headaches. But when we let loose a thousand eugenical* speculations, all adopted before they are verified and acted on even before they are adopted, he is just as likely as not to find himself separated from the woman for those or any other reasons. Similarly there was something to be said for restrictions, even rather puritanical and provincial restrictions, upon what children should read or see, so long as they fenced in certain fixed departments like sex or sensational tortures. But when we begin to speculate on whether other sensations may not stimulate as dangerously as sex, those other sensations may be as closely controlled as sex. When, let us say, we hear that the eye and brain are weakened by the rapid turning of wheels as well as by the most revolting torturing of men, we have come into a world in which cart-wheels and steam-engines may become as obscene as racks and thumbscrews. In short, so long as we *combine* ceaseless and often reckless scientific speculation with rapid and often random social reform, the result must inevitably be not anarchy but ever-increasing tyranny. There must be a ceaseless and almost mechanical multiplication of things forbidden. The resolution to cure all the ills that flesh is heir to, combined with the guesswork about all possible ills that flesh and nerve and brain-cell may be heir to – these two things conducted simultaneously must inevitably spread a sort of panic of prohibition. Scientific imagination and social reform between them will quite logically and almost legitimately have made us slaves. This seems to me a very clear, a very fair and a very simple point of public criticism; and I am much mystified about why so many publicists cannot even see what it is, but take refuge in charges of anarchism, which firstly are not true, and secondly have nothing to do with it.

* Relating to, or suited for the production of good offspring.

The Conscript and the Crisis

VERY FEW of us ever see the history of our own time
happening. And I think the best service a modern journalist can
do to society is to record as plainly as ever he can exactly what
impression was produced on his mind by anything he has
actually seen and heard on the outskirts of any modern problem
or campaign. Though all he saw of a railway strike was a flat
meadow in Essex in which a train was becalmed for an hour or
two, he will probably throw more light on the strike by
describing this which he has seen than by describing the steely
kings of commerce and the bloody leaders of the mob whom he
has never seen – nor anyone else either. If he comes a day too
late for the battle of Waterloo (as happened to a friend of my
grandfather), he should still remember that a true account of the
day after Waterloo would be a most valuable thing to have.
Though he was on the wrong side of the door when Riccio was
being murdered, we should still like to have the wrong side
described in the right way. Upon this principle I, who know
nothing of diplomacy or military arrangements, and have only
held my breath like the rest or the world while France and
Germany were bargaining, will tell quite truthfully of a small
scene I saw, one of the thousand scenes that were, so to speak,
the anterooms of that in most chamber of debate.

In the course of a certain morning I came into one of the
quiet squares of a small French town and found its cathedral. It
was one of those grey and rainy days which rather suit the
Gothic. The clouds were leaden, like the solid blue grey lead of
the spires and the jewelled windows; the sloping roots and high-
shouldered arches looked like cloaks drooping with damp; and
the stiff gargoyles that stood out round the walls were scoured
with old rains and new. I went into the round, deep porch with
many doors and found two grubby children playing there out of
the rain. I also found a notice of services etc., and among these

I found the announcement that at 11.30 (that is, about half an hour later) there would be a special service for the Conscripts, that is to say, the draft of young men who were being taken from their homes in that little town and sent to serve in the French Army; sent (as it happened) at an awful moment, when the French Army was encamped at a parting of the ways. There were already a great many people there when I entered, not only of all kinds, but in all attitudes, kneeling, sitting, or standing about. And there was that general sense that strikes every man from a Protestant country, whether he dislikes the Catholic atmosphere or likes it; I mean, the general sense that the thing was 'going on all the time'; that it was not an occasion, but a perpetual process, as if it were a sort of mystical inn.

Several tricolours were hung quite near to the altar, and the young men, when they came in, filled up the church and sat right at the front. They were, of course, of every imaginable social grade; for the French conscription is really strict and universal. Some looked like young criminals, some like young priests, some like both. Some were so obviously prosperous and polished that a barrack room must seem to them like hell; others (by the look of them) had hardly ever been in so decent a place. But it was not so much the mere class variety that most sharply caught an Englishman's eye. It was the presence of just those one or two kinds of men who would never have become soldiers in any other way.

There are many reasons for becoming a soldier. It may be a matter of hereditary luck or abject hunger or heroic virtue of fugitive vice; it may be an interest in the work or a lack of interest in any other work. But there would always be two or three kinds of people who would never tend to soldiering; all those kinds of people were there. A lad with red hair, large ears, and very careful clothing, somehow announced across the church that he had always taken care of his health, not even from thinking about it, but simply because he was told, and that he was one of those who pass from childhood to manhood without any shock of being a man. In the row in front of him there was a very slight and vivid little Jew, of the sort that is a tailor and a Socialist. By one of those accidents that make real life so unlike anything else, he was the one of the company who seemed especially devout. Behind these stiff or sensitive boys were ranged the ranks of their mothers and fathers, with knots and bunches of their little brothers and sisters.

The children kicked their little legs, wriggled about the seats, and gaped at the arched roof while their mothers were on their knees praying their own prayers, and here and there crying. The grey clouds of rain outside gathered. I suppose, more and more; for the deep church continuously darkened. The lads in front began to sing a military hymn in odd, rather strained voices; I could not disentangle the words, but only one perpetual refrain; so that it sounded like:

> Sacrarterumbrrar pour la patrie,
> Valdarkararump pour la patrie.

Then this ceased; and silence continued, the coloured windows growing gloomier and gloomier with the clouds. In the dead stillness a child started crying suddenly and incoherently. In a city far to the north a French diplomatist and a German aristocrat were talking.

I will not make any commentary on the thing that could blur the outline of its almost cruel acruality. I will not talk nor allow anyone else to talk about 'clericalism' and 'militarism'. Those who talk like that are made of the same mud as those who call all the angers of the unfortunate 'Socialism'. The women who were calling in the gloom around me on God and the Mother of God were not 'clericalists'; or, if they were, they had forgotten it. And I will bet my boots the young men were not 'militarists' – quite the other way just then. The priest made a short speech;

he did not utter any priestly dogmas (whatever they are), he uttered platitudes. In such circumstances platitudes are the only possible things to say; because they are true. He began by saying that he supposed a large number of them would be uncommonly glad not to go. They seemed to assent to this particular priestly dogma with even more than their alleged superstitious credulity. He said that war was hateful, and that we all hated it; but that 'in all things reasonable' the law of one's own commonwealth was the voice of God. He spoke about Joan of Arc, and how she had managed to be a bold and successful soldier while still preserving her virtue and practising her religion; then he gave them each a little paper book. To which they replied (after a brief interval for reflection);

> Pongprongpereesklang pour la patrie,
> Tambraugtararronc pour la patrie.

which I feel sure was the best and most pointed reply.

While all this was happening, feelings quite indescribable crowded about my own darkening brain, as the clouds crowded above the darkening church. They were so entirely of the elements and the passions that I cannot utter them in an idea, but only in an image. It seemed to me that we were barricaded in this church, but we could not tell what was happening outside the church. The monstrous and terrible jewels of the windows darkened or glistened under moving shadow or light, but the nature of that light and the shapes of those shadows we did not know and hardly dared to guess. The dream began, I think, with a dim fancy that enemies were already in the town, and that the economous oaken doors were groaning under the hammers. Then I seemed to suppose the town itself had been destroyed by fire, and effaced, as it may be thousands of years hence, and that if I opened the door I should come out on a wilderness as flat and sterile as the sea. Then the vision behind the veil of stone and slate grew wilder with earthquakes. I seemed to see chasms cloven to the foundation of all things, and letting up an infernal dawn. Huge things happily hidden from us had climbed out of the abyss, and were striding about taller than the clouds. And when the darkness crept from the sapphires of Mary to the sanguine garments of St. John, I fancied that some hideous giant was walking round the church and looking, in at each window in turn.

Sometimes, again, I thought of that church with coloured windows as a ship carrying many lanterns struggling in a high sea at night. Sometimes I thought of it as a great coloured lantern itself, hung on an iron chain out of heaven and tossed and swung to and fro by strong wings, the wings of the princes of the air. But I never thought of it or the young men inside it save as something precious and in peril, or of things outside but as something barbaric and enormous.

I know there are some who cannot sympathize with such sentiments of limitation; I know there are some who would feel no touch of the heroic tenderness if some day a young man, with red hair, large ears, and his mother's lozzenges in his pocket, were found dead in uniform in the passes of the Vosges. But on this subject I have heard many philosophies and thought a good deal for myself; and the conclusion I have come to is 'Sacarterumbrrar pour la Patrie', and it is not likely that I shall alter it now.

But when I came out of the church there were none of these things, but only a lot of shops, including a paper-shop, selling papers which announced that the negotiations were proceeding satisfactorily.

The Lion

IN THE town of Belfort I take a chair and I sit down in the street. We talk in a cant phrase of the Man in the Street, but the Frenchman is the man in the street. Things quite central for him are connected with these lamp-posts and pavements; everything from his meals to his martyrdoms. When first an Englishman looks at a French town or village his first feeling is simply that it is uglier than an English town or village; when he looks again he sees that this comparative absence of the picturesque is chiefly expressed in the plain, precipitous fronage of the houses standing up hard and flat out of the street like the card-board houses in a pantomime – a hard angularity allied perhaps to the harshness of French logic. When he looks a third time he sees quite simply that it is all because the houses have no front gardens. The vague English spirit loves to have the entrance to its houses softened by bushes and broken by steps. It likes to have a little anteroom of hedges half in the house and half out of it; a green room in a double sense. The Frenchman desires no such little pathetic ramparts or halting places, for the street itself is a thing natural and familiar to him.

The French have no front gardens; but the street is every man's front garden. There are trees in the street, and sometimes fountains. The street is the Frenchman's tavern, for he drinks in the street. It is his dining-room, for he dines in the street. It is his British Museum, for the statues and monuments in French streets are not, as with us, of the worst but of the best, art of the country, and they are often actually as historical as the Pyramids. The street again is the Frenchman's Parliament, for France has never taken its Chamber of Deputies so seriously as we take our House of Commons, and the quibbles of mere elected nonentities in an official room seem feeble to a people whose fathers have heard the voice of Danton like a trumpet under open heaven, or Victor Hugo shouting from his carriage amid the wreck of the second Republic. And as the Frenchman drinks in the street and dines in the street so also he fights in the street and dies in the street, so that the street can never be common place to him.

Take, for instance, such a simple object as a lamp-post, in London a lamp-post is a comic thing. We think of an intoxicated gentleman embracing it, and recalling ancient friendship. But in Paris a lamp-post is a tragic thing. For we think of tyrants hanged on it, and of an end of the world. There is, or was, a bitter Republican paper in Paris called *La Lanterne*. How funny it would be if there were a Progressive paper in England called *The Lamp Post!* We have said, then, that the Frenchman is the Man in the Street; that he can dine in the street, and die in the street. And if I ever pass through Paris and find him going to bed in the street, I shall say that he is still true to the genius of his civilization. All that is good and all that is evil in France is alike connected with this open-air element French democracy and French indecency are alike part of the desire to have everything out of doors. Compared to a *cafe,* a public-house is a private house.

There were two reasons why all these fancies should float through the mind in the streets of this especial town of Belfort. First of all, it lies close upon the boundary of France and Germany, and boundaries are the most beautiful things in the world. To love anything is to love its boundaries; thus children will always play on the edge of anything. They build castles on the edge of the sea, and can only be restrained by public proclamation and private violence from walking on the edge of the grass. For when we have come to the end of a thing we have come to the beginning of it.

Hence this town seemed all the more French for being on the very margin of Germany, and although there were many

German touches in the place – German names, larger pots of beer, and enormous theatrical barmaids dressed up in outrageous imitation of Alsatian peasants – yet the fixed French colour seemed all the stronger for these specks of something else. All day long and all night long troops of dusty, swarthy, scornful little soldiers went plodding through the streets with an air of stubborn disgust, for German soldiers look as if they despised you, but French soldiers as if they despised you and themselves even more than you. It is a part, I suppose, of the realism of the nation which has made it good at war and science and other things in which what is necessary is combined with what is nasty. And the soldiers and the civilians alike had most of them cropped hair, and that curious kind of head which to the Englishman looks almost brutal, the kind that we call a bullet-head. Indeed, we are speaking very appropriately when we call it a bullet head, for in intellectual history the heads of Frenchman have been bullets – yes, and explosive bullets.

But there was a second reason why in this place one should think particularly of the open-air politics and the open-air art of the French. For this town of Belfort is famous for one of the most typical and powerful of the public monuments of France. From the *cafe* table at which I sit I can see the hill beyond the town on which hangs the high and flat-faced citadel; pierced with many windows, and warmed in the evening light. On the steep hill below it is a huge stone lion, itself as large as a hill. It is hacked out of the cock with a sort of gigantic impressionism. No trivial attempt has been made to make it like a common statue; no attempt to carve the mane into curs, or to distinguish the monster minutely from the earth out of which he rises, shaking the world. The face of the lion has something of the bold conventionality of Assyrian art. The mane of the lion is left like a shapeless cloud of tempest, as if it might literally be said of him that God had clothed his neck with thunder, Even at this distance the thing looks vast, and in some sense prehistoric. Yet it was carved only a little while ago. It commemorates the fact that this town was never taken by the Germans through all the terrible year, but only laid down its arms at last at the command of its own Government. But the spirit of it has been in this land from the beginning – the spirit of something defiant and almost defeated.

As I leave this place and take the railway into Germany news comes thicker and thicker up the streets that Southern France is in a flame, and that there perhaps will be fought out finally the awful modern battle of the rich and poor. And as I pass into quieter places, for the last sign of France on the skyline, I see the Lion of Belfort stand at bay, the last sight of that great people which has never been at peace.

Hilaire Belloc[1]

WHEN I first met Belloc he remarked to the friend who introduced us that he was in low spirits. His low spirits were and are much more uproarious and enlivening than anybody else's high spirits. He talked into the night, and left behind in it a glowing track of good things. When I have said that I mean things that are good, and certainly not merely *bons mots,*[2] I have said all that can be said in the most serious aspect about the man who has made the greatest fight for good things of all the men of my time.

We met between a little Soho paper shop and a little Soho restaurant; his arms and pockets were stuffed with French Nationalist and French Atheist newspapers. He wore a straw hat shading his eyes, which are like a sailor's, and emphasizing his Napoleonic chin. He was talking about King John, who he positively assured me, was *not* (as was often asserted) the best king that ever reigned in England. Still, there were allowances to be made for him, I mean King John, not Belloc, 'He had been Regent,' said Belloc with forbearance, 'and in all the Middle Ages there is no example of a successful Regent'. I, for one, had not come provided with any successful Regents with whom to counter this generalization; and when I came to think of it, it was quite true. I have noticed the same thing about many other sweeping remarks coming from the same source.

The little restaurant to which we went had already become a haunt for three or four of us who held strong but unfashionable views about the South African war, which was then in its earliest prestige. Most of us were writing on the *Speaker,* edited by Mr. J. L. Hammond with an independence of idealism to

1 Joseph-Pierre Hilaire Belloc (1870-1953), French-British poet, historian, essayist and Catholic apologist. His 4-volume *History of England* is among several works remembered for lucidity and graceful versatality.
2 A clever remark: witticism

which I shall always think that we owe much of the cleaner political criticism of today; and Belloc himself was writing in it studies of what proved to be the most baffling irony. To understand how his Latin mastery, especially of historic and foreign things, made him a leader, it is necessary to appreciate something of the peculiar position of that isolated group of 'Pro-Boers'.[1] We were a minority in a minority. Those who honestly disapproved of the Transvaal adventure were few in England; but even of these few a great number, probably the majority, opposed it for reasons not only different but almost contrary to ours. Many were Pacifists, most were Cobdenites;[2] the wisest were healthy but hazy Liberals who rightly felt the tradition of Gladstone to be a safer thing than the opportunism of the Liberal Imperialists. But we might, in very real sense, be more strictly described as Pro-Boers.

That is, we were much more insistent that the Boers were right in fighting than that the English were wrong in fighting. We disliked cosmopolitan peace almost as much as cosmopolitan war; and it was hard to say whether we more despised those who praised war for the gain of money, or those who blamed war for the loss of it. Not a few men then young were already predisposed to this attitude; Mr. F.Y. Eccles, a French scholar and critic of an authority perhaps too fine for fame, was in possession of the whole classical case against such piratical Prussianism; Mr. Hammond himself, with a careful magnanimity, always attacked Imperialism as a false religion and not merely as a conscious fraud; and I myself had my own hobby of the romance of small things, including small commonwealths. But to all these Belloc entered like a man armed, and as with a clang of iron. He brought with him news from the fronts of history;

1 The Afrikaans-speaking descendants of the Huguenot or of the Dutch origin who had fought and lost against the British in 1902.
2 After British politician and a champion of free trade Richard Cobden (1804-1865). The term Most Favoured Nation coined by him continues to rule the international trade and commerce even today.

that French arts could again be rescued by French arms; that cynical Imperialism not only should be fought, but could be fought and was being fought; that the street fighting which was for me a fairy-tab of the future was for him a fact of the past. There were many other uses of his genius, but I am speaking of this first effect of it upon our instinctive and sometimes groping ideals. What he brought into our dream was this Roman appetite for reality and for reason in action, and when he came into the door there entered with him the smell of danger.

There was in him another element of importance which clarified itself in this crisis. It was no small part of the irony in the man that different things strove against each other in him; and these not merely in the common human sense of good against evil, but one good thing against another. The unique attitude of the little group was summed up in him supremely in this; that he did and does humanly and heartily love England, not as a duty but as a pleasure and almost an indulgence; but that he hated as heartily what England seemed trying to become. Out of this appeared in his poetry a sort of fierce doubt or doubt-mindedness which cannot exist in vague and homogeneous Englishmen; something that occasionally amounted to a mixture of loving and loathing. It is marked, for instance, in the fine break in the middle of the happy song of *camaraderie* called *To the Balliol Men Still in South Africa.*

> I have said it before, and I say it again,
> There was treason done and a false word spoken,
> And England under the dregs of men,
> And bribes about and a treaty broken.

It is supremely characteristic of the time that a weighty and respectable weekly gravely offered to publish the poem if that central verse was omitted. This conflict of emotions has an even higher embodiment in that grand and mysterious poem called

The Leader, in which the ghost of the nobler militarism passes by to rebuke the baser:

> And where had been the rout obscene
> Was an army straight with pride,
> A hundred thousand marching men,
> Of squadrons twenty score,
> And after them all the guns, the guns,
> But She went on before.

Since that small riot of ours he may be said without exaggeration to have worked three revolutions: the first in all that was represented by the *Eye-Witness,* now the *New Witness,* the repudiation of both Parliamentary parties for common and detailed corrupt practices; second, the alarum against the huge and silent approach of the Servile State, using Socialists Anti-Socialists alike as its tools: and third, his recent campaign of public education in military affairs. In all these he played the part which he had played for our little party of Pro-Boers. He was a man of action in abstract things. There was supporting his audacity a great sobriety. It is in this sobriety, and perhaps in this only, that he is essentially French; that he belongs to the most individually prudent and the most collectively reckless of peoples. There is indeed a part of him that is romantic and, in the literal sense, erratic; but that is the English part. But the French people take care of the pence that the pounds may be careless of themselves. And Belloc is almost materialist in his details, that he may be what most Englishmen would call mystical, Not to say monstrous, in his aim. In this he is quite in the tradition of the only country of quite successful revolutions. Precisely because France wishes to do wild things, the things must not be too wild. A wild Englishman like Blake or Shelley is content with dreaming them. How Latin is this combination between intellectual economy and energy can be seen by comparing

Belloc with his great forerunner Cobbett, who made war on the same Whiggish wealth and secrecy and in defence of the same human dignity and domesticity. But Cobbett, being solely English, was extravagant in his language even about serious public things, and was widely romantic even when he was merely right. But with Belloc the style is often restrained; it is the substance that is violent. There is many a paragraph of accusation he has written which might almost be called dull but for the dynamite of its meaning.

It is probable that I have dealt too much with the phase of him, for it is the one in which he appears to me as something different, and therefore dramatic. I have not spoken of those glorious and fantastic guide-books which are, as it were, the textbooks of a whole science of Erratics. In these he is borne beyond the world with those poets whom Keats conceived as supping at a celestial 'Mermaid.' But the 'Mermaid' was English – so was Keats. And though Hilaire Belloc may have a French name I think that Peter Wanderwide is an Englishman.

I have said nothing of the most real thing about Belloc, the religion, because it is above this purpose; and nothing of the later attacks on him by the chief Newspaper Trust, because they are much below it. There are, of course, many other reasons for passing such matters over here, including the argument of space; but there is also a small reason of my own, which if not exactly a secret is at least a very natural ground of silence, It is that I entertain a very intimate confidence that in a very little time humanity will be saying, 'Who was this So-and-So with whom Belloc seems to have debated?

The Slavery of Free Verse

THE TRUTH most needed today is that the end is never the right end. The beginning is the right end at which to begin. The modern man has to read everything backwards; as when he reads journalism first and history afterwards – if at all. He is like a blind man exploring an elephant, and condemned to begin at the very tip of its tail. But he is still more unlucky; for when he has a first principle, it is generally the very last principle that he ought to have. He starts, as it were, with one infalliable dogma about the elephant; that its tail is its trunk. He works the wrong way round on principle; and tries to fit all the practical facts to his principle. Because the elephant has no eyes in its tail-end, he calls it a blind elephant; and expatiates on its ignorance, superstition and need of compulsory education. Because it has no tusks at its tail-end he says that tusks are a fantastic flourish attributed to a fabulous creature, an ivory chimera that must have come through the ivory gate. Because it does not as a rule pick up things with its tail, he dismisses the magical story that it can pick up things with its trunk. He probably says it is plainly a piece of anthropomorphism to suppose that an elephant can pack its trunk. The result is that he becomes as pallid and worried as a pessimist; the world to him is not only an elephant, but a white elephant. He does not know what to do with it, and cannot be persuaded of the perfectly simple explanation; which is that he has not made the smallest real attempt to make head or tail of the animal. He will not begin at the right end; because he happens to have come first on the wrong end.

But in nothing do I feel this modern trick, of trusting to a fag-end rather than a first principle, more than in the modern treatment of poetry. With this or that particular metrical form, or unmetrical form, or unmetrical formlessness, I might be content or not, as it achieved some particular effect or not. But the whole general tendency, regarded as an emancipation, seems to me more or less of an enslavement. It seems founded on one subconscious idea; that talk is freer than verse, and that verse, therefore, should claim the freedom of talk. But talk, especially in our time, is not free at all. It is tripped up by trivialities, tamed by conventions, loaded with dead words, thwarted by a thousand meaningless things. It does not liberate the soul so much, when a man can say, 'You always look so nice,' as when he can say, 'But your eternal summer shall not fade.' The first is an awkward and constrained sentence ending with the weakest word ever used, or rather misused, by man. The second is like the gesture of a giant or the sweeping flight of an archangel; it has the very rush of liberty. I do not despise the man who says the first, because he *means* the second; and what he means is more important than what he says, I have always done my best to emphasize the inner dignity of these daily things, in spite of their dull externals; but I do not think it an improvement that the inner spirit itself should grow more external and more dull. It is though right to discourage numbers of prosaic people trying to be poetical; but I think it much more of a bore to watch numbers of poetical people trying to be prosaic. In short, it is another case of tail-foremost philosophy; instead of watering the laurel hedge of the cockney villa, we bribe the cockney to brick in the plant of Apollo.

I have always had the fancy that if a man were really free, he would talk in rhythm and even in rhyme. His most hurried postcard would be a sonnet; and his most hasty wires like hardstrings. He would breathe a song into the telephone; a song which would be a lyric or an epic, according to the time involved in awaiting the call; or in his inevitable altercation with the telephone girl, the duel would be also a duet. He would express his preference among the dishes at dinner in short impromptu poems, combining the more mystical gratitude of grace with a certain epigrammatic terseness, more convenient for domestic good feeling. If Mr. Yeats can say, in exquisite verse, the exact number of bean rows he would like on his plantation, why not the number of beans he would like on his plate? If he can issue a rhymed request to pleasure the honey-bee, why not to pass the honey? Misunderstandings might arise at first with the richer and more fantastic poets: and Francis Thompson might have asked several times for 'the gold skins of undelirious wine' before anybody understood that he wanted the grapes. Nevertheless, I will maintain that his magnificent phrase would be a far more real expression of God's most glorious gift of the vine, than if he had simply said in a peremptory manner 'grapes; especially if the culture of compulsory education had carefully taught him to pronounce it as if it were 'grapes'. And if a man could ask for a potato in the form of a poem, the poem would not be merely a more romantic but a much more realistic rendering of a potato. For a potato is a poem; it is even an ascending scale of poems; beginning at the root, in subterranean grotesques in the Gothic manner, with humps like the deformities of a goblin and eyes like a best of Revelation, and rising up through the green shades of the earth to a crown that has the shape of stars and the hue of heaven.

But the truth behind all this is that expressed in that very ancient mystical notion, the music of the spheres. It is the idea that, at the back of everything, existence begins with a harmony and not a chaos; and, therefore, when we really spread our wings and find a wider freedom, we find it in something more continuous and recurrent, and not on something more fragmentary and crude. Freedom is fullness, especially fullness of life; and a full vessel is more rounded and complete than an empty one, and not less so. To vary Browning's phrase, we find in prose the broken arcs, in poetry the perfect round. Prose is not the freedom of poetry; rather prose is the fragments of poetry. Prose, at least in the prosaic sense, is poetry interrupted, held up and cut off from its course; the chariot of Phœbus stopped by a block in the Strand. But when it begins to move again at all, I think we shall find certain old-fashioned things move with it, such as repetition and even measure, rhythm and even rhyme. We shall discover with horror that the wheels of the chariot go round and round; and even that the horses of the chariot have the usual number of feet.

Anyhow, the right way to encourage the cortege is not to put the cart before the horse. It is not to make poetry more poetical by ignoring what distinguishes it from prose. There may be many new ways of making the chariot move again; but I confess that most of the modern theorists seem to me to be lecturing on a new theory of its mechanics, while it is standing still. If a wizard before my very eyes works a miracle with a rope, a boy and a mango plant, I am only theoretically interested in the question of a sceptic, who asks why it should not be done with a garden hose, a maiden aunt and a monkey-tree. Why not, indeed, if he can do it? If a saint performs a miracle tomorrow, by turning a stone into a fish, I shall be the less concerned at being asked in the abstract, why a man should not also turn a camp-stool into a cockatoo; but let him do it, and not merely explain how it can be done. It is certain that words such as 'birds' and 'sweet', which are as plain as 'fish' or 'stone' can be combined in such a miracle as 'Bare ruined quires where late the sweet birds sang'. So far as I can follow my own feelings, the metres and fall of the feet, even the rhyme and place in the sonnet, have a great deal to do with producing such an effect. I do not say there is no other way of producing such an effect. I only ask, not without longing, where else in this wide and weary time is it produced? I know I cannot produce it; and I do not in fact feel it when I hear *vers libres*. I know not where is that Promethean* heat; and, even to express my ignorance, I am glad to find better words than my own.

---

* Relating to, or resembling Prometheus (who in Greek religion is a god of fire and is associated with the creation of humans. He stole fire from the gods and gave it to humans). Promethean thus connotes anything that is daringly original or creative.

The Surrender of a Cockney

EVERY MAN, though he were born in the very belfry of Bow and spent his infancy climbing among chimneys, has waiting for him somewhere a country house which he has never seen; but which was built for him in the very shape of his soul. It stands patiently waiting to be found, knee deep in orchards of Kent or mirrored in pools of Lincoln; and when the man sees it he remembers it, though he has never seen it before Even I have been forced to confess this at last, who am a Cockney, if ever there was one, Cockney not only on principle, but with savage pride. I have always maintained, quite seriously, that the Lord is not in the wind or thunder of the waste, but if anywhere in the still small voice of Fleet Street. I sincerely maintain that Nature-worship is more morally dangerous than the most vulgar man-worship of the cities; since it can easily be perverted into the worship of an impersonal mystery, carelessness, or cruelty. Thoreau would have been a jollier fellow if he had devoted himself to a green-grocer instead of to greens. Swinburne would have been a better moralist if he had worshipped a fishmonger instead of worshipping the sea. I prefer the philosophy of bricks and mortar to the philosophy of turnips. To call a man a turnip may be playful, but is seldom respectful. But when we wish to pay emphatic honour to a man, to praise the firmness 'of his nature, the squareness of his conduct, the strong humility with which he is interlocked with his equals in silent mutual support, then we invoke the nobler Cockney metaphor, and call him a brick.

But, despite all these theories, I have surrendered; I have struck my colours at sight; at a mere glimpse through the opening of a hedge. I shall come down to living in the country, like any common Socialist or Simple Lifer. I shall end my days in a village, in the character of the Village Idiot, and be a spectacle and a judgment to mankind. I have already learnt the rustic manner of leaning upon a gate; and I was thus gymnastically occupied at the moment when my eye caught the house that was made for me. It stood well back from the road, and was built of a good yellow brick; it was narrow for its height, like the tower of some Border robber; and over the front door was carved in large letters '1908'. That last burst of sincerity, that superb scorn of antiquarian sentiment, overwhelmed me finally. I closed my eyes in a kind of ecstasy. My friend (who was helping me to lean on the gate) asked me with some curiosity what I was doing.

'My dear fellow,' I said with emotion, 'I am bidding farewell to forty-three hansom cabmen'.

'Well, he said, 'I suppose they would think this country rather outside the radius.'

'Oh, my friend' I cried brokenly, 'how beautiful London is. Why do they only write poetry about the country? I could turn every lyric cry into Cockney.

> My heart leaps up when I behold
> A sky-sign in the sky.

as I observed in a volume which is too little read, founded on the older English poets. You never saw my *Golden Treasury Regilded: or, The Classics Made Cockney* – it contained some fine lines.

O Wild West End, thou breath of London's being,......
or the reminiscence of Keats, beginning:

> City of smuts and mellow fogfulness.

I have written many such lines on the beauty of London; yet I never realized that London was really beautiful till now. Do you ask me why? It is because I have left it for ever.'

'If you will take my advice,' said my friend, 'you will humbly endeavour not to be a fool. What is the sense of this mad modern notion that every literary man must live in the country, with the pigs and the donkeys and the squires? Chaucer and Spenser and Milton and Dryden lived in London; Shakespeare and Dr. Johnson came to London because they had had quite enough of the country. And as for trumpery topical journalists like you, why they would cut their throats in the country. You have confessed it yourself in your own last words. You hunger and thirst after the streets; you think London the finest place on the planet. And if by some miracle a Bayswater omnibus could come down this green country lane you would utter a yell of joy.'

Then a light burst upon my brain, and I turned upon him with terrible sternness.

'Why, miserable aesthete,' I said in a voice of thunder, that is the true country spirit. That is how the real rustic feels. The real rustic does utter a yell of joy at the sight of a Bayswater omnibus. The real rustic does think London the finest place on the planet. In the few moments that I have stood by this stile, I have grown rooted here like an ancient tree; I have been here for ages Petulant Suburban, I am the real rustic. I believe that the streets of London are paved with gold; and I mean to see it before I die.'

The evening breeze freshed among the little tossing trees of that lane, and the purple evening clouds piled up and darkened my Country Seat, the house that belonged to me, making, by contrast, its yellow bricks gleam like gold. At last my friend said: "To cut it short, then, you mean that you will live in the country because you won't like it. What on the earth will you do here; dig up the garden?'

'Dig!' I answered, in honourable scorn 'Dig! Do work at my Country Seat; no, thank you. When I find a Country Seat, I sit in it, And for your other objection, you were quite wrong I do not dislike the country, but I like the town more. Therefore the art of happiness certainly suggests that I should live in the country and think about the town. Modern nature-worship is all upside down. Trees and fields ought to be the ordinary things; terraces and temples ought to be the extraordinary. I am on the side of the man who lives in the country and wants to go to London. I abominate and abjure the man who lives in London and wants to go to the country; I do it with all the more heartiness because I am that sort of man myself. We must learn to love London again, as rustics love it. Therefore (I quote again from the Great Cockney version of *The Golden Treasury*)

> Therefore, ye gas-pipes, ye asbestos stoves,
> Forbode not any severing of our loves.
> I have relinquished but your earthly sight,
> To hold you dear in a more distant way.
> I'll love the buses lumbering through the wet,
> Even more than when I lightly tripped as they.
> The grimy colour of the London clay
>   Is lovely yet.

because I have found the house where I was really born; the tall and quiet house from which I can see London afar off, as the miracle of man that it is.'

On Lying in Bed

LYING IN bed would be an altogether perfect and supreme experience if only one had a coloured pencil long enough to draw on the ceiling. This, however, is not generally a part of the domestic apparatus on the premises, I think myself that the thing might be managed with several pails of Aspinall and a broom. Only if one worked in a really sweeping and masterly way, and laid on the colour in great washes, it might drip down again on one's face in floods of rich and mingled colour like some strange fairy rain; and that would have its disadvantages. I am afraid it would be necessary to stick to black and white in this form of artistic composition. To that purpose, indeed, the white ceiling would be of the greatest possible use; in fact, it is the only use I think of a white ceiling being put to.

But for the beautiful experiment of lying in bed I might never have discovered it. For years I have been looking for some blank spaces in a modern house to draw on. Paper is much too small for any really allegorical design; as Cyrano de Bergerac* says, 'Il me faut des geants'. But when I tried to find these fine clear spaces in the modern rooms such as we all live in I was continually disappointed. I found an endless pattern and complication of small objects hung like a curtain of fine links between me and my desire. I examined the walls; I found them to my surprise to be already covered with wallpaper, and I found the wallpaper to be already covered with very uninteresting images, all bearing a ridiculous resemblance to each other. I could not understand why one arbitrary symbol (a symbol apparently entirely devoid of any religious or philosophical significance) should thus be sprinkled all over my nice walls like a sort of smallpox. The Bible must be referring to wallpaper, I think, when it says, 'Use not vain repetitions, as the Gentiles

* French satirist and dramatist (1619-1655).

do'. I found the Turkey carpet a mass of unmeaning colours, rather like the Turkish Empire, or like the sweetmeat called Turkish Delight. I do net exactly know what Turkish Delight really is; but I suppose it is Macedonian Massacres.* Everywhere that I went forlornly, with my pencil or my paint brush, I found that others had unaccountably been before me, spoiling the walls, the curtains, and the furniture with their childish and barbaric designs.

Nowhere did I find a really clear space for sketching until this occasion when I prolonged beyond the proper limit the process of lying on my back in bed. Then the light of that white heaven broke upon my vision, that breadth of mere white which is indeed almost the definition of Paradise, since it means purity and also means freedom. But alas! like all heavens, now that it is seen it is found to be unattainable; it looks more austere and more distant than the blue sky outside the window. For my proposal to paint on it with the bristly end of a broom has been discouraged – never mind by whom; by a person debarred from all political rights – and even my minor proposal to put the other end of the broom into the kitchen fire and turn it into charcoal has not been contended. Yet I am certain that it was from persons in my position that all the original inspiration came for covering the ceiling: of palaces and cathedrals with a riot of fallen angels or victorious gods. I am sure that it was only because Michaelangelo was engaged in the ancient and honourable occupation of lying in bed that he ever realized how the roof of the Sistine Chapel might be mare into an awful imitation of a divine drama that could only be acted in the heavens.

The tone now commonly taken towards the practice of lying in bed is hypocritical and unhealthy. Of all the marks of modernity that seem to mean a kind of decadence, there is none more menacing and dangerous than the exaltation of very

---

* Three devastating wars were fought by Philip V of Macedonia and his successor, Perseus, against Rome (215-205 BC, 200-197, and 171-167 BC).

small and secondary matters of conduct at the expense of very great and primary ones, at the expense of eternal ties and tragic human morality. If there is one thing worse than the modern weakening of major morals it is the modern strengthening of minor morals. Thus it is considered more withering to accuse a man of bad taste than of bad ethics. Cleanliness is not next to godliness nowadays, for cleanliness is made an essential and godliness is regarded as an offence. A playwright can attack the institution of marriage so long as he does not misrepresent the manners of society, and I have met Ibsenite pessimists who thought it wrong to take beer but right to take prussic acid. Especially this is so in matters of hygiene; notably such matters as lying in bed. Instead of being regarded, as it ought to be, as a matter of personal convenience and adjustment, it has come to be regarded by many as if it were a part of essential morals to get up early in the morning. It is upon the whole part of practical wisdom; but there is nothing good about it or bad about its opposite.

Misers get up early in the morning; and burglars, I am informed, get up the night before. It is the great peril of our society that all its mechanism may grow more fixed while its spirit grows more fickle. A man's minor actions and arrangements ought to be free, flexible, creative; the things that should be unchangeable are his principles, his ideals. But with us the reverse is true; our views change constantly; but our lunch does not change. Now, I should like men to have strong and rooted conceptions, but as for their lunch, let them have it sometimes in the garden, sometimes in bed, sometimes on the roof, sometimes in the top of a tree. Let them argue from the same first principles, but let them do it in a bed, or a boat, or a balloon. This alarming growth of good habits really means a too great emphasis on those virtues which mere custom can ensure, it means too little emphasis on those virtues which custom can never quite ensure, sudden and splendid virtues of inspired pity

or of inspired candour. If ever that abrupt appeal is made to us
we may fail. A man can get used to getting up at five o'clock in
the morning. A man cannot very well get used to being burnt for
his opinions; the first experiment is commonly fatal. Let us pay
a little more attention to these possibilities of the heroic and the
unexpected. I dare say that when I get out of this bed I shall do
some deed of an almost terrible virtue.

For those who study the great art of lying in bed there is one
emphatic caution to be added. Even for those who can do their
work in bed (like journalists), still more for those whose work
cannot be done in bed (as, for example, the professional
harpooners of whales), it is obvious that the indulgence must be
very occasional. But that is not the caution I mean. The caution
is this: if you do lie in bed, be sure you do it without any reason
or justification at all. I do not speak, of course, of the seriously
sick. But if a healthy man lies in bed, let him do it without a rag
of excuse; then he will get up a healthy man. If he does it for
some secondary hygienic reason, if he has some scientific
explanation, he may get up a hypochondriac.

About the Workers

IT IS often said, truly, though perhaps not often understood rightly, that extremes meet. But the strange thing is that extremes meet, not so much in being extraordinary, as in being dull. The country where the East and the West are only is a very flat country. For such extremes are generally extreme simplifications; and tend to a type of generalizations flattening out all real types, let alone real personalities. Two of the dreariest things in the world, for instance, are the way in which the snobs among the rich talk about the poor; and the way in which the prigs who profess to have an economic cure for poverty themselves talk about the poor. On the one side, we have the class of people who are always talking about 'the lower classes', thereby proving that they belong to a class very much lower; a class so low that it almost deserves to be called classy. It is sufficiently weak-minded to be proud; but this type is generally merely purse-proud; and as Thackeray said, 'it admires mean things meanly'; for example, it admires itself. To hear such people talking about servants or about working men will be enough to send the wise and good away with a wild impulse to make, if not a barricade, at least a butter-slide. But, curiously enough, there is something that produces almost exactly the same impression on my own feelings; and that is the pedantic way in which all people who happen to by poor are classified by some professors of Socialism or social reform; and even some who are supposed to be working-class representatives themselves. Somehow they seem to talk about the Proletariat* in exactly the same tone of voice in which the wealthier snobs talk about the lower classes. Why, for instance, is it never correct to call them 'the workmen' or 'the working men'; but always crushingly correct to call them 'the workers'? Somehow that word alone, and the ritual repetition of it, seem to discolour and

---

* The lowest-ranking socio-economic classes. Karl Marx's term refers only to the class of wage-earners engaged in industrial production, while for the unemployable workers, paupers, beggars, and criminals, Marx has: *Lumpenproletariat* (lumpen: *rags*).

drain the whole subject of any human interest. To be a workman is perhaps the noblest of all human functions; and I was delighted the other day to hear a speaker describe Mr. Eric Gill, the great sculptor, as 'the first workman in the land.' But the person swallowed up in these sociological generalization is no more the last than the first. He is not a working man became he is not a man; he is not any workman anybody has ever known; he is not the funny Irish bricklayer you talked to when you were a little boy; he is not the plumber of the mysterious plumber's mate; he is not the gardener, who was rather cross; he is not the needy knife-grinder or the romantic rat-catcher. He is one of The Workers; a vast grey horde of people, apparently all exactly alike, like ants; who are always on the march somewhere; presumably to the Ninth or Tenth International. And this dehumanizing way of dealing with people who do most of the practical work on which we depend; merely because they unfortunately have to do it for a wage, is really quite as irritating to anybody with any real popular sympathies as the ignorant contempt of the classes that are established and ought to be educated. And both fail upon the simple point that the most important thing about a workman is that he is a man; a particular sort of biped and that two of him are not a quadruped nor a hundred of him a centipede.

These amusing but annoying habits are but the outer expression of a social truth, which will grow more and more obviously true; but which very few people of any political or social group have yet seen to be true at all. Talking as if I were myself a wild Communist, the voice of the rough and simple masses of the poor, and therefore using the longest words I can and putting what I mean as pedantically and polysyllabically as possible. I might state the matter thus. The sociology of capitalistic industrialism began with an identification with individualism; but its ultimate organization has corresponded to a complete loss of individuality. So far so bad. But what is even worse, the sort of constructive discontent, in revolt against it, which is still most common in the varieties of popular opinion, has itself inherited and carried on this indifference to individuality. For Communism is the child and heir of Capitalism; and would still greatly resemble his father, even if he had really killed him. Even if we had what is called the Dictatorship of the Proletariat, there would be the same mechanical monotony in dealing with the mob of Dictators as in dealing with the mob of wage-slaves. There would be, in practice, exactly the same sense of swarms of featureless human beings, swarms of human beings who were hardly human, swarms coming out of a hive, whether to store or to sting. And when I thought of that word, I suddenly realized why I so intensely disliked the other words I have mentioned; for, now I come to think of it, I believe there is one whole section of such insects that is called 'the workers'.

Upon this similarity, generally called a conflict, between an industrial order and an equally industrial revolution, is largely founded that third thesis, on which I have sometimes touched; the insistence on true individualism instead of false individualism; the distribution of private property to the individual citizens and individual families, I am not now arguing about its political prospects or economic effectiveness; though they are much more hopeful than most modern people suppose. I am thinking of it merely in relation to the sweeping criticism and the swarming crowd; the general tendency of people at both extremes to simplify the problem either by contempt or by pedantry. I mean that some of us think the Irish bricklayer might be even funnier if he were as free as the Irish peasant; that if the plumber always owned his own tools, he might sometimes neglect to leave them behind; that though, a man can be cross as well as contented with his own garden, the fact of ownership itself tends on the whole to contentment; and that even discontent of that sort does not mean that a man is at once discontented and indistinguishable or invisible; or reduced to making a vague noise out of the voices of many nameless men, like the buzzing of bees in his back garden. For I do not believe that any human being is fundamentally happier for being finally lost in a crowd, even if it is called a crowd of comrades; I do not believe that the humorous human vanities can have vanished quite so completely from anybody as that; I think every man must desire more or less to figure as a figure, and not merely as a moving landscape, even if it be a landscape made of figures. I cannot believe that men are quite so different that any of them want to be the same I admit that the brigading of men for the purposes of social protest may have some of the justification of a just war. I even admit that the menace of such a war may palliate the panic-stricken arrogance of some of the ignorant rich, who do not know what the war is about. But I repeat that in both cases I think the habit of dealing with men in the mass, not merely on abnormal occasions, as in a war or a strike, but in normal circumstances and as a part of ordinary social speech, is a very bad way of trying to understand the human animal. There are only a few animals, and they are not human animals, who can be best judged or best employed in packs or herds. Some may compare the workers of a Communist state to a pack of wolves; I should very strongly suspect that they bear more resemblance to a flock of sheep. But neither of these animals can be said to have a very complex or entertaining type of mentality; few of us would be eager to listen, even if we could to the flowing and continuous reminiscences of a sheep; and St. Francis* seems to have been the only man who was ever on intimate terms with a wolf. It is precisely because man is the most interesting of the creatures, that he finds his proper place among those creatures who dig a domestic hole or hang up an individual nest; and the disgrace of our society is not when he has not a hive or an ant hill; but when, among so many nests and holes, he has not where to lay his head.

---

* Italian saint and founder of the Franciscan religious order, St. Francis of Assisi; orig. Francesco di Pietro di Bernardone (1181-1226). He stressed the need to imitate the life of Jesus. In many ways a mystic, Francis viewed all nature as His image, treating all creatures as his brothers and sisters.

The Tower

I HAVE been standing where everybody has stood, opposite the great Belfry Tower of Bruges, and thinking, as everyone has thought (though not, perhaps, said) that it is built in defiance of all decencies of architecture. It is made in deliberate disproportion to achieve the one startling effect of height. It is a church on stilts. But this sort of sublime deformity is characteristic of the whole fancy and energy of these Flemish cities. Flanders has the flattest and most prosaic of landscapes, but the most violent and extravagant of buildings. Here Nature is tame; it is civilization that is untamable. Here the fields are as flat as a paved square; but, on the other hand, the streets and roofs are as uproarious as a forest in a great wind. The waters of wood and meadow slide as smoothly and meekly as if they were in the London water-pipes. But the parish pump is carved with all the creatures out of the wilderness. Part of this is true, of course, of all art. We talk of wild animals, but the wildest animal is man. There are sounds in music that are more ancient and awful than the cry of the strangest beast at night. And so also there are buildings that are shapeless in their strength, seeming to lift themselves slowly like monsters from the primal mire, and there are spires that seen to fly up suddenly like a startled bird.

This savagery even in stone is the expression of the special spirit in humanity. All the beasts of the field are respectable; it is only man who has broken loose. All animals are domestic animals; only man has remained ever undomestic. All animals are tame animals; it is only we who are wild. And doubtless, also, while this queer energy is common to all human art, it is also generally characteristic of Christian art among the arts of the world. This is what people really mean when they say that Christianity is barbaric, and arose in ignorance. As a matter of historic fact, it didn't; it arose in the most equally civilized period the world has ever seen.

But it is true that there is something in it that breaks the
outline of perfect and conventional beauty, something that dots
with anger the blind eyes of the Apollo and lashes to a cavalry
charge the horses of the Elgin Marbles. Christianity is savage, in
the sense that it is primeval; there is in it a touch of the nigger
hymn. I remember a debate in which I had praised militant
music in ritual, and someone asked me if I could imagine Christ
walking down the street before a brass band. I said I could
imagine it with the greatest ease; for Christ definitely approved a
natural noisiness at a great moment. When the street children
shouted too loud, certain priggish disciple did begin to rebuke
them in the name of good taste. He said: 'If these were silent the
very stones would cry out.' With these words He called up all
the wealth of artistic creation that has been founded on this
creed. With those words He founded Gothic architecture. For in
a town like this, which seems to have grown Gothic as a wood
grows leaves, anywhere and anyhow, any odd brick or
moulding may be carved off into a shouting face. The front of
vast buildings is thronged with open mouths, angels praising
God or devils defying Him. Rock itself is racked and twisted,
until it seems to stream. The miracle is accomplished; the very
stones cry out.

But though this furious fancy is certainly a speciality of men
among creatures, and of Christian art among arts, it is still most
notable in the art of Flanders. All Gothic buildings are full of
extravagant things in detail: but this is an extravagant thing in
design. All Christian temples worth talking about have
gargoyles; but Bruges Belfry is a gargoyle. It is an unnaturally
long-necked animal, like a giraffe. The same impression of
exaggeration is forced on the mind at every corner of a Flemish
town. And if anyone asks, 'Why did the people of these flat
countries instinctively raise these riotous and towering
monuments?' the only answer one can give is, 'Because they
were the people of these flat countries.' If anyone asks, 'Why

did the men of Bruges sacrifice architecture and everything to the sense of dizzy and divine heights?' we can only answer, 'Because Nature gave them no encouragement to do so.'

As I stare at the Belfry, I think with a sort of smile of some of my friends in London who are quite sure of how children will turn out if you give them what they call 'the right environment'. It is a troublesome thing, environment, for it sometimes works positively and sometimes negatively, and more often between the two. A beautiful environment may make a child love beauty; it may make him bored with beauty; most likely the two effects will mix and neutralize each other. Most likely, that is, the environment will make hardly any difference at all. In the scientific style of history (which was recently fashionable, and is still conventional) we always had a list of countries that had owed their characteristics to their physical conditions.

Thus Spaniards (it was said) are passionate because their country is hot; Scandinavians adventurous because their country is cold; Englishmen naval because they are islanders; Switzers free because they are mountaineers. It is all very nice in its way. Only unfortunately I am quite certain that I could make up quite as long a list exactly contrary in its argument, point-blank against the influence of their geographical environment. Thus Spaniards have discovered more continents than Scandinavians, because their hot climate discouraged them from exertion. Thus Dutchmen have fought for their freedom quite as bravely as Switzers, because the Dutch have no mountains. Thus pagan Greece and Rome and many Mediterranean peoples have specially hated the sea, because they had the nicest sea to deal with, the easiest sea to manage. I could extend the list for ever.

But however long it was, two examples would certainly stand up in it as pre-eminent and unquestionable. The first is that the Swiss, who live under staggering precipices and spires of eternal snow, have produced no art or literature at all, and are by far the most mundane, sensible, and business-like people in Europe. The other is that the people of Belgium, who live in a country like a carpet, have, by an inner energy, desired to exalt their towers till they struck the stars.

As it is therefore quite doubtful whether a person will go specially with his environment or specially against his environment, I cannot comfort myself with the thought that the modern discussions about environment are of much practical value. But I think I will not write any more about these modern theories, but go on looking at the Belfry of Bruges. I would give them the greater attention if I were not pretty well convinced that the theories will have disappeared a long time before the Belfry.

On Leisure

A GREAT part of the modern thought arises from confusion and contradiction about the word 'leisure'. To begin with, of course, it should never be confused for a moment with the word 'liberty'. An artist has liberty, if be is free to create any image in any material that he chooses. But anyone who will try to create anything out of anything will soon discover that it is not a leisurely occupation. On the other hand, a slave may have many hours of leisure, if the overseer has gone to sleep, or if there is no work for him to do at the moment, but he must be ready to do the work at any moment. The point is not so much that the master owns his toil as that he owns his time. But there are other difficulties and double meanings about the term, as it is used in a society like ours at present. If a man is practically compelled, by a sort of social pressure, to ride in the park in the morning or play golf in the afternoon or go out to grand dinners in the evening or finish up at night clubs at night, we describe all those hours of his day as hours of leisure. But they are not hours of leisure at all, in the other sense, as, for instance, on the fanciful supposition that he would like a little time to himself, that he would like to pursue a quite solitary and even unsociable hobby, that he would like really to idle, or, on a more remote hypothesis, that he would like really to think. Now when modern social philosophers are generalizing about labour and leisure and the greater or less degree of liberty for men and women in the modern world, they necessarily lump all these different meanings of leisure together and bring out a result that is not really representative. The weakness of all statistics is that, even when the numbers are generally right, the names are generally wrong. I mean that if somebody says there are so many Christians in Margate or in Mesopotamia, it is obvious that they are assuming that everybody is agreed on what is meant by a Christian. And we have sometimes seen even Christians who appeared to differ on the point. If somebody says that there is a certain percentage of educated people in Heliopolis, Neb., he will very likely say it as firmly as he would say that there are so many negroes in that Nebraskan seat of culture. Whereas it is rather as if he were saying that there were so many opinionated people, which is a matter of opinion. Even the negro question, now I come to think of it, is considerably less concrete than such severe statisticians make it. There are probably almost as many shades of brown as there are shades of education. Before I went to America, I always thought the expression 'coloured people' was as fantastic as a fairy-tale; it sounded as if some of the people were peacock green and others a rich mauve or magenta. I supposed that it was either a sort of joke, or else a sort of semi-ironical euphemism or parody of politeness. But when I went there, I found that it was simply a dull description of fact. These people really are all colours; at least they are all shades of one colour. There must be many more coloured people than there are black people. I will not insist on the delicate parallel between colour and culture. I will not inquire whether a completely educated person is a more or less rare and refreshing sight than a completely coal-black negro. I merely point out that when people talk about 'educational statistics' and make tables of the condition of culture in Nebraska or anywhere else, there is really nothing in their statements that is exact except the numbers; and the numbers must be inexact when there is nothing to apply them to. The statistician is trying to make a rigid and unchangeable chain out of elastic links.

All this is obvious enough; but it has been less generally noticed that the same applies to the legal and economic statements made nowadays about work and recreation and the rest. In their nature they deal exclusively with the quantity and not at all with the quality. Least of all has anybody dealt adequately with the effect of a social system on the quality of leisure. When we say lightly about a man in some employment or other, 'What holidays does he get? we only mean it in the sense of 'How many holidays does he get?' or 'How long are his holidays? We do not put the question to ourselves in the form, 'What sort of holidays does the general system of society allow him to get? I am not arguing at the moment that anybody is indifferent to the welfare of any other person in particular; or that any other persons, past or present, had better holidays or ideal holidays; all that is connected with very much wider controversies. I am only pointing out that the structure of society does determine the nature of a man's leisure, almost as much as the nature of his labour. And I am pointing out that of all such statistical tables the most misleading may be a time-table.

It is obvious enough that there are men in the world who seem to labour in a very leisurely way. It is still more obvious that there are men who seem to enjoy their leisure in a very laborious way. And of course it is a very difficult question of psychology to consider which of them gets the most out of life, or whether either of them gets as much as there is to be got. But when people come to making magnificent and sweeping generalizations about history and progress, when they tell us emphatically that science declares this and that about the relative wisdom or welfare of different societies it is obvious that these sociological dogmas are very lax and inconclusive indeed. We have no exact way of testing the proportion of people in any society who really enjoy its social institutions more than they had been trained with a different social sense. Nobody knows, for instance, whether the noise of modern London is not actually a friction to the nerves, which diminishes pleasure even while it drives people on to more pleasure. It is no answer to say that the people are driven to become yet noisier in order to forget the noise. It is no answer to the question of whether, as a fact, people would be happier if they had less friction, even if they seemed to have less fun. There is no way of measuring happiness in that scientific sense; and the scientists who try to do it do not prove anything, except that they have never had any. Nobody can prove positively, for instance, whether the strategical excitement of organized games is great enough to outweigh the loss of personal self-determination and adventure. A man can only say which of the two he likes best himself;, and I have no difficulty at all in saying that. But in modern schools, for instance, what is called playtime has become a sort of extended work-time though both have probably been turned into rather more pleasant work. But none of it is so pleasant as playing alone to the sort of child who likes playing alone. Some of it is acutely and painfully unpleasant to that sort of child. It is obvious that sumptuous preparations for playing the latest professional form of American baseball are no consolation to one who has a solitary genius for playing the fiddle or playing the fool. It may even be questioned whether playing tennis is always a substitute for playing truant. Since education permitted more play, it has perhaps permitted less leisure; and certainly less liberty.

I think the name of leisure has come to cover three totally different things. The first is being allowed to do something. The second is being allowed to do anything. And the third (and perhaps most rare and precious) is being allowed to do nothing. Of the first we have undoubtedly a vast and very profitable increase in recent social arrangements. Undoubtedly there is much more elaborate equipment and opportunity for golfers to play golf, for bridge-players to play bridge, for jazzers to jazz or for motorists to motor. But those who find themselves in the world where these recreations are provided will find that the modern world is not really a universal provider. They will find it made more and more easy to get some things and impossible to get others. The second sort of leisure is certainly not increased, and is on the whole lessened. The sense of having a certain material in hand, which a man may mould into *any* form he chooses, this is a sort of pleasure

now almost confined to artists. Private property ought to mean
that a man feels about bricks and mortar as an artist feels
about clay and marble, It ought to mean that gardening,
whether or no it can be landscape-gardening, is as personal as
landscape-painting. But this special sentiment can hardly
flourish among those who live in public gardens or large
hotels. And as for the third form of leisure, the most precious,
the most consoling, the most pure and holy, the noble habit of
doing nothing at all – that is being neglected in a degree which
seems to me to threaten the degeneration of the whole race. It
is because artists do not practise, patrons do not patronize,
crowds do not assemble to reverently worship the great work
of 'Doing Nothing' that the world has lost its philosophy and
even failed to invent a new religion.

On Monsters

I saw in an illustrated paper – which sparkles with scientific news – that a green-blooded fish had been found in the sea; indeed, a creature that was completely green, down to this uncanny ichor in its veins, and very big and venomous at that. Somehow I could not get it out of my head, because the caption suggested a perfect refrain for a Ballade: A green-blooded fish has been found in the sea. It has so wide a critical and philosophical application. I have known so many green-blooded fish on the land, walking about the streets and sitting in the clubs, and especially the committees. So many green-blooded fish have written books and criticism of books, have taught in academies of learning and founded schools of philosophy, that they have almost made themselves the typical biological product of the present stage of evolution. There is never a debate in the House of Commons, especially about Eugenics or The Compulsory Amputation of Poor People, without several green-blooded fishes standing up on their tails to talk. There is never a petition, or a letter to the Press, urging the transformation of taverns into teashops or local museums, without a whole string of green-blooded fish hanging on to the tail of it, and pretty stinking fish too. But for some reason the burden of this non-existent Ballade ran continually in my head, and somehow turned my thoughts in the direction of poisonous monsters in general; of all those dragons and demi-dragons and devouring creatures which appear in primitive stories as the chief enemies of man. It has been suggested that these legends really refer to some period when prehistoric man had to contend with huge animals that have since died out. And then the thought occurred to me: Suppose the primitive heroes killed them just when they were dying out. I mean, suppose they would have died out, even if the Cave Man had sat comfortably in his Cave and not troubled to kill them.

Suppose Perseus* turned the sea-monster into a rock at the very moment when it was well on its way to becoming a fossil. Suppose St. George arrived, not only just before the death of the Princess, but just before the death of the Dragon. Suppose he burst in, rather tactlessly, so to speak, on the deathbed of the dragon, and only finished him off with a lance when the dragon-doctor had done the real work with a lancet. In short, is it possible that the heroes might have saved themselves the trouble of fighting, if they had only felt the pulse or taken the temperature of the expiring foe of mankind? The dragon is always represented with wide-open jaws, darting out a forked and flaming tongue. But perhaps he is only putting his tongue out to be examined by his private physician. Perhaps all the monsters, when they appear in song and story, were in a bad way, physically as well as morally. Now I come to think of it, that might explain the green-blooded fish that was found in the sea. Perhaps he is not a species, but a disease. Perhaps the green-blooded fish was suffering, if not exactly from anæmia, at least from some subtle form of chloraemia pisciana, or whatever this obscure malady will be called when it is discovered. I suppose a fish in the sea could hardly be green with sea-sickness. Anyhow, there are biological theorists even on land, who have lately begun to look rather fishy.

The fancy might make many variants in the fairy-tales. They always narrate how the cavern of the monster or giant is surrounded by the bones of thousands of victims. We can imagine the hero carefully counting them and making calculations about the stage of indigestion at which any monster must have arrived after such a meal. In the special department of Giants there is a story about Jack the Giant-killer and a hasty-pudding, which the Giant at least devoured. I do not know what a hasty-pudding is, but I gather that in this case the meal was somewhat hasty. All this could not be good for the health of Giants as a class. And

---

* In Greek mythology he is the son of Zeus the chief deity of the pantheon, and Danaë, and was thrown into the sea by his grandfather to escape a prophesy of death.

Dickens, who had known several Giants, as they appear in travelling-shows, testified to their delicate constitutions. But I admit that, while my rambling subconsciousness ran on this ancient theme, I was beginning to think of its modern application I sometimes wonder whether it is worth while to attack every monster of modern anarchy and absurdity as it appears in the realm of thought, or whether they would kill themselves even if they were not killed. Sometimes they seem to kill themselves almost too fast to be killed. Some I can remember making war on for months who have now been dead for years. I can remember giants of blasphemy or barbican philosophy; giants so gigantic that they seemed not only darken the earth, but block out the heavens. They defied the world like Goliath, and all were warned against accepting the challenge in sight of all the bones about their caverns. But now it is their own bones that are scattered, and even a rag-and-bone man will hardly stoop to pick them up.

For instance, there was Haeckel* and the hard concrete Materialism of his day. For years on end I filled my life with fighting Mr. Blatchford and others about it, and pointing out the fallacies, not to say falsehoods, of Haeckel. And where is he now? Mr. Blatchford has forgotten all about Haeckel, and so has everybody else. The new men of science have completely repudiated him. But I remember when every new man of science, and especially of the new science of sociology or eugenics (a green-blooded fish has been found in the sea), accepted him as the founder of a new religion. And when Mr. Belloc wrote the envoi of another Ballade – '

> Prince, if you meet upon a bus
> A man who makes a great display
> Of Dr. Haeckel, argue thus,
> The wind has blown them all away —

---

* Ernst Haeckel (1834-1919), famous German zoologist and evolutionist who created the first genealogical tree of the entire animal kingdom, drawing attention to many vital biological questions.

it really sounded like an audacity or a daring prophecy. Whereas now it sounds like a truism, because it has come true.

Then there came Lombroso,[1] and all the quackery that was called Criminology. I can remember when the name of Lombroso was like the name of Newton or of Faraday; but I do not often see it mentioned now, least of all among men of science. It is to the enduring glory of Mr. H. G. Wells that even in those days, though on the materialist side in many matters, he protested against the premature dogmatism of the prigs who talked about 'the criminal skull' or 'the criminal ear', and who called the young and earnest to stamp out hereditary criminal tendencies by selection or segregation (a green-blooded fish has been found in the sea). Was it worthwhile to argue against the great Science of Criminology in the later nineteenth century? the dragon would have died a natural death, if anything about him could be natural.

I could give any number of other cases; of other controversies with things I thought dominant which were in fact dying; which are in fact dead. There was the proposal that people too poor to bring actions for libel should be put on a Black List as blackguards who were too fond of beer (a green-blooded fish has been found in the sea); there was the absurd theory that being too fond of beer is hereditary, and the proposal (moved by the fish) that the beer-drinker should be forbidden children. There was the whole assumption that anything done by a State Department would be perfect and that Supervisors are Supermen. That was once our nightmare; but flogging it was flogging a dead horse, or at least a dying horse, and I rather repent of my inhumanity.

1 Cesare Lombroso's *Crime* (1876), was an acclaimed work in early penology (science of punishment of crime and management of prisoners).

A Dead Poet

WITH FRANCIS Thompson we lost the greatest poetic energy since Browning. His energy was of somewhat the same kind. Browning was intellectually intricate because he was morally simple. He was too simple to explain himself; he was too humble to suppose that other people needed any explanation. But his real energy, and the real energy of Francis Thompson, was best expressed in the fact that both poets were at once fond of immensity and also fond of detail. Any common Imperialist can have large ideas so long as he is not called upon to have small ideas also. Any common scientific philosopher can have small ideas so long as he is not called upon to have large ideas as well. But great poets use the telescope and also the microscope. Great poets are obscure for two opposite reasons; now, became they are talking about something too large for anyone to understand, and now again because they are talking about something too small for anyone to see. Francis Thompson possessed both these infinities. He escaped by being too small, as the microbe escapes; or he escaped by being too large, as the universe escapes. Anyone who knows Francis Thompson's poetry knows quite well the truth to which I refer. For the benefit of any person who does not know it, I may mention two cases taken from memory. I have not the book by me, so I can only render the poetical passages in a clumsy paraphrase. But there was one poem of which the image was so vast that it was literally difficult for a time to take it in; he was describing the evening, earth with its mist and fume and fragrance, and represented the whole as rolling upwards like a smoke; then suddenly he called the whole ball of the earth a thurible, and said that some gigantic spirit swung it slowly before God. That is the case of the image too large for comprehension. Another instance sticks in my mind of the image which is too small. In one of his poems, he says that abyss between the known and the unknown is bridged by 'Pontifical death'. There are about ten historical and theological puns in that one word. That a priest means a pontiff, that a pontiff means a bridge-maker, that death is certainly a bridge, that death may turn out after all to be a reconciling priest, that at least priests and bridges both attest to the fact that one thing can get separated from another thing – these ideas, and twenty more, are all actually concentrated in the word 'pontifical'. In Francis Thompson's poetry, as in the poetry of the universe, you can work infinitely out and out, but yet infinitely in and in. These two infinities are the mark of greatness; and he was a great poet.

Beneath the tide of praise which was obviously due to the dead poet, there is an evident undercurrent of discussion about him; some charges of moral weakness were at least important enough to be authoritatively contradicted in the *Nation;* and, in connexion with this and other things, there has been a continuous stir of comment upon his attraction to and gradual absorption in Catholic theological ideas. This question is so important that I think it ought to be considered and understood even at the present time. It is, of course, true that Francis Thompson devoted himself more and more to poems not only purely Catholic, but, one may say, purely ecclesiastical. And it is, moreover, true that (if things go on as they are going on at present) more and more good poets will do the same. Poets will tend towards Christian orthodoxy for a perfectly plain reason; because it is about the simplest and freest thing now left in the world. On this point it is very necessary to be clear. When people impute special vices to the Christian Church, they seem entirely to forget that the world (which is the only other thing there is) has these vices much more. The Church has been cruel; but the world has been much more cruel. The Church has plotted; but the world has plotted much more. The Church has been superstitious; but it has never been so superstitious as the world is when left to itself.

Now, poets in our epoch will tend towards ecclesiastical religion strictly because it is just a little more free than anything else. Take, for instance, the case of symbol and ritualism. All reasonable men believe in symbol; but some reasonable men do not believe in ritualism; by which they mean, I imagine, a symbolism too complex, elaborate, and mechanical. But whenever they talk of ritualism they always seem to mean the ritualism of the Church. Why should they not mean the ritual of the world? It is much more ritualistic. The ritual of the Army, the ritual of the Navy, the ritual of the Law Courts, the ritual of Parliament are much more ritualistic. The ritual of a dinner-party is much more ritualistic. Priests may put gold and great jewels on the chalice; but at least there is only one chalice to put them on. When you go to a dinner party they put in front of you five different chalices, of five weird and heraldic shapes, to symbolize five different kinds of wine; an insane extension of ritual. A bishop wears a mitre; but he is not thought more or less of a bishop according to whether you can see the very latest curves in his mitre. But a swell is thought more or less of a swell according to whether you can see the very latest curves in his hat. There is more *fuss* about symbols in the world than in the Church.

And yet (strangely enough) though men fuss more about the worldly symbol, they mean less by them, it is the mark of religious forms that they declare something unknown. But it is the mark of worldly forms that they declare something which is known, and which is known to be untrue. When the Pope in an Encyclical calls himself your father, it is a matter of faith or of doubt. But when the Duke of Devonshire in a letter calls himself yours obediently, you know that he means the opposite of what he says. Religious forms are at the worst, fables; they might be true. Secular forms are falsehoods; they are not true......

Now, poetical people like Francis Thompson will, as things stand, tend away from secular society and towards religion for the reason above described: that there are crowds of symbols in both, but that those of religion are simpler and mean more. To take an evident type, the Cross is more poetical than the Union Jack, because it is simpler. The more simple an idea is, the more it is fertile in variations. Francis Thompson could have written any number of good poems on the Cross, because it is a primary symbol. The number of poems which Mr. Rudyard Kipling could write on the Union Jack, is, fortunately, limited, because the Union Jack is too complex to produce luxuriance. The same principle applies to any possible number of cases. A poet like Francis Thompson could deduce perpetually rich and branching meanings out of two plain facts like bread and wine; with bread and wine he can expand everything to everywhere. But with a French menu he cannot expand anything; except perhaps himself. Complicated ideas do not produce any more ideas. Mongrels do not breed. Religious ritual attracts because there is some sense in it. Religious imagery, so far from being subtle, is the only simple thing left for poets. So far from being merely superhuman, it is the only human thing left for human beings.

On Mammoth Portraiture

WHEN I first heard of the scheme for carving colossal heads of American heroes out of the everlasting hills, the scheme (I think) of the American sculptor, Mr. Borglum,* I felt again the thrill first given to me in childhood in reading Nathaniel Hawthorne's fantasy of *The Great Stone Face*. It is not unnatural that two great American artists, in different departments, should have dreamed similar dreams; for the whole conception not only arises out of but really requires the vast American background of prairies and mountain-chains. Any one will feel, I think, that it would be rather too big for England. It would be rather alarming for the Englishmen returning by boat to Dover, to see that Shakespeare's Cliff had suddenly turned into Shakespeare. We had a distinguished portrait-painter named Beechey, but none of his portraits is quite on the scale of Beachy Head. And the most intrepid mountaineer might well be staggered if, when scaling the steep face of Snowdon, he saw the cold and stony face of Lord Snowden, that far from extinct volcano. Though the heads in the American experiment are those of statesmen, they are mostly those of statesmen who have passed to where politician cease from troubling and, at any rate, cease from taxing. But this does not altogether get rid of a further difficulty, even in the more appropriate and spacious American atmosphere.

It is unlucky that at the moment when America can carve permanent historical monuments there has been some loss of permanence in historical theories. America is stronger than any other State just now in certain kinds of architecture and architectural sculpture, suggestive of the stark and starry altitudes of Egypt and Assyria. But the ideas in those designs are

* John Gutzon (de la Mothe) Borglum (1867-1941) born to Danish immigrant parents; famous for his carving of Lincoln bust and making of Mt. Rushmore Memorial in South Dakota, USA.

either dead or indestructible. In modern history, however, one man has been trying to 'debunk' Washington in a book, while another man has been moulding him out of a mountain. What does the 'debunker' do in this contest? Does he buy another mountain; and carve another and less pleasing portrait of Washington? Will he prove that the great man was small, by exhibiting his smallness on a large scale? There remains a very fine head of Rameses III, the Pharaoh of the – Exodus. But we have got a colossal caricature of him – by Moses.

That is the mischief with the modern world. We might make more permanent records of our opinions. But we have not got more permanent opinions to record. In every sense we are strong in the concrete; but very wobbly in the abstract. But that is a large matter than the largest statue, and we cannot conclude upon it here. For my part, I sometimes think public monuments ought to be too large to be seen. I suggest that there should be a now art, plotting out large spaces of the earth in coloured pictures of turf or clay, only to be seen from a skyscraper or a flying-ship. Instead of disfiguring the sky with aviators writing advertisements that everybody can see, let us plan out the earth in gigantic figures that only aviators can see. Then anybody who wants to be an aesthete, and talk about Art, can pay a stiff sum to go up to a dizzy and uncomfortable height, and see his own very exclusive portrait gallery spread out before him, over hill and dale, or even over country and province. For things can be kept secret by being large as well as by being small. Hitherto it has been assumed that size and scale in the arts belonged only to things vertical and solid; to architecture, or at least to sculpture, and that pictures painted in the flat belonged to a world of smaller things, in some cases even concentrating in illuminated missals or in miniatures. By the trifling reform or experiment which I suggest, it would be possible to make pictures more colossal than the most colossal buildings I will even confess to a weakness for the fancy; there is something faintly stirring to the imagination in the notion of the whole earth traced out in the shapes of Titans, the earth's huge but forgotten children; or in using the raw colours of geology and the vaster forms of vegetation to fit together into the unity of a sprawling figure or a staring face it would hardly be safe, of course, to assume that geological areas are plainly coloured like a map; I do not know whether Yellowstone Park is really yellow or the Black Forest really black; in spite of my simple and romantic mind, I am aware that the Red Sea is not red. But, the reds and browns and purples of the desert beside the Red Sea would make excellent material for a certain style of portrait-painting; an admirable if not an enviable complexion. Only, as I say, the aesthete would have to be an aviator, and this alone would probably diminish the number of aesthetes. So that, in a sort of way, I should be a reformer after all. As these vast portraits would be invisible, in a general sense, I suppose it would not matter very much whose portraits they were. But, as a general principle of propriety I suppose they should only represent men whose names have really gone to the ends of the earth, figures of great national and international power. Meanwhile, the rest of us would never see them and never trouble about them. We should go on living happily and innocently in the woodlands of Abraham Lincoln's whiskers, or in the pleasantly shady district not far from the eyebrow of Charles James Fox, without being presented about Art at all.

It is a fine, large scheme, and more sensible than most large schemes I know. For that would appear to be the logical end of all that pursuit of pure largeness, as such, which has been so much the mark of our time; and has even intoxicated some of the finest intellects of our time, like that of Mr. H.G. Wells. The end of the process of expansion would seem to be disappearance; the vanishing of these vast things from the restricted senses and calculations of man. It is the ultimate upshot of the skyscraper; and upshot seems to be an oddly appropriate term. It is the end that the edifice should tower so high that we cannot see its towers; that the sky-sign should sprawl so wide that we cannot read its lettering: that we should be left, exactly like the people in my parable of the painted earth, living too close to things that are too large. I do not say it is very probable that things will ever go as far as that chiefly because I think it much more probable that, long before that happens, people will have developed a taste for something totally different; perhaps for things that are microscopically small. But the builders, of the big buildings, and the painters of the huge hoardings, do not propose to themselves any logical process except that of making things larger and larger, and therefore have no logical end except to make them too large to bother about.

There is another way in which the parable is really a plain truth; and, indeed, a practical problem. Our relation to modern schemes and systems, to the institutions under which we live and the international influences by which they are extended, is very like the relation of a man living like a pigmy in a city of giants. We have lost the power to control things, largely because we have lost the power to oversee them; that is, to see them as a whole. The economic disasters we suffer are largely due to the operations having grown too large even for the operators. We are all dotted about like little pins stuck in a vast map of financial statesmanship, or rather, financial strategy; it is a plan or chart far too voluminous and bewildering to be at present mastered by any public opinion, and the pins cannot use their pin's heads. If there are any persons who do understand it, they are much fewer than the aviators who would mount aloft to see the picture of the whole earth.

On Turnpikes and Medievalism

OPENING MY newspaper the other day, I saw a short but emphatic leaderette entitled 'A Relic of Medievalism'. It expressed a profound indignation upon the fact that somewhere or other, in some fairly remote corner of this country, there is a turnpike-gate, with a toll. It insisted that this antiquated tyranny is insupportable, because it is supremely important that our road traffic should go very fast; presumably a little faster than it does. So it described the momentary delay in this place as a relic of medievalism. I fear the future will look at that sentence, somewhat sadly and a little contemptuously, as a very typical relic of modernism. I mean it will be a melancholy relic of the only period in all human history when people were proud of being modern. For though today is always today and the moment is always modern, we are the only men in all history who fell back upon bragging about the mere fact that today is not yesterday. I fear that some in the future will explain it by saying that we had precious little else to brag about. For, whatever the medieval faults, they went with one merit. Medieval people never worried about being medieval; and modern people do worry horribly about being modern.

To begin with, note the queer, automatic assumption that it must always mean throwing mud at a thing to call it a relic of medievalism. The modern world contains a good many relics of medievalism, and most of us would be surprised if the argument were logically enforced even against the things that are commonly called medieval. We should express some regret if somebody blew up Westminster Abbey, because it is a relic of medievalism. Doubts would trouble us if the Government burned all existing copies of Dante's *Divine Comedy* and Chaucer's *Canterbury Tales,* because they are quite certainly relics of medievalism. We could not throw ourselves into unreserved and enthusiastic rejoicing even if the Tower of

Giotto were destroyed as a relic of medievalism. And only just lately, in Oxford and Paris (themselves, alas! relics of medievalism), there has been a perverse and pedantic revival of the Thomist Philosophy and the logical method of the medieval schoolmen. Similarly, curious and restless minds, among the very youngest artists and art critics, have unaccountably gone back even farther into the barbaric period than the limit of the Tower of Giotto, and are even now telling us to look back to the austerity of Cinabue and the Byzantine diagrams of the Dark Ages. These relics must be more medieval even than medievalism.

But, in fact, this queer phrase would not cover only what is commonly called medievalism. If a relic of medievalism only means something that has come down to us from medieval times, such writers would probably be surprised at the size and solidity of the relics. If I told these honest pressmen that the Press is a relic of medievalism, they would probably prove their love of a cliche by accusing me of a paradox. But it is at least certain that the Printing Press is a relic of medievalism. It was discovered and established by entirely medieval men steeped in medieval times, stuffed with the religion and social spirit of the Middle Ages. There are no more typically medieval words than those noble words of the eulogy that was pronounced by the great English Printer on the great English poet; the words of Caxton upon Chaucer. If I were to say that Parliament is a relic of medievalism, I should be on even stronger ground; for, while the Press did at least come at the end of the Middle Ages, the Parliaments came much more nearly at the beginning of the Middle Ages. They began, I think, in Spain and the provinces of the Pyrenees; but our own, traditional date, connecting them with the revolt of Simon de Montfort, if not strictly accurate, does roughly represent the time. I need not say that half the great educational foundations, not only Oxford and Cambridge, but Glasgow and Paris, are relics of medievalism. It would seem rather hard on the poor journalistic reformer if he is not allowed to pull down a little turnpike gate till he has proved his right to pull down all these relics of medievalism.

Next we have, of course, the very considerable historical doubt about whether the turnpike is a relic of medievalism, I do not know what was the date of this particular turnpike; but turnpikes and tolls of that description were perhaps most widely present, most practically enforced, or at least, most generally noted in the eighteenth century. When Pitt and Dundas, both of them roaring drunk, jumped over a turnpike-gate and were fired at with a blunderbuss, I hope nobody will suggest that those two great politicians were relics of medievalism. Nobody surely could be more modern than Pitt and Dundas, for one of them was a great financial statesman, depending entirely on the bankers, and the other was a swindler. It is possible, of course, that some such local toll was really medieval, but I rather doubt whether the journalist event inquired whether it was medieval. He probably regards everything that happened before the time of Jazz and the Yellow Press as medieval. For him medieval only means old, and old only means bad; so that we come to the last question, of whether a turnpike really is necessarily bad.

If we were really relics of medievalism – that is, if we had really been taught to think – we should have put that question first, and discussed whether a thing is bad or good before discussing whether it is modern medieval. There is no space to discuss it here at length, but a very simple test in the matter may be made. The aim and the effect of tolls is simply this; that those who use the roads shall pay for the roads. As it is, the poor people of a district, including those who never stir from their villages, and hardly from their firesides, pay to maintain roads which are ploughed up and torn to pieces by the cars and lorries of rich men and big businesses, coming from London and the distant cities. It is not self-evident that this is a more just arrangement than that by which wayfarers pay to keep up the way, even if that arrangement were a relic of medievalism.

Lastly, we might well ask, it is indeed so certain that our roads suffer from the slowness of petrol traffic; and that, if we can only make every sort of motor go faster and faster, we shall all be saved at last? That motors are more important than men is doubtless an admitted principle of a truly modern philosophy; nevertheless, it might be well to keep some sort of reasonable ratio between them, and decide exactly how many human beings should be killed by each car in the course of each year. And I fear that a mere policy of the acceleration of traffic may take us beyond the normal modern recognition of murder into something resembling a recognition of massacre. And about this, I for one still have a scruple; which is probably a relic of medievalism.

On Abolishing Sunday

THE REPORT that the Bolshevist* Government had abolished Sunday might be read in several ways. Some of the Bolshevists were of the race which might be expected to substitute Saturday. Others have a marked intellectual affinity to the great religion which, oddly enough, selects Friday. The Moslem day of rest is Friday; and when I was in Jerusalem, very quaint results sometimes followed from the three religious festivals coming on the three successive days. It was complained that the Jews took an unfair advantage of the fact that their Sabbath ceases at sunset; but, anyhow, it was highly significant of a universal human need that the three great cosmopolitan communions, which all disagreed about the choice of a sacred day, all agreed in having one. They had fought and persecuted and oppressed and exploited each other in all sorts of ways. But they all had the profound human instinct of a Truce of God, in which men should, if possible, leave off fighting, and even (if the thought be conceivable) leave off exploiting.

If the Bolshevists have really declared war on the intrinsic idea of a common Day of Rest, it is not perhaps the first point in which they have proved themselves much stupider than Jews, Turks, infidels and heretics. We all tend to talk naturally about antiquated pedantry. But the most pedantic sort of pedant is he who is too limited to be antiquated. He is cut off from antiquity and therefore from humanity; he will learn nothing from things, but only from theories; and, in the very act of claiming to teach by experiment, refuses to learn by experience. There could hardly be a stronger example of this sort of deaf and dull impatience than a merely destructive attitude towards; Sabbaths and special days. The fact that men have always felt them

* Bolshevik in Russian is 'member of the majority'. When Lenin seized control in the Russian Revolution in 1917, his consolidation of power became one prototype of totalitarianism. (The other form that followed suit was fascism of Mussolini and Hitler.)

necessary only makes this sort of prig more certain that they are unnecessary. Their universality, even in variety, ought to warm him that he is dealing with something deep and delicate – something at once subtle and stubborn. I do not say that he is bound to consider them right; but he is bound to consider them. And he never does consider them, because he finds it the line of least resistance to condemn them. It is almost enough for him that mankind has always desired something; he will instantly set to work to deliver mankind from anything that it has always desired. Sooner or later, we shall doubtless see a movement for freeing men from the old and barbarous custom of eating food. We have already, for that matter, seen something like a movement for delivering them from the fantastic habit of drinking drinks. We shall have revolutionists denouncing the degrading necessity of going to bed at night, After all, the prostrate posture might be considered servile or touched with the superstitions of the suppliant. The true active, alert, and self-respecting citizen may reasonably be expected to stand upright for twenty-four hours on end. The progressive philosopher may be required to walk in his sleep, and even to talk in his sleep; and, considering what he says and where he walks to, it seems likely enough. Anyhow, the same sort of dehumanized philosophy which destroys the recurrence of one day in seven may well disregard the recurrence of six hours in twenty-four. We may see a vast intellectual revolt against the Slavery of Sleep. I can vividly imagine the pamphlets and the posters; the elaborate statistics showing that, if people never stopped working, they would produce more than they do at present; the lucid diagrams setting forth the loss to labour by the fact that few men are actually at work in their factories while they are asleep in their beds. These scientific demonstrations are always so close and cogent. I can almost see the rows of figures showing successively in the case of coal, cotton, butter, boot-laces, pork and pig-iron, that in every single example more work would be done if everybody could only go on working. It is true that this sort of argument is generally of most ultimate use to Capitalism. But so is Bolshevism.

But these true friends of Capitalism, who still call themselves Communists, do not, of course, mean that nobody should have any leisure, any more than that nobody should have any sleep. The Communists would say that there should be shifts of labour, and frequent recurrences of leisure; but so would the Capitalists. They would say that the labour should be organized for all, and the leisure given in turn to each individual; but so would the Capitalists. There is really not much difference in the general plan of the factory system presided over by the collectivism of Moscow and the individualism of Detroit. It is only fair to say that Mr. Ford has forgotten what anybody ever meant by Individualism, quite as completely as the Bolshevist leaders have forgotten what they themselves originally meant by Bolshevism. The holiday is given to the individual, but there is nothing individual about it. It is given by an impersonal power by a mechanical rotation over which the individual himself has no power. It is not given to him on his birthday, or the day of his patron saint, or even on the day that he would personally prefer; God forbid! – or, rather (as the Bolshevists would say), Godlessness forbid.

But, even apart from the failure of the solitary holiday to be a personal holiday, there is a deeper objection to the disappearance of a social holiday. It lies deep in the mysteries of human nature, the one thing which the pedantic revolutionist is always too impatient to understand. He will study mathematics in a week and metaphysics in a fortnight; and as for economics, he has picked up the whole truth about them by looking at a little pamphlet in the lunch-hour. But he will not study Man; he dodges that science by simply dismissing all the elements he cannot understand as superstitions. Now one thing that is essential to man is rhythm; and not merely a rhythm in his own life but to some extent in the living world around him. I will even remark, chiefly for the pleasure of annoying the scientific sociologist, that the most profound and practical truth of the matter is found in the statement that God made the world in six days and rested on the seventh day. In other words, there is a rhythm at the back of things, and in the beginning and nature of the universe; and there must be something of the same kind in the social and secular manifestations of the world. Men are not happy if things always *look* the same; it is recognized in practice in the common medical case for what is called a 'change'. The mere fact that a man has not got to do any work himself on Tuesday is a very small part of the general sense of release or refreshment that exists in an institution like Sunday. I once ventured to use the expression (though I put it into the mouth of a bull-terrier), 'the smell of Sunday morning'. And I am prepared to say that there is such a thing, though my own sense of smell is very deficient compared with a bull-terrier's. There is something in the very light and air of a world in which most people are not working, or not working as much or in the same way as usual, which satisfies the subconscious craving for crisis and fulfilment. If men have nothing but an endless series of days which look alike, it would matter little whether they were days of leisure or labour. They would not give that particular sense of something achieved, or, at least, of something measured; of the image of God resting on the seventh day. It is a psychological fact that such monotony would take on a character as of mathematical insanity. It would be like the endless corridors of a nightmare. Men have always known this by instinct, Pagans as well as Christians. And when all humanity has agreed on the necessity for something, we may be perfectly certain that some sort of humanitarian will want to destroy it.

On Pleasure-Seeking

THE DENUNCIATION of pleasure-seeking is rightly suspect, because it is itself so often the seeking of the very basest of pleasures. I mean, of course, the pleasure of being pained; I mean, the pleasure of being shocked, the pleasure of being censorious – in a word, the pleasure of scandal. But there are criticisms of modern pleasure-seeking which are not merely the scandal-mongering of old women, which is a permanent temptation to men as they grow old. There are criticisms that rest on reasonable and eternal principles. And one of them, I think, is this – that so many modern pleasures aim at indiscriminate and incongruous combination. They are colours that kill each others; they are like the action of a musician who should try to express his universality by listening to five tunes at once.

For instance, it is not greedy to enjoy a good dinner, any more than it is greedy to enjoy a good concert. But I do think there is something greedy about expecting to enjoy the dinner and the concert at the same time. I say trying to enjoy them, for it is the mark of this sort of complex enjoyment that it is not enjoyed. The fashion of having very loud music during meals in restaurants and hotels seems to me a perfect example of this chaotic attempt to have everything at once. Eating and drinking and talking have gone together by a tradition as old as the world; but the entrance of this fourth factor only spoils the other there. It is an ingenious scheme for combining music to which nobody will listen with conversation that nobody can hear. Recall some of the great conversations of history and literature; imagine some of the great and graceful impromptus, some of the spontaneous epigrams of the wits of the past; and then imagine each of them shouted through the deafening uproar of a brass band. It seems to me an intolerable insult to a musical artist that people should treat his art as an adjunct to a refined gluttony. It seems a yet more subtle insult to the musician that people should require to be fortified with food and drink at intervals, to strengthen them to endure his music. I say nothing of the deeper and darker insult to that other artist, the cock, in the suggestion that men require to be inspired and rallied with drums and trumpets to attack the dangers of his dinner, as if it were a fortress bristling with engines of death. But in any case it is the combination of the two pleasures that is unpleasant. When people are listening to a good concert they do not ostentatiously produce large pork pies and bottles of beer to enable them to get through it somehow. And if they do not bring their meals to their music, why should they bring their music to their meals?

I have noticed many other examples of this kind of luxury in the wrong place. I mean, the elaboration of enjoyments in such a way that they cannot be enjoyed. A little while ago I happened to be dining in the train; and I am fond of dining in the train – or, indeed, anywhere else. I know that people sometimes write to the papers, or even make scenes in the railway carriage, complaining of the railway dinner service; but my complaint was quite different – and, indeed, quite contrary. I did not complain of the dinner because it was too bad, but because it was too good. The pleasure of eating in trains is akin to the pleasure of picnics, and should have a character adapted to its abnormal and almost adventurous conditions. This dinner was what in called a good dinner – that is, it was about twice as long as any normal person would want in his own home, and a great deal longer than he would want even in an ordinary restaurant. The train was also what is called a good train – that is, it was a train that swayed wildly from side to side in hurtling through England like a thunderbolt. Nobody who really wanted to enjoy a long and luxurious dinner would dream of sitting down to it under those conditions. Nobody would desire the restaurant tables to be shot round and round the restaurant like a giddy-go-round. Anybody would see in the abstract that it is foolish to attempt to possess simultaneously the advantages of luxury and leisure with the other advantage of speed. It is merely paying for a luxury and purchasing an inconvenience. Add to this the fact that, though the dinner was long, the time given for it was short. For there were other eager epicures waiting to be flung against windows while balancing asparagus or dissecting sardines. Other happy gourmets were to have the opportunity of spilling their soup and upsetting their coffee on that careering vehicle. Everybody concerned in that trainload of banqueters was in as much of a hurry as the train.

As a fact, these combinations are simply conventions. It is not that anybody, left to his own intelligence, would prefer to enjoy a concert in a restaurant, or a dinner in a railway-carriage. It is that some rather vulgar people do not think a restaurant is conventionally complete without a programme of music, or a dinner without a catalogue of courses. These conventions are in their result quite cold and uncomfortable. They entirely neglect the art of pleasure-seeking, in the only intelligent sense of seeking pleasure, where it is to be found. It is generally to be found much more in isolation, in distinction, and even in contrast. There was some Oriental sage or other who said. 'If you have two pence, buy with one a loaf and the other a flower.' I would myself venture to substitute for the flower a cigar or a glass of wine, only that it would be rather ascetical to consume these things at the price. But I am sure it is a sound principle to have one luxury accompanied by plainer things, like a jewel in a simple setting. This is not identical – indeed, it is inconsistent – with what is commonly called the simple Life, which generally means a monotonous mediocrity of experience, without either luxury or austerity. The real pleasure-seeking is the combination of luxury and austerity in such a way that the luxury can really be felt. And any sort of crowding together of more or less contradictory pleasures, in contempt of this principle, is not so much pleasure-seeking as pleasure-spoiling. Those who allow the colours of enjoyment thus to kill each other can with strict propriety be called kill-joys.

There is another moral which I have more than once noted, though it is not generally understood. The sort of ceremony that the world complains of as antiquated and artificial is really much more fresh and simple than the ceremonies of the world. The old pageantry of heralds or priests was really more elementary, almost in the sense of elemental, than the pomps and vanities of the modern world; it was more elemental because it dealt more directly with elements. That sort of ritualism might almost be called a rule for keeping ritual simple. Left to itself, in our secular and social life, it becomes extravagantly complex. The old systems had much more sense of the necessity of doing one thing at a time. They had much more of the national notion of knowing what they were doing.

Thus one of the old Parliaments or Church Councils might have many formalities; but there was nothing corresponding to the noisy band in the crowded restaurant. They did not bang drums and blow bassoons while they argued with their enemies as the others do while they talk to their friends. An ecclesiastical ceremony, like the assumption by a bishop of his mitre and pastoral staff, may seem to some elaborate and extravagant; but there is nothing in it comparable to the elaborate and extravagant city banquet served on an express train. The bishop seldom prides himself on putting on his mitre in a motor-car travelling at any number of miles an hour. What is the matter with the modern ceremonies is that they have not only become elaborate but become entangled. We have the complication of two complicated things caught and hooked in each other, like two gigantic clocks wrestling. Moreover, there is the further complication produced by rapid change combined with rigid discipline. The old customs were at least old enough to become second nature. But a fashion is always sufficiently new to be unnatural. We may think it a meaningless pomposity that a judge should assume a black cap or a cardinal be presented with a red hat. But the judge does not have to change his cap every season, and there is no necessity for the red hat to be a stylish hat. The combination between the rigidity and the rapidity of fashions leads to a mobilization of an almost military type; and, compared with that, the things that were more old-fashioned were also more free.

On Algernon Charles Swinburne*

I

MOST modern titles and slogans have to say the precise opposite of what they mean, for the sake of brevity. Sometimes the organizers are so sincere as to explain this immediately afterwards; and use the sub-title to prove that the title is not true. A little while ago a series of short stories appeared, proclaiming in its editorial title that each author had chosen his best story. But the editor, who evidently suffered from intelligence (and it does sometimes entail suffering) was perfectly well aware that no such author would say that any one story was absolutely and in all aspects the best; indeed, a sane author is more likely to be hag-ridden with the horrid memory of the worst. So the editor put in a note to explain his own title, which he said was necessary, because it was so much shorter. It is true that the phrase 'My Best Story' is very much shorter than the more accurate phrase, 'I think this story is one of the relatively few by which I might possibly consent that people should judge my general intelligence, such as it is.' It is also true that the phrase 'This story is utter trash' is very much shorter than the phrase 'This story is not, fairly considered, quite absolute and utter trash.' But they do not, to say the least of it, mean the same thing. And selecting the shorter would be unwise, even in a publicity expert.

A rather similar problem arose about a recent selection of English essays, made and introduced by the late Lord Birkenhead; it was a very good selection, and it was not alone in suffering from the particular problem. In large letters on the title-page it had to bear the title of 'The Hundred Best English Essays'; and in the very first words of the introduction Lord Birkenhead very sensibly said that there could not possibly be

* English poet and critic (1837-1909), noted for his innovative prosody in verse.

any such thing as 'The Hundred Best English Essays.' He proceeded, in a very frank and sympathetic manner, to explain that it was not only impossible for anybody to do anything except make a reasonable collection of very good essays, but that he (for his part) had practically put in all the essays simply because he liked them. I really do not know what else anyone can do with essays but like them – except, of course, if one has such darker reactions, dislike them. Of all forms of literature they are perhaps the least to be fitted into the old standards of judgement, by which it was in some sense possible to legislate for the drama or the ode. But, anyhow, there is something a little amusing about the claims of publicity and business requiring us to reverse all that we mean, in order to get anybody to listen to what we say. There is something comic about sacrificing everything to the headline, and letting it insist that the article should stand on its head.

It did not mention this book of essays, however, with the purpose of passing in review all its essays, still less the nature of the essay. I have to thank the complete for bringing back many good things I may have missed or forgotten; but the one which especially caught my eye and concerns my pen is an excellent study by a critic lately dead of a poet whom he knew well and of whom he writes admirably. I refer to the essay on Swinburne by Sir Edmund Gosse.* It contains any amount of matter upon which others could pronounce with much more authority than I. I only met Swinburne once; and though I met Gosse a great many times, I would never claim to have got past the guard of that polished rapier any more than anybody else. I had one letter from him about Stevenson, which I count one of the great honours of my life; for the rest, I was only one of a crowd of younger men to whom he was both ironical and kind. But there is something in the general and very vivid picture of Swinburne which he presents, which makes me inclined to linger perhaps

* British historian and critic (1849-1928).

belatedly on that name; and on the poetry which as poetry, was as straight as a singing arrow, but, considered as philosophy, has always puzzled me very much. In other words, if we consider the target of the arrow, we find that there is nothing to consider, it is not even so clear a concentric scheme as a labyrinth; it is rather a labyrinth without a centre.

In plain words, after reading Gosse's essay again, I asked myself: What on earth did Swinburne mean? Or did he mean anything? It is easy enough after reading some of the poems, especially the later, longer and generally lesser poems, to say that he did not mean anything; that he was simply a musician gone wrong; a lunatic with something singing in his head a creature throbbing with suppressed dancing; a creature who could not help foaming at the mouth with flowers and flames and blood and blossoms and the sea. But it is not easy, after reading Gosse's essay, to deny that he did in some way take something seriously; and something not himself, if his contemporaries doubted whether it was something for making righteousness. He did take counsel with Landor[1] and Hugo as if they were grave gods making a world of justice or right reason. He did seem really to believe that some Utopia depended on the success of Cavour[2] or the failure of Louis Bonaparte. But exactly how he connected in his own mind with the queer licentious pessimism, like the last debauch of a suicide, which fills his other verses, I cannot make out, nor how he supposed that anything, even a Utopia, could be made of such flames and foamings. Surely he was not hoping for a republic in which all the citizens should be free to bite each other. Surely the hounds of spring, so hopefully upon writer's traces, were not all of them frothing at the mouth like mad dogs?

1 Walter Savage Landor (1775-1864) who authored several works in Latin; his best
   being *Imaginary Conversations,* prose dialogues between historical personages.
2 Camillo Benso conte di Cavour (1810-1861), Italian Statesman who brought about
   the unification of Italy and became her Prime Minister.

Yet it is his taste in virtue rather than his taste in vice that puzzles me. In the worst and most world-famous of all his lines he wrote something about the raptures and roses of vice and the lilies and languor of virtue. The obvious thing to say is that he cannot have known much about virtue, if he thought it was languid. But, to do him justice, his own appeals to public virtue were anything but languid. When talking of his own favourite type, which used to be called Republican Virtue, he seems to have understood all that Roman dignity and decency which he tore to rags in his ravings about sex. He used another nonsensical tag about somebody being 'noble and nude and antique'. So good a scholar ought to have known that, in the real world of the antique, a noble would never have desired to be nude. He would have regarded it as the mark, not of a noble, but a slave. In reality Swinburne knew all this; indeed one could hardly be a friend of so very ancient a Roman as Landor without knowing it.

Then, again, the Pagan philosophy he pitted against Christianity is a mass of such inconsistencies. In *Songs Before Sunrise* he offers Pantheism* as the religion of the revolution. Pantheism may or may not be a good creed for a philosopher; Pantheism is certainly in one sense a very good creed for a Pagan philosopher. But Pantheism is a hopeless creed for a revolutionist. If all things are equally divine, then the tyrant and the bigot are as divine as the tribune and the truth-seeker. In 'Hertha' he imagines the universe as a vast tree, out of which all things in turn bud and bloom; and then takes refuge in the miserable metaphor of saying that 'creeds' are merely worms that have got into the bark – the devil knows how. If all things are equally unfolded from one natural root, the worms of oppression are as natural as the flowers of freedom. If they come otherwise, then the universe is not universal; and the worm in the tree of

---

* Doctrine that the Universe is God and, conversely, that there is no god apart from the substance, force, and Universally manifested laws.

nature is as theologial as the snake in the tree of knowledge. There might indeed be a war of spring sproutings against dead leaves or decayed fruit; but that only means that each is equally good in its reason. And what is the good of a revolutionary creed that cannot denonuce a tyrant in his season of strength? I believe that this folly of making Pantheism the creed of liberals has a great deal to do with the decline of liberal politics and the reactions against it today. Hertha, explaining (at some length) that she is everything, remarks, if I remember right;

> I the mark that is missed
> And the arrows that miss.

It will strike a thoughtful mind that such arrows are rather likely to miss. William Tell* will not fight well for Freedom, if he thinks that he and his bow and the target and the tyrant are all the same thing.

* * *

II

When I say that Swinburne's praise of virtue puzzles me more than his praise of vice, I do not (I may respectfully explain) mean that my natural taste in villainy makes me regard it as normal to be a villain, or that my brain reels with mystification when I contemplate any proved and public act of decency. I do not mean that crime is second nature to me, or that I set myself like a sleuth or track down a man and discover why he is not a murderer. What I mean is this: that in the case of Swinburne the loose poetry was really loose. It was flowing, both in form and spirit, and rather after the

---

* A legendary Swiss hero of the 14th century who had defied the occupying Austrian authority, and when forced to shoot an apple placed on the top of his son's head, he shot the governor instead.

fashion of the flowing of tears. It was self-expression, but it was not self-assertion; and it certainly was not any other kind of assertion, like the assertion of a definite heresy or sophistry. In so far as there was something indefensible, he was not defending it. He was, perhaps, describing it, and it may be a bad thing that such things should be described; but such things are not in any case the materials of a moral or political system. Such hysterical, half-involuntary confession is not uncommon in literature, especially when as is almost certainly the case with Swinburne) the literary man is confessing what he has never done. Anyhow, over the whole of this department of the poet's work there is a spirit of appealing and almost engaging despair, a pessimism about the impotence of man. He does not pretend that the pagan gods are good; he only confesses that they are stronger, in other words, that he is weak. What puzzled me was how he really reconciled this past of his work with the other part, in which he professed to see a new hope for men in the virile and universal Republic, in which men should become heroes in becoming citizens. There is hardly a hopeful line in *Songs Before Sunrise* that could not be answered with a hopeless line from *Poems and Ballads.* Perhaps the most musical and magical verse in 'Dolores' is that in open glorification of 'the implacable beautiful tyrant'; and what is the use, after that, of denouncing all tyrants as implacable? What is the good of remaining rigid with horror of Napoleon, when you have flung yourself in a lyric ecstasy before Nero? What is the use of saying that you bring seed by night to sow, that men to come may reap and eat by day, when it is apparently so very easy for anybody at any moment to be tired of 'what may come hereafter to men that sow and reap?' What is the sense of shouting about crowing man as the king of all things, if 'the crown of his life' as it closes, is darkness; the fruit thereof dust?'

Nevertheless, there is another sense in which I would not dwell harshly upon the looser type of verse, as part of the real problem of this strange personality. I say that the poet in the poem does not defend himself. The poet in prose was less wise, and defended himself indefensibly. I do not care so much as Gosse did for the ranting and railing prose in which Swinburne accused his critics of being unjust to him; nevertheless, I think that they were unjust to him. I do not mean that he was right; but I do mean that they were wrong. The critic were wrong in the worst way in which a critic can be wrong about a poem; in being wrong about the point of it. The poem may contain a great deal that is pointless or beside the point; it may contain a great deal that is lawless and shameless and really at enmity with morals – in which case I am old fashioned as to think that it ought to be denounced and even destroyed as such. But even in condemning if we must condemn its point; and to condemn its point we must comprehend its point. We must understand what the man has really said, and not hang him as a heretic for saying something he never said. Now much of the wilder part of *Poems and Ballads* is not meant to describe merely a rush towards the antics of animal love, but a reaction from the tragedy of true love. The poet, in a morbid mockery, is bitterly professing (we might say pretending) to prefer the gutter to the palaces of ideal enchantment, from which he has been cast forth by fickleness or pride. It is not a nice state of mind. It is a very nasty state of mind; but it is that state of mind and no other, and not the state of one who always preferred gutters because he was a gutter snipe To put the point shortly, we cannot understand the poem called 'Dolores' without reading it side by side with the poem called 'The Triumph of Time'. For instance, I have condemned, as every sane critic has condemned, all that hydrophobiac nonsense of Swinburne about people 'biting' each other. But it is not quite fair, even to that infernal nonsense to read it without remembering the verse to which it in some sense leads up, and which is the true inner burden of the poem;

> In yesterday's reach and to-morrow's,
> Out of sight though they lie of to-day,
> There have been and there yet shall be sorrows
> That smite not and bite not in play.
> The life and the love thou despisest,
> These hurt us indeed, and in vain —
> O wise among women, and wisest,
>   Our Lady of Pain.

I do not think the heartless woman is the wisest woman; I venture to doubt whether Swinburne thought so. But Swinburne did say so; and this is what he said; and what he meant was that the pains of a nobler love are so much more terrible that perhaps the coarse person has the best of it, after all. He repeats this main theme again and again in the poem, so that it is incredible that the critics did not see the point, even if they were right to condemn. He says it plainly in the lines;

> No thorns go as deep as a rose's,
> And love is more cruel than lust;
> Time turns the old days to derision,
> Our loves into corpses and wives,
> And marriage and death and division
>   Make barren our lives.

And it is *then* only that he says, in words horrible enough but with something of a moral horror:

> And pale with the past we draw nigh thee
> And satiate with comfortless hours:
> And we know thee, how all men belie thee.
> And we gather the fruit of thy flowers. . . .

Or again elsewhere:

> Of languors rekindled and rallied,
> Of barren delights and unclean;
> Things monstrous and fruitless; a pallid
> And poisonous queen.

This is not praising sin, though it may be practising it. This is rather emphasizing the disgust that is the alternative to the disappointment. It is about as idolatrous as a disappointed lover talking to a bottle of gin, and saying, 'Damn your ugly face, I believe you're my only friend, after all!'

I have dwelt a little on this particular point about the poet, because it involves this very vital matter of the point about a poem. Even when it is understood, the attitude may be condemned – indeed, it should be condemned. But it should not be condemned for being something else. It is a morbid view, an unmanly view, a view immoral in its practical effects. But, above all as seems to me most striking in this connexion, it is the very worst possible view of life for anybody proposing to raise political revolution and to found a perfect Republic. This is the question which I asked first; why it is that men who seem so keen on reforming the world equip themselves with the worst possible philosophies for doing so? It is hard to say whether poor Swinburne was a more hopeless revolutionist in being a pessimist or in being an optimist. His Pantheism could only prove that the worst things are good, because they are a part of nature; and his pessimism only proved that the best things are bad, because they are doomed to disappointment and sorrow. It seems either way a weak motive for doing on a barricade for the belief that one thing is better than another. We need a more fixed idea of truth to establish a reign of justice. But though Swinburne could hardly have given justice to men, he has a right to get justice from them. And I say this to show that on one point he did not receive justice – not even the justice that condemns.

* * *

III

'I have lived long enough to have seen one thing; that love hath no end'; so runs, as every one will remember, the first line of Swinburne's beautiful 'Hymn to Proserpine*', the dirge of a Pagan farewell to Paganism. I have lived long enough to have seen one thing; that the love of Swinburne hath an end. Not the admiration for Swinburne; not the reasonable appreciation of Swinburne; but that particular sort of love of Swinburne which is like first love in youth; perhaps (one is sometimes tempted to think) the only sort of real love that Swinburne had ever known anything about I mean that sort of mere magic spell or enchantment by Swinburne which so many young people had in the period when, as Mr. Maurice Baring has very truely said, Swinburne seems to them not so much the best as simply the only poet. That sort of love certainly hath an end, and most of us have lived long enough to have seen it. But it is symbolic of something larger; something that is connected not only with Swinburne but with Swinburianism.

Any man who has 'lived long enough', and not exactly stiffened with negative prejudices, must know by this time that the modern movement, and every sort of movement, revolves round and round the central pillar of the old Christian tradition. It is emphatically *not* leaving the pillar behind and rushing right away towards some winning-post. He knows it for the perfectly simple reason that he has seen it careering in two totally opposite directions, and neither of them has succeeded in getting away from the post. He knows by this time, if he is honest with himself, that the whole thing is like a Giddy-go-Round at a country fair; full of rush and romantic enjoyment, but revolving upon one centre that supports all the movement by being immovable. It is a glorious experience for children, and therefore for poets, who share some of the wisdom of

* The daughter of Zeus and Demeter, Proserpine was abducted by Pluto to reign over -- the underworld.

children. It consists of concentric rings of hobby-hours, and a hobby-horse, like a hobby, is a very good thing to make a thinking man happy. In most Giddy-go-Rounds there are outer and inner rings of horses, nearer or farther from the centre; and this also is an allegory. In some Giddy-go-Rounds there are revolving rings going opposite ways which greatly increase the godlike quality of giddiness. In youth or childhood especially it is quite natural to be giddy, even if it sometimes being to approximate to being sick. Of recent literature we might not unfairly say that for the first half of the time most of the modern poets were giddy; and now, in the second half of the time most of the modern poets are sick.

Anyhow, Swinburne certainly rode his hobby-horse with great fire and galloping energy; but, when he fancied that he was leaving the central pillar of his childhood and his ancestry far behind him, he was really very far from the truth and very close to the pillar. And this is proved by the fact that both poetical and political energy has since galloped in exactly the contrary direction, and is still at about the same distance from: the ancestral pillar as before. If anything, the more recent poets have tended to take their seats in the ring rather nearer to the pillar. I imagine that, if a man had gone round during; the last ten years asking the young people in the literary world whom they regarded as their hope and hero and leader, as the young of my youth regarded Swinburne, it is about ten to one that most of them would mention Mr. T.S. Eliot. Wilde said that Swinburne was the only true Laureate, for the poet praised by all other poets must always wear the laurel. Laurels and Laureates are not so much in the style of our more cynical and realistic time. But the young would probably support a young writer like Mr. Eliot, even it both the young writer and the young admirers strike older people as being rather prematurely old. Anyhow, the two poets will serve very well for the purpose of the parallel about poetry, or even about politics.

Swinburne was quite certain that he and the world were galloping nearer and nearer to the new Republic and farther and farther from the old Church. If he had been right, it would follow that, by this time, a man like Mr. Eliot would be even more Republican than Swinburne. As a matter of fact Mr. Eliot has actually walked out of a real live Republic and loudly announced that he is a Royalist. He has also declared himself an Anglo-Catholic; but I will leave the religious issue as far as possible on one side, because though even more cogent, it is much more controversial. But even in the matter of politics alone it is quite obvious that there has been a complete turn of the tide. The Giddy-go-Round is going round in the reverse direction, but I am glad to say, almost as giddily. The wooden horses are galloping with their accustomed fervour, and I hope the children who ride on them are happy. But one who has seen this complete reversal of direction since his own childhood will not be able to believe that the horses broke loose from the post and fled farther from it for ever merely because he was told so in childhood. Swinburne's hobby-horse, for instance, had a perpetual impulse to gallop away over the Alps into Italy. But suppose he were really still galloping into Italy, like Hannibal or Nepolean, what sort of Italy would he find? The political ideas of Swinburne were the ideas of the period of Mazzini.* and The political ideas of T.S. Eliot are the ideas of the period of Mussolini. It might be maintained that the new poet is nearer than the old poet to the old Roman Pillar of the past. It is stark nonsense to pretend that he is farther away.

I am not dealing directly here with things that I myself accent or reject. Many people know that my own religion is more Roman than Mr. Eliot's. Yet in many ways my politics are much more Republican than Mr. Eliots perhaps much more really Republican than Swinburne's. But I am not arguing about what is right or wrong in any of these views, I am merely

---

* Patriotic Italian revolutionary and lawyer Giuseppe Mazzini (1805-1872), credited with the honour of making Italy a modern state.

remarking on an actual revolution in the ideas of a large number of other people, and nothing that it is more like the real revolution of a Giddy-go-Round than the mere riot of a gallop. In one sense it has been revolution against revolution; that is, revolution in one sense reversing revolution in the other. But nobody who notes the real movements in the intellectual world just now can doubt that there has been a reaction, either practical or theoretical in the direction of order or authority or classical proportion. In France there has been the influence of Maurras[1] in politics or Maritain[2] in religion. In Germany the Director is a vision; in Italy he is a fact. In America, the very last place where most people would look for classicism, there has arisen an influential school of classicists. Those who most fiercely denounce the fact most clearly confess the fact, and even their denunciations are witness that it is a universal fact. The enemies of Humanism denounce it as intellectual Fascism. The enemies of Fascism make fun of its appeal to classicism. Of course a man may quite reasonably like some of these things and dislike others, or like some parts of these things and dislike others as I do, this moment, most certainly going round from left to right. The sort of political party that used to be called the Extreme Right contains more of the really original modern thinkers than the party called the Extreme Left. I only say that the return to traditionalism is obviously strong enough to be recognized. I think it very possible that it may soon be strong enough to be resisted. But when strange survivals of the Swinburnian epoch, imagining themselves to be young, actually come and tell me that the world is on an endless march towards wild liberty and indefinite relaxation of everything, I really do not know how to answer, except with a melancholy smile. 'I have lived long enough to have seen one thing. . . .'

THE END

1 French writer and political theorist Charles-Marie-Photius Maurras (1868-1952).
2 Jacques Maritain (1882-1973), French philosopher and a devout Roman Catholic.